ONWARDS AND UPWARDS

ARABELLA
WEIR

ONWARDS
AND
UPWARDS

HAMISH HAMILTON · LONDON

For Jeremy, Isabella and Archie – the nicest things that ever happened to me.

HAMISH HAMILTON LTD

Published by the Penguin Group
Penguin Books Ltd, 27 Wrights Lane, London w8 5tz, England
Penguin Putnam Inc., 375 Hudson Street, New York, New York 10014, USA
Penguin Books Australia Ltd, Ringwood, Victoria, Australia
Penguin Books Canada Ltd, 10 Alcorn Avenue, Toronto, Ontario, Canada m4v 3b2
Penguin Books (NZ) Ltd, Private Bag 102902, NSMC, Auckland, New Zealand

Penguin Books Ltd, Registered Offices: Harmondsworth, Middlesex, England

First published 1999
10 9 8 7 6 5 4

Copyright © Arabella Weir, 1999

The moral right of the author has been asserted

Grateful acknowledgement is made for permission to reprint extracts from the following:

'Don't Go Breaking My Heart'. Words and Music by Ann Orson and Blanche Carte. Copyright Big Pig Music/Intersong Music Ltd, Warner/Chapell Music Ltd, London w6 8bs. Reproduced by permission of IMP Ltd.

'When Will I See You Again?'. Words and music by Leon Huff and Kenneth Gamble. Copyright 1974 Warner-Tamerlane Publishing Corp., USA, Warner/Chappell Music Ltd, London w6 8bs. Reproduced by permission of IMP Ltd.

'D.I.S.C.O.'. Words and music by Kluger and Vangarde. Reproduced by kind permission of Bleu Blanc Rouge Editions and R & E Music Ltd.

Set in 11/14.75 pt Monotype Sabon
Typeset by Rowland Phototypesetting Ltd, Bury St Edmunds, Suffolk
Printed in Great Britain by Clays Ltd, St Ives plc

A CIP catalogue record for this book is available from the British Library

isbn: hardback   0–241–14024–2
        trade paperback 0–241–14095–1

Acknowledgements

The following people (not in this order) have been great sources of support, advice and encouragement during the writing of this book and I would like to thank them very much: Simon Prosser, Lesley Shaw, Sarah Lutyens, David Tennant, Soozie Waxler, Tracy Hargreaves, Jon Canter, Alison Weir, Roxane Vacca, Pearl Norton, Rachel Norton, and, naturally, 'Les Biches' – they know who they are – the best friends anyone could want and more.

1977

Have You Seen My Fettucine?

'Elvis is dead!'

  'Fuck off!'

  'No, he is, he is!'

  'He is not.'

  'He fucking well is!'

  'He fucking well is not!'

  'Look I'm telling you Elvis is fucking well dead, all right?'

  'Really?'

  'Wow!'

Nobody moved a muscle. Bert and Vicky were sunbathing nude, in the middle of doing their fronts and it wasn't really worth moving – not even for the King's death.

  'How do you know?' asked Vicky.

  'I saw it in the paper, didn't I?'

Tess was tearing off her clothes at full speed, knickers, bra, cap-sleeved T-shirt, scattering them willy-nilly on the borrowed villa's terracotta tiles. Tess did not want her friends to get browner than her.

From the first day the three had met, Albertine had become known as Bert. Her parents had loathed the masculine abbreviation to the beautiful French name they had carefully chosen from Proust's book. Bert, suspecting all along that it had been her mother's choice, always thought it was yet another example, amongst the legion, of her mother's embarrassing pretentiousness. And, naturally, if her parents didn't like it then that made the nickname all the more attractive to Bert and her friends. Tess was panicking that Bert and Vicky were going to get browner than her.

'But you can't speak Italian,' Bert observed.

'I think I can manage, "Elvis *é morto*",' Tess snapped.

'Oh, so you weren't talking all the way through Latin, then?' Bert retorted.

'No, Bert, that was you. And when you paused for breath me and Vicky occasionally managed to let some basic education slip in.'

Vicky couldn't resist. She had to join in now, even if a little late. 'Yeah, do you know? When you were off sick we even cracked reading and writing.'

'Hah bloody hah, I only talked all the time because you made me. Anyway, I had more to talk about, I had . . . have always had, the most interesting life.'

'Mmm, well, if you call snogging every boy south of Edgware interesting, then, yes, you are definitely Empress Most Extra Especially Interesting.'

'Piss off, Tess!' Tess had stripped right off and plastered herself on to the mat placed in the section of the terrace she had marked out for herself with religious obsession right at the beginning of the holiday. Within half an hour of their arrival she'd worked that it was the bit that got full sun for most of the day. She was stretched out to the point of breaking.

'You look like you're on one of those medieval torturing racks,' Bert observed.

Vicky looked over and burst out laughing.

'I just want to make sure I don't get any white bits.'

'Why? It's not like anyone's going to see you naked, are they?' Bert had decided to address the uncomfortable and always spiky topic of Tess's sex life – or, rather, lack of it. It was always Bert who thought the subject ought to be faced head on, never Vicky. Vicky, as always, jumped in to avoid any unpleasantness.

'What did he die of?'

'Don't know, I caught something about hamburgers and toilets,' Tess informed them casually, trying to give a blasé impression of someone who was privy to secret information. She was very relieved and grateful that Vicky had saved her from another jousting match with Bert about why she was still a virgin. It was something she couldn't explain.

'God, there's a hamburger restaurant where they serve you on the toilet?' Vicky asked innocently.

'I didn't say anything about a hamburger restaurant, you stupid idiot. There was just something about Elvis and hamburgers and toilets – separate, but related, issues.' Tess was beginning to regret bringing this up. 'Christ, you can be slow on the uptake sometimes,' she fumed, 'and you're driving me mad just getting all bogged down in details,' she added, pointing at Bert. 'Bloody hell, you're both so annoying!'

It was all backfiring. Tess had planned to swan in, announce the earth-shattering bit of information, get loads of attention, being the only one who knew anything, and then finish the conversation when she felt like it. She did not want other people contributing, getting involved or asking for petty details – especially as she couldn't provide them.

'So what would that be in our host language, then?' Bert couldn't resist it.

Tess intended to surpass herself with sarcastic inflexion. 'What would *what* be in our *what* language?'

'Host language. What would hamburgers and toilets be in our host language, then, clever clogs?'

'You don't say host for a language, you only say host for someone having a . . . erm . . . a party or something.'

'You can say host for languages, diseases, countries. All sorts

3

of things apart from parties. Well, and I thought I was the one not paying attention at school.'

'Fucking hell, you're an annoying pedant sometimes.'

'Pedant? Pedant? Oooooh, aren't we grown-up?'

'Oh, both of you, shut up!' Vicky yelled suddenly. 'Blimey, you two could row about anything, even what time of day it was. You're both being really irritating and I'm trying to read my book, so shut up!'

For Tess and Bert it was one thing rowing between themselves. It was a way of life for them and they rarely meant anything by it. But Vicky had a tendency to be a little high and mighty and her friends never let her get away with it. They simultaneously rounded on her. 'Ooooh, aren't we machwuuure,' they cried, as they flopped about making their favourite, and well practised, over the last seven years, sarcastic faces.

Vicky raised her eyes to the heavens. She *was* trying to read her book and she didn't want to spend the rest of the day listening to them trying to outsmart each other. A similar row the other day about nothing at all had led to hours of listening to them searching through an English dictionary they'd found and scoring points every time the other couldn't spell a word like 'pusillani-mous' or 'kudos' and neither of them had even known what any of the words meant. However, Vicky didn't want to read her book enough to be sent to Coventry. Anyway, whenever any of them sang out the word 'mature' it always made them laugh.

Tess was encouraged to concede. 'Oh, all right, Miss Bi-lingual, I read it in an English newspaper in one of the cafes in the Piazzale Michelangelo when I went to get fags.'

'That's pronounced "Mickleangelo", not Michael-Angelo, like it's a hairdressing salon in Hampstead,' Bert corrected. She had an inclination to pepper her conversation with foreign words which her friends found embarrassingly lah-di-dah at times.

Vicky and Tess could stand no more. This *was* worth getting up for. In one united move they jumped up, not a thing covering them apart from Ambre Solaire, and started dancing around, making exaggerated 'Italian' gestures. 'Porsche *per favore*, cappuccino *prego*, pizza, I think you'll find that's my Lancia if you don't mind, do you know the way to fettucini? have you seen my spaghetti? *Ciao, pronto, arrivederci Roma . . .*'

Eighteen years old, the summer they'd left school and not a care in the world. There they were, confident that they were quite simply the most sophisticated people on earth. They just knew that they had everything to look forward to. And why not? Between them they had a handful of O levels, a few A levels and more experience in the use of drugs and birth control than a caravan full of prostitutes at a hippie convention. With all that, the world was surely their oyster.

Big School 1970

'Please, please, please don't make me go to my new school in this, *please*, I'm begging you . . .' Albertine was desperate, completely desperate. She was looking at the crumpled used green serge pinafore her mother had produced from her embarrassing hessian woven-by-Biafrans-bought-only-by-middle-class-lefties shopping-bag. The pinafore wasn't just second-hand but advertised this shameful fact by being bobbled all the way down the front. Albertine just knew she'd look like she was wearing an old sofa cover that cats had been scratching. 'Please, Mum, please don't do this to me. Buy me a new uniform, I'll pay you back when I'm older. Just please, pleeeease don't make me go there in that.'

Albertine was starting secondary school in a day's time. She'd been rejected by her mother's first two choices, a trendy mixed boarding-school in Sussex and a much less trendy but high-achieving all girls day-school in London. But Albertine didn't wonder why they didn't want her: she was accustomed to being rejected. She knew that the kids granted entry into those schools were cool and brilliant and had great lives with Real Mums, who had nice biscuits for tea and made proper dinners, and that they probably, definitely weren't fat like she was. Until they'd divorced, her parents had rowed all the time – and in front of people as well. By witnessing these scenes she'd somehow got herself into the line of fire and found that her parents had focused on what they didn't like about her, rather than on their marriage.

6

Albertine's brother Marcus had escaped all this by being away at school and, on top of that, good at everything.

Finally a school had been found that was prepared to take her. Albertine wasn't pleased that it was another all girls one but at least they actually seemed to want her and that was good enough. The divorce had been recent, six months ago, and her mother, Angela, was not taking it well, but she was bearing up by doing a good job of making sure that her two children, in particular Albertine, took it worse.

'Don't be so bloody silly! Why on earth should I spend money on a new uniform when there were heaps of perfectly good ones at the school jumble sale?'

'Because everyone else will be wearing one! I'll be the only one in a second-hand uniform, everyone will look at me, everyone will know that my mum is a cow and doesn't even care enough about me to spend any of her precious money and then I'll have no friends and it'll all be your fault!' Albertine screamed at the top of her voice, hoping that, if nothing else, sheer volume might help her win the argument.

'You really are a mind-numbingly crashing bore! I don't want to hear any more of your *petit-bourgeois* moanings. You are going to school tomorrow wearing this,' Angela said, hurling the pinafore at Albertine, 'and that's that!'

Petit bourgeois? Petit bourgeois! Albertine had no idea what *petit bourgeois* meant apart from knowing that it was the insult her mother always used to describe any attitude held by somebody she didn't like. Still, she didn't see what being *petit bourgeois* had to do with not wanting to go to school in an old potato sack. Typical of Mum to throw some pathetic rubbish into an argument when she doesn't have a leg to stand on, Albertine thought. She had a vague idea that being *petit bourgeois* had something to do with using salad cream instead of French dressing, saying toilet instead of loo and having a cover for your toaster. But she didn't understand how her mother had managed to work up this collection of, to her, very enviable comforts, into an insult. She was aware that since her parents had divorced and they'd moved to North London, her mother had reinvented herself as a bleeding-heart who cared only about art, literature and starving Africans. She was also aware that she was constantly embarrassed by this new incarnation.

'I'll never forget this! I hate you! I'll hate you for the rest of my life, you wait and see!' Albertine shrieked, slamming the living-room door behind her with as much force as she could manage and stomping up the stairs as stompingly loudly as possible.

As she lay on her bed in the tiny box-shaped room at the top of the thin, narrow house her mum had thought was such a great find, miles from their old house, Albertine mulled over her defeat. It had been caused by a lack of ammunition, she decided. She was pretty sure that her mum couldn't care less whether she hated her or not. Her mum never did anything she wanted and was always in a bad mood. To her, it seemed that the more badly she wanted something the less likely she would be to get it. She also suspected that the reverse was true, and that this had been her downfall in the battle over the uniform – if she didn't want to do something then it became her mother's mission to make sure she did it. At eleven years old Albertine was resigned to the fact that her mum didn't put her first, had never put her first and what's more didn't see why being her mother meant that she should.

The next day as she finished getting ready, hoicking the wretched pinafore over her head with all the contempt she could muster, she steeled herself for what she felt was inevitably going to be a tough day at her new school.

Albertine entertained murderous thoughts of her mum as she did up the straps to her sandals. She only thinks about her own problems, she wouldn't care if I killed myself. In fact, she'd prefer it if I did then she could spend even more time talking to her drunken, craggy old friends about their horrible husbands leaving them for stupid little tarts. She wasn't entirely sure if all her mum's friends' husbands had left for stupid little tarts but that's how she'd heard her mum refer most often to the woman her dad was now living with.

As the school was within easy walking distance of their home Angela saw no reason to accompany Albertine. In her heart of hearts, knowing that Real Mums did that kind of thing, Albertine had hoped that her mother would want to go with her. However, she was relieved that Angela hadn't offered to, as that morning she'd come down to breakfast wearing her orange and white Mary Quant towelling kaftan with the scalloped hem and cuffs. Albertine would rather have gone to school naked than accompanied by her mum looking like the melted beach-hut she resembled in that thing. Added to that, she was consumed with the I'm-not-talking-to-you-because-I'm-completely-ignoring-you performance she'd managed to keep up since the row. And she wasn't about to spoil it all by breaking the silence with a request that her mum walk her to school on her very first day. As she put on her coat, she reckoned her mum would have refused anyway, no matter how plaintive her appeal.

Albertine left her house without saying goodbye. She felt that was a nice touch. She reached the main road and turned left. The large Victorian building surrounded by several glass extensions and various patches of lawn that was to be her new school loomed into view. Albertine felt a mixture of nerves, defiance and hope. In an effort to control herself, she made a bet. If I don't step on any of the cracks in the pavement and keep my feet inside the paving stones only, all the way there, then today's going to be OK.

Having succeeded in this task for a few yards she began to

feel a little more confident. Seeing a bus in the distance as she neared the school, she decided to double her odds and guess its number. OK, if it's a 29 then today's definitely going to be OK *and* no one's going to say anything about my pinny. It was an added safety measure on top of the not-stepped-on-cracks. The bus hurtled towards her and Albertine's heart sank. Oh, no, God, it's a two five three. I might as well have stepped on all the cracks all the way here. This is going to be the worst day of my life. She decided that it was going to be worse even than the day her brother Marcus had farted in the middle of the session at that awful family counselling place they'd been forced to go to just before their dad had left. Everyone had thought it was her and Marcus had refused to own up. It had been a really smelly, squeaky fart too, one of those ones that you try to trap in by squeezing your bum cheeks together but which escapes anyway, making a noise like air being let out of the neck of a balloon when someone's holding it very tight.

Albertine soon reached the entrance gates and looked up at the building towering above her. Well, this is it. She sighed, giving one last forlorn look at her pinafore. She crossed her fingers as she went in and made a mental note to cross one foot over the other if she had to let the fingers go at any point later on. Upon entering the main gates she saw a sign saying 'New Girls' and an arrow pointing to what she guessed was an assembly hall. At its entrance she noticed a woman looking remarkably like a man in a dress holding a clipboard. Albertine assumed she had better make herself known to this tall, bony, strange-looking person. 'I'm new. Do I go in there?' she asked.

'Do I go in there . . . what?' the woman replied snippily.

Albertine had no idea what she could possibly mean. Is this some sort of hideous test? She panicked, deciding to take a guess. 'Do I go in there . . . now?'

'Oh dear, I'm going to have trouble with you, aren't I, young lady? "Do I go in there, *please, Miss*?" would have been a polite, well brought-up way of asking me.'

For God's sake, Albertine thought, isn't it enough that you look so ugly? Do you actually have to be horrible as well? I should have just stuck doing the cracks in the pavement. The 29 bus ruined everything. She looked down at the ground and decided not to respond, having found that when she answered back adults invariably accused her of being cheeky.

The teacher finally relented. 'Yes, go in there and find the letter of the alphabet that corresponds with your surname. They're stuck up underneath the stage. Stand in front of it and await registration.' Albertine paused for a moment to gather her strength. 'Well, off you go!'

I hate you, you – you – you man-in-a-dress, Albertine seethed silently. She gave the teacher an insincere farewell smile and slipped into the assembly hall. Oh dear, she thought, as she looked around the huge hall. The place seemed to be filled with perfectly formed little girls, each wearing creakingly new pinafores and crisp white blouses. Their uniforms appeared to be screaming, 'I'm new, I've never been worn before and I was bought by someone who didn't care how much it cost because they think I'm special!' Although Albertine's blouse was new it wasn't ironed, since ironing was another thing her mum considered *petit bourgeois*. Albertine looked around for the letter P, shuffling inconspicuously in its direction, desperately hoping that once she'd found it no one would notice her. But someone did.

Best, Best Friends in the Whole Wide World For Ever

'So your mum and dad divorced too then, are they?' Tess said to Albertine, poking her hard in the back. She was another P and had been loitering aimlessly round their designated area until she spotted this girl, who she knew was just like her. Albertine spun round. She hadn't noticed Tess until this moment.

'How did you know?' she asked, impressed.

'I dunno, you can just tell, can't you? Bet everybody else in here's parents are still together.' Tess sniggered.

'God, how incredibly *petit bourgeois*,' Albertine whispered back.

'Incredibly what?' Tess hissed.

'Erm . . . *petit bourgeois*. It's French for . . . er, stupid.' She hoped that in this context her mother's favourite insult would be appropriate. If not, she was counting on Tess not knowing what it meant either but being impressed that she knew some French words. Judging by Tess's expression it looked as if her gamble had paid off.

'So, what's your name?' Tess asked Albertine.

'Albertine Plummer.'

'Albertine? So are your parents French, then?'

'No. I know, stupid, isn't it? My mum did a degree in French and they chose it from some dead French bloke's only book . . . so, you know.'

'But still, *Albertine*,' Tess said, pronouncing it as if it smelt bad. 'Well, I suppose it's not your fault. Anyway, I'm going to call you Bert, OK?'

Albertine loved the idea. No one had ever come up with that abbreviation: it sounded really matey, much better than the excruciating Apple her mum called her in a rare moment of maternal affection. Besides she didn't care if Tess called her Shitface as long as she was going to be her friend and not mention the bobbled uniform.

'What's your name then?'

'Tessa Pile, but everyone calls me Tess and don't say something stupid about piles, all right?'

I might, when I find out what piles are, Albertine thought, but in the future, if we get to be better friends.

The teachers began to divide the assembled girls into three classes – One, One A and One Alpha. Albertine couldn't work out what system they were using and was terrified that she and her new friend would be split up. What was the point of making us stand in front of those letters? she thought crossly. She still had her fingers crossed and quickly crossed all her remaining ones and her legs too. As they awaited their fate in silent terror, their immediate neighbour, another P, a blonde wisp of an angel, started recounting her journey to school that morning. She told them that her mum and dad had both taken the morning off work to drive her to her first day at big school. Tess and the newly christened Bert listened with identical exaggerated expressions of fake awe. Upon finishing her story the girl trotted off in her effortlessly fitting pinafore. Instinctively, Tess and Albertine knew they'd just been given a golden opportunity to cement their friendship and turned to each other, pulling grotesque faces.

'Yuk,' Bert howled, while Tess stuck her finger down her throat and mimed puking. Bert took up the cue and started to mime puking even more theatrically than Tess, causing the latter to laugh loudly. They both knew they were going to be best, best friends in the whole wide world – for ever.

Suddenly Bert heard.

'Albertine Plummer, Class One A. Over there.' The teacher was pointing towards a small group that had already formed, standing alongside a vast stretch of windows. They looked out on to a concrete patio with an awful modern sculpture in the centre of it.

Bert was thrown into a terrible dilemma. She didn't want to uncross her legs until she'd heard that Tess was going to be in the same class as her, but equally she didn't want to draw attention to herself by trying to walk across the hall with her legs still crossed. She'd done it once before and she'd discovered that although you could actually move like that it took ages and you looked a bit stupid. She'd been with her mum who'd gone berserk at her for 'showing off and holding us up' the last time she'd tried it. Bert uncrossed her legs and walked over to the group, hoping that just the crossed fingers would be enough.

No one seemed to notice her arrival. She didn't mind one bit as long as it meant they wouldn't notice the bobbly pinny. She decided that she'd better find something to occupy her during the agonizing wait that yawned ahead of her until she heard which class Tess was going to be in. She plumped for looking out of the window at the awful sculpture. As she stood there she noticed another girl from her new class already staring at the thing. The girl was very slim and beautiful with dark eyes. She was wearing impossibly elegant pale brown suede shoes. Bert looked down at the shoes with envy and when she looked up the girl was smiling at her. For a moment she was embarrassed that she'd been caught coveting the shoes but then she noticed that the girl's smile wasn't an I've-got-expensive-shoes-on-I'm-not-fat-and-every-school-I-applied-for-wanted-me kind of smile. She thought there was something slightly sad and grown-up about it and immediately realized that Tess was right, you could sort of tell. She was one of them. This girl was like her and Tess, despite being pretty and refined.

'Hi, I'm Bert,' Bert ventured.

'Bert? Is that your real name?' The elegant girl seemed impressed and Bert was delighted.

'No, it's Albertine but everyone calls me Bert.' Everyone? Everyone! Bert panicked. Why did I say everyone? I'm going to look really stupid if we bump into Tess and she's forgotten the new nickname she gave me.

'I like it, it's much better than mine. My name's Vicky.'

'Oh, that's not bad,' Bert said. Actually, she thought, it probably is because loads of people are called Vicky. But Bert liked this girl and she particularly liked the idea of having not just another friend but one who was beautiful too.

'Do you know anyone here?' Vicky asked.

'Yeah, my best friend Tess is over there. I'm hoping she'll be in our class too.' Best friend Tess? Best friend Tess! Oh, God, what am I doing? First I say everyone calls me Bert and now I'm calling Tess my best friend! She was beginning to break into a sweat. Then Tess rolled up. In her panic, Bert hadn't noticed that her new friend's name had been called out and that she was going to join her in Class One A.

'Hi, Bert. God, I'm glad I'm in the same class as you. Thought I might end up having to make friends with that creep – Perfect Parents Girl,' Tess said, with bravado, but Bert could see that she was nervously taking in the elegant new girl.

'This is Vicky, we're all going to be in the same class,' Bert said, as casually as she could, with a hand gesture that was, she hoped, both throwaway enough to make Tess feel OK and yet not dismissive of Vicky. Tess gave Vicky a measured smile and looked down at her shoes, raised her eyebrows and shot Bert a conspiratorial smirk.

Bert experienced a divided loyalty between her new best friends and it made her very uncomfortable. She wasn't new to the predicament of being torn between loved ones – there'd been many similar moments with her parents. But, for Bert, this was much more vital than pretending to her mum that her dad's girlfriend was *petit bourgeois* or to her dad that his happiness was as important to her as her own. She didn't want to give Tess a conspiratorial smirk back in case Vicky saw. In fact, she didn't want to give Tess a smirk back at all because she envied the shoes and thought that, worn by Vicky, they didn't mean what they would have meant if worn by another girl, who wasn't like them. Bert finally decided that the best tactic was to divert their attention out of the newly formed and evidently still precarious circle and on to something they could loathe as a united gang.

'See that pathetic, horrible statue thing? Well, my mum would think that was brilliant. She'd go on and on about it – especially if I said it was horrible.'

'Yeah, my mum would like it too – yukky, isn't it?' Vicky said.

Bert decided that she'd love that statue for ever. She'd be eternally indebted to it for having provided a much-needed object of derision in a moment of crisis; it only needed for Tess to join in and everything was going to be great.

'My mum made it,' Tess said.

Oh, no, Bert thought. I'm going to die. Now I'm going to lose my new best friend and be left with just Vicky. She didn't think she and Vicky would make it on their own. Instinctively she felt that you had to be part of a gang to survive at big school especially if you had the kind of mum who might turn up to a parents' evening in a mini-skirt or offer to sing at a school concert. She knew that two people didn't make a gang, you needed at least *three* people to make a gang. She just knew it. Vicky and Bert threw each other embarrassed glances and stood there for a couple of seconds not knowing what to say.

'Yeah, my mum made it and then donated it to the school because she used to go here too. Disgusting, isn't it?'

Bert's relief was tremendous, she felt like falling to her knees and giving a prayer of thanks.

The trio hunched their shoulders over like a gaggle of old witches and broke into wild laughter – they were all in agreement, a shared agreement that bonded them: Tess's mum made embarrassing sculptures.

A few minutes later a middle-aged woman, whom Bert recognized from her interview as the headmistress Mrs Fowler, got up on to the stage at the far end of the assembly hall and started a welcoming speech. She had a mild manner with a fittingly quiet voice. Most of what she said was completely inaudible to the assembled throng. Bert, Vicky and Tess were standing near the back and Bert couldn't hear a single word. As she never liked being left out and invariably did something about it, irrespective of how inappropriate the moment, she leant over and whispered in Vicky's ear, 'What's she saying?'

'Sssh, don't talk, we'll get into trouble.'

Bert was outraged. She hadn't bargained on one of her new friends being sensible. Tess caught the exchange and shot Bert another conspiratorial look, raising her eyes to the heavens. This time Bert felt justified in responding and amused Tess greatly by silently baring her teeth at Vicky in the style of a rabid dog. As Bert had intended, Vicky saw the display out of the corner of her eye, but wouldn't be budged, resolutely persevering in trying to make sense of their headmistress's address. Bert continued to snarl at Vicky but found that secretly she admired her determination not to be distracted. She decided that Vicky must have a very strong character to be able not to join in even under pressure and Bert liked that.

As soon as the speech was over, the man-in-a-dress woman stepped into the middle of the stage and made an announcement that couldn't fail to be heard, even at the back, where the new little gang stood. Her voice was so sharp it immediately silenced the low hubbub of chat the girls had broken into.

'My name is Miss Jay. Welcome to the North London Girls' College. I'm sure you're all going to be very happy here. Adhere to the school motto "Onwards and Upwards" at all times and you can't fail. Now, could you please form three orderly lines according to the classes you've been given? One over here,' she barked, pointing to the left of the hall. 'One A here,' she indicated the middle, 'and One Alpha there,' she said, pointing to the right. Miss Jay then gave a tight smile, like a facial version of a full stop, conveying that she'd finished speaking and now expected her orders to be acted on immediately and with military precision.

Bert thought Miss Jay looked very forbidding and wondered what subject she taught.

'I bet she teaches maths,' Tess muttered, as the three made their way towards the line in the middle of the hall already taking obedient shape.

'Yeah, or religious knowledge,' Bert said. She was delighted to discover that she and Tess had been thinking exactly the same thing. Vicky smiled in agreement. Maths and religious knowledge were the most awful subjects they could think of, and they just knew that no one nice would actually choose to teach them.

Once the lines were complete, three different teachers appeared and instructed the girls to follow them. Bert felt that things hadn't been going badly so far. In fact, she thought, they've been going pretty well. No one has said anything about my scabby uniform and I've made two brilliant, brilliant new friends *and* we're all in the same class! It was more than she'd ever dared hope for. She was thrilled that they could stay being her friends for seven years. Seven whole years! she thought excitedly. Her father worked for a big oil company and while her parents had still been married they'd moved around all the time. Bert had learnt early on that making proper friends wasn't possible because sooner or later there'd come a time when she'd never see them again.

When they arrived at their form classroom Bert immediately took in the three lines of individual desks divided by aisles of about eighteen inches. 'Please, God, please, God, I'll never be horrible to my mum again, please let me be sitting with Tess and Vicky, I'll do anything, please, God,' Bert prayed. She had no views on God except as the man to whom pleas were made when you wanted something very badly. This God isn't half bad, she decided, that morning, as she settled into her allocated desk directly behind Tess's and one across from Vicky's.

'Why's the front of your pinafore all bobbly?'

Bert's new world crashed around her as she heard these words emerge from the mouth of a devastatingly pretty girl standing at the desk behind Vicky's.

'Yeah, why is it?' chipped in another girl, clearly the pal of the first tormentor and equal to her in prettiness and confidence. The pair were standing up and lolling casually on the backs of their chairs. Bert looked hopelessly at them and realized in a split second that they were the kind of girls accepted by all the schools that had rejected her. She didn't think she had a hope pitched against them.

'It's not second-hand, is it?' the first girl said, with a loud snort. Bert was in a whirlwind of panic – she didn't know whether to confess and throw herself at their mercy or tough it out. They were in her class, she was going to know them for ever – whatever she did now would decide her fate for eternity. As she sat mute, grappling for an explanation, she couldn't think of any, other than it being second-hand. She was stumped. I *can't* tell them the truth. I just can't, she moaned to herself, as the seconds creaked by while they stood arms crossed, waiting for an answer.

'She was climbing a tree this morning and fell down along the side of it. The bark scratched the whole front of her new pinafore.'

Bert thought she must have passed out with terror and was now having a lovely dream.

'Oh, yeah,' the second girl said, with obvious disbelief.

'Yeah,' Vicky replied, standing up and turning around to face her new friend's persecutors.

They were clearly thrown. They'd picked on Bert because she looked like an outsider, an easy target, they hadn't anticipated her being defended by a cool, elegant beauty.

A weighty silence hung in the air as the three girls fronted it out – to Bert, it felt like a million years. She was so unaccustomed to having someone stick up for her that she'd already resigned herself to Vicky changing her mind and switching to her attackers' camp.

'Oh, right, I see, well never mind. Anyway, my name's Charlotte, call me Charlie and this is Georgina, call her Georgie. We're best friends from primary school.'

'I'm Vicky and these are *my* best friends, Bert and Tess.'

Bert had never felt so happy in her life.

1972

Too Fat for a Mini

'You are not going to school in that!'

Bert's morning had not started well. Her mother was trying her hand at being an authoritative parent.

'I bloody well *am* going to school in this and you can't bloody well stop me!'

'Oh, yes, I can, and stop that wretched swearing. You are not going to wear that!'

'Yes, I am, and I'm not going to stop bloody well swearing either, so bloody there!'

'I can't believe you mutilated it. That wretched thing cost three pounds. You are not going to wear it. I'm sorry, but that is final!'

Bert and Angela were rowing about the skirt Bert was wearing. With enormously bad grace Angela had finally agreed to replace the, by now, threadbare second-hand pinafore, which Bert had been forced to wear up to this point. The skirt was the correct colour and material for the school uniform. The only way in which it deviated from the norm was that it was shorter than its original length. Bert had chopped it in half, in keeping with current fashion. She couldn't work out whether her mother was trying to stop her wearing the skirt as punishment for adjusting it or whether she was just being bloody-minded.

'If you care so much about how much it cost then you should want me to wear it!' Bert had developed the knack of being logical in a row with her mother, having found that it always threw her off-course. This wasn't difficult to do as Angela made up the rules as she went along. Today she had decided that, at thirteen, Bert was too young to wear a mini.

'Don't be so infuriating. You are not wearing it and that is final.'

'You've said, "That is final," about a trillion times already and it's not final because I am wearing it actually and you can't stop me!' Bert knew she had a good point. Her mother couldn't physically stop her wearing the skirt.

'All right, then, darling, I wasn't going to say anything but if you must know you look terribly silly in it. Mini-skirts are for girls like your friend Victoria, not girls like you. Your legs look like little cocktail sausages. You are not doing yourself any favours.'

Angela and Bert's relationship was characterized by aggression and competition, and Bert had been fully prepared for her mother's attack to turn personal. At one stage during their rows her mother invariably resorted to making a comment about Bert's appearance, her compulsion to win an argument being far greater than her concern for other people's feelings.

It was precisely the knowledge that her un-Twiggy-like legs were an embarrassment to her mother that had spurred on Bert's resolve to wear the skirt in the first place. Although she wanted to dress like the other girls she didn't really have the inherent confidence required to wear a mini. However, her mother's fierce objections made wearing one possible because instead of being a fashion statement it turned into an act of defiance.

'Yeah, well, when you wear those disgusting horrible kaftans, you like you're wearing a tent. You're fat and ugly and I never say anything!'

Angela wasn't actually overweight at all but she was fairly unkempt. The general effect, to her daughter, was that of a slob which, as far as she was concerned, equalled fat and ugly.

'You're so rude and horrid to me. I don't know what I've done to deserve such an unpleasant daughter.'

When she felt she was losing a row, Angela would often resort to self-pity in a last-ditch attempt to make Bert give in and it never failed to astound her. All the same, it was always a waste of time. Bert firmly believed that the way she behaved was entirely her mother's own fault. She was convinced that she'd never be rude to her mum if her mum weren't always so mean to her.

Angela wasn't deliberately a bad mother. She simply didn't know how to be a good one. She had never planned on doing the job single-handed and deeply resented the position she found herself in. Marcus was easy: he was seventeen and at boarding-school, and even when at home for the holidays seemed to have no apparent expectations of her. On the other hand, to her, Albertine felt like a black hole of voracious need.

Having got no response, Angela panicked and tried to retreat. 'Look, darling, I didn't mean to say that about your legs looking like sausages. I'm just trying to protect you from being hurt by unpleasant comments from the other girls at school.'

If Angela fancied this as an apology, Bert did not. She was infuriated by her mother's pretence that her insults were really a gentle device to protect her from other people's unkindness. Bert knew very well that Angela was not in the habit of protecting her from anything. 'Well, I can look after myself, thank you very much. Anyway, no one will say anything because everyone likes me.'

Bert was popular at school by this stage but she knew it was for being funny and rude not for being thin and pretty, like Vicky.

Her mother responded by giving her one of her special looks. It perfectly conveyed total incredulity that her daughter should have any foundation for such self-confidence and it crushed Bert. Her mother had finally lit upon her one area of real vulnerability:

the fear that she wasn't really and truly loved by the people who mattered to her most on earth – her friends.

'Don't give me that look!'

'What look? I didn't say anything.'

'You know what look. That look you do of if-you-really-think-your-friends-like-you-that-much-then-go-ahead-and-do-what-you-want-but-you're-really-making-a-big-mistake. That look!'

'I did not give any such look. You're being terribly silly.'

'I am not being silly. You know you gave me that look and now you won't bloody well admit it!' Bert was apoplectic with rage and Angela was thrilled that she'd managed to turn the tide. 'This is absolutely typical of you,' Bert continued to scream. 'You start a row and then when you're losing you pretend you weren't rowing all the time and start giving those looks instead. I hate you. You're ruining my life, you're a liar, you did give me that look and you know it!'

'Really, darling, I think you're overreacting just a tad. If you ask me, you're getting this cross because you feel guilty that you were so rude and nasty to Mummy.'

Bert thought she was going to pass out with fury. 'I don't bloody well feel guilty. You always do this, you make me angry and then say it's because I feel guilty, well, I don't. I really, really do hate you and I wish you were dead!' Bert yelled as she stormed out of the kitchen, leaving Angela with a smirk on her face. When she got to the top of the stairs, she shouted down as loudly as she could. 'And I am going to wear this skirt for the rest of my life, so bloody there!'

'Vic, do you think my skirt's too short?' Bert asked, as casually as she could manage, while filing into assembly later that morning. Having won the argument Bert had no choice but to go to school wearing the controversial garment. Although she was technically the victor, her mother as ever, had emerged as the real champion, having succeeded in planting a hefty seed of self-doubt in Bert. She was now petrified that she looked stupid and was, in fact, too fat for a mini. Knowing that Vicky was always honest Bert was looking to her, out of her two best friends, to make her feel better. She didn't want to ask Tess who, she knew, would say something stupid just for the hell of it. Vicky never lied, even to be liked.

'No, it's fine, you look fine.'

Bert sensed that the reply lacked conviction but she couldn't face dwelling on it and decided instead to focus on her friend's commitment to truth at all times.

Towards the end of assembly, something of fascinating interest grabbed Tess's attention. 'Claire Sutherland is wearing a bra!' she hissed, managing to sound both lewd and sarcastic at the same time.

'No, she isn't,' Bert retorted, craning her head to get a view of the girl in question.

'She *is*, she definitely is.'

'No, she bloody well isn't.' Despite not being able to tell whether Claire was wearing a bra or not Bert was instinctively taking up the opposition. Since the day the pair had met, they argued about anything and everything, finding it a source of endless entertainment. Irrespective of whether they knew what they were talking about or not both of them would cling resolutely to the I'm-right-you're-wrong position. It wasn't Vicky's style to get involved and, unless provoked, usually just let her friends slug it out until they got bored. 'Anyway, you can't tell from here.'

They were sitting in the back row of the hall listening to the ritual morning address given by the headmistress, Mrs Fowler. As usual, they were actually pretending to listen because, as they'd discovered on their first day, her voice was virtually inaudible. The entire school went through the same routine every morning, with Mrs Fowler blissfully unaware that practically everything she said fell on deaf ears. However, the girls had developed a gift for picking out intermittent words they found amusing – the most memorable, so far, being 'dog excrement' and 'smoking pot'.

Unless they spotted a teacher sitting near them, Bert, Vicky and Tess invariably spent the entire duration of assembly chatting, catching up from the day before and discussing items of great interest to them, such as fellow pupils' underwear. Today, Claire Sutherland from Three Alpha was in the line of fire.

'Yes, I can. She's a moron, she doesn't need a bra. She hasn't even started her periods.' Tess was indignant that the girl should have on anything she wasn't yet qualified for.

A frantically competitive needing-to-wear-a-bra race had started around the time the second year was ending. Every single girl yearned for a Teenform – the definitive teenager's bra. It consisted of two Airtex triangulars stitched on to stretchy cotton straps and, for a girl with breasts of any note, was less effective than a couple of sticking plasters. However, until the time a proper one was essential, it was a much-coveted item, housing teenage girls' hopes and dreams as well their non-existent breasts.

Some of the more developed girls already had a self-evident necessity for restraining underwear. But in case they hadn't noticed it themselves, this fact was brought to their attention in the showers after PE by the gym teacher, Mrs Pringle, known to all as Twin-set. Seeing no call for discretion she would bark out the names of the chestier girls, followed by commands that they immediately equip themselves with the kind of bra no one under eighty years old would be seen dead in. Mrs Pringle was a hearty tweed jacket and thick-tights type. Although she was married, most of the girls, feeling self-conscious as signs of puberty emerged, were convinced that she lingered around the changing rooms longer than she really needed to.

'Albertine Plummer, will you be *quiet!*' the biology teacher, Miss Laver, hissed, poking Bert hard in the back with her finger.

She whipped round and hissed back, 'It wasn't me, it was Tess.' Bert wasn't ordinarily disloyal, her sense of outrage at being wrongly accused had caused her to betray Tess.

'Well, it usually is you, so shut up anyway.' Having been sneaked on, Tess was delighted that her friend had ended up getting ticked off. She elbowed Bert in the ribs and gave her a smug so-there look.

Bert ignored Tess and flashed her teacher a look of murderous rage. It was the fierce facial cast she was accustomed to giving the large number of staff who had occasion to reprimand her. Unfortunately for Bert, unlike most of her colleagues Miss Laver wasn't the slightest bit intimidated by her or the reign of terror she and her little gang wielded throughout the school. After two and a half years of attempting to educate her, Bert was generally agreed to be the naughtiest girl any of them had ever come across. However, having met her mother, some of them felt sorry for her and understood how she had developed such a feisty character. Miss Laver was more old-fashioned than the majority of leftie-lenient types the school employed and had no time for mollycoddling an unruly pupil who, as far as she was concerned, needed nothing more than strict discipline to whip her into shape.

Later that day, during lunch-break, the trio repaired to their lair, the lower years' cloakrooms. It was a large, dingy room with a low ceiling. On each wall there were rows of hooks, below which ran wooden benches. The middle of the room was occupied by six long narrow islands made up of more benches above which wooden frames held more hooks on either side. During the day, when all the pupils' coats were hanging up, the camouflage was extensive – it was the perfect den for the three friends. They were sitting on the bench attached to the wall furthest from the door. Each of them had arranged the bottom hem of the coat hanging directly above their heads around their hairlines. They looked like they were wearing nuns' wimples made of green gabardine.

'I don't believe it! Twin-set's let Claire off netball because she feels sick. She reckons it's her "time of the month",' Tess sneered, giving an impressive imitation of the PE teacher's deep, booming voice.

'Bloody liar, she can't have started her periods. Katy hasn't and her tits are huge.' Bert hadn't shown any evidence of puberty yet and reviled all those who had.

'I don't think it goes by the size of your breasts,' Vicky said, ever the voice of reason.

'Course it does, you idiot. Vic, you're such a know-it-all sometimes.'

'So I suppose flat-chested girls don't ever get periods, then?'

'Yes, actually, smarty-pants, they do, of course, but not until much later than girls with big tits, all right?'

'Don't be silly. My dad's girlfriend's got no tits at all and she's twenty-six, she must have started her periods by now.'

'Yeah, all right, *probably*. But only just recently, I bet.'

Bert and Tess thought Vicky's dad was a real swinger. They'd only met him once, when he'd come to pick her up from Bert's house. He'd arrived in a pale yellow Ford Capri and they thought he looked just like Simon Templar. 'What on earth does that man think he looks like, racing around in a sports car, dressed like that at his age and with young daughters as well?' Angela had remarked, once he'd left.

Bert and Tess suspected that dads weren't really supposed to wear velvet loons and polo-necks and Afghan waistcoats or drive cars like his, but knowing he was an artist they figured he didn't have to be all stuffy. They envied Vicky for having a father who not only dressed so trendily but also took her to groovy parties in Chelsea filled with pop stars and models. And whenever he wanted to introduce her to a new girlfriend he'd take her to posh restaurants like Mr Chow's. However, although she never complained they sensed that Vicky didn't like going to all these places that sounded, to them, so glamorous, and that she would much prefer it if he were less flamboyant.

'I still can't believe you sneaked on me to Red Hot Lava,' Tess said, clutching her improvised headdress and leaning forward so far from the wall that the coat was stretched almost to the point of ripping.

'Look, stop going on about it, I had to. She's got it in for me, she always picks on me and I'm hardly doing anything wrong. She just really, really hates me, I can tell.'

Tess and Vicky snorted with laughter at the feebleness of Bert's excuse. Their friend was invariably doing something she shouldn't be and most of the teachers knew that. At that moment, Claire Sutherland walked into the room. Bert knew what was expected of her.

'Claire, are you wearing a Teenform?'

'Um, yeah, my mum thought it was time,' Claire mumbled, her face turning bright pink as she spoke.

'Why? You haven't got anything, not big tits like Katy from your class. She needs a couple of cranes, not a bra!'

Bert's friends met her witticism with peals of hysterical laughter.

'Well, you know, they're sort of starting, and I don't want to get hangy-down, saggy tits like Red Hot Lava,' Claire said, shrewdly drawing attention away from the dangerous subject of her entitlement to wear a bra and on to the chest of the universally loathed biology teacher.

Miss Laver's breasts were a constant source of hilarity to her pupils. She possessed an unfortunate mountain of bosom, which emerged horizontally from her neck and undulated without restraint until it collapsed around her knees. The girls spent hours speculating over what kind of undergarment she wore that allowed such freedom of movement. Greater amusement still was derived by thrilling themselves with the possibility that she went about braless because nothing big enough to house her massive mammaries existed. Based on the assumption that any woman with huge breasts must be desperate for sex all the time, they had come up with the nickname Red Hot Lava.

'Yeah, you've got a point, Claire, and you don't want to get banana tits either,' Bert replied, earning more laughter. A few months before during geography Bert had been leafing through a *National Geographic* magazine and had come across a photograph of group of topless Nigerian women. She had sent her classmates wild with mirth describing them as having 'banana tits' and the term had instantly become part of their everyday language. It perfectly described the kind of long, droopy breasts they found hilarious. Their breasts were never going to look like that.

Bert was very relieved that Claire had shifted the focus away from herself, she'd felt bad taking the piss out of her. But, she doesn't really need to wear it, so she was kind of asking for it, Bert thought defensively. She was deeply envious to learn that Claire had the kind of mother who'd buy her a Teenform, and resolved to save up and buy one for herself.

The Untouchables

By the time lunch-break was over Bert had managed to rid herself completely of the vulnerable feelings the mini-skirt had generated. She had cooked up a prank for the first lesson after the break – religious knowledge. Much to the delight of her pupils, Miss Jay (whose subject had indeed turned out to be RK, just as Bert had guessed) looked more and more like a man in a dress as the years had gone by. Bert, Tess and Vicky were convinced that she shaved. The low-heeled brown shoes she wore were the crowning glory sealing her fate as a lesbian in their eyes. Just before they went into her class the three of them sneaked into the lavatories to prepare themselves for their latest wheeze.

'Take those pencils out of your hair, Albertine and Tess. Yes, and you too, Victoria.' Miss Jay was red in the face and rigid with tension. Her entire body was quivering as if she was in the process of being electrocuted.

Bert was thrilled. Only fifteen minutes into RK and I've already managed to get J-cloth [as Miss Jay was unsurprisingly known] to boiling point.

'I am not starting this lesson until those pencils are out of your hair.'

Bert looked at Tess and Vicky and smirked. The rest of the class giggled. Everyone felt the same, the threat of withdrawing half an hour's worth of religious knowledge wasn't going to force anyone to do anything.

'*Quel horreur!* Not going to teach us all about baby Jesus – now I'm really worried,' Bert muttered, under her breath, to her friends. Ever since she had got away with saying *petit bourgeois*, Bert had decided to memorize other French phrases, which she would drop into conversations now and again. She'd decided it made her sound very sophisticated.

'Albertine Plummer, take that pencil out of your hair *this minute*.' Miss Jay was making a pathetic attempt to sound as if she was in control. Unfortunately for her, the entire class, and in particular Bert, could smell her fear. She didn't have a prayer – she might as well have been a bleeding antelope surrounded by a pride of starving lions.

'What pencil, Miss Jay?' Bert, and most of her peers, had by now developed a distinct style of speaking that simultaneously conveyed contempt, disdain and, most importantly, a been-there-done-that attitude.

'You know very well what I'm talking about. You have a pencil, or by the looks of it two pencils, sticking out of your hair. I suppose you think I'm stupid?'

'Oh, no, Miss Jay,' Bert said, making much of the four words, having recently discovered that the more often she used the name of her victim the more contemptuous she could sound. 'Not *stupid*, Miss Jay, no,' Bert drawled, grimacing with faked incredulity. 'Perhaps you're just not *au fait* with the latest fashions that's all . . . Miss Jay.'

The class burst out laughing. Tess had been hoping not to draw attention to herself but was laughing so hard that she had to clutch her fanny in an attempt to suppress her giggles and not wet herself. Sometimes Tess actually did wet herself if she laughed too hard.

Bert was in seventh heaven. Her classmates were laughing, even 'those two' – the pair that had nearly ruined her first day at school and therefore her life – Charlie and Georgie, they were admiring her performance. She was on a roll.

32

'You see, at the moment, Miss Jay, there is a fashion to put your hair up in a bun with pencils. Would you like me to show you how to do it?' Most of the girls in the class were openly guffawing by this stage. Miss Jay had lost control and they knew it.

'No, I would not. I have just about had enough of you, young lady.'

'Oh, all right, I'm sorry.' Bert paused for just long enough to allow her teacher to think that this was an apology. 'Shall I go, then?' Bert had developed the timing of a professional comedian.

'What are you talking about? You are not going anywhere, you little madam.'

'I'm sorry, Miss Jay. I'm a bit confused now. You see, just now you said you'd just about had enough of me. I must have misunderstood.' She paused again, allowing the class to enjoy Miss Jay's puzzled look. 'Can you let me know when you've *actually* had enough of me and *then* I'll get out of your way?'

Wild laughter rang out throughout the room, Bert couldn't stop herself now even if she wanted to. The drive to humiliate Miss Jay was primal. While it was true that she had never been very nice to Bert, it wasn't so much for that as for what she represented that she was now being sacrificed. As a teacher who'd allowed her class to humiliate her, Miss Jay represented every figure of authority who'd ever been given the task of caring for kids and failed. In Bert's mind she stood for every parent whose job it had been to protect the welfare of their children but had decided to put themselves first instead. Miss Jay was showing that she was human and they weren't interested. Bert, Tess and Vicky had no time for an adult's vulnerability. They weren't interested in why a grown-up was failing, they'd seen so much failure in their young lives already they were hardened to it. The power to shake Miss Jay's authority was thrilling beyond compare to them, they were untouchable.

Miss Jay burst into tears and blurted out, 'That's it, I've had enough. You can teach your bloody selves for all I care.'

The entire class broke into a loud cheer as she stormed out of the room. Once the laughter had subsided they fell into hushed silence.

'Blimey, she said bloody. Can you believe it? J-cloth said bloody.' Tess was genuinely shocked. She and her friends were already at the stage of saying 'bloody' all the time. It was practically every second word they used, having decided that swearing made you sound very grown-up. All the same, they'd never heard a teacher swear. They were thrilled and a bit frightened.

'She must be really, really cross to swear,' Vicky opined.

'And cry!' Tess added.

Bert was worrying that she'd pushed J-cloth too far and that it was going to backfire on her but if it did she knew she'd have to tough it out. To back down was unthinkable. She'd lose all the extra approval she'd gained with today's display.

By the next day the story of Miss Jay's storming out had evidently spread round most of the school and Bert was being greeted like a conquering hero. A few girls from the fourth year smiled at her in the corridor, and even one fifth year gave her an approving nod as they filed into assembly. Bert was thrilled to bits.

As Bert and her friends sauntered out of assembly, the deputy head, Miss Barton, an unprepossessing woman in her late fifties with stooped shoulders, approached the group. 'Albertine, Mrs Fowler would like to see you in her office during first break.'

Before moving off, Miss Barton stood there for a moment looking meekly at Bert as if she needed her agreement. Miss Barton was wholly unsuited to the teaching profession: she had a constant look of fear mixed with obsequiousness. In fact she hardly ever taught any classes and none of the pupils was sure what her subject was, assuming she had one at all. Bert and her friends had decided that she was really Mrs Fowler's lesbian love-slave and that's how she kept her job. The three of them stood in shocked silence for a few minutes.

'Blimey, you're really in for it now,' Tess commented.

'What do you mean I'm in for it? Everyone had done their hair up with pencils, it wasn't just me!' Bert cried, vainly hoping that her friends would volunteer to come to Mrs Fowler's office with her.

'After all, it *was* your idea, Bert.' Vicky seemed to think this point needed making.

It really irritated Bert, particularly as it was true. 'Thank you very much, Miss Machwuurre. Everyone else did it, though, I didn't force them to, everyone else was laughing and stuff. God, I always get picked on.'

'That's because you're always doing the most mucking about.'

'You do, too, Tess.'

'Yeah, but you make me. I bloody wouldn't if you weren't a-bloody-round.'

'God, you are such a bloody creep! I don't make you muck about, you want to. You just haven't got the bloody guts to do it on your own.'

'Oh, so it's really brave to muck about, is it?'

'Stop it, you two! Shut up. You'll be fine, Bert. You know what Mrs Fowler's like – she won't do anything really bad.'

Bert wasn't sure that Vicky was right in this case but she was extremely grateful that she'd stepped in. Tess had a tendency to absolve herself of responsibility from unpleasant scenes, pretending that she'd had nothing to do with them all along and Bert loathed it.

At first break Bert swaggered up to Mrs Fowler's office door.

She was nervous but she didn't want anyone to know it. Vicky knew – Bert hadn't told her, she just knew. She knocked on the door and waited. Finally she heard Mrs Fowler's reedy voice squeaking something she assumed to be 'Come in.'

Bert had only been in the headmistress's office once before, when she'd come with her mum for the pre-entry chat. Although Mrs Fowler's voice was reasonably audible when you were alone with her up close, Bert hadn't heard anything she'd said on that occasion either. Desperation that this school, her last chance, would accept her had been coursing through her veins like boiling oil and she hadn't been able to hear a word, not even when Mrs Fowler had said they looked forward to seeing her in September. That occasion was all Bert could think about as she stood in the doorway waiting to be told what to do.

'Shut the door, Albertine, please.'

Oh, God, Mrs Fowler's so nice, Bert thought. Why can't she be more like J-cloth?

'Please sit down.' Bert sat down in the plastic-imitation-leather brown chair facing the headmistress. 'Miss Jay is very upset with Class One A, Albertine, and with you in particular. Can you tell me why that might be?'

Bert hated this style of reprimand. She was at her best on the attack: the constant battling with her mother had honed her warrior skills. Bert had refined an if-you-think-that's-bad-watch-this style of fulfilling her mother's low expectations of her, and she was completely lost when faced with a kind and reasonable approach.

'I dunno,' was the best she could manage by way of a reply. She was careful, though, to make sure that she didn't sound sulky.

'But you don't like her, is that right?'

This must be a trap, Bert thought. She can't really be asking me to honestly tell her what I think of a teacher. Why would she care? I'm not supposed to like them, am I? I'm supposed to learn things off them and that's it, isn't it?

'She's a very good teacher, if you give her a chance, you know, Albertine.'

More reasonableness, Bert thought. This is terrible. 'Thing is, Mrs Fowler, I'm not really interested in RK, you know, so maybe that's the problem.' Bert had decided to take a chance on being mildly cheeky just to see what happened. If she could get a little conflict going, she'd be more comfortable.

'Well, you can give it up when you get to the fifth form. That's only a year and half away.'

'Oh, right . . .'

'But until then I would ask you to give Miss Jay a chance. She's an interesting woman and she really does know her subject very well. Did you know that the background for most literature is found in the Bible?'

Yeah, like I care, thought Bert.

'We'll leave it at that, then, Albertine, and I'll tell Miss Jay I've spoken to you and that you're going to try harder, OK?'

As Bert walked back down the hall to her class she thought about the difficulties presented by being at a liberal school. There were practically no real opportunities for rebellion. The thing was you *had* to make them yourself because no one was ever threatening you with expulsion or caning or things like that. At the North London Girls' College you could sort of do what you wanted. Here they believed in personal accountability, which was all very well but when you were trying to make a name for yourself it wasn't much use. Still, Bert was doing all right: after all, that fifth former nodded at me, so I must be quite important, she decided.

Maggoty Bacon

'Are you coming back to mine after?' Tess whispered to Bert.

They were in the middle of domestic science making rock cakes, which weren't coming on very well as they'd eaten half the uncooked mixture while attempting to wrestle it into a feasible consistency. They were feeling a bit sick by this stage but they couldn't stop.

'Is your mum going to be there?' Bert didn't like Tess's mum much and the feeling was mutual. Tess's mother still made all Tess's friends call her Mrs Pile and no one else's mum did and on top of that when you went round there the fridge was always full and there were loads of biscuits and everything but you weren't allowed to eat anything. At least my mum never has any food, Bert thought, so you know where you stand. Bert had made her own arrangements for survival since the day, during the first term of her second year, when she'd asked her mum what was for supper and Angela had replied, 'How the fuck should I know?'

This had happened around the same time that Angela's ex-husband had got a new girlfriend after a period of prolonged singledom. Bert was pretty sure that Angela had been hoping he'd ask for a reconciliation. She'd always known her dad wasn't ever coming back – why would he? Her mum was bad-tempered all the time and wore kaftans and let her hair go frizzy and wore it up in horrible old bits of leather with pieces of twigs stuck through them. She never made supper and the house was always messy and filled with other women like her wearing awful beads and leather sandals and they all had hairy legs. When they came round they would go on and on about being freed from shackles and quote stuff from some book about eunuchs. Bert didn't know what shackles or eunuchs were but she was absolutely sure they weren't things her dad was going to be interested in.

Her dad had stayed exactly the same as he was before the split, except that he now lived in a flat. It was smart and neat and he had a cleaning lady who also cooked for him. Most importantly, as far as Bert was concerned, it was in the same area they'd lived in as a family. It wasn't like where they lived now. There weren't gangs of skinheads hanging around street corners, drunks in the parks and old Greek ladies dressed in black sitting outside all the local shops. Bert had never spent the night at her dad's flat because he didn't have a spare room. She'd overheard her parents rowing about this once when her father had dropped her off after a visit. He'd said that he couldn't afford to live where he wanted to live if he had to have spare rooms. Angela had screamed at him. Bert couldn't make out exactly what, but had caught something about him being a selfish pig and Angela wanting some time off herself from 'that wretched child'. Bert found it galling that her mother was pretending that she was a burden. She hadn't told her dad that she mainly fended for herself, having learnt long ago that talking about either parent in front of the other usually led to trouble or embarrassing questions. Bert would have liked to spend the night with him sometimes but she didn't blame him for not wanting to live in their area. She didn't either. Even where Tess and Vicky lived was nicer, though still close by. Staying at her dad's would have meant that she was too far away to see her friends every day after school and she didn't want that.

'I think Mum's going to be in, she's doing some commission for someone. A baby's head or something.'

'Bet they'll be pleased with that,' Bert sneered.

'Yeah, they can use it as a door-stop or a football.' Tess always felt she had to join in with nasty comments about her mum's sculptures. After all, she'd set the whole thing up on the first day. She felt a bit guilty doing it but at least she wasn't horrible to her mother's face, like Bert, she reasoned.

'Well, then, let's go back to mine.' They usually went back to Bert's anyway. Bert had found that the one advantage of Angela's lack of domesticity was that she could trail in and out with her friends whenever she liked and her mother never seemed to notice.

'But there won't be anything to eat. There's *never* anything to eat at your house,' Vicky said. She hadn't been eating the cake mixture like the others. Vicky never picked at food, snacked between meals or pigged out.

'No, it's all right. Mum did some shopping the other day. I don't know what came over her,' Bert said. She was stretching the truth slightly as she wasn't absolutely sure her mother had done any shopping, but she'd noticed some stuff in the fridge recently that she hadn't bought and she really wanted her friends to come back to her house. From experience, Vicky knew there was no guarantee that they'd find anything edible but she didn't fancy going straight home after school.

'Are you three going to chat throughout this *entire* lesson?' Mrs Cartwright's enormous voice came booming across the room. Mrs Cartwright was a caricature of a domestic science teacher. She was short and large with big, solid breasts, wide hips and red knobbly hands, and she was usually good-tempered.

'Erm, sorry, Mrs Cartwright, we were just discussing what temperature rock cakes probably got done at,' Bert lied quickly.

'Very well and what have you decided?' Tess snorted under

her breath, she knew her friend hadn't a clue: Bert was useless at cooking.

'Erm, yeah, we thought that probably about . . . the ideal temperature would be about . . . erm . . .' Bert shot her friends a look entreating them to come to her aid. They just looked back at her blankly. '. . . erm . . . six hundred degrees Fahrenheit, or so.'

'Six hundred degrees Fahrenheit . . . or so,' Mrs Cartwright repeated.

'Yeah, erm . . . yes, for about half an hour.' Although Bert was floundering she didn't feel the need to be rude to Mrs Cartwright. No one ever was. It wasn't necessary. You didn't score points answering back to jolly old Mrs Cartwright.

'Do you know what you'd get if you put your rock cakes into the oven at that temperature, Albertine? That is, assuming you could find an oven that went up as high as six hundred degrees?'

'Nice hot rock cakes, erm, quite quickly, Mrs Cartwright?' A few girls nearby grunted with laughter.

'No, Albertine, you would be lucky if you got pure carbon. More likely you'd get a pile of soot. Now if you want to learn how to cook then you'll have to concentrate. Cooking is a skill and you'd be wise to acquire it. Men like a woman who can cook, you know,' Mrs Cartwright said, with a suggestive smile, turning her attentions to a couple of girls who were trying to extract a wooden spoon embedded deep into their cement-like cake mixture. Bert shot Tess and Vicky a look of incredulity and pulled a grotesque face, sticking her tongue out as far as possible. She could believe that men liked women who could cook, but not if they looked like Mrs Cartwright.

'Where's the food? You said your mum had been shopping.'

'I dunno. Look in the bloody fridge,' Bert snapped back.

Vicky's suspicions had been well founded: they were back at Bert's house, she couldn't seem to find any food, and she was hungry.

'I'll look.' Tess was nearest. She stood up and opened the fridge door. The light didn't come on; it hadn't worked for ages. 'There's some eggs, a bit of old rancid butter, a jar of marrons glacés – yuk, I hate those and . . . God, Bert, this fridge stinks!'

'It always stinks. Mum never cleans it – she says it's *petit bourgeois* to worry about clean fridges.'

'I'm glad my mum's *petit bourgeois* then,' Tess remarked. 'Oh, and there's something in a white paper bag.'

'Oh, yeah, that's bacon. Get it out. I'll make bacon sandwiches.' Bert was relieved that she was going to be able to feed her pals after all. She was still embarrassed by her mum's inability to provide even the most basic comforts. Tess reached for the white paper bag and let out a bloodcurdling, ear-piercing scream, recoiling violently, leaving the fridge door swinging open.

'What? What?' Bert and Vicky cried out, jumping up simultaneously.

'It moved! The packet moved! It moved when I touched it! Oh, my God, I'm going to be sick, the packet moved!'

'What do you mean moved? Don't be so stupid, it can't have moved! How could it have moved?' Bert didn't know what Tess was on about.

'I'm telling you it moved! If you don't believe me then have a look yourself. It moved!'

'All right, I will.' Bert marched over to the fridge and bent down to have a look. She leapt back, hitting the heavy pine kitchen table with enough force to make it wobble.

'Yurgh, she's right, it's moving – Vicky, do something, the packet's moving.' Bert and Tess were helpless when it came to practical matters. They always deferred to Vicky who was level-headed and not at all squeamish.

'Why should I?'

'Please, pleeeeease. I'll be your best friend in the whole wide world for ever and ever, cross my heart and hope to die, if I don't.'

'You're already my best friend in the whole wide world for ever and ever.'

'Yeah, OK . . . but please do it. I can't, I'll puke,' Bert wailed.

Vicky shrugged her shoulders and resigned herself to the task. Armed with a fork she made her way towards the fridge. She bent down to have a look and gently tore back the white paper bag using the fork as a prong. 'When did your mum do this famous shopping?' Vicky asked, turning her head back to Bert.

'I dunno, couple of days ago maybe, why?'

'Because this bacon is crawling with maggots.'

'Yeurgh!' Bert and Tess shrieked at the top of their voices. Using the fork as a miniature crane Vicky lifted up the paper bag with its wriggling contents and inched herself round away from the fridge, chucking the pulsating packet on to the table. It lay there, throbbing silently. A tremendous pong began to fill the room. Bert and Tess threw themselves back against opposite walls of the kitchen, squealing wildly through their hands, which were clasped firmly over their mouths and noses.

'Stop it, you two, they're only maggots, they won't kill you,' Vicky said calmly.

At that moment Angela burst into the kitchen. 'What the hell is going on down here?'

'Mum, there were maggots in that bacon, we nearly ate them!'

'What bacon?' Angela managed to make the word bacon sound not only as if she'd never heard it before but as if it was something akin to pus.

43

'The bacon that was in the fridge, in the white paper bag. Look, it's on the table, it's moving, can't you see it?'

Angela looked at the table and saw the heaving packet. 'Oh, that. Well, of course it's got maggots. I bought it weeks ago when I thought Marcus was coming home for half-term – he loves bacon. Stop being so silly and just throw it away, although I'm sure it would be perfectly all right if you took the maggots out. They probably die in the cooking. I've never heard such a performance. Serves you right – you shouldn't have been eating it anyway, it was for Marcus.'

'But it's all right for *me* to eat now that it's got maggots!' Bert was enraged that her mother had managed to make the effort of buying something special for Marcus when she provided barely enough for Bert to live on.

Vicky and Tess started to giggle, which encouraged Angela.

'Oh, don't be so childish! Didn't you have lunch at school? I don't know why on earth you should want bacon now. It's five o'clock in the afternoon.'

'Because we felt like it, you stupid old cow!' Bert screamed back at her mother.

Tess was hanging on to her fanny tightly: she was laughing so hard that she was close to wetting herself. Vicky was also laughing out loud.

'Honestly, there's no need to get so het-up, darling. You really are making a nit-wit of yourself in front of your friends.'

'They're laughing at you, not me!' Bert screamed even louder.

'I don't think so!' Angela said, as she turned to exit the kitchen, giving her daughter a sarcastic smile.

Bert rounded on her friends. 'Why are you laughing? What's so funny?'

'You shouldn't let your mum wind you up like that – she does it on purpose. You two are just so funny together.' Vicky wasn't being unkind to her friend, just stating a fact.

'Anyway, you probably shouldn't call your mum an old cow, you know. She is your mum and she's all right, you know,' Tess said sanctimoniously.

'She *is* an old cow and she's not all right and I'll call her what I want OK, Miss Perfect?'

'Look, never mind that. Let's get rid of this,' Vicky intervened. Bert and Tess let out groans of revulsion, indicating that they couldn't be counted on to help out in the disposal.

'It's OK, I'll get rid of it. Bert, open the bin, then stand back both of you,' Vicky said, taking control of the situation.

Bert went over to the bin, threw open the lid and ran across to join Tess, who was plastered up against the wall furthest away from the procedure. Vicky took the broom out of the cupboard, from where it was rarely moved, and holding the brush end, slid the top of the handle into the packet of bacon. Once it was secure she lifted it up off the table and moved it round towards her target with careful precision, she looked like she was manoeuvring a gunner tank, finally dropping the packet into the bin. She put down the broom, picked up the lid and jammed it firmly on.

'Right. Shall we have the rock cakes I made instead?' Vicky said, producing a bulging paper bag from her satchel.

'Great. But not with that scabby butter from the fridge, please.' Tess was disinclined to eat anything ever again that came out of Bert's fridge.

'Oh, Vicky, weren't you taking them home for your mum?' Bert was touched that, as ever, Vicky was saving the day.

'Yeah, but she won't know.'

'Shall we watch *Blue Peter*?' Tess said through a mouthful of rock cake. The rock cakes were exactly as they ought to be, delicious and still a bit warm. Vicky always did everything well.

'No, John Noakes makes me sick and I hate Shep. Let's watch *Magpie*.' Bert knew that *Magpie* was much trendier.

45

'*Magpie*'s not on today, let's watch *Blue Peter*. You never know, they might have something really interesting you could do with sticky-back plastic,' Vicky said.

The girls all smiled. The three of them often made each other laugh just saying 'sticky-back plastic'.

'Yeah, you could use it for wrapping up stinky old bacon crawling with maggots,' Bert quipped.

Chewed-up bits of rock cake spewed across the table out of Vicky's and Tess's mouths as they burst out laughing. Bert had regained face and was happy.

1973

How To Ruin Your Daughter's Life

As Bert returned from Vicky's house, where she'd managed to stay for supper for the third time that week, she opened the front door to find her mother standing in the hall. Bert was not accustomed to being greeted by her mother upon her return, and even less accustomed to find her mother actually waiting for her. In fact, she often thought her mother wouldn't notice if she didn't come home at all. She must have heard my key in the door, Bert thought. She can't have been standing there all day. Bert knew that her mother wouldn't have had the patience.

'Well, I've just come back from a parents' meeting,' Angela announced, with theatrical gravity. Bert wasn't too concerned, though the look on her mother's face didn't bode well. She considered mimicking Angela's voice and responding sarcastically, 'Oh, really? And I've just come back from Vic's,' but decided against it. Instead she shrugged her shoulders as she shook off her coat and said, 'Oh, yeah,' in her most devil-may-care manner.

'I could barely hold my head up talking to the members of staff'.

Bert was about to ask if that was because she was drunk, but again decided against.

'Every single teacher I spoke to named you as the worst pupil they had ever had the misfortune to teach.'

Bert didn't respond. Her head was swimming. Bloody hell, that's not bad! 'Worst pupil ever', and the school's been there for a hundred years and some of the teachers nearly as long as that, so that's pretty amazing. Wow, wait till Tess and Vicky hear this. She was puffed with pride.

Angela mistook the silence for mortification and continued, for once confident of her ground. 'I am not prepared to be humiliated by your behaviour. I want to know what you've got to say for yourself,' she demanded.

'Um, I dunno. Maybe . . . don't go to the parents' evenings any more?' Encouraged by the news that she'd really made her mark, Bert had decided that the time was ripe for some of her wit.

Angela was taken aback: she had confidently assumed that Bert would be deeply shamed to hear that her teachers didn't like her. Angela had been an exemplary student at her school ending her days as head girl, after which she had gained unconditional entry to Girton College, Cambridge. These achievements had given her no greater sense of personal worth, her parents having made it clear that she had achieved no more and no less than was expected from a girl with her background and, as such, should not expect praise. However, Angela could not conceive of a world in which academic failure combined with notoriety constituted the deliberately chosen route to popularity. 'Doesn't this mean anything to you . . . *at all*?' was all she could say, faced with the defiant, brazen glare her daughter was giving her.

'Nope,' Bert answered truthfully. She didn't care: she didn't want teachers to like her, she wanted her friends to like her, and her friends' mums to like her. She wanted people who didn't have maggots in their fridges to like her. She wanted people with organized lives to like her, people who bought biscuits for tea, people who made meals for their children. She wanted a Real Mum.

Angela let out a plaintive sigh. 'Good God, what have I done to deserve this?'

Bert realized that her mother was defeated and replied, 'I think we all know the answer to that, Mummy,' as she skipped two by two up the stairs to her bedroom.

She never asks where I've been, how my day was, what I'm doing at school. She wouldn't care if I was dead or alive, Bert thought crossly, as she lay on her bed listening to Neil Young's *After the Goldrush*, her current favourite album. Now she suddenly expects me to be the perfect daughter when she's been a crap mum all along. Huh, she's got a nerve! Notwithstanding her conviction that all responsibility for the way she behaved lay at her mother's door Bert had found herself feeling sorry for Angela. She was instantly made very uncomfortable by the sensation of pitying her own mum. Occasionally her father engendered the same feeling and it always made her feel funny inside. She didn't know quite why but she was sure that young children weren't supposed to worry about their parents. She stomped on the sensation quickly, turning up the volume on her record player and singing along loudly. Bert was aware that her mother could probably hear her, and thought that this would further prove just how little she cared what her teachers thought about her.

A while later, feeling a little guilty, she decided to go downstairs and be nice to her mother for a bit. She found Angela in the living room, smoking and reading a book as usual. Bert plopped herself casually on to the sofa. She didn't sit too close in case her mum thought she was after a cuddle.

A few months previously Bert had had an experience she'd found depressingly educational. Her father had just dropped her off at home after their day out together. He hardly ever came into the house any more, and they tended to say their goodbyes in the car. Just as she was about to get out, he had leant over and patted her on the knee saying, 'You're a good girl for never making a fuss and it's very nice for Daddy always to have a cheery, well-behaved girl to look forward to seeing.' Her father's words, no doubt intended as a compliment, had made her feel sad and isolated. She knew that this view of her was not accurate but she'd understood his message: this was the daughter he wanted to be presented with and nothing else. As she'd entered the house her mother had noticed that she looked deflated and thinking it might be caused by some juicy tit-bit about Charles had asked her what the matter was. Bert, forgetting her rule about not speaking about either parent to the other, had tried to explain how she felt, hoping to solicit some comfort from her mother.

Angela had listened for a moment and then cut in, 'I don't know why you're feeling so sorry for yourself. That's nothing compared to what it was like being married to him! You should count yourself lucky you only have to see him once in a blue moon. He wants a perfect wife and model children. He's not interested in real people, with thoughts and feelings of their own. Don't come looking to me for sympathy: he's a cold bastard and the sooner you realize it the better off you'll be.'

Bert had felt crushed and furious. She was mainly angry for having allowed herself to seek emotional support from her mother but also for having given her the opportunity to criticize her dad, something for which she needed little encouragement. Although her father's methods were more subtle than her mother's, both were quick to embark on listing each other's faults if given half a chance.

After a couple of minutes' silence Angela made an announcement. 'Well, I've decided to get more involved at your school. I'm going to help out as a sort of stand-by supervisor.'

'What?' Bert exclaimed, with total disbelief, sitting bolt upright (not easy, considering the uneven depths to which the ancient sofa's springs had sunk).

'Well, at the parents' evening they asked for volunteers to help out from next year with supervising classes when teachers were absent and on school trips to museums and galleries, that sort of thing, where an extra pair of hands might be helpful.'

Bert realized her mum was serious, and she saw her life flash before her eyes. 'Mum, you can't, I'll – I'll – run away – I'll kill myself, you *can't*!' Bert put all the pathos she could muster into the last 'can't', choking back tears of frustration and despair as she spoke. But she knew her mother was going to go through with her plan.

'Don't be so silly – kill yourself indeed! I've never heard such nonsense in all my life. I'm only sorry I can't start straight away. At least I'll be around from when you start your O levels, so that's something. It strikes me that if this is the only way I can make sure you start behaving at school then so be it. It appears that giving up my valuable time helping out is the only means of ensuring that you get an education!' And with that Angela lit a fresh cigarette and returned to her book, with an emphatic and-that-I'm-afraid-is-that flick of her head. Bert felt like hurling herself on to the floor and screaming until her lungs burst. She couldn't believe that Angela had not only landed finally upon the perfect way to ruin her life but was having the nerve to act like she was doing her a favour as well.

The next day after assembly, as Bert, Vicky and Tess trooped up to their classroom to collect their books for the morning's classes, Bert broke the news.

'God, that'll be brilliant,' Tess exclaimed.

'Brilliant? Brilliant? Are you fucking mad or what? My life is over and you're saying it's going to be brilliant?' Bert couldn't believe her ears.

'Your mum is so funny, it'll be fantastic seeing her with the teachers. Imagine what she'd be like with Miss Barton!' Vicky was evidently inclined to agree with Tess on the amusement

Angela's presence at their school might provide. She could see why Bert was agonized at the idea of her mother invading her turf but she did think it might be very entertaining. 'Miss Barton, you are soooo *petit bourgeois*. You should read Mozart's letters – they give you such a wonderful insight into the composer's mind. By the way, I heard you say, "pardon", the other day and one should only say "I beg your pardon", or "What?" "Pardon" really is completely non-U.' Tess was doing an impressive rendition of Angela and her likely first encounter with the headmistress's lesbian love-slave.

'Don't,' Bert pleaded. 'That's exactly what she'll be like, I'm going to have to run away or kill myself or – or – or –'

'Start behaving yourself.' Tess finished her friend's sentence.

'Very funny, hah, hah, I'm sure. Look, what am I going to do?'

'Don't be such a drama queen. Your mum's hardly ever going to be here. You said she was only helping out now and again. God, honestly, my mum used to go here, she bloody well comes to old girls' reunions – most of the teachers remember her and liked her, what's worse. You want to try living with that.'

'That's hardly the same as your mum coming in all the time and snooping around. Oh, my God, I've just thought, what if she makes friends with some teachers and they start coming round our house?'

'Well, I'd start with cleaning the fridge,' Tess advised.

As they shuffled off to French, the first class that morning, Bert could not see how, in a few short months, her beloved school life, where she had found everything she had ever wanted, would be anything other than over.

Big Willies 1974

'So we're at his house, right, in his parents' bedroom, on their waterbed, which is, like, the most totally amazing thing, right, and we've been smoking loads of that Moroccan black and suddenly all the lights go out . . .' Bert was treating her friends to a blow-by-blow account of the weekend just gone.

'Another power-cut?'

'No, his parents don't pay the electricity bill.'

'Really?'

'No, you idiot, of course it was another power-cut! Honestly, don't interrupt. So the lights go out, right, and we're sitting there, well, actually you can't really sit on a waterbed so we're slopping on the bed, right, and –'

'What's slopping?' Tess interrupted.

'Tsk, you know, sort of not sitting up and not lying down. If you ever go on a waterbed you'll find out – you can't sit up properly, it's too wobbly. Anyway, do you want to hear what happened or not?'

'Yeah, yeah, go on,' Tess said dismissively, feeling she'd had a right to know what slopping was.

'So we're slopping there on the bed in total darkness, right, and we're both really, really stoned and then he sort of rolls over and kisses me, right and we start really snogging, which was really nice, and then I could feel his willie and it was all hard, right, and . . .' Vicky looked impressed and Tess giggled. 'Tess, you do know it's supposed to get hard, don't you? It means

Adam really, really fancies me a lot, because they don't always get really hard just from kissing, OK?'

The three were huddled in their lair, the cloakrooms. Bert was relishing every second of her story and her friends were hanging on to every word. The girls were very used to talking about boys and snogging but the real thing, SEX, was only now being contemplated as the next possible step. Bert had snogged a couple of boys previously at parties they'd all been to, but hurriedly and standing up and there'd never been any suggestion of below-the-waist activity. Vicky had snogged one boy and Tess hadn't snogged anybody. None of them could accurately be described as an expert on the subject, despite Bert's firm belief that, out of all of them, she qualified as one.

After her eventful weekend Bert realized that, from their class, it looked like she was going to be the first to go all the way and she was thrilled. Strictly speaking, she wouldn't be because Georgie had been sleeping with her boyfriend for a month now, or so she said. Bert and her pals weren't convinced, however, despite witnessing the great display she'd made the other day, before gym, of accidentally-on-purpose spilling the contents of her satchel out on to the floor and asking one of them to pass her pill pack back, even though it'd actually been nearer to her. Bert reckoned that although she might be sleeping with him she hadn't actually let him put it in yet. And Charlie, Georgie's best mate, was sleeping with her boyfriend but admitted that for now she was holding off having full sex. All the same, as 'those two' weren't part of Bert's inner circle, she felt she had a right to her anticipated claim of being the first.

'So did you touch it?' Tess was keen to carry on getting all the gory details.

'Yuk, no, I could just feel it through his trousers.'

'God, it must be enormous.'

'Yeah, I reckon. It felt pretty big. I mean, even though I didn't touch it I could still feel it even through his trousers and my skirt so that means it's probably quite big, right?'

'Did you . . . erm . . . do it?'

'No, but we snogged for ages. It's really brilliant snogging on a waterbed and being stoned at the same time. I'm definitely going to get a waterbed when I get my own flat. His willie stayed hard the whole time, then the lights came back on, right, and we sort of stopped and then we had another joint and then I walked home.'

'Didn't he walk you home?' Vicky said.

'No – don't be so old-fashioned. Why should he? I only live round the corner.'

Tess and Vicky looked at each other. Bert caught the look and knew what they were thinking. She didn't live round the corner from Adam. He lived in the same area as Vicky and Tess, in the really smart part. But she often walked home from their houses hoping to prove that she really did live close by – even though it was quite a trek.

'So are you going to sleep with him?' Tess had been disappointed that her pal hadn't done it on Saturday and wanted to know when she could look forward to hearing the facts about penetrative sex.

'Yeah, of course I am. We talked about it and I told him I'd go and see the doctor and then we could do it.'

'That's a bit swotty, isn't it? Planning it all in advance?' Vicky thought it ought to be a bit more spontaneous. That's how she'd imagined it would be for her. A bit more wild and frantic, she hoped anyway.

'Well, there's no point in being childish about birth control. We may as well plan everything in advance.'

'Oooh, machwuuurre,' Vicky and Tess cried out.

Bert didn't respond except to give her pals a grimace, baring her teeth with a false smile. They're bound to be a bit silly about this because I know more about sex than either of them and they're probably a bit jealous, she thought.

Bert's haste to arrange birth control wasn't driven by wild passion for Adam, nor by a thoughtful concern to avoid pregnancy. It was a result of her conviction that using contraception and having sex would turn her into a grown-up and that was that. She'd enjoyed kissing Adam but hadn't felt anything earth-shattering apart from his hard-on, and she hadn't really thought that was the most amazing thing in the world either – more just something boys get when they kiss girls whether they want to or not.

By this stage, Bert had become very organized in some areas of her life. This unlikely attribute had come about as a response to the increasingly chaotic home life her mother continued to provide. Bert made her own suppers, generally from tins. She'd steal money out of her mother's purse to pay for them, a theft she saw as entirely justified, particularly as her mother didn't know what was in there half the time anyway. If her mother's purse was empty she'd use the pocket money her dad gave her, reimbursing herself when her mother's purse had money in it again. More frequently, she'd hang around at Tess's or Vicky's as long as possible after school until one of their mums would get the hint and feed her along with the rest of their family. Vicky's mum, Julia, never seemed to mind her staying but often Mrs Pile would say something like, 'Isn't it time you were getting home for your own supper?' Bert sometimes thought that Mrs Pile would be happy if she and her daughter were the only people on earth. Tess, embarrassed by her mother's behaviour, would always sneak something out of the fridge for Bert before she left.

Julia was much nicer than Mrs Pile, which Bert had decided was because she had a boyfriend. However, they all thought Julia's boyfriend Stewart, who was something to do with politics, a real wanker. Vicky and her friends couldn't bear him because even though he was ancient he insisted on wearing flares, which he looked stupid in, and tried to be all young and groovy when talking to them, always saying that it was 'cool' for them to smoke dope in the house if they wanted to. They didn't want an adult's permission to smoke. There was practically no point in taking drugs at all if adults were going to let you. To them he was deeply embarrassing in every way but at least he kept Julia distracted. As far as Bert knew, neither her mum nor Mrs Pile had had boyfriends since their divorces. She and her friends had decided that most women over forty probably just *couldn't* get boyfriends. They guessed that it was one of those things that just happens in life – women don't get a bloke after they're forty unless he's also really ancient. They also reckoned people that old probably didn't want sex anyway.

'Mum . . .' Bert was leaning on the door of the living room. She was attempting to look casual and wanted to strike as uncombative an attitude as possible. She was hoping that she looked as if the question she was about to pose was one of the most normal, everyday, banal kind. Angela was sitting in the deflated calico-covered Habitat sofa that dominated the living room. It was a huge grey semi-circle that had been the height of fashion a couple of years previously but was now as grubby and unkempt as most other items of furniture in their house.

'Yes, what?' Angela said looking up from the huge book she was reading.

She does nothing but read all day long, Bert thought. This is probably another one like the last – *Sirens through History*, whatever that means. Since seeing the 'eunuch' book Bert had noticed that the titles of all the things her mother read contained weird words like 'captive' and 'emasculation'. One in particular she remembered was 'jar', she didn't know what that one was about but she was sure her mother wasn't about to start making jam.

An ashtray piled high with cigarette stubs sat next to Angela on the coffee table and she had one on the go in her hand. It had just turned six o'clock in the evening and a large gin and tonic stood next to the ashtray. Angela was wearing an ill-fitting Moroccan dress with little bits of mirror and thread woven into the yoke, ash was scattered wantonly on her lap and down her front, and Bert could see a ladder in her tights. Angela's *laissez-faire* attitude to the way she looked appalled her daughter, but on this occasion Bert was determined not to convey her revulsion. She needed to get her mother to agree to something.

'Erm, you know Adam, right?'

'No,' Angela said abruptly, returning to her book.

Bert was cross. She knew that her mother knew who Adam was because his dad was some famous poet and Angela had been impressed when she'd heard his name. Bert contained herself. She had to get her mother on her side. 'You know Adam de la Sour . . . my, er, my, um, my friend Adam. Look, you do know him – he's been round here a couple of times.'

Angela could tell that Bert was feeling uneasy and had something she wanted to get off her chest. She was enjoying dragging it out and was being deliberately obtuse. 'Oh, yes, I remember him, scrawny-looking thing, like a six-day-old string bean.' Angela looked up and smiled at her daughter as she delivered her insult.

Bert was fit to explode, letting rip a torrent of insults, the theme of which would be her mother's own physical appearance. However, she needed her mother's consent and she knew that her mother was trying to lure her away from this mission and into a heated row. 'Well, I don't think he looks like a string bean but anyway, thing is, right –'

'Oh, darling, I do wish you wouldn't say "right" after every second word, it really is infuriating.'

Bert persevered. Yeah, well, anyway, thing is, I –'

'Not only is it infuriating, it's also grammatically incorrect. One doesn't need to hear an interrogative after every word particularly one that isn't even a question.' Angela spoke with a smile in her voice and a condescending tone, a combination usually guaranteed to send Bert into a frenzy of rage.

Bert felt like jumping up and down on the spot and screaming her head off but she wasn't going to let her mum win this time, it was too important. 'Erm, the thing is Mum, right, er, sorry, the thing is Adam and me have decided –'

'Adam and I! Adam and I! Me and Adam, or Adam and I! Really, darling, do you ever pay attention at school? I do wonder sometimes.'

'Mum,' Bert raised her voice but refrained from shouting, 'will you shut – be quiet and listen? I'm trying to talk to you about something important!'

'All right, darling, calm down. Goodness, there's no need to fly off the handle like that, you *are* in a tizz.' Angela was satisfied now that she had succeeded in ruffling Bert's feathers.

Bert made a superhuman effort to contain herself. Even though she knew what her mother was up to she found it maddening to be deliberately wound up by her only to be told to calm down.

'Yeah, well, anyway, ri– Thing is, Adam and I have decided to sleep together, OK, and I want to go to the doctor's – all right?'

'No.' Angela's response was instant.

'What do you mean no?' Bert raged.

'No, I mean, no, you can't. You're only fifteen, it's illegal –'

'Oh, for Christ's sake, you can't be serious. Illegal? Don't be ridiculous. I can and I'm going to!'

'You can't, I'll stop you, you can't sleep with him, or with anybody – Oh, I don't know. Is everyone else at school sleeping with boys?' Angela had no idea how to respond to her daughter's request but she felt she just ought to say no. Her mind went into a spin: one wasn't supposed to just let one's children start having sex whenever they wanted to! Wasn't one supposed to impose laws and rules that they then adhered to? When had children started announcing to their parents that they were going to have sex? She would never have dreamt of doing anything of the kind.

Angela wished she had some guidance, someone she could turn to for advice. Her marriage had failed because although she and Charles had come from identical, austere backgrounds she had changed and he hadn't. He had always lived very comfortably in the grin-and-bear-it world, and in spite of her attempts to stamp on the feelings, Angela had begun to yearn for someone she could talk to about how unfulfilled she felt at just being a wife and mother. Charles had told her she was whingeing and to pull her socks up. When she couldn't, he'd found someone else whose socks were in a permanent state of pulled-upness. Angela knew that he would blame her for not being able to cope if she even attempted to discuss with him their daughter's hopes to lose her virginity with him.

Bert could tell her mother's mind was wandering and she wanted to capitalize on it.

'Georgie and Charlie from school are sleeping with their boyfriends and their parents know. Georgie is even on the pill.' Bert thought she'd better give some examples of well-behaved girls already having sex.

'You're not going on the pill.'

'I don't want to go on the bloody pill – it makes you fat, or it can. I want to get a diaphragm!'

Angela was dumbstruck. A diaphragm! How on earth did her daughter know about diaphragms? She hadn't known about sex, never mind birth control, until the first time it had happened to her and she hadn't known or learnt much more thereafter. 'Why can't you wait?'

'Because I don't bloody well want to!'

'There's no need to be so unpleasant.'

'You're trying to control my life and I only want to sleep with my boyfriend and you're trying to stop me!'

'I'm your mother, I'm supposed to! Look, I'm just trying to do what's right and I don't know what that is!'

Bert had one of her rare moments of sympathy for her mum. She could tell she didn't have a clue what to do. On the other hand, Bert thought, it's not my fault she's a crap mum. I didn't ask to be born. Seeing that her mother was wavering, Bert sensed that it was a good time to make another assault. 'Look, Mum, I'm going to do it sooner or later so you might as well let me take the proper precautions and then you don't have to worry about me getting pregnant or anything.'

Angela whipped round and gave Bert a horrified look. 'Is that supposed to be funny? There'll be no pregnancies round here! I'm not going through all that again, you mark my words.'

Bert had intended the mention of pregnancy as a little joke and it was painful to her to hear yet another reminder of how much her mother disliked being a mother.

'Yeah, well, there won't be if I go to the doctor's and sort it out, OK?' Bert felt she was getting nearer to winning the argument.

'All right, but I'm coming with you in case Dr Manning says you're too young. You might be physically too young for sex – have you thought of that? The doctor might say you can't have sex because your body isn't fully formed yet, you never know.' Bert raised her eyes to the heavens and gave her mother a long-suffering, knowing smile.

'Really, Mum, people aren't too young for sex. They're too old, not too young.'

As she walked up the stairs headed for her bedroom to attempt some homework Bert felt that she deserved a medal for not ending her parting sentence with 'and you should know that by now'. Tonight, however, she didn't feel her mother deserved the full extent of her vitriol.

Bert got out her schoolbooks and arranged them on her orange-painted wooden desk. It was covered in flower-power Fablon stickers with a large picture of the Bay City Rollers glued on in the centre. Bert had already grown out of them but having failed to get the picture off she'd defaced it instead as a mark of how much more sophisticated she was now. Got to admit, Les is still pretty tasty, though, she thought, as she opened a book on to his face. Bert never put her heart and soul into her homework but always did the minimum amount required to avoid detentions or more meetings about her dismal attitude with Mrs Fowler. She was trying to muster some interest in *Northanger Abbey* when she noticed that she was feeling a bit deflated, despite having won the right to embark on the journey to shed her unwanted hymen. Bert realized that if her mum had been more adamant that she shouldn't sleep with Adam it would actually have made her happier. It scared her that she was completely on her own when it came to managing life. Her mum didn't know what to do – ever.

Enormous Fannies

A few weeks later, following a visit to the doctor's, Bert was equipped with a diaphragm and some peculiar jelly. Dr Manning had told her that she must use the jelly or she might as well use half a scooped-out orange and throw away the diaphragm. Bert had assumed that she was joking, but intended to use the jelly anyway. To her delight Dr Manning had asked Angela to wait outside while she and Bert discussed the purpose of her visit. Bert had felt terribly grown-up and on the way home refused to discuss the details of what had happened in the consultation room on the grounds of privacy. Bert enjoyed telling a story too much to be discreet but she didn't want to go into the details of the jelly and stuff with her mum. Anyway I'd die, she thought, if Mum said something like 'I used to use that.' Yuk. Not only had Bert and her friends decided that sex for women over forty was an impossibility but they'd made each other screech with horror by conjuring up the image of their respective mums and dads doing it at all. The only thing they found more horrifying was the spectre of their parents ever having done it with each other in the first place.

'So can Adam stay this Friday?' Bert ventured, as they approached their house.

'Yes, very well.' Angela had decided that as she knew about everything and, indeed, had been involved in the preparations there was little point in refusing to allow the 'string bean' to spend the night. She felt uncomfortable about the whole episode and although she didn't disapprove morally she resented the uncomplicated way her daughter was breezily entering into what had been for her and most of her generation a torturously awkward and unsatisfactory stage of adulthood.

However, she was mistaken. Bert wasn't entering into sex with Adam with a breezy air at all. Bert was petrified and not at all sure she even really fancied Adam that much. Bert and her peers were driven to embark on sex as soon as possible by what having sex offered – sophistication, superiority and a huge step further away from childhood and all its uncomfortable associations. Ever since Bert had started having to look out for herself she hadn't really felt like a child. She knew she wasn't an adult but she realized that she had more responsibilities and worries than most children. She longed to come home from school to find that her mother had transformed, cleaned up the house and made fish fingers and baked beans for supper, going on later to nag her about homework and ending the day chatting to her in the bath before bed. As Angela hadn't done that sort of thing before the divorce, Bert didn't know why she hoped that her mum would suddenly start doing so now, but she couldn't help fantasizing sometimes.

'So, come on, what happened, *what happened*?' Tess was panting. It was the following Monday morning at first break and Tess, Vicky and Bert had torn down the corridor to stake themselves out in their lair for the next twenty minutes. They were desperate to hear how the great virginity loss had gone. They hadn't spoken over the weekend because Bert had had to spend Saturday and Sunday with Adam and hadn't wanted to talk to her pals in front of him. In fact, she wished he'd gone home the morning after the deed was done so that she could go straight round to her friends and spend the weekend telling them all about it, which she knew would have been much more fun. After all, Bert had decided, one of the main reasons for doing it in the first place was so that you could talk to your friends about it.

'OK, so we watched a bit of TV, right . . .' The three of them had settled down in their usual corner, coats-acting-as-wimples in place and Bert was embarking on her tale.

'Was your mum in the room?' Tess was a stickler for details.

'No, course my bloody mum wasn't in the room. Don't interrupt!'

'I didn't mean in the bedroom. I meant before, when you were watching TV.'

'I knew you didn't mean the bedroom – even you couldn't be that stupid. No, she wasn't with us – I don't know where she was. Just shut up and listen, will you?'

'OK, but she was in the house, yeah?' Tess felt this was an important detail.

'Yes, she was in the fucking house! What is the matter with you?' Bert screamed.

'I just wanted to get an idea of the atmosphere,' Tess said sulkily. Bert and Vicky looked at each other and raised their eyes to the heavens. They were in silent agreement: Tess just didn't understand what the important stuff was sometimes.

'Just let her get on with it. You know how easily distracted she gets,' Vicky said, intending to appease Tess by teasing Bert.

'Thank you very much. Anyway, so we're watching TV and then we start snogging, which I didn't really want to do in the TV room in case Mum came in and said something stupid, which she definitely would have done, and then, after a bit, he goes, "Shall we go up?"'

'Oh, darling, I wish you wouldn't say "goes" instead of "says", it's absolutely awful.' They all laughed at Tess's perfect imitation of Angela.

'Anyway, anyway, so we go upstairs and luckily he went to

the bathroom first so I quickly got undressed and jumped under the covers.'

'Why? Didn't you want him to see you naked?' Tess knew the answer to this perfectly well but she was paying Bert back for earlier.

'Course I didn't want him to see me naked – blimey, the whole thing's weird enough as it is without having to stand about looking at each other in the nude as well. So, anyway, he comes back into the room and he obviously couldn't see anything 'cos he trips over something on the floor.'

'Was the light off?' Vicky had guessed the answer but wanted to know for sure.

'Course.'

'Why?' Tess really didn't know.

'Because it's well known you always do it in the dark. People don't do it with the lights on, no one does, it's one of those things.' Bert was sure of herself.

'What about in the daytime? What do people do then?' Tess was puzzled.

'I dunno. You close your eyes or something. Anyway, people don't do it in the daytime. Not normally – it's understood, it's another one of those things, yeah?'

'Oh.' Tess seemed unconvinced but was prepared on this occasion to bow to Bert's recently established superior knowledge.

'Anyway, so he trips up and falls over – God, he made a right thump. I was terrified Mum was going to come in and complain about the noise. I knew she was probably lurking about some-where waiting to pounce.'

'Didn't you get up and help him?' Tess interrupted.

'No, course not! I didn't have anything on, remember? Anyway I think he must have hurt himself because I could sort of hear him swearing under his breath. After a bit I could feel him getting

66

into the bed, but he was trying to get in at the wrong end first 'cos he couldn't see, so then I had to tell him where I was.'

'Hadn't you said anything up till then?' Vicky seemed surprised.

'For Chrissakes, do you want to hear what happened or not?' Bert was losing her patience.

'Yeah, all right, keep your hair on, but, you know, you do always take ages to get to the point.'

'That's because you're always interrupting me.' Bert was a natural story-teller, and although it did take her a long time to get to the crux of a tale she was convinced that was the fault of her friends' interruptions, not because she was a waffler. 'Anyway,' she recommenced where she'd left off, 'I could feel his hard-on through his pants and we started kissing.'

'He still had his pants on?' Tess thought it sounded a bit peculiar to get into bed with your pants on if you knew you were going to have sex.

'Course he did.' Bert thought it was perfectly normal.

'Did you have your knickers on?'

'No, I had a T-shirt on, so that covered my fanny and stuff. Anyway, we just sort of lay there for a bit, not doing anything, and then he held my hand . . .'

'Ooer, sweet,' Vicky cooed.

'Yeah, it might have been but my hands were all sweaty and . . .'

'Why were you sweating?' Tess inquired.

Bert was reluctant to admit she'd been nervous. 'Cos I was all hot, yeah, under the duvet with him as well and everything. Anyway so we start kissing and then I could feel his hard-on through his pants.'

'Wasn't it sticking out if it was hard?' Tess thought this was a fair point.

'Shut up, will you? I'm trying tell you about my first time and

67

you're asking stupid things like that. I'm going to strangle you in a minute!'

'I only asked,' Tess moaned.

'Did you touch it?' Vicky would have been very impressed if Bert had.

'No, I didn't really want to and he didn't ask me to.' Bert didn't mind admitting this, as she didn't think there was anything unusual about not touching it. 'So after a bit I think he'd got it out or pushed his pants down a bit or something . . .'

Tess made a face, sticking her tongue out a tiny way between her teeth and screwing up her nose, finding the idea of Adam inelegantly struggling out of his pants while trying to mount Bert silly.

Bert ignored her and continued, '. . . so he sort of gets on top of me and –'

'Had you put the thingy in?' Tess interrupted, suddenly realizing that she hadn't established that before the story had begun.

'Of course I had the diaphragm in! Wouldn't have been much point in getting it, would there, if I wasn't going to use it?'

'Sorry, go on,' Tess said.

'Where was I? Oh, yeah, so he gets on top of me and after a bit of fumbling about he pushes it in.'

'Did it hurt?'

'Erm, no, not really.' Bert hadn't thought about it hurting until Vicky'd asked. They'd all assumed it would hurt because that was the perceived intelligence, and Bert was surprised to find herself realizing that it hadn't hurt at all.

'Probably means you've got an enormous fanny or something,' Tess said idly. She wasn't intending to insult Bert but she didn't see how it could not hurt unless you were very roomy down there.

'Piss off, will you? Anyway, he sort of bounced around for a bit, like he was dancing but lying down and then he kind of made a noise that sounded like a cross between a squeak and as if someone had stood on his foot, and then it was over and we had a bit of a cuddle, but I had to go to the bathroom 'cos I could feel all the stuff coming out.'

'Yeurgh!'

'Tess, it's just part of having sex, you know. It is natural,' Bert said. Secretly she agreed with Tess that the spunky stuff was disgusting but she thought she'd better not admit it. She feared that not liking that part made her a bit immature.

'Did it last long?' Vicky wanted to know.

'No, not really, erm, normal time, about . . . er, three or four or five minutes, you know.' Bert thought that anything between three and five minutes was probably normal. She couldn't imagine people wanting to do it for much longer.

'Was it great?' Tess asked.

'Oh, yeah, fantastic, really, really brilliant. I really, really love Adam. He's great.'

Bert was lying, which she wasn't accustomed to doing, not to her best friends. I'm not really lying, she thought, on her way home after school. I suppose I do love him or something. Well, I'm supposed to, aren't I? The truth that Bert had held back from her friends, and hardly dared admit even to herself, was that her first go at sex had been singularly uneventful.

Although Angela hadn't given her a mother-to-daughter pep talk, for which Bert had been grateful, she instinctively suspected that the episode should have been more interesting than she'd found it. She knew Adam was keen on her but she'd been disappointed to discover that the entire event seemed to be focused on his climax and nothing else. It was supposed to have been a momentous moment in her life: she had banked on feeling like a completely different person, on actually *being* a completely different person. God, it's hardly worth doing if it's always going to be that boring, Bert thought, as she opened her front door.

She heard her mother calling from the living room, 'Albertine, is that you? Well, don't slam the door!' She decided that, if for no other reason, it was worth doing to hasten the onset of adulthood and the inevitable distance that it would provide between her and her mother.

The Wanker 1975

'I'm not going to bother going to double Blogs, I can't face Red Hot Lava. Do you fancy going up to the Heath for a smoke this afternoon when lunch-break is over instead?' Bert was always the first to propose bunking off, which, by now, mid first term of their fifth year, took up as much of their time as the few selected classes they did attend.

'Well . . .' Vicky hesitated '. . . thing is, it's only a few weeks until the mocks and I don't want to do badly in them. They are supposed to be practice for the O levels, you know.'

'Oooh, machwuuurre,' Tess and Bert sneered loudly. Vicky really wanted to do well in her exams but found it increasingly hard to apply herself in the face of pressure from her friends. Unlike Bert, Vicky was doing well at school and was generally popular with the teachers. They considered her quiet and polite, and if she ever did get into trouble, they unanimously agreed that she wasn't to blame and must have been led astray by her unfortunate, and to them inexplicable, friendship with the unruly Albertine Plummer.

Vicky had a fiercely strong character and was never led astray by Bert. She loved Bert's ability to clown around at any time, no matter how inappropriate the moment. But for herself, she'd chosen a different path. Long ago she'd worked out that if she allowed people to believe she was compliant, she was much more likely to achieve her own aims than by drawing unnecessary attention to herself. This steely characteristic had been developed

71

and refined in the course of the hysterical rows her parents had indulged in leading up to their divorce. Neither parent had ever thought to temper their aggression towards each other to protect their daughters. In fact more often than not both parents would attempt to enlist the support of whichever child was present. Rather than taking sides, Vicky had elected to abstain.

'You're not even doing biology O level, are you?' Bert asked, in a contemptuous tone.

'Of course I am. Why else would I want to go?'

'I dunno. Because you're a swot?' Bert was trying to shame her friend into missing the class.

'I'm not a bloody swot, I happen to like biology actually, madam, thank you very much! You know, it is possible to enjoy learning sometimes, you know.'

'Ooooooh, well, pardon me for breathing.' The pair fell into a sulky silence, which both were equally resolute not to be the first to break.

The three friends were sitting in a row on the bench that looked on to the school's only tennis court, which, as usual, was unoccupied. Formal tennis lessons weren't included in the curriculum so the court was only used for its intended purpose on rare occasions by the school's few seriously sporty pupils. Everybody else used it either to sunbathe on or, if bored enough, to thrash balls violently back and forth at each other until they caused injury or ran out of energy. Tess was sitting between Bert and Vicky. The sun was hot and they had kicked off their once-much-prized Kickers boots. To ensure total exposure to the sun they had rolled up the sleeves of their shirts and tucked the hems of their skirts into their knickers all the way round. They looked like they were wearing improvised doublet and hose.

The court was situated at the back of the school, having been added on to the original Victorian lay-out of the grounds. Two sides of it were surrounded by high brick walls separating it from the outside world and making it ideal for sunbathing. Behind the bench was a large piece of grass that normally served as the venue for unauthorized games of rounders, and seemed to have no other purpose. No one was playing today. On the remaining side of the court, to the right of the bench, stood a high wire fence dividing it from the small garden at the rear of the caretaker's house. The caretaker, Mr Baker, was an officious short, stocky man, who sported a small, neat black moustache. He lived alone with his adored bulldog called Willie, which always accompanied him on his frequent, and regimentally timed, patrols of the school grounds. Mr Baker was convinced that he and his dog were the only obstacles standing between the school's safety and imminent hostile invasion.

After studying the Second World War in history, the girls had decided that Mr Baker was actually Hitler, who, having escaped from Germany, had disguised himself as a school caretaker while awaiting the perfect moment to relaunch his quest for world domination. Meanwhile, he was keeping up his dictatorship skills yelling at first-years who inadvertently left gates open or dropped sweet wrappers. Their fantasy was lent further support by the fact that he was constantly bursting into the cloakrooms shouting, 'I know what's going on in here, you can't fool me. I can smell drugs a mile off.' On one occasion, he had entered shouting, 'You won't get away with your law-breaking this time – I've trained my Willie to sniff out drugs. I'm on to you now!' Every single girl present had erupted into uncontrollable laughter, and this time Tess had actually wet herself. Their amusement had been made all the more raucous by the fact that Mr Baker had remained glued to the spot with a bemused expression, lead in hand, tethering his loyally snarling dog and clearly ignorant of what had made the girls laugh.

While it was true that the vast majority of the school's postpubertal pupils were in the habit of smoking dope by now ('It's absolutely *de rigueur*,' Bert had taken to saying), hardly anyone ever smoked on the school grounds unless they were hoping to be expelled. At the North London Girls' College, where making allowances for and understanding even the most antisocial behaviour were considered paramount, it was one of the few activities that would result in immediate expulsion. However, Bert and her pals so enjoyed Mr Baker's outbursts that they had taken to smoking herbal cigarettes in great quantities, even though they made them feel sick. They'd worked out that if Mr Baker's Willie was really trained to sniff out drugs he evidently hadn't been trained very well as he couldn't differentiate between marijuana and a pot-pourri of dried herbs. The dog's poor drug-detecting skills ensured that, during the fifth year, a high proportion of the gang's breaks were spent entertaining themselves taunting the caretaker and his Willie.

'All right, come on, then, let's go to the Heath. It's too hot to be in the biology lab all afternoon. I can't face having to look at Red Hot Lava's huge sweaty tits all day,' Tess said, finally breaking the silence. She had got bored waiting for one of her sulking friends to concede defeat.

'Yeah, all right.' Vicky was relieved that she hadn't had to lose face by either volunteering not to go to biology or speaking first. Bert was glad that her plan had come to fruition and resisted the temptation to rub Vicky's nose in it by asking what had happened to her determination to go to the class.

The Heath was a short journey away but too far to walk, so they decided to take a bus. As they jumped off the moving vehicle they congratulated themselves on having avoided paying the fare. The threesome had sat on top and fled past the conductor down the stairs when he'd come up. They were convinced that their genius had ensured the success of the heist. In fact, the conductor on this particular route was so weary of wisecracking schoolkids that he rarely bothered attempting to collect their fares at all.

The little group tramped across the Heath, heading towards their usual destination, a large tree in the middle of a small copse on the top of a low hill. They had discovered this tree a few years ago and considered it their own property. It was particularly well suited to their clandestine dope-smoking sessions as it had mutated into a kind of enormous stool on which they could sit well out of view. Instead of growing up towards the sky, the tree's branches had grown to half the height they should have and then turned outwards at right angles, forming a large round seat of intermeshed branches, twigs and leaves circling the top of the trunk. As they approached the tree they found a park bench which they dragged along the ground behind them to use as a ladder.

'Onwards and upwards,' Tess said, mimicking Miss Jay, as they clambered up the bench and into the tree. Once she'd settled into her chosen position, Bert, who was the last up, kicked away the bench. It was easy enough to jump down and by kicking over the bench they reckoned that anyone who came along wouldn't guess that people were up in the tree. Bert produced a joint and some matches. Having planned in advance to suggest bunking off biology, she had rolled a couple at home that morning before setting off for school. Bert always kept a ready supply of hash, skins and fags stashed in a special box at home. In common with most of her dope-smoking peers Bert went to the lengthy precautions of ensuring she bought the packets of No. 10s at a different newsagent from the one where she got her cigarette papers. They felt you could never be sure who was going to report you to the 'pigs'.

It was still warm and they lay back on the branches passing round the joint in silence. To make sure they got stoned as quickly as possible they had learnt to inhale taking enormous drags, which they then held in their lungs for so long that conversation was rendered impossible. Expertise at dope-smoking was one of the few things all three took equally seriously.

Suddenly Tess noticed something, by the edge of the pond that lay at the bottom of the hill. 'What's that bloke doing?' she asked.

Bert and Vicky looked over in the direction that Tess was pointing. They could see a man in a belted raincoat. He seemed to be rooting about in his pocket for something, while looking furtively around him.

'He's just stopping to blow his nose,' Vicky said, seeing him produce a large handkerchief from the pocket.

'You don't stop walking along to blow your nose, you keep going. It's not a stopping thing, like tying up a shoelace or hoicking your knickers out of your crack,' Bert hissed. She didn't want the man to hear them. 'And why would he look around him like that before he did it. It's not illegal to blow your nose!'

'Maybe he's got a joint in his handkerchief or something,' Tess had started whispering too.

'Men that age don't smoke dope, and definitely not if they wear raincoats like that, you idiot.' Bert was confident that, like sex, drugs were only for young, trendy people like them.

'What's the kind of raincoat you wear got to do with whether you smoke dope or not?' Vicky thought Bert was being a bit narrow-minded.

'It's obvious, isn't it? That's the sort of raincoat my dad wears and he's probably never even *seen* a joint.'

'Well, that bloke might have borrowed the raincoat off some-one who doesn't smoke dope, but he does,' said Tess, who loved finding an obscure and unlikely line of argument to pursue.

As Tess and Bert began a heated whispered debate about what kind of person wore raincoats and also used drugs, Vicky continued to watch. Just as they were getting under way, they heard Vicky hiss, 'Look, look, you two! Look, he's wanking.'

Bert and Tess whipped their heads round and saw that the man had pulled his penis out of his raincoat, which remained done up, and was indeed masturbating furiously.

All three girls were dumbstruck and stared at him in silence. It was clear to them that the man was oblivious to their presence. The trio were completely blasé faced with the spectacle.

'There's no one around, so why's he wanking into a bush?' asked Tess, bemused.

'Maybe he finds foliage erotic,' Bert quipped.

They started giggling but with their hands clamped over their mouths so as not to draw his attention. They carried on watching until Bert suddenly realized something. 'Yurgh, he got the handkerchief out to spunk into.'

'Yuk!' Tess agreed.

'Well, that's better than him doing it all over the bushes. It wouldn't be very nice brushing past that, would it?' Vicky had an eye for practicality.

Suddenly they all noticed his body stiffen – he was about to reach his climax. They were transfixed. As the man ejaculated into his handkerchief, throwing back his head in ecstasy, the three friends erupted into a spontaneous loud cheer, waving their arms and clapping. The man spun round and looked up towards them. They continued to wave and cheer. A look of appalled horror and shame spread over the man's face and he immediately took flight. As he went he frantically tried to push his penis back into his trousers. However, in his haste he got it and his flies tangled up together hampering his flight and causing him to drop the soiled handkerchief. He eventually made his escape with his penis flapping from side to side and leaving his hanky behind.

The girls' glee was unbridled.

'Stop, stop,' Tess was urging, clutching her fanny. 'I can't wet myself up here, I've got nothing to dry it with.'

'You could always use his hanky,' Bert said, laughing hysterically at the revolting suggestion. Their amusement kept up for ages. The unfortunate masturbating man, compounded by the giggles the dope had given them, made stopping impossible.

Once they finally regained their composure Vicky said, 'So, he wasn't really a proper wanker, was he?'

'What do you mean? Course he was a proper wanker,' Bert replied, still laughing.

'No, I mean, he wasn't doing it so that anyone would see. He was just having a wank.'

'Oh, I see. You mean he's just an ordinary bloke out for a walk on the Heath and suddenly he comes over all horny so he stops to have a wank in the middle of a public park. *Bien sûr*, what could be more normal?' Bert sneered.

'Well, mmm, s'pose.' Vicky could see her argument was flawed.

'Makes him a better sort of wanker, though, doesn't it?' Tess piped up.

'Eh?' Bert had no idea what Tess could possibly mean.

'Well, if you're going to be a wanker then it's better to be a wanker who just likes doing it in the open, right, with no one looking, yeah, you know, better than the sort of bloke who wants to do it at you, you know, who gets his kicks because he wants you to see his prick and stuff, right?'

Vicky and Bert agreed that Tess had a point.

'I feel a bit sorry for him now.'

'Honestly, Vic, you're so pathetic sometimes. He might not have been doing it *at* someone but he still had his prick out. Anyone could have come round the corner, an old lady or something.' Bert was exasperated that Vicky's natural inclination to be kind was being extended even to a man who masturbated in public.

'Yeah, s'pose so.' They were too stoned by this time to continue the debate and decided to repair to their respective houses, much cheered by the afternoon's events.

As Bert neared her home she realized something that made her very pleased: God, just think, Vic nearly missed seeing that and now she'll always have me to thank for seeing that bloke wanking.

These Boots Weren't Made for Walking

'Wow, it's amazing . . .'

'Absolutely fantastic.'

'Completely and totally out of this world!'

Bert, Vicky and Tess were dazzled. They were standing in the entrance hall of the newly done-up, bigger, grander Biba store on Kensington High Street, staring up, eyes and mouths wide open, at the massive black and gold vaulted ceiling. On either side of the entrance hall were vast rooms also painted black and gold, filled with outlandish merchandise. They found the opulence awe-inspiring, a feast of black silk, fake fur rugs and reproduction art deco, with the atmosphere of a twenties bordello. To the three girls it seemed like the most amazing place in the whole wide world.

Until now they had usually spent their Saturdays mooching round Kensington Market, the hippie Mecca. Dope could easily be scored there and, almost as importantly, it was the only place on earth they knew of where you could buy flared loons in every single colour you might want. Although loons were on their way out by now they were still an acceptable alternative to jeans, especially if worn with a really funky pair of platform boots. No one wore them with cheesecloth smocks any more, though, a teaming which, until eighteen months previously, had been the very last word in style.

Bert and her friends were dressed in all their weekend finery. Each of them wore the essential Biba puffed-sleeved T-shirt. At first they had rowed about all buying the same T-shirts but no self-respecting follower of fashion could be without one, and the range wasn't extensive enough for Bert, Vicky and Tess to choose different styles. After a while they had decided it was funny all to wear the same tops, although they'd agreed on different colours.

The moment they'd bought the T-shirts they'd set about modifying them to suit the current trend. This involved pulling the drawstring out of the cuff, ditching the puffed sleeve in favour of a floppy, flared, medieval look. The cuffs became wide and unruly and frequently trailed in food when they were eating, not something they cared about but which drove their mothers mad.

They were all wearing their platform boots. Characteristically, Vicky had the most elegant pair: pea green suede with a modest platform, not too high but not so low as to look like someone's mum might wear them. She was wearing a tight pair of purple loons and her Biba T-shirt, which was chocolate brown. As always she looked like something straight off the fashion pages of *Jackie* magazine. Tess and Bert wore identical T-shirts, which had originally been black but were now a washed-out grey. Tess was wearing black loons and black leather boots, the platforms of which were too high and made walking very difficult. This had not escaped Bert and she was fond of saying at the very moment Tess was looking most wobbly, 'Better not fall off those, Tess, you'll break your neck.' Despite the perambulatory handicap Tess persevered with the boots, partly because she knew her mother wouldn't ever buy her another pair and partly because she thought she looked slimmer with the extra height.

Bert was wearing loons of a deep blood-red colour, and although they weren't hugely flattering she'd been emboldened to wear them by Vicky's assurances that she looked fine in them. Anyway, Bert felt that anything she wore with her new boots looked fantastic. The boots, made of burgundy-coloured leather, were her pride and joy and Bert was enraptured by them. In a rare moment of kindness (generated by hearing that Charles had been dumped by his latest girlfriend) Angela had suggested that she pay for Bert to have a pair made by the Greek cobbler whose shop was down the road from their house. He had started making platform boots to order, having enterprisingly noticed that there was a demand for them in a wider variety of colours than was available in most shops. Bert had been overcome with gratitude, particularly as she'd discovered that her calves were a little too chunky to get shop-made boots properly done up without a struggle and, even accompanied by Vicky and Tess, she found attempting to force herself into them too humiliating. Her gratitude had been short-lived, evaporating into thin air the instant her mother, upon seeing the boots for the first time, had cried out, 'What an appalling colour! Had I had any idea you were going to choose such a dreadful colour I'd never in a million years have offered to pay for them. Maroon leather, dear God! You look like you've got a couple of cheap wine bottles strapped to your lower legs. What were you thinking of? And the expense!'

Bert had felt like strangling her but made do with shouting at the top of her voice, 'You have no idea what it's like to be me – you don't care about anybody but yourself. I love these boots and they're not fucking maroon they're burgundy, which is really bloody trendy, and I was looking forward to wearing them for the first time and now you've ruined it for me, like you ruin everything! Every time I go out in them now I'll be wondering if everyone thinks they look like wine bottles!' To Bert's relief her friends had heaped much admiration on the boots and the height of the platforms had been deemed 'just right'.

'So where are we going to go first?' asked Tess, who always deferred decisions to Vicky and Bert.

'I dunno. Let's just wander around and see what's here,' Vicky suggested.

'Yeah,' Bert agreed. 'I bet everything's great. There's, like, five floors or something. We can sort of explore.' So far they had studiously ignored their companions for the day: Adam, now officially Bert's boyfriend, his cousin Mark, and a friend of Mark's called Barney. Bert had never seen either Mark or Barney before but had told Vicky and Tess, as they made their way to meet the boys, that as long as they didn't turn out to be gargoyles then they should probably get off with them when they all went back to Adam's later that night as they'd already planned. Vicky hadn't reacted to the suggestion while Tess had told Bert to mind her own fucking business and pulled a theatrical I'm-going-to-puke face.

Vicky and Bert knew that Tess hadn't yet snogged a boy and they were concerned that she get the ball rolling. 'After all,' they had said to each other in Tess's absence, 'she's fifteen years old, for Chrissakes. Fifteen!'

Vicky's style of encouraging her friend was sensitive and discreet, gently mentioning a potential candidate here and there, without necessarily identifying him as a likely first snog. Bert, however, had little patience and couldn't see what was holding Tess back: 'Look, you've got to start somewhere. It doesn't matter what the first one's like, you've just got to get a feel of the whole thing, you know, sort of get the thing off the ground, honestly it's not that big a deal, the longer you hold off, the more weird it's going to be! You don't want people to think you're some sort of freak or, worse still, a lezzie!'

It wasn't that Tess was biding her time: she just could not imagine how the whole embarrassing kissing thing started. She knew a few boys, mainly Adam and his friends, and they usually all hung around together every weekend and during holidays. She was quite comfortable sitting chatting with them, but the idea of going from that into a frenzied snog seemed ludicrous. As far as she could tell, Vicky and Bert were genuinely immersed in the whole science, but when she wasn't with boys she never thought about them even though her two constant companions talked about little else.

Tess was an only child and rarely saw her father, who lived abroad and her mother liked privacy. Consequently Tess had learnt early on in her life to make her own entertainment. She'd been regarded as 'odd' at primary school but as she'd never been aware of how she was perceived it hadn't bothered her. She much preferred her life since meeting Vicky and Bert and loved belonging to a gang but she couldn't pretend to be interested in all the same things as them. Well, she'd found that she could pretend, and did when necessary, but she'd also decided that she'd get off with someone when she felt like it and not before.

Once inside the Biba lift they decided to start on the top floor and work their way down. This decision had been made unanimously by means of a few grunts, ensuring that the girls had still not exchanged a word with the boys. Ordinarily Bert wouldn't have said much to Adam anyway, seeing as her girl-friends were present, but casual conversation had been rendered impossible by the presence of Barney. Bert could not believe how tasty he was. He was tall, with a huge mop of light brown curls, just like Marc Bolan's. He was wearing tight deep green velvet trousers tucked into the most amazingly fantastic knee-high boots Bert had ever seen in her life – a pair of the actual Mr Freedom appliquéd leather Stars and Stripes platforms. Bert knew they cost a fortune and had assumed that only pop stars and models could afford them. She was absolutely sure that David Bowie had worn some on *Top of the Pops*. It didn't seem possible that a friend of someone she knew could actually be in possession of a pair of those boots.

Later on, when they were having a cup of tea in the deco tea rooms filled with huge palms and waitresses wearing twenties outfits, Vicky mentioned that she liked the cups they were drinking out of. They were large black china cups with the Biba motif in gold on the side. Without saying a word Barney leant over the table, picked up Vicky's now empty cup and popped it into his shoulder-bag, which was hanging off the back of his chair. The assembled group was speechless. Barney shrugged his shoulders, looked at Vicky and said, 'If you like it, you should have it.'

Bert thought she was going to pass out with envy. She turned to Adam and said, 'I like them too. Get me one.'

He replied, in his usual bland tone, 'No, I'll get caught, I'm not nicking it.' Bert wanted to kill him for his fearfulness.

Barney made matters worse by chipping in casually, 'You only get caught if you think you'll get caught. Watch this.'

At that moment the waitress approached their table; everyone's eyes except Barney's were glued to her face as she piled the used cups on to a tray. 'There should be six cups here. Where's the sixth cup?' she asked suddenly, looking at Barney.

He paused for a moment, giving her a beatific smile, and said, 'Oh, yeah, I took it back up to the counter earlier. The tea wasn't right.'

The waitress smiled back at him and said, 'Sorry about that, I'll take it off your bill.' Bert and Vicky looked at each other. Both knew instantly what the other was thinking: this boy was a Prince Amongst Men.

Barney had secured his position – with the girls at any rate – as the one person everyone wanted to stick closest to and they spent the rest of the afternoon trailing after him as he charmed shop assistant after shop assistant whilst secreting miscellaneous items in his bag. During the shoplifting spree Barney would occasionally turn to acknowledge his entourage. Bert and Vicky were impressed beyond belief by his cool demeanour, but by mid-afternoon Tess had clearly become less enamoured of him. 'Don't you think he's a bit full of himself?' she whispered to her friends, but they both ignored her.

Adam and Mark were happy to talk to each other while lurking in the background, having made sure there was enough distance between themselves and Barney to avoid arrest should he get caught.

'Right, shall we go back to your place, Adam, and see what I got?' Barney said, when he'd had enough.

Bert couldn't believe that he didn't even know what stuff he'd got, that he'd just nicked it because he could. He really is amazing, she thought, before glancing over at Adam sitting opposite her in the tube carriage trundling its way back up to North London. More boring sex with him tonight, if he doesn't get too stoned, she moaned to herself. They'd been sleeping together for a while now and every single bonk (once on a Friday night, once on a Saturday morning, once on a Saturday night and once on a Sunday morning because weekends were the time they spent together) was exactly the same as the first time. Bert could not believe it hadn't got more eventful; the regularity and monotony of the sex was a huge disappointment to her. Once or twice, while they were doing it, Bert had felt something unexpected, a bit like she was going to pee, followed by an itchy and restless feeling, but she hadn't known what it meant. It had occurred to her that it might go away if they did it again and, on one occasion, she suggested this to Adam who told her that she was an insatiable nymphomaniac and that no normal girl wanted to do it twice. Bert had been shamed by the idea of being thought sex mad. Notwithstanding, she remained puzzled by the itchy, restless thing. All she knew for sure was that it had motivated her to make demands of Adam that she would never have ordinarily dared make. Bert's sense of shame had restrained her from asking him how come he was such an expert on what other girls did or did not do. She knew he'd been a virgin until they slept together and resented him suggesting that there was something wrong with her, but as she feared there might be she didn't want to push it.

Too Special For That

Adam's parents were away for the weekend and his two younger brothers were staying the night with friends so the house was at their disposal. The prospect of an empty house held no great thrill for Bert, as she already knew what lay in store for her, but for Vicky it was electrifying. Both she and Bert had picked up on Barney's interest in her and Vicky was very much hoping that things were going to develop between them.

Barney put on the latest Emerson, Lake and Palmer record and they all settled down in Adam's parents' living room to smoke their way through the motley collection of bits of grass and hash they'd pooled. The house stood in a large garden and was made up entirely of huge sheets of glass, instead of conventional windows, and timber instead of bricks and mortar. Bert thought it was a bit like a spooky treehouse and wasn't comfortable with the whole open-plan lay-out. The living room was U-shaped and occupied about half of the first floor, the remaining area given over to bedrooms and bathrooms. In the space underneath the U was the kitchen, which you could see down into from the living room.

As they all got progressively more stoned Vicky announced she had the munchies; Adam managed to summon up just enough energy to tell her to help herself to whatever was in the kitchen. As she stood up Barney suggested he go with her. Bert instinctively knew what was going to happen and she felt jealous. She didn't like the feeling. Despite having increased the number of boys she'd snogged, Vicky was still a virgin, and Bert couldn't help resenting that Vicky's first time was going to be with someone like Barney rather than with someone like Adam.

After a while it was clear that Vicky and Barney weren't coming back up and Bert announced, to deaf ears, that she was going to bed. Mark had disappeared and Adam had passed out on the sofa. Tess looked like she was watching telly with the sound off but on nearing her Bert realized that her friend had fallen into a vegetative state: her eyes were glazed over and staring fixedly at the flickering screen. Bert thought she looked like the waxwork of the dying Admiral Nelson they'd seen at Madame Tussaud's. She decided to leave her there. She headed off for Adam's bedroom but couldn't stop herself shooting a quick glance over the balcony down into the kitchen where she saw what she had known she'd see: Barney and Vicky locked in a passionate embrace. As she drifted off to sleep she consoled herself, thinking, Well, at least I'll get to hear what he's like to bonk.

The next morning Bert awoke to find Tess exactly where she'd left her and in the same state. Adam and Mark were in the kitchen scoffing a huge fried breakfast. Bert asked Mark where he'd gone last night and he revealed that he'd fallen asleep in the bath having got into it for '. . . a little nap 'cos I thought the sides of the bath would feel nice and cool on my face, which was feeling a bit hot'. Bert thought he was a bit weird, and that as such he'd probably have got off with Tess if only she hadn't turned into a dummy. Some time ago Vicky and Bert had decided that the boy Tess finally did get off with would have to be a bit strange because as she never showed any interest in boys the one who went ahead regardless would *have* to be weird. Bert didn't really want to be alone with the two lads and decided to wake Tess. She shouted loudly up the well, hoping that the racket would also wake up Vicky and Barney. She couldn't stomach the idea of them lounging around in bed all day enjoying copious amounts of rampant sex – something she and Adam had never even contemplated. Eventually Tess leant over the balcony.

'Make us a cup of tea. I feel sick.' Bert was pleased to have something to do as she'd felt increasingly lemon-like hanging around waiting for Adam or Mark to say something, and agreed instantly. While she was making it Vicky entered the kitchen behind her.

'Ooh, make us a cup too, will you?' she said. 'And one for Barney. I'll take it to him.'

'No, he can make it him-fucking-self. What am I? His bloody maid?' Bert snapped.

Vicky was stunned. 'Don't be so stupid, you're already doing it. Just make us a couple of extra cups, all right?'

'No, make it yourself, if you want it that badly.'

'Blimey, what's the matter with you? It's only a cup of tea! God, if you're going to be like that I *will* make it myself.' Vicky said, pushing crossly past her friend to get at the tea-bags. Bert turned round with two cups in hand and saw that Tess, who had joined them in the kitchen by now, was giving her a puzzled look. Bert hadn't intended to be quite so childish: it had just come out that way. Anyway, why should I make His Majesty a fucking cup of tea? she reasoned, as she and Tess trampled back upstairs.

Vicky returned to Barney and didn't emerge until a couple of hours later. During this time Bert, Tess, Adam and Mark sat silently in front of the TV, not knowing quite what to say to each other. On the occasions that they were alone Adam and Bert talked a bit, or rather Adam responded to Bert's recurrent and favourite line of questioning, the theme of which was getting him to quantify how much he loved her by comparison to dope, his mum, football, King Crimson, good grass, his brothers, his

Yes poster, and any other objects or people she could think of. Bert didn't care whether he loved her or not, but it made her feel good to hear him *say* he loved her.

Eventually while Bert and Tess were discussing going home Vicky and Barney emerged and Vicky told them she was coming with them. Bert went over and gave Adam a kiss.

'I'll see you next weekend, yeah?' he said, giving her a little wink which she assumed he thought was sexy. Oh, God, he's so pathetic, she grumbled to herself, as they prepared to leave.

She and Tess hung about awkwardly in the hall while Vicky and Barney went through protracted goodbyes. Bert was convinced that Vicky was making more of a meal of it than was strictly necessary, just to pay her back for the tea episode. In return she made an ostentatious display of not paying attention to their passionate farewells. Tess, who was still stoned, genuinely wasn't paying any attention, being absorbed by the Escher print hanging next to the front door. Finally Vicky and Barney managed to prise themselves apart and the three girls set off. At first no one spoke: Bert was waiting sulkily for Vicky to volunteer some information about what had gone on with Barney, and Tess was worrying about whether her mum had phoned Vicky's mum to check whether she really had spent the night there. Eventually Bert could bear it no longer. She thought she'd burst if she didn't find out.

'*Eh bien*. So?' she said, to Vicky.

'So what?' Vicky replied, irritating Bert enormously.

'So? So? What happened with erm . . . thingy . . . erm . . . you know.' Bert thought that casually pretending she'd forgotten Barney's name would disguise any hint of jealousy.

'Barney,' Vicky said, making it sound like she was eating a Flake.

'Yeah, him, well, what happened? Did you . . . you know . . . did you do it?' Bert said, in a tone she hoped was funny.

'I don't think I should talk about what me and Barney did together,' Vicky said sanctimoniously.

'What?' Bert shrieked, at the top of her voice. 'What are you on about? You're not going to tell us? Are you fucking joking?'

'No, I'm not. All I'm going to say is it was absolutely fantastic and I'm not going to spoil it by, you know, talking about it and stuff. It was too special for that.'

Other than looking at Bert and raising her eyes to the heavens Tess didn't seem too bothered by Vicky's reticence. Bert, however, was seething with indignation and a heated sense of betrayal. She could not believe her best friend in the whole wide world – apart from Tess and when it comes to sex she doesn't count, Bert always reasoned when privately listing them in order of best-friendness – was going to keep something secret from her.

'So it's all right for him to know all about it, special Prince fucking Barney, but I can't know about it, not little old me?' Bert shouted at Vicky.

'Of course *he* knows about it, he was there. Look, I just want to keep it special and it won't be so special if I tell everyone about it, all right?'

'Everyone? Everyone? "Tell everyone about it" – oh, so I'm *everyone*, am I?' Bert's rage was making her splutter.

'Oh, you know what I mean,' Vicky replied dismissively.

Bert was so upset she couldn't formulate another coherent sentence and stomped off, leaving Vicky and Tess to make the rest of the way alone. She was petrified that this might be the beginning of the end of their friendship.

The Blow-job

For the next couple of months, as Christmas approached, the frost that had set in between Vicky and Bert continued to harden. Bert and Tess were still hanging around together as much as ever, spending all their time in and out of school in each other's company, but Vicky had moved on. She spent every spare moment she had with Barney, who was often to be found waiting outside the gates for her, now wearing a very hip patchwork velvet floor-length coat. Few girls had boyfriends who waited outside school for them and none as cool as Barney. The rest of the time Vicky appeared, much to Bert's disdain, to be working towards getting good O levels. She'd stopped sitting with Bert and Tess in class, joining Georgie and Charlie instead.

Tess had ended up siding with Bert, not out of contempt for Vicky (although she'd been relieved that she hadn't had to listen to weeks of what Barney was like at snogging) but because Bert was still the central linchpin. Bert and Tess still needed each other and the security their friendship offered in equal measure. Vicky, now Officially In Love (as Bert referred to her), didn't appear to need anything except to be with Barney. She certainly didn't seem to need best friends and all the childish, silly things associated with having them. She appeared to have become more sophisticated and ethereal and not just in spirit: she had adopted a new look and wore many of the latest fashions. Uniforms for fifth formers were no longer compulsory and Vicky floated into school each day wearing a variety of beautiful outfits. On one of the rare occasions that she and Bert spoke, Bert asked her where all these clothes were coming from. Vicky replied loftily that they were presents from Barney. 'I'll bet he nicked them all,' Bert said later with obvious contempt to Tess. To her, Barney's shoplifting skill, like his Mr Freedom boots, had now become an object of derision rather than an admirable attribute.

Bert hadn't anticipated ever falling out with Vicky and she was desperately worried that the rift might be permanent. She'd made a decision not to let herself focus intensely on the issue, having found it made her too unhappy. Her childhood experiences had led her to believe that broken things don't ever get mended. In the years leading up to her parents' divorce Bert had watched her mother become increasingly miserable and had found it too painful to bear. To block this out she'd learnt to appear oblivious and insensitive to emotional dramas going on around her. As far as the rift with Vicky went, Bert had worked it all out: 'If I act like the whole thing is no big deal it'll go away and the three of us will end up just the way it was . . .' In the back of her mind, Bert feared that her planned outcome wasn't very likely, judging by the way things were going at the moment. However, she didn't think the whole thing was entirely her fault. She knew she'd been a bit silly that day at Adam's and afterwards. 'But it was Vicky who suddenly went all mature and lah-di-dah . . .' she reasoned, when thinking about how she and Vicky had fallen out. 'She could have made it up with me any time and didn't even have to tell me about the sex!' Bert had decided crossly. 'She obviously only cares about Barney now – who she thinks is so fucking fantastic!'

Bert and Vicky were still going to the same parties and pubs, although no longer as a gang. They didn't yet know enough people to provide them with different places to go where they could be sure of not bumping into one another. Instead they'd taken to ignoring each other, Bert making more of an ostentatious display of it than Vicky who, thanks to her new status, felt above the need to make too much of it.

One Saturday, a couple of weeks before Christmas, just before the school term ended, Adam's other cousin Jessica, Mark's sister, was having a party. Bert was going with Adam and she was taking Tess, who hadn't been invited, partly because she took her everywhere and partly because she knew she'd need someone to talk to. The party turned out to be a real trek: they had to get two buses and ended up going much further than they'd meant to on the second because they hadn't known precisely where to get off. Adam had only ever been there with his parents in the car.

Eventually Bert, Tess and Adam arrived pissed, even later than the deliberately late they'd planned on being. They'd already finished the Party Seven can of beer they'd brought with them in case the party had been drunk dry by the time they got there. Once inside, Bert and Tess left Adam to his own devices, having decided to look round the house to see if they could find anyone they knew. The house was packed to the rafters with teenagers in varying states of intoxication. Every single room was filled with gyrating, sweaty dancers and people lying about in piles on the floor smoking drugs. With some difficulty the two girls squeezed themselves through the various rooms searching in vain for a familiar face.

Once they'd had a nose around upstairs Bert turned to Tess. 'Let's find Adam and get a joint. I'm going to have a slash first, OK?' She'd decided that even if they did find someone they knew there'd be no point in trying to talk to them as everyone was too far gone.

Bert looked around, found the only door that was shut and assumed that it must be the bathroom. She knocked on the door to make sure someone hadn't gone in but forgotten to lock it. There was no answer. Bert opened the door and was stunned by the scene that confronted her. A tall boy was standing facing the lavatory which was side-on to the door. He was fully dressed except for his trousers which, although technically he was still wearing them, were crumpled around his ankles. He was clutching the cistern in front of him so hard that Bert could see the whites of his knuckles, his pelvis was rocking backwards and forwards and his eyes had glazed over making him look like he'd taken an overdose. Seated on the lavatory, facing the boy's groin, was a girl with long blonde hair. As far as Bert could tell, she had most of the boy's penis in her mouth. Bert stood there with her jaw gaping wide open, wondering how the girl was managing to breathe. Although neither the boy nor the girl seemed to be aware that she'd entered the room, Bert suddenly realized that she was staring at them. She mumbled an apology while backing out. Not until that moment did it dawn on her that she knew the boy. It was Barney. Barney, fantastic Barney, he's-so-great, we're-so-in-love Barney. Oh dear, she panicked, as she raced downstairs, what am I going to do? What the fuck am I going to do?

Although Bert loathed Barney for having come between her and Vicky she'd had no desire to find out that he was a creep. When she'd fantasized about how she and Vicky would make up, her best-case scenario had been that Vicky would come to her senses and either chuck Barney or relegate him to Adam's level, a necessary accessory, a boy you slept with regularly to ensure your continued status as hip, cool, and in-the-know but definitely not someone you held in higher regard than your best friends. Squeezing her way with difficulty through the throng Bert rushed around in a frenzy trying to find Tess. Eventually she located her slumped on the floor in the TV room sharing a massive joint with a bunch of people Bert had never seen before.

'Tess, Tess,' Bert hissed, 'I've got to talk to you – *now*.'

'Look, relax, I'll pass it to you next, just relax,' Tess drawled.

'I'm not worried about the fucking joint, I need to talk to you now. Have you seen Vicky? Is she here?' Bert started dragging Tess to her feet with some difficulty, she felt like a dead weight. 'Look, I have got to talk to you – fucking well *now*!'

Tess grunted a few times, handed the joint to the person nearest her and staggered out of the room with Bert half supporting her and half dragging her by the elbow. Once they reached the hall, the least well-populated area of the party, Bert delivered her news. 'Barney is upstairs in the toilet –'

'Don't say "toilet", darling, it's so *petit bourgeois*, only common people say "toilet", either say "lavatory" or "loo".' Tess sniggered at her own impressive rendition of Angela.

'Shut up, this is serious. Barney is upstairs in the toi – lavatory with his prick in some girl's mouth!'

'Eh?' Tess didn't seem able to envisage the scene Bert had described.

'Barney, fantastic Barney, Vicky's boyfriend Barney, is upstairs with his prick inside some girl's mouth and the girl is not Vicky, OK?'

'Oh . . .' was all Tess could manage at first.

Bert stood waiting for her reaction. She had an idea that she'd know what to do once she found out what Tess was going to suggest: she would automatically do the opposite.

Tess paused and appeared to think of something she needed clarifying. 'Why is he doing that?'

'For fuck's sake, I dunno – because he likes it, I suppose. Maybe Vicky refuses to do it. I know I would – yuk.' Bert made the face you make when you smell a carton of off milk. 'Anyway, is Vicky here? Have you seen her?'

'No, I don't think so. I saw Georgie and Charlie, they're here, they said they'd seen Barney but no Vicky. Maybe she didn't come, maybe they've broken up . . .'

'What are Georgie and Charlie doing here?' Bert's focus on

the immediate problem was diverted by the news that those two were at the party.

'I dunno. They said they'd heard about it from Vicky but they couldn't find her and they don't know anyone here. Still, Charlie's snogging Mark in the kitchen.'

Bert was irked to learn that Vicky was not just sitting with those two at school but was even telling them about parties she was going to. For a moment her sense of injury at Barney's betrayal to Vicky was cooled by the wrath she felt upon hearing how chummy she was with that loathed pair but she quickly got things into perspective. Bert was a loyal person and she knew that the crime of being friendly with a couple of pretty swots didn't mean that you deserved to have your boyfriend put his prick in someone else's mouth.

'Do you think he washed it first?' Tess asked, as they walked home from the party, having waited in vain for a night bus. The two girls had left shortly after Bert had discovered Barney and his friend. To Bert's relief, Adam had elected to stay behind.

'I doubt it,' she replied confidently.

In truth, she had absolutely no idea what etiquette was involved: there had never been even the faintest allusion to oral sex by either her or Adam. Penetration being the sole and only known route into the select non-virgins club, was all that she had ever fixed her sights on. She had never given any thought, before or since, to other types of love-making. For Bert, sex had been a means to an end not a recreation in itself. She knew oral sex went on in the world but she had assumed that it was something other sorts of people did. Nonetheless, Bert was reluctant to reveal her ignorance.

'Don't you think you're supposed to?' Tess continued.

'Maybe, I dunno, depends on who's doing it. I expect if you really like someone you wash it, and if you don't, you don't bother,' Bert ventured.

'Well, what's someone doing letting someone do that if they don't really like the person doing it in the first place?' Tess seemed concerned.

'Oh, I dunno. Look not *that* many people do it, you know. Most blokes don't even like it, only weirdos like Barney,' Bert said dismissively. She was keen to divert Tess from a line of questioning that might reveal her lack of knowledge on the current topic.

'Oh, right,' Tess said, and Bert was relieved that she seemed to be satisfied with that. Bert had not yet shared with anybody the whole truth of how uneventful her sex life was. It didn't occur to Tess that there might be areas of sexual expertise that Bert was not familiar with and she happily deferred to her companion's superior knowledge.

There were only two days of school left after the weekend and Bert had resolved to speak to Vicky before term was over. She knew that the way things were between them made it unlikely that they'd be seeing each other over the Christmas holidays, and Bert thought she ought to tell her what was going on while she had a chance. She took no joy in the prospect. In fact, she felt sick to her stomach at the idea. She was nervous that Vicky would accuse her of lying and making up stories to ruin her Perfect Love. Nevertheless Bert felt that it was the right thing to do, even if Vicky never spoke to her again. She felt that Vicky deserved better than this.

On the last day of school Bert steeled herself to confront Vicky. At first break, after a seasonally relaxed maths class, she fixed her sights on her ex-friend, who was walking ahead of her as they left the classroom. Bert had told Tess what she was going to do and the latter, foreseeing an almighty row, had predictably absented herself. Bert walked alone down the corridor, trailing a few steps behind Vicky, trying to summon up the courage to approach her. Her task was made doubly difficult by the fact that Vicky was accompanied by Georgie and Charlie. As Bert neared the group she could hear them discussing Charlie's snog with Mark and she thought angrily, Oh, so she'll talk about snogging and stuff but only with *those two*, not with me.

The little rush of indignation gave her the spur she needed. 'Hey, erm, Vicky, can I have a word with you?' Bert called, casually as she could manage. In one simultaneous move all three girls turned round and looked at her. Bert fixed her eyes on Vicky's, willing her to break away from her companions.

Vicky saw herself now as a chosen one, inhabiting the world of the beloved, replete with all the hallowed superiority that a person in love for the first time perceives themselves as embodying, but she wasn't malicious and had no wish to punish Bert. 'Yeah, what?' she replied.

Bert did not want to have this conversation in the corridor. 'Not here . . . erm . . . in the . . . in the . . . science lab?' It was the nearest place she could think of where they might get some privacy. There might be other people in the common room and, anyway, she thought, it'd better be somewhere neutral.

'The science lab?' Georgie sneered. 'Why? Do you need someone to show you how to use a Bunsen burner?'

Charlie sniggered at her friend's witticism.

'Piss off, Georgie. This has got nothing to do with you,' Bert retorted, angry that these creeps were attempting to thwart her mission.

Vicky had no desire to participate in a full-scale scrap and jumped in. 'Yeah, all right, come on, then,' she said, walking towards Bert. When she reached her she turned to the others and, much to Bert's chagrin, said, 'See you both later, yeah?'

The pair set off in embarrassed silence towards the laboratory. Vicky assumed that Bert was going to ask to be friends again and was embarrassed that she was going to have to explain to her that when you were really in love with a proper boyfriend it meant that you didn't have time for best friends any more and that one day she'd understand that. Bert, on the other hand, was consumed with embarrassment that she was going to have to tell her friend something she definitely wouldn't want to hear. They entered the empty science lab, Vicky going in first. She pulled out one of the high wooden stools, which slotted under the long desks that ran the length of the room, climbed up on it, turned to Bert and said, in a tone of gracious tolerance, 'I think I know what you want to say, Bert.'

Bert was taken aback. She can't! How could she possibly know and be acting like this? she panicked.

'It's about us . . . not . . . well, not being best friends any more, isn't it?' Vicky was being intentionally gentle.

'No,' Bert blurted out dismissively. She didn't like the idea that Vicky had presumed that she had come grovelling back to beg forgiveness.

Vicky didn't believe her. 'OK, well, what *is* it about then?'

'Ah, look, it's . . . erm . . . it's about . . . Oh, look, I'm sorry, it's about you and Barney . . .'

Vicky knew she'd been right. Bert did want to talk to her about their friendship. 'Bert, I'm sorry that me and Barney being in love has meant that I don't spend time with you and Tess any more but the thing is when you fall properly in love you just don't –'

Bert hastily cut her off. She couldn't face a lecture on what being Officially In Love meant, least of all from someone whose boyfriend clearly had a completely different take on the whole subject. 'Vicky, it's not about you and Barney in that way, it's about . . .' Bert didn't know where to start '. . . it's about . . . about . . . Look, do you and Barney have . . . erm . . . Does Barney . . . Oh, God, listen, do you let Barney put his prick in your mouth?' Bert couldn't believe she'd asked that question. That wasn't what she wanted to know. She couldn't believe her nerves had thrown her so off-course. Vicky drew up her body into a schoolmarmy stance and said, 'Bert, I've told you before I'm not telling you what Barney and I –'

Bert jumped in. 'Listen, I'm sorry, I didn't mean to ask that. I meant to say, oh, fuck, look I saw his prick – I mean Barney's prick – in some girl's mouth on Saturday night at Mark's sister Jessica's party.' The horrible truth was out and Bert was finally able to take a breath.

'What?' Vicky's cry was incredulous and withering at the same time.

Oh, God, here we go. Bert sighed. Now I've got to explain everything. She plunged in without formulating her thoughts properly. 'In the bog at Jessica, Mark's sister's, party, I saw Barney with his prick, erm ... willie ... you know, anyway, inside some girl's mouth . . .' Bert's voice trailed off at this point, then she added faintly '. . . and ... erm ... she wasn't ... erm ... it wasn't you.' Bert looked up at Vicky for the first time since she'd started speaking to see a picture of rage.

Vicky replied, in a steely tone, 'No, you didn't. You're making this up. You want to break me and Barney up so that you can have your gang back. You're just jealous because Barney is a million times better than Adam and – and . . .' Vicky's tirade ended abruptly at this point, she didn't seem to be able to come up with a fresh accusation to follow the unfavourable comparison between their two boyfriends.

'I knew you'd say this, I almost didn't tell you because I knew instead of believing me you'd say that I was doing it to be horrible. Well, thanks a lot! I'm telling the truth. Some blonde girl was eating your fantastic boyfriend's prick in the toilet at Mark and Jessica's house on Saturday night and I'm not making it up!'

Vicky stood up and barked, 'I'm not going to bother even answering you back because it's not true and I'm never, ever going to speak to you again. You're mean and jealous and a liar.' She marched out of the room and slammed the door behind her.

Bert felt crushed. She'd guessed that Vicky might react this way but she'd hoped that she'd also know that Bert would never do something to hurt her deliberately and, because of that, realize that she must be telling the truth.

Even If He's David Cassidy, David Soul and That Bloke Out of Wizzard All Rolled Into One

'Told you . . .' Tess sneered unhelpfully, as they walked back to her house for tea later that same afternoon. 'You shouldn't have said anything. She was never going to thank you for that, even if it was true.'

'What do you mean "even if it was true"? Of course it's bloody true. Do you think I made it up for a laugh?' Bert had guessed that Tess might not be very supportive.

'Well, I know you *think* it was Barney but how could you be sure? Maybe it wasn't.' Tess didn't really believe this: she was just feeling argumentative.

'Oh, fuck off! I know what I saw. It was Barney – and stop trying to deliberately annoy me.' Bert was pissed off that, unlike Vicky, Tess could never be relied upon to be sympathetic in a crisis. It backed up her increasingly painful realization that as a threesome they had formed a perfect circle, each one providing essential qualities and faults that either negated or complemented the others. Deprived of one element, the individual personalities didn't match up quite so well and their perfect circle was broken.

Vicky was never going to be pleased to hear that her boyfriend was being unfaithful. Who would be? Bert reluctantly admitted to herself as she made her way home soon after arriving at Tess's. She hadn't stayed long as Mrs Pile had been there unexpectedly and had been even more unwelcoming than usual. She'd kept going on about how much she and Tess had to do to get ready for Christmas. It's eight days away, for Chrissakes, Bert sneered, as she walked along. What's she planning on doing – making a giant Christmas tree out of empty washing-up bottles? *Blue Peter* was currently advising its viewers on the imaginative and fun things that could be done with an empty washing-up bottle, and by now, in second place to 'sticky-back plastic' the words 'empty washing-up bottle' always raised a laugh.

Marcus came home for the Christmas holidays, which meant that Angela behaved like a semblance of a mother for the duration. Bert noted with contempt that the house got cleaned up, the fridge was full of delicious things to eat (minus maggots), Angela's stockings didn't have ladders in them and she wasn't wearing her usual foul kaftans and Moroccan smocks. Marcus was very like Charles, having, by paternal design, been shaped by the same public school. He kept himself to himself and said little which, as with Charles during their marriage, Angela interpreted as disapproval. The effect was to make her try harder and want to do everything better. It was a bitter pill for Bert to swallow, understanding that disapproval from her earned her mother's sarcasm and disinterest, while from Marcus it earned clean ashtrays, hoovered stair carpets and a host of other *petit bourgeois* conveniences and even an attempt to behave like a Real Mum.

However, one day Marcus and Bert shared a moment of sibling unity over lunch, which Bert was sure her mother had intended to have alone with Marcus as there was barely enough food for three. Angela was telling Marcus about her plans to do voluntary work at Bert's school and what ideas she had in mind (to ruin my life, Bert thought). As their mother rattled on, Marcus, keeping his head facing downwards to his plate, moved his eyes up slowly to catch Bert's, at which point he'd crossed them and raised his eyebrows. The whole manoeuvre took less than a second but Bert was thrilled that her brother had finally shown a sign of solidarity. From then on the prospect of Christmas seemed a little less grim.

On the afternoon of Christmas Eve Bert was in her bedroom wrapping the presents she'd bought. She'd got Adam a record token, a perfunctory choice she'd made after briefly considering buying him a book she'd seen called *The Joy of Sex*. The cover had a drawing on it of a couple copulating and she'd been too embarrassed to buy it. She knew that she'd have been even more mortified by what Adam might think the gift meant. Leafing through it in the bookshop she and Tess had had to suppress raucous giggles, finding each suggested activity hilarious particularly as it was accompanied by explicit drawings. Despite the amusement the book had caused, Bert had been privately alarmed to learn that not only was the act she'd caught Barney enjoying at the party obviously considered perfectly normal but it was also highly recommended as an alternative to penetration and/or something you broke off penetration to indulge in and/or something you did prior to penetration. Her horror was topped off when she saw that there was a similar activity for men to do to women.

Bert had bought Tess some Fenjal bubble bath, which she knew she'd like, and as she wrapped it she remembered with sadness that it was the first Christmas in five years she hadn't got something for Vicky. At that moment the doorbell rang. Bert decided she wouldn't bother going down to answer it as her mother was in the living room. After a few seconds it rang again, this time for longer, and Bert cursed her mother as she got up to go downstairs.

'Well, it's not going to be for me, is it? It'll be one of your ghastly friends or worse still some godforsaken carol singers collecting for some wretched woebegone local charity I have absolutely no interest in!' Angela called out, hearing her daughter stomping down the stairs. Bert didn't respond and made a V sign in the direction of the living room as she approached the front door.

'Err . . . hello,' Vicky said, shuffling nervously from side to side on Bert's front doorstep.

'Fuck!' Bert exclaimed. She was genuinely surprised. Vicky was the last person she'd expected to see.

'Who is it?' Angela barked out, still seated in the living room.

'It's none of your business,' Bert called back, making a face at Vicky to indicate to her friend that, as ever, her mother was driving her nuts.

'It's my house and if I want to know who it is then I shall damn well know who it is. Now, who is it?' Angela had roused herself and was approaching the living-room door, delivering her rant. 'Oh, it's you, Victoria, come in. Why haven't you asked her in, Albertine? Really, you are so rude sometimes. Come in, come in.'

Vicky appealed to Angela on many levels, not least because she was elegant and restrained and the opposite of her own bellicose daughter. Vicky looked tentatively at Bert, who gave her a guarded smile, meaning it to convey that she should come in.

'Albertine, give Victoria a mince-pie in the kitchen. I've got some lovely Fortnum's mince pies, Victoria, they're heavenly – and, Albertine, *you* are not to have any!' Angela commanded, as she walked back into the living room. Despite her recent adoption of all things connected with women's liberation, aiding the Third World and made of cane, Angela had seen no reason to relinquish her account at Fortnum and Mason. It had been one of her few married-life perks and, to Angela, particularly worth hanging on to as by some quirk of fate her ex-husband, in ignorance, still seemed to be paying the accounts. As far as she was concerned just because she now lived in a mixed area and had seen the light (with the help of some other sisters) in respect of oppressive marriages it didn't mean she had to eat lower-quality fare than she had prior to her unsought freedom. As Bert knew to her cost, most of the year the orders were made up of Gordon's gin and Persian cashew nuts, but when Marcus was home for his holidays the delivery boxes heaved with goodies.

Bert put some mince-pies on a plate and plonked it, unceremoniously, in the middle of the kitchen table. Vicky leant up against the sideboard and looked down at the floor. Bert had mixed feelings. She felt sorry for her friend but nervous in case she'd come round to have another go at her.

'Do you want a cup of tea?' Bert decided she'd better say something, anything.

'Yeah, that'd be great, thanks,' Vicky said, sitting down tentatively.

'You'd better have one of those mince-pies or Mum'll accuse me of poisoning you against them,' Bert said, as she placed two cups of tea on the table. Vicky laughed and picked one up; Bert took one too. 'I'll stuff a couple down in here and then say you ate them if Mum asks, otherwise I'll never hear the end of it. She wouldn't care if you ate the whole box as long as there were a few left for Marcus.' Bert was aware that she was struggling to make conversation.

'Bert . . . look . . . I'm sorry.' Vicky spoke through a mouthful of mince-pie. Although Bert's heart leapt at hearing these words she couldn't help noticing at the same time that Vicky even managed to look elegant when talking with her gob full. 'You were right, erm . . . Barney.' Vicky seemed to have difficulty saying his name and Bert suspected that it wasn't because of the pie. 'Erm, he was sleeping with someone else – well, I don't know about sleeping but . . . erm . . . you know, well, you saw and that wasn't the first time . . . well, not with that cow . . .' At this point Vicky trailed off and sipped her tea.

The two girls sat in silence. Bert was resisting the temptation to ask Vicky if she'd known all this when she'd had a go at her in the science lab but decided that it would be insensitive and, strictly speaking, not relevant at this particular moment in time.

'Anyway, I've chucked him now and I'm sorry I was horrible to you – and – to Tess . . . and . . .'

'And that you became a swot and super-pally with those spotty creeps, Georgie and Charlie,' Bert added, but in a tone intended to tease rather than admonish her friend. She made herself sound deliberately silly using a nah-nah-nah-nah-nah inflection when pronouncing the names of her two erstwhile rivals.

Vicky laughed. 'Yeah, I'm sorry about that too. Oh, Bert, I was madly in love with him and I thought he was with me as well and I'm really unhappy now, but I couldn't carry on going out with him.'

'Look, I'm sorry it happened and I'm sorry I told you as well. Tess said I shouldn't but I thought you ought to know . . . that he . . . well, you know,' Bert explained.

'No, I was really angry when you told me and I didn't believe you but I'd sort of thought he was up to something a bit before but he always seemed so keen and everything and . . . and . . . you know.' Bert guessed Vicky didn't know what else to say.

The pair spent the rest of the evening in Bert's bedroom listening to records and going over the whole thing in detail. It turned out that Barney had told Vicky that, although he'd slept with a couple of girls before her, he'd never done *that* thing properly and had always wanted to but only with someone he really loved. After some persuasion Vicky had eventually agreed to do it. To Bert's amazement she told her that, after a while, she'd grown to enjoy it, particularly as it made Barney so happy.

Apparently one day Vicky had dropped round at Barney's house unannounced and his little sister, unaware of what he was up to, had let her in. She had gone up to his bedroom and found

Barney and the girl from the party enjoying more of the same activity. Vicky informed Bert that what she'd found most painful was that Barney had told her it was the greatest gift she could ever have given him and had once sworn that whatever happened to them he was never, ever going to let another girl do it to him. Privately Bert thought that Vicky had been a bit of a twit to believe that, but she kept her opinion to herself, remembering that her friend had, after all, been Officially In Love. She reasoned that being like that probably makes you believe all sort of things that aren't actually true.

Just before midnight Vicky decided that she'd better go home. The two girls parted company crossing their hearts and hoping to die and solemnly vowing and swearing to God that they'd never, ever let a boy come between them again – no matter how madly, *madly* in love they fell. Even if he was David Cassidy, David Soul and that bloke out of Wizzard all rolled into one, they pledged, he still wouldn't be able to break them up. Bert went to bed that night very happy and feeling like her whole world had come together again but in an even better way.

The Price of Eggs

Angela had been doing her bit as a standby supervisor for a little under two terms by now but, much to Bert's relief, the headmistress had given her duties confining her dealings to the first and second years so she and Bert hardly ever ran into each other. As the months went by without event, Bert had been gradually and cautiously more and more relieved to note that her peers, and in particular Georgie and Charlie, didn't seem to be aware that her mother was working at the school. Tess and Vicky, knowing Bert's feelings on the subject, had loyally kept quiet and told no one. On the increasingly rare occasions when Bert and her mother bumped into each other at home, to give herself a cheap thrill Angela would pretend that there was a possibility she might be supervising one of Bert's classes in the near future, but by this stage Bert was wise to her mother's games replying, 'Oh, good. That'll be great because then I can be rude to you in front of thirty people instead of just in the privacy of our own home.'

Although theirs was still wholly unlike any normal mother–daughter relationship, Bert and her mother had slipped into a relatively easy co-existence. Angela had little to do all day other than read and smoke. Her alimony, although not huge, precluded any need to work. However, when she was bored and depressed, which was most of the time, she would seek entertainment by attempting to goad her daughter into a fight.

The school staff boasted one male member, the music teacher

Mr Hatton (that was if you didn't count Mr Baker and no one did). Mr Hatton was a well-built, swarthy-looking man in his mid-forties. To the uncritical adult eye he would have been considered a good-looking, pleasant man, but to his highly critical teenage pupils, with an exclusive set of criteria that only they appreciated as to what constituted good-looking, he was a smarmy wanker. One of the things that contributed to this view was his insistence that the older girls call him by his first name, Richard. As far as Bert and her friends were concerned he might as well have asked them to do the Twist with him in the school play.

Mr Hatton was known amongst the girls as Randy Richard, for no reason other than that he was single – a state that, at his advanced age, must surely mean an unusually high interest in bonking, or so reasoned Bert, who'd coined the nickname. She and her friends were generally rather scornful of him but didn't disrupt his classes excessively, partly because he never put up any resistance to bad behaviour, rendering it embarrassingly redundant, and partly because he occasionally played their kind of music, which they enjoyed. His pupils considered it impossible that he could be genuinely familiar with the Who, Pink Floyd and Janis Joplin but assumed he'd asked someone young what to bring in. It also meant that they didn't always have to listen to classical music, which they thought of as deeply boring and depressing. Mr Hatton's classes took place once a week in the large music room, housed in one of the annexes. The room also housed the school grand piano, a huge black thing which, unless it was being used for a performance, was always concealed beneath a moth-eaten cover. When they were bored during these lessons, Bert, Vicky and Tess amused themselves by watching Mr Baker doing the rounds with his beloved Willie in the courtyard below. Even parading an empty piece of tarmac he was the picture of paranoid erectness. Encouraging Willie to sniff around in every nook and cranny in the unlikely hope of discovering a stash of heroin, Mr Baker lived for the day he could make his name by busting a teenage gang of major drug smugglers who had infiltrated their way into the school.

One day, towards the middle of the spring term, Bert, Vicky and Tess were lounging around in the fifth-form study room, which although more public had inevitably succeeded the cloak-rooms as their lair. As none of them was taking any of the sciences for O level they had a free period straight after lunch-break, which they never used for its intended purpose: study. Vicky was revising for her exams but in her own time at home, not wanting to risk alienating her friends again.

'Let's go up to the music room and listen to records,' Bert suggested, breaking a bored silence.

'Are we allowed to?' Tess asked.

'Why not? God, it's not like we're going to do something bad. We're just going to listen to records. That's what they're there for, isn't it?' Bert reasoned.

'Isn't that room locked when no one's in it?' Vicky interjected. She wasn't averse to the suggestion but she didn't want to tramp all the way up there to find that they couldn't get in.

'Not always. Anyway, I've seen where he keeps the spare key, up on the doorframe, so we can easily get in and if anyone comes along we'll say it was never locked in the first place, right?' Bert had it all worked out.

'Yeah, all right, but if Randy Richard finds us and says anything I'm going to say it was your idea, yeah?' Tess replied.

'Typical! God, you are pathetic sometimes. You know Randy Richard won't care, and anyway if he does come in, which he probably won't, he'll say something twatty, like it's really inspiring to find us appreciating his input during our own free time and that's the kind of thing that makes teaching worthwhile.' Vicky and Tess sniggered at Bert's rendition of Randy Richard's cringingly self-conscious laid-back style of speech.

The three girls shuffled out of the study room and trooped across the playground to the annexe. The stairs and corridors were deserted, as everybody else was occupied with their various classes. The trio was uncharacteristically hushed as they made their way up the stairs to the music room. Although technically, not having a class, they were at liberty to do as they pleased, they knew they were supposed to be studying and had no wish to draw attention to themselves. They especially wanted to avoid being discovered by one of the more irritating teachers who would interrogate them as to their destination and purpose in such great detail that they'd end up wishing they had been studying after all.

To their great surprise, when they reached the music room they found the door locked and the blind drawn. All of the school's interior doors, except those leading into rooms from which pupils were permanently excluded, like the staff room and the headmistress's office, had glass in the top half affording a comprehensive view into the room. Each door was equipped with a blind on the inside, but no one ever used them. This was the first time the girls had ever come across a classroom with one actually pulled down. They looked at each other, exchanging mildly puzzled expressions.

Bert was the first to proffer a theory. 'You know what? The blind's probably broken and it's just fallen down. Half of them are like that at our house.'

'No. No. What if it means someone's in there?' Tess hissed. Bert had retrieved the key from the top of the door and was unlocking the door. 'Don't be so fucking stupid! The door's locked. How *can* someone be in there?'

The threesome stepped into the room and, in unison, let out a loud scream. Nobody moved, they were frozen still – transfixed by the sight that greeted them. A few seconds later the door of a nearby classroom flew open and Miss Jay steamed in behind them, all fired up to take control of the situation. She stopped dead in her tracks, a couple of feet behind the girls, and gasped out loud as she took in the spectacle that had made the girls scream.

Angela was facing the door, her voluminous frock spread out around her, sitting on top of the grand piano. She was straddling a man whose naked torso was poking out from underneath her dress. His identity was initially unclear, from the group's point of view, as they could only see the crown of his head. Angela, uncharacteristically athletic, leapt off the piano, adjusting herself as she flew, to reveal a completely nude man. Remaining prone, he grasped the piano cover hurriedly with both hands and frantically clutched it around himself. After a few moments of clumsy shuffling, the improvised toga clearly hampering fluid movement, he managed to slip down on to the ground next to Angela. Quickly composing himself, while checking that the piano cover was concealing his genitalia and summoning up what little dignity he had left to him, Randy Richard straightened himself up to face the gathered company.

'What on earth is going on in here?' Miss Jay demanded.

'Ah, well, it's not quite as bad as it appears, Miss Jay. You see . . . I well . . .' Randy Richard was grappling for a reasonable explanation.

'I don't want to hear your excuses. I think we'll see what the headmistress has to say about this!' Miss Jay said, in a cool, threatening tone.

'Now, listen here, this has got absolutely nothing to do with you. It's a private matter between myself and Richard and, unfortunately, it would now appear, my daughter. Other than having happened upon the scene you are not involved in any way whatsoever. I think it would be a good idea for you to leave the room and leave us to sort it out ourselves, in the manner we see fit.' Angela was in no mood to be vilified.

'Well, I never!' Miss Jay exclaimed indignantly. She stood still for a moment, not knowing quite what to do. She then made an emphatic turn to go, whipping her shoulders round as she went, making it clear, she hoped, that they had not heard the last of this.

Vicky and Tess looked at Bert, waiting for her to take the lead. Both desperately wanted to flee the scene but they knew that their friend, as the injured party, had to make the first move. Bert couldn't budge herself, she was dumbstruck. Her mind was whirling. Her mum was over forty, Bert couldn't believe she was having sex at all, let alone with one of her teachers. Finally, a question plopped limply out of Bert's mouth. 'Is this the first time?'

'Oh, for God's sake, what on earth has that got to do with the price of eggs? This is none of your business. Now, go away. And, for the record, I don't expect to hear a word of recrimination from you about this.' Angela, as usual, was attempting to cover up her own discomfort at Bert's expense.

'Steady on, Angela. I don't think snapping at Albertine is going to help matters,' Richard piped up.

Bert was so filled with disgust by the scene she'd just witnessed that she had no room for any gratitude she might otherwise have felt for Richard's attempt to defend her. 'It *is* my bloody business! You are pathetic and old and disgusting, and you should know better!' Bert shouted, directing her tirade at both her mother and Richard. 'Come on, let's go,' she barked fiercely at her friends, turning to leave.

As the trio shuffled out, Tess glued her eyes resolutely to the floor. She was panic-stricken with embarrassment and wanted to be absolutely sure of not catching either adult's eye. Vicky, however, surreptitiously shot Angela a sympathetic look. She didn't want to be disloyal to Bert but she knew that Angela was going to get into awful trouble and she couldn't help feeling a bit sorry for her. From the vantage-point she had of not being Angela's daughter, Vicky had always been able to see that she wasn't a complete demon. Half the time, she thought that the way Angela went on at Bert was just her way of trying to be funny. But she also understood why Bert couldn't see that.

Once outside the room, Bert burst into tears. 'I *hate* her guts! I wish she was dead! I'll never ever get over this, I'm going to die. God, she is disgusting. I bet J-cloth tells everyone my mum is a slag!'

'She isn't going to do that, Bert,' Vicky said comfortingly, 'but she will probably tell Mrs Fowler.'

'I couldn't care less about that 'cos that means Mum'll have to stop coming here, which would be great. I just don't want anyone else to find out about this. Oh, God, how could she do it?' Bert sobbed.

'She probably fancies him, I reckon,' Tess opined.

'Well, that's pretty obvious, Einstein,' Bert snapped, 'but she's not supposed to do anything about it, is she? People that age aren't supposed to be doing that sort of thing. God, it makes me sick, the pair of them, behaving like – like – like fucking teenagers. If they absolutely *have* to do it, which they don't, they should be doing it in the dark, in their bedrooms, in the middle of the night, not at *my* fucking school on the bloody, fucking piano!'

'Maybe they had to do it here. Maybe Randy Richard's got a girlfriend or something and this is the only place they can do it.'

'Don't be ridiculous, Tess! They did *not* have to do it here. They shouldn't be doing it at all. It's not natural!' Bert screamed.

'All right, calm down, Bert. I know this is horrible and your mum definitely should not have done it here, but you know . . .' Vicky intervened.

'No, she shouldn't have been doing it anywhere!' Bert insisted hotly.

'Look, there's no reason why your mum shouldn't have a

boyfriend. Your dad's always got a girlfriend,' Vicky said gently. She was hoping that helping Bert see logic might erase the image of her mother sitting astride Randy Richard.

'It's different with Dad – I don't live with him, I don't have to see his laddered tights and dirty old bras and pukey friends and all that revolting stuff every single day.'

Bert couldn't bear, yet again, having her faced rubbed in her mother's inability to behave like a Real Mum. She yearned for someone solid to offer her stability and security. Someone who didn't expose her to their frailties and offered her the chance to get to grips with her own. Bert was sure that Real Mums did not have sex at all. And if they did it would definitely not be on top of the piano at their daughters' schools.

Coo, Coo, Coo, Cachoo

After school, Bert and Tess went back to Vicky's, there being obviously no question of going to Bert's. As usual, Vicky's mum Julia was welcoming and unfussed when her daughter announced that they'd all be staying for supper. There'd been no group plan to do so but Vicky guessed that Bert would want to stay away from home for as long as possible. By this stage in her life, Vicky preferred to make supper for herself anyway, finding that it meant she didn't have to fall in with her mother's meal-times. Julia didn't mind when Vicky brought her friends home – she never complained or said things like 'I'm being eaten out of house and home' like Tess's mum did.

'Anything interesting happen at school today, girls?' Julia asked innocently, as she was leaving the kitchen. Bert had often noticed, with envy, that she always took an interest in Vicky's day.

All three burst into spontaneous laughter. Eventually Vicky composed herself enough to be able to reply, 'No, nothing, Mum. Just an ordinary day,' she said, giving her friends a knowing look. Bert and Tess started laughing again. Julia shrugged her shoulders, smiled at the giggling teenagers and left the room. As she went Bert noticed that she hadn't taken offence at Vicky's secretiveness. She thought how great it would be to have a mum just like her.

When Bert finally made her way home, it was quite late and she was hoping that her mother would be so drunk she wouldn't hear her come in. Angela wasn't a heavy drinker but she always had a few over the odds whenever she felt stressed. Bert opened the front door quietly and hovered silently between it and the porch listening out for any sign that her mother was lurking about. Hearing nothing, she shut the door as gently as she could, and headed straight up the stairs still wearing her coat. She wanted to avoid making any unnecessary noise by taking it off in the hall.

She got as far as the fourth step before being heard. Bert had forgotten that the step, no matter how gingerly you stood on it, always gave out a long, squealing creak, like a sound effect from a horror film. In fact, she often made a point of landing on it deliberately forcefully because the noise, like so many other minor things, was guaranteed to send her mother into a flurry of irritation. Bert cursed under her breath and stood, statue-like, mid-ascent, waiting for the inevitable.

'Albertine, I know that's you. I am perfectly aware that you are trying to avoid seeing me. Well, believe you me, I have no great desire to see you either, but unfortunately there's nothing that can be done about that, at least for the foreseeable future, so you may as well come in here and face the music,' Angela barked from the living room.

For a few moments Bert remained totally silent and didn't move – her right leg bent, suspended mid-air on its voyage up to the next step and her left hand hovering a few inches above the banister. She was considering making a dash for her bedroom and barricading herself in.

'Albertine, stop being so bloody childish and get in here. Good God, I haven't got a contagious disease, I've had consensual sex with a grown man. Something, I'd like to point out, that I am perfectly entitled to do as a single woman!'

Bert raised her eyes to the heavens and prayed that the neighbours couldn't hear. 'I think we all know that by now, thanks to your brilliant choice of location,' she sneered, stomping into the living room. She advanced a few feet into the room, crossed her arms and took up a hostile stance. She gave her mother a defiant glare, making it clear that she was waiting for the contrition to begin.

'Well?' Angela was the first to speak.

Bert was thrown. What could she mean, saying, 'Well?' like that? she thought. 'What do you mean "well?"? If anyone should be saying "well?" like that, it's me!' Bert was careful not to raise her voice too high. She didn't want the neighbours to get the rest of the details, assuming they'd heard her mum's first load of ranting.

'Well, what were you doing going into the music room when it was locked?'

'What was *I* doing in the music room? Is this a joke? What was *I* doing in the music room? I can't believe you're asking me what I was doing in the music room!' Bert was losing her cool very rapidly.

Angela, on the other hand, was completely composed. 'It's a perfectly simple question that even you should be able to grasp. What were you doing going into the music room when it was locked? You weren't supposed to be in there.'

'That's perfectly obvious now and you'd better believe I wish I'd never gone in. I suppose you think I wanted to see you – you – you –' Bert was unable to find a word that she could bring herself to utter.

'– me making love. Your mother making love and having a nice time for once in her life and, what's more, with someone who likes her,' Angela said, finishing Bert's sentence for her. 'It's high time you accepted your mother as a grown woman with needs of her own and –'

Needs! Needs! Bert's mind was reeling. Oh, my God, now she's going to talk about her needs and go into the details of sex with Randy Richard. I'm going to puke. She didn't seem to be able to move herself from the spot.

'You ought to be pleased I've met someone I like. Good God in heaven, it's not as if your father isn't at it with all and sundry, night and sodding day. The whole world doesn't revolve around you and your petty preoccupations, you know! I have a right to some fun too. You might like to know that, miserable as it may be in many respects, life after forty doesn't necessarily mean that your interest in sex dries up like a rain-soaked Ordnance Survey map left in the boot of a car, *much* as your children might prefer that to be the case!' Angela was up and running. She carried on reeling off a list of home truths but Bert had stopped listening. She was humming, 'Coo, coo, coo cachoo' loudly in her head, she'd been singing it from the second her mother had mentioned her needs and brought up her ex-husband's sex life. For Bert it was bad enough trying to fight off the repulsive vision of what she'd seen in the music room – she couldn't stomach being forced to wrestle with a picture of her dad on the job as well.

By the time her mother had come to the end of her lengthy catalogue of sexual entitlements Bert didn't have the energy to pursue her own claims to outrage. She waved Angela a limp goodnight and sloped off to bed. As she drifted into sleep she thought how ironic it was that the basis of her mother's defence had hinged upon her description of herself as a woman who'd sacrificed everything for her children and, after years of thinking only of their welfare, was finally treating herself to the most meagre indulgence.

A few days later it became obvious that, as she had threatened, Miss Jay had told Mrs Fowler what she'd witnessed. Randy Richard and Angela were nowhere to be seen, clearly having been discharged. Music theory was cancelled without explanation. As a result the upper-years' conversations were running amok with rumours as to the possible reasons for the music teacher's sudden disappearance. Gossip about Angela didn't appear to be rife as she hadn't come into contact with the older girls and, to Bert's relief, the lower-years had obviously not yet developed a taste for salacious speculation.

Although Bert, Vicky and Tess knew perfectly well why Randy Richard had been sacked they didn't divulge their secret to anyone. The possible reasons put forward for his removal ranged from drug-dealing to getting an upper-sixth-former pregnant. As far as anyone knew, no one in that year was actually up the duff but it had been noted that a few of them had been very chummy with Randy Richard. The friendships in themselves would not have warranted dismissal so those girls applying themselves to the topic had naturally leapt to the most sinister conclusion. Bert felt uncomfortable on the occasions she was party to these conversations not because she felt protective of her mother but because she was terrified that she might hear something about Randy Richard that would compromise her. Although she was delighted that her mother would no longer be a threatening presence at school, Bert sincerely wished she'd had to leave for different reasons.

Over the next few weeks Bert pointedly avoided her mother. Every day she thanked her lucky stars that Randy Richard had not, so far, put in an appearance at their house. Occasionally her mother would spend the night out, and Bert assumed that she was staying at his place. As she had no wish to be treated to another roller coaster ride through her mother's rights to carnal desires she never asked her where she'd been. This uncharacteristic discretion greatly irked Angela, who made flashy attempts to lure her into asking questions about her love affair. Angela wanted Bert to take notice of it. She didn't know that Bert had resolved not to acknowledge the relationship if it killed her. The whole thing made Bert feel sick and she had no intention of indulging her mother by giving her an opportunity to boast about it. She knew she ought to be relieved that her mother had met someone who was, at the very least, distracting her. But she deeply resented having to take on her own mother as sexually active just when she'd started exploring the same thorny territory herself.

How Do You Get an Orgasm?

'Of course, if I'd still been helping out at your school this would never of happened. Well, I hope you're proud of yourself!'

Angela was nagging Bert yet again about her O level results as she prepared to leave for school one morning. Bert herself had been surprised at her wholesale failure to pass even one O level. She'd imagined that at least she'd get English literature. After all, she thought indignantly, as she made the short walk to school, it's not like I hadn't read *Northanger Abbey*! Bert had actually enjoyed reading Jane Austen and had been irritated to discover that enjoying something wasn't enough to get you through a tedious exam paper.

Vicky had passed all of the five she had taken. This didn't really surprise or bother Bert, who rarely felt competitive towards her. However, Tess had managed to pass four out of her five O levels and Bert was outraged. 'How the fuck could you have passed four and me fail all of them?' Bert railed at her, not for the first time. They'd only got their results a few months before and Bert still couldn't take it in.

Tess, who wasn't letting on that she was also amazed at her passes, had chosen to behave as if she'd been expecting them all along and was very pleased with herself. She didn't respond to Bert's question, but arched her eyebrows and gave her friend a do-you-really-want-me-to-answer-that? look instead.

'What's that look supposed to mean?' Bert snapped.

'Don't have a go at me because you failed all your O levels

and I didn't. It's not my fault, I didn't make you fail them. Me and Vicky did some work and you didn't – simple as that.'

'But when were you two doing all that work? You must have been doing it behind my back. Why didn't you tell me you were swotting in secret?'

'We weren't swotting in secret, Bert, it wasn't a plot. It's just one of those things, you know . . . maybe you had a different marker . . . you know, a harder one.' Vicky was pleased that she'd done well but didn't want it to come between them.

Tess, however, was very keen to lord it over Bert. 'You know what? Maybe me and Vic are just naturally more intelligent than you, so . . . you know . . . a little work from us helped us pass the exams whereas you'd need to do loads of work in comparison to our little to have any chance of passing . . . yeah?'

'Piss off, clever clogs!'

The girls were now in the first term of the lower sixth and Bert was having to endure the ignominy of retakes as well as study for her two chosen A levels. She found the retake classes even more boring than she'd found the classes the first time round. Added to that she did not like having to attend lessons without her pals *and* do more work than them into the bargain.

Bert wouldn't have minded failing her O levels if it weren't that her friends had passed theirs. She felt betrayed by their achievements. Up until this stage in their lives the girls had done more or less everything as a single unit, except for when she and Vicky had lost their virginitys. For Bert, on the occasion of that particular achievement it had seemed to her merely a practical necessity that she leave her friends behind. Aside from having them present at the actual event she had otherwise involved them in every possible way. Bert wanted to continue to do every last thing as a gang.

126

She was still going out with Adam, whom she'd come to regard as similar to an old family pet – around and comfy but not worth playing with. He continued to spend most weekends at her house, but they rarely bothered to have sex any more. Bert felt increasingly like an ancient married woman instead of the teenage hell-raiser she'd worked so hard to become and partly blamed the tedium of her limited sexual experience to date. One day when she, Vicky and Tess were lounging around in the sixth-form common room between classes Bert suddenly decided to pick Vicky's brains on the subject of sex. She was sure that there must be more to it than she had so far discovered.

'You know when you were going out with Barney, right?' Bert ventured tentatively.

'Yeah, what about it?' Vicky replied. She was over Barney now but still didn't relish talking about him.

'Well, did you . . . you know *like* doing it?'

'Yeah, it was all right, he was pretty good at it and – you know – did lots of different stuff . . .' Bert was puzzled. She couldn't think what her friend meant by 'different stuff'. She was desperate to know, but terrified that if she probed Vicky would clam up and refuse to divulge the details.

Tess's curiosity came to her aid. 'What sort of different stuff?'

Vicky looked at both of her friends and considered not going on but she felt no loyalty towards Barney any more and, after a couple of minutes' pause, decided to continue. 'You know . . . ah, not just sex . . . you know . . . not just fucking . . . different stuff . . . Oh, you know . . . stuff . . .' Vicky was embarrassed and shot Bert an imploring look, entreating her to show that she understood. She assumed that, between Tess and Bert, at least Bert must know what she was talking about.

'What, like . . . doing it with the lights on?' Tess ventured.

'No . . . oh . . . yes, that as well . . . no, I mean . . . you know

. . . oh, you know . . . doing it from behind . . . me going on top . . . blow-jobs . . . that kind of thing.' Vicky rattled hastily through the list of things that, for her, constituted 'different stuff'. Bert was stunned. She could tell Vicky hadn't completed her list when she'd eventually trailed off. Vicky'd already told her about the oral sex with Barney but she simply could not believe that she'd done all that other stuff too.

'Did you *want* to do all those things?' Bert was hoping that Vicky's answer was going to be no and that it had all been undertaken reluctantly under pressure from Barney.

'Yeah, of course I did. It gets boring just doing it one way the whole time.' Vicky was less inhibited now that she'd got the naming of the actual acts out of the way.

'So did you always come with him, then?' Tess asked matter-of-factly.

Bert was stunned. Tess was still a virgin. Before she could stop herself she blurted out, 'How do you know about orgasms, Tess?'

Tess's face turned bright red and she replied tartly, 'How do you think?'

'I dunno.' Bert's answer was genuine. She couldn't figure out how Tess could possibly know anything about orgasms, particularly when she herself knew absolutely nothing about them despite having been thrashing away with Adam for all this time.

'Well, work it out.' Tess was deeply embarrassed, and although she was quite happy to listen to Vicky talk about her colourful sex life with Barney she had no intention of revealing her own private goings-on.

Bert looked at Vicky and pulled a bemused face. 'She's talking about wanking . . . you know . . . herself . . . Come on, you know, haven't you ever done it?' Vicky whispered theatrically to Bert. She wasn't imagining that Tess wouldn't hear, she just hoped that by whispering it might make it all a bit less embarrassing for her.

'Oh,' Bert eventually replied lamely. She was completely taken aback. She'd heard that boys apparently spent every waking moment wanking but it had never occurred to her that girls did it. She had always imagined that if girls had orgasms then it was solely from having sex and, she guessed, with someone a lot more adept than Adam. All of a sudden it dawned on her that the itchy, restless feeling she'd experienced during and after sex was the result of not having an orgasm. She immediately felt as if somebody had just turned on the light in a darkened room she'd spent years flapping about in, bumping into furniture and stubbing her toes.

'Don't you have orgasms with Adam?' Tess asked, using an exaggeratedly incredulous tone, intending to transfer her own embarrassment on to Bert.

'Erm . . .' Bert hesitated, reluctant to admit that this was the case. She knew that once she did so her long-held claim of sexual expertise was going to appear very lame.

'Erm . . . not very often . . . no . . . sometimes but . . . you know . . . not a lot . . .'

Vicky and Tess knew Bert was lying but didn't pursue it. Tess would have been happy to embark on haranguing her friend over what she'd been doing in bed with Adam all this time if she hadn't been having orgasms. She was being held back by the knowledge that Bert would instantly throw in her face the fact that she was a virgin, and therefore completely unqualified to talk about sex at all.

Bert's classes finished before Vicky and Tess's that day and as she made her way home that afternoon, she wondered if masturbation and orgasms were something else Real Mums told their daughters about. If so, then, for once, she was relieved that her mum wasn't a Real Mum. Bert hadn't thought to ask her friends how they'd found out about them. Applying herself to it now, Bert reckoned that Tess had probably been driven to experiment with masturbation by despair at still being a virgin, and Vicky had probably got the idea off Barney. Spontaneous self-exploration had never occurred to Bert and she could not imagine her friends having come up with the idea themselves either. Bert resolved that she was going to find out what having an orgasm was like if it killed her. Her first major hurdle in achieving this end was that she wasn't very keen on the idea of doing it to herself. Adam wasn't entirely to blame for the uneventful sex life he and Bert had. Bert was squeamish about the messy aspects of sex and had always anticipated that the male partner would be familiar with all that was required – simply by dint of being a man and therefore more interested in the act itself. She was slowly realizing that she might have to take more of an active role in the whole thing if she wanted to get rid, once and for all, of that itchy, restless feeling.

'My friend Richard is coming to dinner on Saturday and he's bringing his godson Jonathon, who's down from Bristol or Bath, one of those ghastly regional towns, to spend the weekend with him. Apparently he's about your age. I would very much appreciate it if you would join us for supper.'

Bert and her mother had bumped into each other in the kitchen, late one evening, while Angela had been getting herself some ice and Bert was making beans on toast. Angela delivered her request in a deliberately off-hand manner. She was hoping to deflect attention away from the fact that she rarely asked her daughter to do her favours, aware, as she was, that they would be likely to be turned down as a matter of principle. Bert was perplexed. To her eternal relief her mother had never mentioned Randy Richard since the whole grand-piano fiasco. Fucking typical, she doesn't mention him all this time and then asks me to sit through dinner with him and some pathetic godson of his, Bert seethed, deciding to decline the invitation.

'Can't. I'm busy on Saturday night.'

'What are you doing?'

'Just busy, all right?'

'No, it isn't all right. I hardly ever ask you to do anything and on this occasion I think you could show me the good manners of staying in at least for supper.'

Bert snorted derisively as she emptied the beans on to the toast she'd made. 'Yeah, 'cos you'd know a lot about good manners!' she sneered, as she sat down.

Angela was primed to start a full-scale row but managed to hold back. She knew she had to get her daughter to agree to stay for supper. She had absolutely no intention of entertaining her lover's godson single-handed. 'Please, Apple darling, just do this one thing for Mummy. I'll order the supper from Fortnum's, I won't make it.' Bert was amused by how much her mother evidently needed her and decided to make the most of it.

'Twenty pounds,' she said, through a mouthful of beans.

'Twenty pounds? What do you mean twenty pounds? And don't talk with your mouth full – it's repellent!'

'Give us twenty pounds and I'll stay in for your pathetic supper, which you have to promise comes from Fortnum's or else. Otherwise no deal,' Bert said, with another mouthful of beans and toast.

'Twenty pounds! Twenty pounds! Are you out of your tiny mind? What on earth makes you think I'd give you twenty pence let alone twenty pounds? You'll stay in for supper because I'm bloody well telling you to stay in and that is that!'

Angela's sense of outrage was making her lose sight of her ultimate goal. She badly wanted to please Richard, who, she suspected, was losing interest in her. He had cooled considerably over the last few months and Angela imagined that he'd met someone else. Bringing his godson over to dinner had been her idea. Richard had been quite happy to entertain him alone but Angela had insisted they come. She couldn't believe that Richard might genuinely enjoy his godson's company and wanted to make sure he wasn't using him as an excuse not to see her.

'Mum,' Bert said, dragging out the word to make herself sound very longsuffering, 'when was the last time I did something just because you told me to?'

Angela didn't have an answer. It still baffled her that she had failed to instil in her daughter the kind of fear and respect her parents had instilled in her. She blamed the failure on her ex-husband and the collapse of the marriage. She fantasized that, united against their children, they could have ruled with a rod of steel, whereas alone she felt clueless. 'Don't be so common, asking for money to come to your own house for supper. The very idea!'

'Twenty quid, take it or leave it.' Bert rarely found herself in a situation where she held all the trump cards and she was loving it, particularly given the opposition.

Angela hesitated for a moment. 'Ten.'

'Fifteen.'

'Ten, and that's my final offer.'

'Fifteen up front or nothing doing.'

'I said ten pounds was my final offer and I meant it.' Angela was desperately hoping that if she stuck to one figure Bert would lose confidence.

'Fifteen, and I won't tell Richard that you didn't make the dinner.' Bert would have been quite happy with ten quid but felt her honour was at stake and that she needed to hold out for a sum nearer her original price.

Angela hadn't anticipated the threat of Bert revealing the supper's true source. 'OK, done. Fifteen pounds, but for that price you stay for the whole evening. No sloping off the moment the food's finished.'

Bert shrugged her shoulders in agreement. She was very chuffed – fifteen quid was more than the monthly allowance she got from her father.

1976

Sidney Poitier

'Guess who's coming to dinner?' Bert announced to Vicky and Tess the next day as they lounged around in the common room.

'Sidney Poitier,' Tess called out. She was standing a few feet away by the table where the kettle and tea-bags lived, making herself a cup of tea.

'What?' Bert said, in her most withering tone.

'Guess who's coming to dinner? Sidney Poitier,' Tess repeated.

'What the fuck are you on about? I go "Guess who's coming to dinner?" meaning to my house on Saturday, and you go, "Sidney Poitier". What's that supposed to mean?'

'Sidney Poitier, a famous film star, stars in a film called *Guess Who's Coming To Dinner*. So, you go "guess who's coming to dinner" and I say, "Sidney Poitier." Do you get it?'

'Is that supposed to be funny, Tess?'

'Well, I thought it was, and if you knew anything about classic cinema then you'd have got the reference and thought it was funny too,' Tess retorted.

'I don't know about crappy old movies because I've got a life and don't spend my whole time in front of the TV!'

Tess had an extensive knowledge of film. She particularly liked the old ones and had watched hundreds since she was a child. Her interest was initially inspired by her father, who had been an editor. When they had lived together as a family the pair of them would often watch old classics together and her father would tell her the names of all the actors, directors, writers and explain how each film had been lit and shot. Over time, Tess had become fascinated by every aspect of film-making. Since her father had left to go and live abroad she had maintained her enthusiasm, chiefly guarding it as a solitary pursuit. Her friends occasionally watched movies with her but they irritated her by talking all the way through.

'*Guess Who's Coming To Dinner* is not a crappy film and, if you must know . . .'

'Will you two pack it in? Blimey, what are you like, the pair of you? Bert, for God's sake, just tell us who is bloody well coming to dinner.' Vicky was exasperated by her friends' bickering.

'Guess.' Bert was determined to make the most of this moment.

'Just tell us,' Vicky snapped. She wasn't in the mood for games after the spat.

'No, guess, guess, you'll never guess, just guess . . .'

'Sidney Poitier?' Tess chipped in.

'Most amusing, no – come on, guess. You'll never guess in a million years.' Bert was thrilled by the prospect of finally telling them who was coming.

'Bert, if we'll never guess in a million years then there's no point in us trying to guess, so just tell us, OK?'

Bert saw that Vicky had a point and mentally kicked herself for having said that guessing would be that hard. 'Yeah, all right. Well, Randy Richard is coming over to dinner on Saturday and he's bringing some pathetic godson of his, and Mum's giving me fifteen pounds so that I'll stay in with them!'

'Fifteen pounds!' Tess was impressed. 'Just to stay in for supper! Wow, that's not bad!'

'Yeah, but I've got to look after his crappy godson so it's not *that* great.' Bert didn't want it to sound like she was getting away with murder.

'How come your mum's giving you money to stay in?' Vicky inquired.

''Cos I said I wouldn't stay unless she paid me and she was desperate so eventually she said yes,' Bert explained proudly.

'Bert,' Vicky said, in way that Bert knew was meant to be disapproving.

'What? Why should I stay in for her poxy boyfriend and his spotty godson?' Bert hadn't anticipated condemnation from her friend.

'Nothing, forget it,' Vicky replied. She wanted to avoid a row.

'Look, there's no reason I should do my mum any favours. She never does anything for me, she's horrible to me all the time, and if I asked her to help me out she'd definitely say no, so, you know . . .' Bert trailed off. She didn't know whether Vicky had deliberately intended to make her feel guilty but she did now and she was loath to admit it.

'God, I'm late for my class. See you later,' Tess blurted out, rolling the last three words together to make them sound like one word – slater. They'd all taken to saying their farewells like that.

'Me too, fuck, bye . . . slater!' Vicky jumped up and ran out of the room. Bert looked at the clock up on the wall, the glass was cracked but she could make out that it had just gone eleven fifteen. She had a class as well, a retake – English lit O level – but she was in no great hurry. She was cross with Vicky for making her feel bad about her mother. She already knew that Vicky thought her mum wasn't as awful as she made out but she really hated it when she stood up for her.

The dreaded Saturday came round and Bert, having heard her mother moving around unusually early that morning, went down to inspect the food she'd ordered. As she entered the kitchen she was stunned by the sight of her mother in the middle of washing the floor.

'I didn't think you knew how to use a mop,' she remarked,

136

as she poured herself some cornflakes from her store of personally bought food.

'Yes, your father sent me to advanced mop-and-bucket efficiency classes as part of the conditions for marrying me.'

Bert shot round to sneak a look at her mother. She needed to check that she was joking – to Bert's amazement, it was clear that she was. She was very cheered. She couldn't remember the last time Angela had made a joke. 'So, what have you ordered?' she asked brightly, nodding in the direction of the two huge boxes sitting on the table.

'*Pâté de foie gras* to start, *canard à l'orange* for the main course. I think I can manage the vegetables and potatoes – and a *mousse au chocolat* for pudding. What do you think?'

Bert detested *pâté* and fervently hoped Angela wouldn't recite the menu tonight, pronouncing all the words in the same stupid French accent but she didn't want to upset her mother's good mood and refrained from voicing any dissent.

'Sounds delicious, Mum. Erm . . . do you want me to help . . . er, do anything?' Bert could barely believe what she was saying.

'Thank you, darling. Perhaps you could get out the good plates and glasses – ooh, and cutlery and give them all a clean. That would be very helpful.'

Bert and her mother set about performing a variety of domestic chores chatting pleasantly like two great friends who always got on like a house on fire. They laid the table together and, to Bert's astonishment, Angela even took her advice about not putting the napkins inside the glasses. Bert loved the unfamiliar feeling of getting on well with her mother. Later that afternoon, when everything was finally ready, Angela went off to have her hair done. Bert was very pleased that she was tidying herself up but worried that it might all look a bit much. Bert felt that it was always a mistake to appear keen. She knew that nonchalance pays dividends, and that letting people know you've made a big effort heightens the pain when you're let down *and* makes you look pathetic into the bargain.

At around seven o'clock that evening Bert and Angela were sitting together in the living room waiting for their guests. The mood had remained friendly between them but Bert couldn't shake off a growing sense of doom. She wasn't accustomed to harmonious times with her mother at all, let alone ones that lasted for an entire day, and she couldn't help having a panicky feeling in her stomach, as if the whole thing might blow at any moment. Bert felt all the trouble her mother had gone to made an eruption all the more likely. She knew that if her mother was headed for a fall then she'd be the first in the line of fire.

'Mum, you know that . . . er . . . the money?' she mumbled.

'Don't worry, I'll give it to you tomorrow, first thing,' Angela said, without malice, Bert noticed.

'No, I was going to say, forget it . . . um . . . I didn't really mean it, you know . . . er . . . I was just mucking about . . . er . . .' Bert had felt secretly guilty about the whole transaction, even before Vicky had said anything. She was glad that her mother's behaviour was making it possible for her to climb down from the belligerent position she'd taken.

'That's very decent of you, darling,' Angela replied.

Bert thought she detected a twinge of sarcasm but not enough, she decided, to make her regret her offer to retract. A moment later the doorbell rang and Angela leapt up to answer it. The display of tangible eagerness made her daughter wince. Bert stayed in the living room while she listened to the greetings and introductions taking place in the hall. She was preparing herself to face Richard for the first time since she'd seen him half naked, draped in a piano cover.

'Hello there, Albertine. You look well. This is my godson Jonathon.' Bert looked up casually from the bowl of nuts she'd been picking through. She had decided that, at all costs, she must be in the middle of doing something when they came in. Bert greeted Richard without standing up and threw his godson, whom he was masking, a cursory nod. As Angela started offering drinks around about Bert's attention was drawn to Jonathon's feet: he was wearing a pair of real cowboy boots and she was very impressed.

'I need to get some fag – er, cigarettes. Is there an off-licence near?'

'Yes, Jonathon, quite near. Albertine will go with you and show you where it is.' Bert shot Angela a look, narrowing her eyes and grimacing. 'Won't you, darling?'

Bert grunted and stood up. She hated being proffered like a child, but she didn't want to look even more like one by making a scene.

She and Jonathon walked out of the house in silence. They were both embarrassed by the situation they'd been forced into, and Jonathon was the first to speak. 'Look, I'm sorry I've been dumped on you like this. You probably had something better to do tonight.'

'It's all right, it's not your fault.' Neither of them spoke again before they got back to Bert's house, by which time Angela and Richard were sitting at the dinner table in the kitchen.

'Goodness, what took you so long? We thought you'd eloped!' Angela sang out with forced hilarity as they entered.

Bert wanted to die. She caught Jonathon looking at Angela like she was mad and took a deep breath, steeling herself for what she now knew would be an excruciating evening.

During the first course, conversation was stilted and there were a few long gaps when no one spoke at all. Bert didn't particularly care, but she noted with dread that it was making Angela flap. She began to over-compensate for the silences and started guzzling down wine like some bloke in a pub drinking competition. As the meal progressed, she produced bottle after bottle, before the one on the table was even half finished. Bert's heart sank. She could tell her mother had lost control and was making matters worse by trying to encourage an obviously reluctant Richard to join in.

I wouldn't blame Richard if he does go off her if she's going to act this desperate, Bert thought, as she heard her mother react over-enthusiastically to some lame comment Richard made. Suddenly to her horror she saw her mother lurch towards Richard and incline her head at him, turning away from the table at the same time. Bert couldn't make out what exactly she was saying but she recognized the hushed, urgent tone from heated conversations she'd overheard between her parents. Bert looked at Richard's face and could instantly tell that this was not a discussion he wanted to have with Angela now or at any other time.

'So, are you doing your A levels at the moment?' Jonathon said, suddenly coming to Bert's rescue.

She was filled with gratitude. 'Yeah, and retakes,' she replied cheerily. She had made no effort to be pleasant to him up to this point, but now she desperately wanted to encourage a conversation between them to avoid having to witness her mother making a fool of herself.

'God, I had to do them too. I only passed one O level. They're a nightmare, aren't they?'

'Albertine didn't even manage to pass one, did you, my darling?'

Angela had got no joy from Richard and was now looking to other quarters for a fight. Bert ignored her mother's jibe and shot Richard a contemptuous look. She was filled with loathing for him for having landed her in the shit just because he didn't have the guts to be straight with her mother.

'Well, the one I passed was only woodwork so it didn't really count . . .' Jonathon piped up gallantly.

'Still, passing one is quite an achievement when you compare it to none at all, isn't it?'

'Angela, please, I don't think Albertine wants us to talk about her exam results,' Richard said, in a gentle but, Bert thought, patronizing voice.

'Oh, doesn't she, Richard sweetheart? Well, then, what do you suggest we *do* talk about? Shall we talk about your new fucking girlfriend? Would that be an interesting topic of conversation? I, for one, would certainly find it most fascinating, assuming that is that you have a new girlfriend and that it's not just my decrepit old body that has ceased to appeal to you. How well I remember when once it drove you to the heights of passion!' Angela was waving her glass around as she spoke and wine was slopping out on to the table.

'For Chrissakes, Angela, calm down. This is neither the time nor the place to talk about this!' Richard said, while giving Bert a sympathetic look.

Bert wanted to hit him. She was disgusted by her mother, but infuriated by Richard's attempt at empathy. 'I'm going upstairs,' she said, as she stood up.

'That's right, off you go. Desert your mother when she needs you most, rats off a sinking ship, just like your father, self-centred and emotionally stunted!'

Bert bolted out of the room, slamming the door behind her. She raced up to her bedroom and threw herself on to her bed, her whole body shaking with shame and fury. She was furious with herself for having let down her guard. She knew she shouldn't ever have trusted her mother.

Do All Boys Look the Same?

I always said he was a smarmy wanker, Bert thought, once she'd calmed down. She sat up cross-legged in the middle of her bed and rolled a joint. There had to be something wrong with him for fancying Mum in the first place. What a tosser! *And* he's got a revolting hairy chest, bleurgh! Bert grimaced as she remembered the sight of Richard's semi-naked body. The moment she lit up there was a quiet knock on her door.

'Go away,' she barked angrily. She'd guessed her mother might come up to make amends and get her to rejoin the party. She knew Angela would regret the outburst sooner or later, not because of her but because of what Richard might think. After a moment's pause the person knocked again. Bert didn't think her mother would knock twice, not quietly anyway.

'Who is it?'

'Um, it's me, Jonathon. I just wanted to see if you were all right.'

'Yeah, I'm fine . . . um . . . thanks,' Bert replied, staying put on her bed. She was a bit puzzled by Jonathon's concern and wondered if he'd been sent up by his godfather.

'Er, um, can I come in?'

Bert raised her eyes to the heavens and made a face but got up and let him in anyway.

'Hi . . . oh, are you having a smoke? Any chance of joining you?' Jonathon said, pointing at the joint Bert was holding.

'Yeah, s'pose so,' Bert said, then she suddenly thought of

something. 'What are Randy – oops, I mean your godfather, er, Richard and – and her doing?'

'Oh, fuck knows, getting more pissed probably. Hopefully they'll pass out and forget everything that happened!'

'Fat chance,' Bert said, laughing.

Jonathon sat down on Bert's bed and looked around the room. After a brief silence he said, 'So you going to light that or what?'

The joint had gone out. Bert had momentarily forgotten about it when Jonathon had sat on her bed. Although there was nothing else to sit on in her room, she was frozen in panic by having to sit down next to him. She was afraid she'd look like she was trying to get off with him. 'Yeah, sorry.' She was relieved to see that her matches were sitting on the shelves that ran down the length of the wall behind where Jonathon was sitting. It meant that she could get on to the bed to fetch them without looking like she was after him, she reasoned. She climbed on to the bed and lit the joint. The pair of them finished it in total silence.

'Shall I roll another one?' Jonathon asked.

Bert had greatly relaxed by this time and, with a lazy smile, handed Jonathon the box she kept her gear in. He's quite tasty, she thought as, out of the corner of her eye, she watched him roll up.

'Is your mum all right about you smoking?' Jonathon asked, as he put the finishing touches to the impressive spliff he'd created.

'I don't care, it's none of her business. Anyway, she doesn't know about half the stuff I do.'

Jonathon nodded to convey that he understood what Bert meant and lit up. Again they smoked in silence until Jonathon suddenly suggested they play a reading game. He explained that they were to take turns reading out backwards the titles of the books on the shelf while the other person looked away and had to guess what the book was. Bert, who was quite stoned by this time, thought it sounded like a great idea and readily agreed when Jonathon suggested she go first. To ensure she didn't sound like an idiot she chose a relatively easy title for her first attempt.

'Did ytak tahw.'

'Never heard of it, it must be a Chinese book, doesn't count.'

Bert smiled. 'No, it isn't, that was *What Katy Did*. You have a go. It's really hard finding one you can actually pronounce.' Jonathon looked around for a suitably complicated title – he'd played this game lots of times before.

'I've got a good one, OK – Dribgnikcom a llik ot.'

Bert let out a snort of laughter. 'You sound like some Russian bloke, say it again!'

Jonathon started to repeat himself but, half-way through the first word, started laughing too. Once they were both laughing they couldn't stop and as soon as one calmed down the other would set them off again. The mattress started shaking and Bert lost her balance. Still giggling, she fell back on to the bed. Jonathon looked down at her and said, 'Dribgnikcom? Dribgnikcom? Dribgnikcom?' over and over again each time making it sound like a question. Every time he said the word Bert found it more and more hilarious. She started to laugh harder and harder and clutched her ribs, which were starting to ache. Without warning Jonathon leant over and planted a kiss on her lips. Bert was very surprised. She hadn't thought about kissing Jonathon even when she'd noticed he was tasty. It wasn't until they'd been kissing for a couple of minutes that Bert grasped she was enjoying herself. He's very good at it, she thought.

Just as Bert was relaxing into the snog she felt Jonathon's hand slide up her T-shirt. Before she knew what was happening he had manoeuvred his hand underneath her bra and was fondling her left breast. In all the time she had been sleeping with Adam he had never touched her breasts. In fact, neither of them had ever deliberately touched any part of each other's bodies other than when contact had occurred by accident. Bert felt like she was going to explode with excitement and responded to Jonathon's kissing with fervour. At that moment, he pulled his hand away from her breast and moved it down the length of her body. Bert gasped as he pushed it past the top of her skirt and into her knickers. She was embarrassed because she could tell she was wet down there, and although this had happened before she'd never known if it was normal or not. Her body stiffened as she anticipated Jonathon whom, she guessed, would know either way, recoiling with disgust. As his hand came into contact with her fanny Jonathon began rubbing it frantically and moaning with what Bert thought sounded like pleasure. She realized that the wetness didn't repel him and that it must be normal.

The familiar itchy, restless feeling was mounting inside her. Bert desperately tried to ignore it. Suddenly she panicked, feeling an uncontrollable urge to pee, and she knew she wasn't going to be able to avoid wetting herself. Jonathon seemed to sense the change and, to her dismay, took his hand away. He sat up and in one skilful movement pulled her knickers off and lunged his face down between Bert's legs. Bert gasped with a mixture of horror and ecstasy, she didn't feel like she could stop him even if she wanted to. She just prayed she smelt all right. A smile beamed across her face as the drawing of the couple performing this act in *The Joy of Sex* popped uninvited into her mind.

A moment later, without warning, Bert felt her fear of wetting herself evaporate and the itchy, restless feeling disappear. Her fanny started to pulsate and felt as if it had burst into flames. Her body began convulsing involuntarily. She was sure she looked like she was having an epileptic fit but she didn't care, she was convinced she was about to die with pleasure. Jonathon kept lapping away eagerly until her body stopped shuddering.

Once she'd come to rest he wiped his face on the hem of her skirt and drew himself up to lie beside her.

'That didn't take long,' he said, evidently very pleased with himself.

Bert gave him a measured smile. She really felt like throwing her arms around his neck and offering herself up as his sex-slave for the rest of her life but she thought he might think it was a bit uncool, particularly as she'd probably have to admit she'd never had an orgasm before.

'So are you on the pill?' Jonathon asked, after kissing her again.

'No, but I've got a diaphragm.'

'Do you want to go and put it in then?'

Bert was awestruck by his confidence. She could tell that he'd assumed they'd shag and, therefore, no persuasion was needed. She wasn't accustomed to spontaneity in this field and didn't want to look prissy by saying no. Bert trotted off to the bathroom, returning a moment later feeling desperately self-conscious. It seemed weird and embarrassing that he knew what she'd gone to do. However, the second she was in the door Jonathon put his arms around her and started kissing her neck and the awkwardness disappeared. To Bert's delight Jonathon pushed his hand back down to her fanny. She'd been resigned to him just jumping straight on top of her and getting the whole thing over and done with in the blink of an eye, like Adam always did. As she began to feel like she was losing consciousness and drifting out to sea again she heard Jonathon speak in a low voice: 'Touch me. Get it out for me.'

Eeeeeeek! Bert screeched, at full volume, inside her head but she managed to stop herself from saying it out loud. She'd never held Adam's penis and he'd never asked her to, for which she'd been very grateful. In general she didn't like the way they looked and really didn't fancy having to handle one, but she didn't see how she could reasonably decline. Bert gritted her teeth and moved her hand gingerly down to the front of Jonathon's trousers where she immediately came into contact with his still clothed hard-on. Jonathon unzipped his fly and his penis popped straight out as if it had just been sprung free from heavy-duty restraints. Bert took a deep breath and thought, Here we go, as she laid her hand on the flesh of his penis. The moment she touched it, he let out a long, throaty groan. Bert was surprised to find that such a simple action elicited such a great response and wondered momentarily if all boys liked having their willies felt this much.

'Hold it. Rub it up and down,' Jonathon moaned. His voice had grown even lower and sounded like he was parched. Bert thought it sounded a bit silly and had to work hard to suppress a giggle. Jonathon seemed not to notice and continued to give her instructions, telling her to rub it and grip it, and she was pleased that, even though he was evidently getting excited, he hadn't stopped touching her. Actually it doesn't feel as bad as it looks ... It's almost nice ... Bert mused dreamily, as she continued with the prescribed hand movements. Jonathon's breathing began to get more urgent and suddenly in one swift movement he swept Bert's hand away from his penis, climbed on top and pushed himself into her. Her whole body felt like she was being wrapped in melted marshmallow while recovering from pins and needles at the same time. It felt completely unlike she'd ever felt before. Bert was amazed that two boys could do the exact same act and yet so wildly differently. She could not believe she'd done it so many times before. Within a few minutes Jonathon's thrusting picked up pace, he gave out a deep grunt then collapsed into a crumpled heap half on and half off her.

As they lay there in silence Bert had to admit that there was one similarity between Jonathon and Adam: she'd noticed that just as Jonathon had climaxed his eyes had suddenly taken on the same glazed look as Adam's when he came. She made a mental note to ask Vicky if she thought all boys looked like rabbits caught in car headlights when they orgasmed.

'What are you thinking?' Bert asked, after they'd lain in the same position long enough for her to get dead-leg. She hadn't wanted to ask him to move in case he thought she was trying to get rid of him.

'I'm wondering what your mum and Richard are up to,' he replied, rolling off her on to his back and putting his penis away as he went.

Bert was very pissed off. She hadn't expected him to say something romantic but she didn't want to hear that he was thinking about something so completely unrelated to what they'd just done.

'Sorry, that sounded a bit funny. I mean, I *was* thinking about that but only because I was trying to work out how I could spend the night with you . . . if you want me to . . . how we could manage that . . . you know . . . if they're still downstairs and stuff . . .' Bert felt like smothering him in kisses. He is just fantastic, she thought.

Bert woke up with a start at six thirty the next morning. After hours of chatting and snogging, she and Jonathon had eventually fallen asleep without taking their clothes off or checking what was going on downstairs. Bert looked at him: he was still fast asleep. She decided that she was madly in love with him and really hoped he felt the same way. Then she began to worry about Angela.

She realized that she had no idea what had happened after she'd left the dinner table and suspected the worst, particularly when she remembered how drunk her mother had been. Bert guessed Angela would be very unpleasant about Jonathon having spent the night if things had gone badly with Richard but wouldn't even notice if they'd gone well. To avoid a disastrous morning, which might ruin everything with her new love, she decided that she had to find out immediately how the land lay.

Bert crept out of her bedroom leaving Jonathon asleep, and hoped that he wouldn't wake up while she was gone. Angela's bedroom was on the floor above but Bert decided to check the kitchen first. She didn't really have a clear idea of what the kitchen would be able to tell her about how last night had ended but as she hadn't fancied creeping into her mother's bedroom to find her wrapped around Richard, it seemed the logical first stop.

She wasn't prepared for the sight that greeted her when she opened the kitchen door. The table was strewn with leftovers, plates with half-eaten food encrusted on them, half-empty serving dishes, several bottles of wine in varying states of emptiness, screwed-up napkins, candles burnt down to the wicks, and Angela's head. Amidst all the debris, she had evidently fallen asleep on the table still clutching her glass of wine.

Bert was appalled. It wasn't finding her mother in that state that particularly worried her, it was what the scene meant. She knew Angela had the gift of being able to fall asleep anywhere and anytime, drunk or not. But she knew her mother wouldn't have fallen asleep at the table if things had gone well with Richard. She decided she'd better get Jonathon out of the house before her mother heaved into consciousness.

'Wake up, wake up,' Bert whispered to Jonathon, who appeared to be even more deeply asleep than when she'd left him. After Bert had given him a few nudges, Jonathon blinked his eyes open and gave Bert a huge grin, stretching his arms out and pulling her to him to plant a kiss on her lips. Bert was delighted that he obviously hadn't gone off her in the night and enthralled by his easy, open, loving manner, but also desperate to get him out before her mum surfaced.

'You are lovely,' Jonathon murmured, as he nuzzled into Bert's neck.

'Erm . . . so are you . . . but you've got to go. My mum's asleep on the kitchen table and I don't want her to wake up and find you here. She's going to be in a foul temper – I don't think things went too well with Richard.'

'Can't have gone too well if she ended up sleeping on the table, eh?' Jonathon said, with a smile, but still not making a move.

'Listen, you've got to get out of here. I'm sorry, I don't mean to be horrible or anything but . . . you know . . . I mean, I do want . . .' Bert trailed off at this point. She couldn't bring herself to say she wanted to see him again.

'Yeah, all right . . . Can we meet up later on? I don't have to go back until this evening.'

'Yeah, yeah, definitely, I'll ring you later on, all right?'

'Yeah, all right, see you later. Erm . . . last night was great by the way.'

Bert felt as if she was going to collapse with joy. God, if only he knew *how* great it was for me too, she thought, but she was too shy to say anything and gave him a big smile instead.

Following her lead, Jonathon crept downstairs behind Bert in total silence. When they came to the creaky step she was very impressed that he understood her exaggerated mime and stepped over the tread as instructed. Bert opened the front door as quietly as she could and watched Jonathon walk down the path. If he turns round before he gets to the gate then we're going to be together for ever and ever . . . she bet. Her heart sank as Jonathon's hand reached out to open the gate but just in time he turned round and blew her a kiss. She was ecstatic. After watching him lollop across the street in his fantastic cowboy boots looking, she thought, just like Robert Redford in *Butch Cassidy and the Sundance Kid*, Bert went back upstairs to bed and fell asleep. She couldn't wait to tell Vicky and Tess what had happened.

When Bert got up later that day there was no sign of her mother in the kitchen. Unperturbed she ate breakfast and went upstairs to find her sitting sedately in the living room. 'All right?' Bert said gruffly, poking her head round the door, leaving the rest of her body in the hall. She wanted to be in a good position to make a hasty retreat in case her mother's mood turned out to be the same as it'd been before she'd passed out.

'I'm fine. Why shouldn't I be?' Angela responded sniffily. Bert didn't like the sound of her voice but decided to continue trying to sound as normal as she could, hoping that this would deter her mother from launching into the tale of how her evening had ended.

'No reason, I was just asking if you were all right, you know. "You all right?" It's a kind of figure-of-speech kind of thing.'

'It might be a figure of speech for you and your friends but it certainly isn't for anyone with a brain!'

Bert instantly recognized what her mother was up to. She had no intention of bringing up last night's performance and was trying to vent her rage by goading her into an argument instead. But Bert wasn't going to waste her time rowing with her mother. She wanted to get straight on the phone to her friends. 'Yeah, well. See you later,' Bert mumbled, as she sloped off.

'And you needn't think you're not doing the washing up!' Angela called out.

'Fine, I'll do it right now.'

Bert could almost smell the disappointment Angela felt in having failed to get a rise out of her. She picked up the phone attached to the kitchen wall and dialled Vicky's number. It was Vicky who answered.

'Canada-a-a-a-a,' Bert sang out in full vibrato, mock-rock-star voice.

'Oh, Canada-a-a-a-a,' Vicky responded, in her own rendition of the same song. Their current favourite way of greeting each other on the telephone was to sing lines from TV advertisements that they found particularly funny, without saying hello or identifying themselves first. Bert's chosen theme this morning was from the ad for the Canadian Tourist Authority. It was a sub-Janis Joplin type of wailing ballad, sung with enormous gusto, to convey fervent national pride. Bert had chosen it because it exactly suited her mood – loud and full of verve. They repeated the refrain, going up an octave each time until they'd reached the top of their vocal ranges. Bert then embarked on a no-holds-barred blow-by-blow recount of the night that had changed her life.

1977

Don't Pee In the Bath

'Right, so shall I get off with Jamie, then?'

'Jamie? Jamie?'

'Yeah, Jamie.'

'Jamie? Who's Jamie?'

Bert knew perfectly well who Vicky was talking about but she wanted to appear disdainful.

'You know, Jamie that Vicky thinks is so fantastic,' Tess added, earning a forced smile from Vicky.

'Oh, yeah, no, I know. Jamie, that wanker with disgusting long hair and the rancid dog?'

'No, Jamie that very interesting person with an individual sense of style and a beautiful Afghan hound.'

'Yeah, that's what I said, that wanker with the disgusting long hair and the rancid dog.'

'Bert, since I've been at art school I've found that most of my fellow students have moved on from such mundanities as following high-street fashion. Everyone at the Foundry has their own way of being that is a unique expression of their talent.'

'Bleurgh.' Bert mimed being sick. 'Vicky, you sound like such a tosser sometimes – "moved on from such mundanity" perrleeeeze. Well, get off with him if you like but I think he looks very weird. Don't come crying to me if he tries to get you to have sex with his dog as well!'

Tess guffawed so hard and so unexpectedly that a great blast of beer shot out of her nose. The three of them collapsed in hysterical laughter as the amber liquid trickled down her face.

It was a few months after they'd come back from their seminal end-of-school-for-ever-life-starts-here holiday in Italy, and Bert, Vicky and Tess were having a drink in a pub near Vicky's art college. Bert thought privately that it was bringing out the worst in her. She felt that her pal's tendency to take herself seriously was running amok now that it was no longer subject to daily restraint from her. Added to that, she had acquired some new friends, who, in Bert's opinion, were real plonkers and this Jamie bloke was a prime example.

Vicky made her way back from the bar, precariously balancing three half pints of lager and lime between her overstretched hands.

'If I hear this song once more I'm going to kill myself,' she said, lowering the drinks delicately on to the table. Last year's big hit was playing on the jukebox for the umpteenth time. It was evidently on automatic re-select.

'Don't go breaking my heart,' Bert started singing along and doing wild disco dancing while remaining seated.

'I couldn't if I tried,' Tess sang out, and joining in with the jigging as well.

'Oh, honey, if I get restless.'

'Baby you're not that kind.'

'Ooh, ooh, nobody knows it.'

'Nobody shows it.'

Both Tess and Bert were prancing away in their seats. Tess had taken Kiki Dee's part and Bert was being Elton John. Their performance was beginning to irritate Vicky. She also didn't really want any of her new art-school friends to witness it.

'Right from the start, you gave me your –'

Suddenly Bert broke off in the middle of her singing. 'You know he's gay don't you?'

'Who's gay?' Tess asked, still jigging. She'd been enjoying the

154

duet, especially since it had clearly been winding Vicky up.

'Elton John. Elton John is gay.'

'He can't be. This is a love song.'

'I'm telling you, Elton John is gay and Kiki Dee is a lesbian.' Bert was adamant.

'How do you know?'

'I just know. All right?'

'Well, then, why are they singing, "Don't go breaking my heart," to each other, clever clogs?'

'Look, dumbo, they don't have to be going out with each other to sing a song together, do they?'

'No, but why would they do a song like this if they were gay?'

'I don't know. Maybe they're really good mates,' Bert blurted out belligerently. She was getting less sure of her assertion about the singers' sexuality.

'We're really good mates and I've never asked you not to go breaking my heart! Mates do not ask each other not to break each other's hearts. Honestly, I bet neither of them's gay and you just made it up to have something to say.' Tess had a strong feeling that she might be going to win this row.

'They might if they really liked each other a lot,' Bert mumbled. She was floundering badly but wasn't yet prepared to concede defeat.

'For Christ's sake, you two, shut up! I said I was going to kill myself if I had to hear this song one more time. Now I've got to listen to you two doing a bloody essay on it!' Vicky burst out, shutting her friends up instantly. They looked at each other and made stupid faces instead.

'So, typical me. I managed to get the most depressing job in the whole wide world today,' Bert announced, after a moment's silence.

'Oh, yeah, what's that?' Tess inquired.

'I'm answering telephones for a message service and it's very, *very* boring.'

'Well, why are you doing it, then?' Tess asked.

'How pointless a question is that? Why do you *think* I'm doing it? I'm doing it because I need money to live and I need to do something, *anything*, until I find out what I really want to do with my life!'

Tess shrugged her shoulders and lowered her head towards the table until her mouth was level with the edge of her glass. She was attempting to take a sip without picking it up.

'Stop that. You look like a sodding camel!' Bert snapped.

Tess laughed again, and this time the force of her laugh shot beer out of the glass and across the table. 'Look what you made me do!'

'I didn't *make* you do that. If you hadn't been behaving like a farmyard animal it wouldn't have happened.'

'I think you'll find a camel is not a farmyard animal, m'lady.'

'I never said it was. I said you looked like a camel first off because that's what came into my head but, now that I think about it, actually you look like a hog, which, I think you'll find, *is* a farmyard animal. Thank you.'

Bert and Tess were up and running again. Given half a chance, they'd embark on a row about animals' dwelling-places for the rest of the evening. However, Vicky's interruption put a halt to that possibility.

'It's not *doing* what you want to do that's hard, it's finding out what it is that you want to do in the first place that's impossible,' she declared, having taken a dainty sip of her lager.

'What?' Bert's face was contorted into a look of exaggerated pain and contempt. By this stage in her life, she had developed an extensive portfolio of extreme facial expressions, each one conveying a specific, usually critical, feeling. This particular look indicated clearly that she thought something was incredibly stupid and that whoever had said it was even more stupid for saying it out loud.

'It's a pity that talking about boys isn't a job qualification because if it was you'd have been beating off job offers with a shitty stick since we left school,' Tess said casually, keen to return to arguing – even if not about camels and farmyard animals.

'Piss off, Tess.' Bert was annoyed but not enough to start another row. Vicky's pronouncement had struck a chord and she wanted her to elaborate. 'What do you mean with all that knowing-what-you-want stuff, Vic?'

'What I'm saying is that working towards getting *it* once you know what *it* is is much, much easier than trying to find out what *it* is you want to do in the first place.'

'God, you're right, yeah, I see what you're saying,' Bert replied. She wasn't entirely sure but she thought she saw what Vicky meant.

'That's quite profound for you. Isn't it, Vic?'

'Piss off, Tess.'

'Oooh, pardon me for breathing. Aren't I allowed to join in this deep conversation about the meaning of life, then?'

'Yes. But only if you say something constructive.'

'Oooh, aren't we machwuuurre?' Tess drawled.

'You know, thinking about it, you've got a point. I don't know what I want to do and that's the main problem.'

Bert hadn't applied for university, chiefly to annoy her mother, which she'd achieved in great measure, but also because she'd no idea what to apply for. As things had turned out she'd have faced great difficulty getting into any university as she'd only scraped by with one A level, getting the lowest mark possible. And she was aware that on its own it wasn't going to get her very far.

Now that Vicky was at art school and Tess was studying

photography at the local polytechnic, Bert felt increasingly isolated by the sense of purpose and direction their respective courses were giving them. She'd spent so much time at school entertaining everyone, ensuring she maintained her naughtiest-girl-ever fame she hadn't ever given a second's thought to adult life and its requirements. She wouldn't really have given up her popularity even if it had occurred to her that life turned out to require more than the ability to make your friends laugh.

'Why don't you do nothing and just marry Jonathon, then get divorced in a few years' time and get loads of money off him?' Having failed to reignite the earlier row Tess was trying a different route to have another enjoyable scrap with Bert.

'Hah bloody hah. I don't think Jonathon would marry me even if I begged him to, and he probably won't have any money until his parents die.'

'O K, so marry Jonathon and kill his parents straight after the wedding. They're still married to each other, aren't they? So it should be easy to kill both of them at the same time. You could accidentally on purpose reverse the wedding car into them as they were waving you goodbye or –'

'Shut up, will you, Tess? I like Jonathon's parents. I don't want to kill them! It's not –' Bert snapped back.

Tess interrupted her before she could go on. 'Is that all that's holding you back? You mean, if you didn't like them you'd be prepared to murder them?'

'No, stop being so fucking stupid! I probably wouldn't mind marrying Jonathon actually but I don't think he'd marry me now anyway.'

Bert had been going out with Jonathon since the night he'd come to dinner and given her an orgasm. She hadn't thrown Adam a backward glance once she'd discovered that Jonathon knew how to do every single thing out of that *Joy of Sex* book. The combination of being able to feast herself on a whole array of new sexual experiences and the pair of them residing in different towns had ensured that the relationship had lasted longer than it ought to. However, much to her surprise, since they'd got used to each other Bert had begun to think there ought to be more. Her friends thought Jonathon was a bit loopy, he didn't talk very much and no one understood why he and Bert were still together – including, by this stage, Bert.

'Why did you say "now" like that? What's going on? What's happened?'

'Ah, well . . . I – I think I might be pregnant,' Bert mumbled sheepishly. She didn't really believe it was possible, even though she hadn't been feeling well for ages. She was hoping that talking about it out loud would somehow dispel the fear and mean that it definitely wasn't true.

'Piss off,' Tess said, assuming that Bert was mucking about.

'Do you really?' Vicky said, with concern.

'Not really, but you know, I suppose I could be – my periods *have* been a bit funny.'

'Does Jonathon know?'

'Er, no, I haven't said anything to him. See, if I am, which I'm sure I'm not, it wouldn't be his.'

'Eh?' Tess and Vicky howled in unison.

'Well, if I am, which I can't be, then it would be . . . erm . . . oh, God . . . don't go berserk, but it would be that bloke Nathan I snogged at Georgie and Charlie's big end-of-school party.'

'You said you didn't shag him!' Tess said indignantly. She was momentarily more concerned by the idea that Bert had kept something from them.

'I didn't really, it was one of those sort of in-and-out shags that don't really count.' Bert could see from Tess's expression that she would need further explanation. 'You sort of getting into heavy snogging and he gets his prick out and you're both sort of fumbling around and he gets on top of you and stuff but

159

it's not like a proper shag and . . .' She trailed off. She was beginning to regret having brought it up: it sounded too cheesy for her to justify.

Nathan had come along to the party with the older brother of someone from school. He'd been wearing leathers and said he had a bike and Bert had been very impressed by him. He'd made a beeline for her and after chatting to her for a while had suggested they go off on their own to smoke his very strong hash. It was the most potent dope she'd ever had and by the time they'd finished off his entire supply she'd been convinced that she'd permanently lost the use of all of her bodily functions. It clearly hadn't had the same effect on Nathan, but Bert didn't feel able to resist his advances, nor did she particularly want to at the time. However, Nathan had proved mighty unappealing the second the whole thing was over, scarpering as soon as he'd shot his bolt, and Bert had instantly decided to forget that the whole thing had ever happened.

'Why couldn't it be Jonathon, if you are, though?'

'Because I've always used my diaphragm with Jonathon and we haven't done it for ages. He hardly comes down any more. Anyway, look, forget about it, I'm sure I'm not pregnant.'

'Yeah, you don't look pregnant and you'd be really big by now if it was that bloke,' Vicky said reassuringly.

'He was disgusting,' Tess added.

'Yes, I remember, thank you, Tess. I was stoned and he sort of jumped on me and, anyway, God, it's not a big deal. Listen, just shut-up about it, OK?' Bert said, standing up to go to the bar. As she made her way towards it, she realized that talking about it hadn't worked; she didn't feel reassured. All the same she decided not to think about it any more.

'Well, I'm never, *ever* getting married,' Vicky announced, as Bert returned with the drinks.

'Getting married isn't a career choice, you know.' Bert was

feeling prickly, having just admitted to something that she wasn't at all proud of. She felt that Vicky might be implying that she would never get a job and might just try to get married instead.

'It is if you're Jewish.'

'Not if you're Jewish like you are, Vic.'

'What's that supposed to mean?'

'It's only a career choice for girls like Jewish princesses. The type that gives her boyfriend blow-jobs round the clock until he proposes and then refuses to do them ever again after the wedding – like your cousin Nil-by-mouth Nadine. You told us she'd lured that poor bloke Jason into marrying her, pretending all she ever wanted to do was suck him off, and from the moment they were married wouldn't open her mouth again,' Bert reminded her.

'Oh, yeah, she is like that,' Vicky conceded. 'Still, I'm never getting married.'

'You could say you don't do blow-jobs from the start and then he'd know where he stood when he asked you to marry him,' Tess piped up.

'If *who* asked me to marry him?' Vicky asked. She couldn't follow Tess's bizarre train of thought.

'Him, I mean he, him, whoever. If he, someone, asked you to marry him you could say that.' As far as Tess could see it was all very straightforward.

'First of all I would never marry a person I didn't want to give blow-jobs to. And second, it's not in case I have to do *that* that I don't want to get married, you dope! I just don't want to be tied down, lose my individuality, the freedom to do whatever I want whenever I want to do it.'

Before Tess could reply, Bert seized the opportunity presented by her simple approach to bedroom etiquette to display her superior knowledge of the subject. 'Tess, you can't go to bed with a bloke and say, "Listen, by the way I don't do blow-jobs," just like that, like, it's something you just don't do, like "I don't drive a car" or "I don't pee in the bath".'

'Why not?' Tess's inquiry was sincere.

Unlike her friends, Tess was still a virgin. Considering how greatly boys and all related issues had featured in their lives, to date, it was an exceptional achievement. Even before any of them had actually done it, it had been a favourite topic of conversation. Although Tess didn't like to admit it, Bert and Vicky knew that she had meant to stay intact. While the rest of her peer group had virtually trampled over each other in the stampede to shed their virginitys, she had held back thinking that she ought to really know and like the boy she was going to sleep with for the first time. Such quaint niceties hadn't ever flashed across her contemporaries' minds for even one second. To the vast majority of the pupils at the North London Girls' College, virginity had been no more a thing to be cherished than leprosy.

'Well, I'm not going to sleep with anyone until we're married,' Tess said.

'What?' Bert howled, screwing up her face like an old chamois leather.

'I've just decided. I'm going to keep my virginity until my wedding night.' Tess didn't know that she'd been going to say that, but she now meant it.

'Oh, perrleeeeze. Right, so shall we just cut out the middle man and start calling you Miss Haversham straight away?'

'No, I mean it. That way it'll be all special and lovely and romantic.'

Bert didn't know how to respond. She was overcome with a horrible sensation that she ought to take Tess seriously. Attempting to negate the feeling Bert looked at Vicky, raised her eyebrows and stuck out her tongue. Vicky's response completely threw her.

'Whatever you feel is right for you, that's what's important,' she said, laying a hand on Tess's shoulder.

Bert couldn't believe her ears. Nervous questions began racing through her mind. What are my mates turning into? What on earth is going on? Vicky's gone all arty-farty and likes some boy who looks like a tramp, and Tess is turning into a fucking nun! She was worried that they were changing into completely different people and that this would inevitably lead to them not being best friends or, worse still, that she wouldn't fit in any more.

1983

Keeping Mum

'You're going out with that Danny again?'

'Yes, and don't say Danny like that.'

'Like what?'

'You know very well. Like it's not a name but another word for shit.'

'Oh, did I say it like that? I didn't mean to. It was meant to sound like I think he's a complete tosser.'

'He is not! Anyway, you hardly know him. You've only met him for a minute a couple of times.'

'Bert, he said, "Catch ya later," when he was saying goodbye . . . "catch ya later"! What is he? A country and western singer? "Catch ya later"? I mean, I know you're desperate but *really*.'

'I am not desperate, I'm just not as picky as you are. Unlike you, I am able to accept that people in general always have *some* things that you don't like about them. It's not that I think it's great when Danny says those kind of things but I also don't think it means he should be dragged out into the street and shot! Anyway, will you babysit or not? I said I'd meet him at eight and I need to ring him if I can go.'

Yet again Bert was asking Tess to babysit with only a few hours' notice. Since Bert had been working at Vicky's restaurant she'd been meeting a wide variety of new people and getting lots of invitations to go out. Tess loved being with Tabatha but didn't like Bert automatically assuming that she would always look after her; she didn't want to be taken for granted. 'Oh, so you made a date with him before checking that I could babysit and wasn't actually doing something else?'

Bert decided to be diplomatic and resist the temptation to tell Tess that the likelihood of her having something else to do was about ten billion to one. 'Only so that I didn't have to ring him up to make arrangements . . .' She decided to flatter Tess a little. 'You know, I said that you might well be busy in which case I'd have to cancel.'

The strategy worked. 'Yeah, all right, I'll babysit, but don't be really late and *don't* bring him back here. It's not a good idea to constantly parade an ever-changing string of awful boyfriends in front of Tabatha.'

'I am not constantly parading an ever-changing string of awful boyfriends in front of Tabatha but she might as well grow up with her eyes open. There's no point in her thinking her mum's a nun!'

'Fat chance of that happening!'

'Hah bloody hah! Anyway, thanks a lot. Listen, you'll do her supper too, won't you? I want to go and get ready.'

Without waiting for an answer Bert skipped out of the room. Tess wouldn't admit it, but she actually preferred making Tabatha's supper herself: that way she knew the child was eating proper food. To her horror, Bert's idea of making her daughter a meal was to empty something out of a tin, defrost a packet from the freezer, or give her leftovers from the restaurant. Although her style was a little haphazard Bert made sure that Tabatha never went without. She saw this as a massive improvement on the sparse provisions Angela had supplied for her survival; by comparison, she saw herself as akin to a Bird's Eye mum.

They were now twenty-four years old and Tess was still living with her mother. She refused to see this as bizarre even though she knew that was what Vicky and Bert thought. Tess justified the situation to them by saying that she didn't see the point of paying rent for some grotty flat when her mother had a house that could easily accommodate two adults. She insisted that the fact they were related was irrelevant.

She had always got on fine with her mother, with whom she had an old-fashioned, unusually formal relationship. Most people had a similar association with Rosemary Pile, her personality forbade any other kind. Being an artist she worked alone, she didn't have colleagues and very few friends, mainly other artists whom she saw infrequently. As Tess had grown up she'd come to realize that her mother was a bit of a hermit but having decided that this was probably by choice she didn't allow it to worry her. Now and again, Tess would wonder if she really knew who her mother was and whether it mattered if she didn't. But most of the time Tess simply accepted that an intimate relationship with your mother wasn't necessary or even desirable. In fact, she often thanked her lucky stars that she was never going to have to listen to her mother talk about the onset of facial hair.

Tess had occupied the same bedroom since childhood, the only one on the top floor. In her view, she'd made enough adult adjustments – putting in a sofa, getting rid of the T. Rex posters and hiring her own TV and video – to be able to dismiss Bert's accusations that she'd turned into a freak. Tess's mother spent most of her days holed up in her studio, which occupied the entire ground floor, so Tess came and went as she pleased. The only room they shared, in effect, was the kitchen/living room. It was filled with Rosemary's sculptures, most of which were rejected commissions, and to Tess, it felt like her mother's domain. However, this didn't bother her since the little time she spent at home was usually in her bedroom.

Tess had enjoyed her time at poly and made lots of friends, but somehow she still hadn't got round to losing her virginity. There'd been a tutor to whom she'd become close but when Tess had found out he was married she'd gone right off him. Sneaking about and shagging other people's husbands did not fit into Tess's highly romanticized view of the world. By this stage, if and when she allowed herself to think about it, she convinced herself that she'd remained a virgin for the simple reason that she'd never met anyone worth bothering with.

Since leaving college Tess's daily life had been largely dominated by looking after Tabatha. She had been in the middle of her degree when Bert's daughter had been born, but she'd managed to make time to help out and as the baby got older and more demanding Tess had become increasingly involved. Neither of them had planned for this to happen but a kind of big-sister Mary Poppins side of Tess had mysteriously emerged in the face of Bert's obvious hopelessness. The first time Tess's inherent capabilities as a surrogate parent were revealed had been while Tabatha was still very little. Tess and Bert had been having coffee together.

'What the fuck are you doing?' Tess screamed lunging across the table and knocking the tart out of Bert's hand.

'Just giving her a bit. She keeps grabbing at it – she obviously wants some. Don't be so neurotic.'

'Bert, it's pecan pie! Tabatha is four months old. She's not on solids yet – are you trying to choke her to death?'

'OK, well, what if I just break off a little bit, then?'

'No, she doesn't eat food, that's what solids mean – food. Don't ever give her that kind of thing, especially not with nuts. Honestly, you're hopeless!'

'When do they start eating, then?'

'I dunno. When they get teeth, I suppose.'

'Oh, right, so when do they get teeth, then?'

Tess sighed and made a longsuffering face. 'Bert, haven't you read that book I gave you? It tells you all about what to expect from nought to five. You should know all this by now.'

'*The Art of Being a Mother*? What do you think? I tried reading it but it was full of a load of bollocks like "Listen to your child, he will tell you what he needs." Bert looked down at her baby. 'She doesn't tell me what she needs, she just lies around like a sack of old potatoes all day long.'

'Bert!' Tess was shocked.

'What? Look, I do love her but if you think I'm going to turn into one of those nut-rissole mothers with a baby hanging off my tit until it's seventeen you've got another think coming!'

Tess laughed at the image Bert had conjured up. 'I'm not saying you should turn into one of those women but, you know, you did have her and stuff. She is your responsibility now, you didn't have to have her.'

'Yes, I did,' Bert interrupted.

'Well, you know what I mean . . .'

Having not discovered that she was pregnant until she'd been five months gone, Bert's choices had been severely limited. She had refused to contemplate adoption, despite the fierce opposition from Angela, having decided, with uncharacteristic maturity, that as she'd made her own bed she'd better lie in it. At the final hour Bert's dad had organized for her to have his girlfriend's old flat since things had deteriorated too badly for her to stay with her mother.

'Anyway, it's not like a driving test or anything. There isn't a set thing you must do or you fail. You just have to do what comes naturally and, you know, that's probably what's best for the baby in the end, I reckon,' Bert said, making a cheery face that didn't go anywhere towards convincing Tess that this was an ideal approach to being a parent. From that moment on Tess had resolved not to let Bert bring up Tabatha unsupervised.

'Oi, I thought I told you not to be late. Anyway how was the Rhinestone Cowboy?' Tess shouted out good-naturedly, the moment she heard Bert entering the front door. Tess loved hearing about Bert's dates and, together, they often had a good laugh at her suitors' expense. Bert popped her head round the door and didn't reply, but made a face, frantically rolling her eyes up, down and sideways. 'What's the matter? Have you taken some speed?'

Bert didn't answer and a second later Danny strolled in behind her. Tess instantly realized what Bert had been trying to convey.

'Hoyadoin', Tess?' Danny said, in his confident, pseudo-American way. Tess didn't respond and stood up to go. She was livid.

'Thanks a lot, see you in the morning,' Bert said, as she saw her out. Tess didn't reply but, for what it was worth, gave Bert a look of exaggerated fury. As she made her way home she fumed quietly over her friend's resolute refusal to be dictated to by her. She felt that, considering how much involvement she had in Tabatha's daily life, her views on what was good for her ought to be taken into consideration. It wasn't that Tess wanted Tabatha to grow up in Disneyworld but she did think Bert could afford to be a little less tra-la-la when choosing what her five-year-old child should be exposed to.

As she lay in bed that night, Tess remembered appreciatively that while she'd been growing up her mother had never brought menfriends home to meet her. Her parents had broken up when she was ten years old and she'd been completely bewildered by it. She'd never heard them argue or even disagree and had assumed, not that she'd really thought about it, that they were happily married. Even after her father had left, nothing had become any clearer. Her mother wasn't given to talking about things, least of all emotional matters, and Tess didn't think, even now, that she'd be inclined to discuss the details of her marriage breakdown, assuming she even knew what they were.

Her father had sat her down one day and told her that he'd

bought a small house in France where he was going to live for a while because he needed time to think. Tess had understood that when he stopped needing this 'time to think' he'd come home. In keeping with the starkly unemotional way in which her parents handled the separation Tess hadn't made a fuss. For the first year, when she found herself worrying that her dad might not be coming back, she'd assured herself that if he wasn't then surely her mother would behave differently. As it turned out she was wrong: he never came back and her mother's behaviour never altered.

Once Tess had met Vicky and Bert and heard their stories about their parents' hysterical rows she found herself envying them. At least they knew why their mums and dads broke up. Her father had kept his promise of frequent visits so she'd seen him fairly regularly, each time always doing the same thing: they'd go to a weekend matinée at the Everyman cinema followed by high tea in the café. But he'd never once mentioned coming home. It didn't occur to Tess to ask either of her parents for an explanation. As she'd got older she decided that she must have misinterpreted what her father had meant by 'time to think' and blamed herself for any false hopes she'd had that he'd return.

1984

Too Many Cooks

'You know, it's lucky for you that Tess hasn't got much of a life, otherwise you'd be really stuck.'

'What do you mean? She *has* got a life. She's doing exactly what she wants to do, which is hanging around with Tabatha all day long. Sounds like a perfect life to me! Yuk, you're not doing that again. It's revolting . . .' Bert said, leaning over Vicky's shoulder and pointing to a starter on the menu that Vicky was writing out.

'It's an acquired taste, Bert, but only people who really know about food appreciate it,' Vicky replied, not looking up.

Bert pulled a face at her. 'Anyway, it's not like it's really hard work for Tess. She pretends that she helps Tabatha with her reading and stuff, but I know they just watch videos and dress up as dead movie stars. Tabatha did some funny accent the other day and said something about being ready for her close-up, Mr De Mille.' Vicky laughed. 'Yeah, cute, except she was frighteningly withering when it was clear I had no idea who she was imitating or what film it was from. She was like a horrible crossbreed of Mum and Tess.'

'Don't be silly, Tabatha's sweet. Anyway you can't fight genes. She's bound to be a bit like your mum, whatever happens.'

'Thanks a lot, Vicky.'

'Oh, you know, I don't think your mum's that bad. Honestly you've always exaggerated how much of a demon she is. I think she's a laugh, particularly since she went religious.'

Bert curled up one side of her lip and crossed her eyes, making it clear that she did not agree.

'Where are the aubergines?' Vicky said, rummaging about in the vegetable box.

'What aubergines?'

'The aubergines, the aubergines!'

'Shouting the word aubergines over and over again at me does not make me have a better idea of what you're talking about.'

'Look, you definitely said you'd ordered the bloody aubergines!'

'I did not say I'd ordered them. You never asked me to order the sodding aubergines, so why would I say I'd ordered them? I don't ever do the vegetable ordering!'

'I know you don't, but I forgot to include the aubergines in the order and that's why I asked you to get them separately!'

'You didn't!'

'I bloody well did!'

'Look, I'm telling you, you bloody well didn't! I don't even like bloody aubergines. They're disgusting, they taste like tarnished metal. I don't know why you're always putting them on the menu,' Bert added sulkily.

'Because they're an essential element of Mediterranean cooking. And I know you don't like them – and that's probably why you deliberately forgot to get them!'

'Don't be so bloody stupid – I wouldn't be that childish.'

Vicky didn't reply but exhaled loudly instead. Bert thought she sounded like an old mare coming to rest after a spurt of hefty galloping. 'You're a nightmare to work for, you know. You're so controlling, everything has to be just so, there's only one way to do things – your way – or it's completely wrong. God, you're like some sort of – of – dictator bloke in a chef's hat!'

'I am not controlling. I am thorough and professional. You can always quit, if I'm so awful.'

'Oh, yeah, 'cos you could easily manage without me, I don't think,' Bert said, with bravado. She had a sneaking suspicion that Vicky probably *could* manage perfectly well without her but she didn't like to dwell on the possibility.

Vicky had been running her own restaurant, La Cantina, for just over a year. She did all the cooking and stuck to a menu of simple Italian food. It was doing well, having become very fashionable amongst trendy young ex-art-college types whom both Tess and Bert thought were excruciatingly pretentious. Vicky had left art school with a good degree but absolutely no interest whatsoever in pursuing a career related to the course she'd taken, having become much more involved in something else. Whilst at college she'd worked as a junior chef in a smart restaurant to supplement her grant. She'd always been good with food and enjoyed the job. After she'd graduated they'd offered her a permanent position, which she'd happily accepted. Vicky had done very well and had quickly been promoted, ending up as the head chef's deputy.

One day Vicky had fallen on her feet – as ever in Tess and Bert's view. Jack, Vicky's father, had loaned money to an old friend who'd done a bunk. Amongst the debts he left behind was a failing restaurant. Jack had gamely suggested that Vicky take it over, seeing as she was, by now, an experienced cook. With all her inherent flair and elegance, Vicky had proved herself a natural at the business. It had taken off from the start. By now, she was enjoying herself enormously and had been particularly delighted that she'd been able to give Bert a job. She and Tess had often discussed what Bert was going to do with her life. For her part, Bert had mixed feelings about being in Vicky's employ, especially as a waitress, and she executed her duties with a grumpy lack of grace that few employers would have tolerated.

However, she was happier being a waitress than a full-time mother and Tess had gladly seized the opportunity to have an even greater influence over Tabatha's development.

'Look, do you want me to go the market and buy all the aubergines I can find?' Bert asked, after deciding she'd had enough of listening to Vicky angrily banging pots about.

'No, it's too late now. They have to be salted and there isn't enough time to do that on top of everything else.'

Bert made a face behind Vicky's back. She was cross that Vicky hadn't thanked her for offering to go to the market, and resented feeling guilty, when she didn't believe that it had been her job to get the aubergines in the first place. But she wasn't going to argue the toss with Vicky. Bert knew that when Vicky thought she was right that was that, and it was a waste of time trying to persuade her otherwise.

The positions each of the trio had held in their group had shifted since school. Vicky had become increasingly confident, having made such a success of herself in the smart restaurant and now in her own. Conversely, Bert had become less self-assured since she had sealed her immediate destiny by becoming a teenage mother, while Tess, having done well at college but nothing of note since, had adopted a kind of lofty, remote, maiden-aunt stance. However, their relationship remained as solid as ever.

Old Hippies 1985

'Better freeze her assets before she goes, Bert,' Tess said casually, with a mouthful of naan bread.

'Eh?'

'That's what happens. All these middle-aged hippies with nothing better to do than go out there to try and find themselves end up being persuaded that they'll only feel better once they've given all their cash away. They troop out to India to live in these ashrams, get brain-washed and wind up penniless. Those guru blokes drive about in Rolls-Royces while all the old farts walk around in tie-dyed sheets and those awful sandals people who make their own crockery wear.'

As usual on a Thursday night, Vicky and Bert had returned to the latter's flat with a takeaway for them all to share. Bert was telling them about her mother's latest plans to go and live in Poona, having recently converted to the Bhagwan Rajneesh's philosophy.

'She hasn't got any money, apart from the house and Dad's alimony – oh, and her account at Fortnum's, but that's not really an asset.'

'Don't know about that, Bert,' Vicky said, with a smile.

'You know what I mean. It's not like I'm going to inherit some amazing fortune.' Bert was preoccupied: she didn't know how seriously she should be taking Tess's account of what went on in these hippie communes.

175

'Still, whatever she's got is a fortune over there and it all adds up. One of them runs a fleet of limos apparently.'

'What do they do all day?' Vicky asked.

'They lie about in the sun looking for their souls by practising free love. Basically shagging each other. And then once a day they go to worship at the feet of the guru, who tosses them a few words of wisdom they don't understand 'cos it's in Urdu, so he could be saying anything like *roshan ghosh*, *aloo gobi* and *peshwari naan*. Then they all think he's a genius and give him more money.'

'How do you know this?'

Tess could tell that Bert was hoping she might be making it all up. 'I saw some documentary a few months ago. It was a right laugh.'

'Well, don't go on about it, Tess. I don't want to have to picture Mum lying about shagging all day, thanks very much. It's bad enough having to see her in all that gear she insists on wearing now.'

'What gear?' Neither Vicky nor Tess had seen Angela much since Bert had been living away from home.

'Oh, God, everything they wear has to be orange, even their shoes.'

'Why? She wasn't wearing it last time I saw her,' Vicky said.

'Yeah, it's a new thing. Apparently it's the colour that protects their karma . . .' Bert said, pulling a repelled expression.

'Yeah, from what I saw in the documentary, it protects their karma because it's the one colour guaranteed to make everyone look shit. That way there's no danger of anyone coming near you to interfere with your karma – or anything else!' Tess snorted.

The three girls laughed in agreement. Although Bert mainly saw the funny side of her mother's conversion she did have some apprehensions. It wasn't that she was really concerned about her mother's money, such as it was, it was more that she couldn't bear the idea of Angela making a fool of herself – yet again.

'So are you going to take over her house while she's away, then? Might as well get out of this place if you've got the chance,' Tess said, curling her lip as she looked round the room that served as her pal's main living space.

As Bert's pregnancy had progressed so had the frequency of Angela's unsubtle remarks about how colossal a mistake she thought her daughter was making. In the end, as the only alternative she could see to matricide, Bert had moved into the teeny flat previously inhabited by her father's current girlfriend. Charles had been stunned to learn that his daughter was to become a single mother and, true to form, had elected not to deal with it. He had offered up the flat in an effort to extend paternal support, thereby, he hoped, liberating himself from any more practical demands that might otherwise be made on him.

'Yeah, probably. She's calmed down a bit since she saw the light. She did offer it to me but then we had a row and I ended up slamming the phone down on her.'

'That wasn't a very good idea, Bert.'

'Do you think not, Vicky? I hadn't planned to do it, you know. She just really annoyed me going on about how I'd cocked up my life.'

'Well, you have, in a way,' Tess said, intending to wind Bert up. She often liked to taunt her friend by going through a wide variety of things she could have done with her life, had she not got pregnant.

'Thank you very much, Miss I'm-just-the-same-as-that-bloke-out-of-*Psycho*-I-still-live-with-my-mother-and-lie-in-bed-all-day-watching-old-films.'

'How many times do I have to tell you? His mother is dead, that's the whole point of the film. So he doesn't *live* with her, in the same way. And, anyway, I spend quite a lot of my time looking after your daughter, thank you very much, so what I do with the rest of my time is none of your business.'

'Oi, ssh, stop it, you'll wake up Tabs. And, anyway, just shut up. You two are so fucking boring sometimes!' Vicky said wearily.

'Ooooh, machwuuurre,' Tess drawled at Vicky, looking at Bert, who smiled back.

'So, are you going to ring her and beg for her forgiveness?' Tess asked Bert, scraping the last bits of *sag bhajee* out of the foil carton. Bert looked at Tess and grimaced, making it clear that she had no intention of doing anything of the sort.

'Do you always have to eke out the last bits? That spinach is probably freezing cold now, assuming it ever was spinach.'

'I'm not forcing *you* to eat it. Owning some restaurant doesn't make you the Galloping Gourmet, you know.'

'S'pose I will have to ring Mum to make arrangements about the house and stuff. It would be nice to have more room. I'm not going to apologize, though.'

'You might have to. She might already have started filling the house with orange lodgers.'

A couple of weeks later, Bert had succeeded in patching things up with her mother and Tess helped her install herself in Angela's house. Keen to avoid overlapping with her any more than was strictly necessary Bert had left the move to the last day before Angela set off on her trek along the road to enlightenment.

'It's a bit cleaner than I remember it, Bert. That's a bit of a result,' Tess said, hoicking another of Bert's bags into the hall.

'Mmm, ish, but it stinks of joss sticks. I'll have to do something about that when she's gone.'

'I like the smell, Mummy. It smells like churches,' Tabatha piped up, emerging from the basement.

'How do you know what churches smell like?'

''Cos Tess takes me in them sometimes.'

'Tess!' Bert scowled at Tess.

'What? We don't go in to witness the sacrificing of human flesh, Bert, we just like to look at the architecture and stuff. I think it's important for Tabatha to have at least an idea of religion and its influences. Just because you're a pleasure-seeking heathen doesn't mean Tabs needs to grow up the same way!'

Bert was about to protest when her daughter spoke. 'If I was going to be a nun I'd like to be just like Deborah Kerr in *Black Narcissus*. She's my favourite.'

Having never seen the film, Bert was bewildered.

'Not Maria in *The Sound of Music*, eh, Tabs? I thought she was your favourite,' Tess said, smiling proudly.

'No, I've gone off her. She's a bit too goody goody,' Tabatha answered, skipping up the stairs on her way to have another look at the room that was to be her new bedroom.

'Tess, what the fuck are you doing to her? Do you two sit around making lists of your favourite religious icons all day? I suppose you're training her up to be Joan of Arc,' Bert hissed.

'Relax, Bert. She's just a normal little girl with a healthy interest in religious idolatry. It's exactly the same passion as she'll have for awful pop stars in a few years' time and then after that boys.'

'Or girls. You never know,' Bert added, shutting the front door, having brought in the last of her bags.

Tess grimaced. Whenever Tabatha's future came up Bert always threw in the possibility of her being gay just to annoy Tess. Tess had plans for Tabatha and they did not include her being different in any way. She wanted her to have as conventional a life as possible. In Tess's view, people who had completely conventional lives were a lot less complicated and consequently less neurotic than people like her and her friends. Vicky and Bert called it her Doris Day fantasy.

Later on while Tess was helping Bert unpack Angela returned. Although her outfit was made up of varying shades of orange Tess thought she looked quite smart and a definite improvement on her previous sloppy self.

'Would you like something to eat? I expect you're hungry after the move,' Angela called up the stairwell.

Bert gave Tess a surprised look and shouted back, 'Yeah, erm, thanks, Mum, whatever's fine . . . you know.'

'I'll see what I've got left in the fridge,' Angela called back.

'Mmm, can't wait. Let's hope it's some maggoty bacon,' Tess said quietly.

Bert burst out laughing and collapsed on the bed. Tess started sniggering and clutched her fanny, still living in terror of wetting herself whenever she laughed.

Later that evening, on the way home, Tess thought about Bert living back at home and decided that it would be nice. It was partly because she and Tabatha would now be much nearer her own house and also that she'd liked things when they stayed the same. Tess hated change. She thought that Bert living back in Angela's house would be like the old days and that felt safe and cosy to her. Although Angela's house had often been the scene of major drama it was familiar territory to Tess and she liked the feeling that gave her.

Spot the Lesbian

'I see the heavenly David's in tonight,' said Tess, smirking conspiratorially at Bert.

'Don't pick at those olives, Tess, thank you very much. You're not even supposed to be here, legally,' Vicky snapped back. Tabatha was spending the night at a friend's and, as usual whenever this happened, Tess came down to the restaurant and hung around the kitchen chatting to her friends while they worked. Vicky didn't really mind but she liked cracking the whip, especially in her own restaurant's kitchen. She had a theory that to be a really good cook you also had to be a tyrant.

'Gorgeous, isn't he? Gosh, what I wouldn't do for a man like that,' Bert said, taking up Tess's lead.

'Look, don't be so horrible, you two. He's perfectly nice – just a little overweight.'

'A little!' Bert cried sarcastically.

'And just a little . . . bald.'

Tess, Bert and Vicky started laughing. The person under discussion was David Winkleman, the lawyer Vicky had inherited with the business. He often came to eat at the restaurant and, much to her friends' joy, had evidently developed a crush on Vicky. The fact that he was way out of the elegant Vicky's league made him a figure of great fun to the girls, particularly Tess and Bert.

'He's very rich, you know,' Vicky said, as if this might make him more attractive.

'He'd need to be, looking like that,' Tess said.

'No, what I mean is, someone is going to want him, you know, seeing as he's rich *and* a nice person,' Vicky responded lamely.

'Oh, well, in that case, I'd get off with him, if I were you. I mean, think of the bills you'd save.'

'Most amusing, Bert. I'm not saying *I* want to get off with him I'm just saying that, you know, he does have some things going for him, you know . . . if you're . . . if you're . . .' Vicky didn't seem to be able to think of anything plausible with which to finish her sentence.

'If . . . you're drinking Bacardi . . . and a fuck of a lot of it as well!' Bert howled. The three of them were now laughing so hard they could be heard through the kitchen doors in the restaurant.

Tess and Bert knew that Vicky wouldn't be likely to get off with the likes of David Winkleman – she was far too busy taking over the world via La Cantina. On the occasions when she did take up one of her many offers, her choice was made from a stable of trendy fashion photographers, rare-mushroom suppliers and other such exotic professionals. All the same Tess and Bert knew that Vicky's inherent niceness made her sympathetic to David and they often teased her that he could be forgiven for thinking she was leading him on.

'There's a group of seven just come in without a reservation, wanting to know if they can eat, and your mate David has asked me if you could pop out for a minute and have a coffee with him,' Petra, La Cantina's other and infinitely more efficient waitress, called to Vicky from between the swing doors that divided the kitchen from the restaurant. Tess and Bert both turned to Vicky and smirked like teenagers.

'Tell David I'll be out in a minute and tell the group if they have one dish, no starters, that'll be fine. I'm not staying here all night.' It was already past ten thirty and the restaurant's popularity meant that Vicky could afford to be choosy.

'OK, I'm sure David will wait . . . no matter how long you are,' Petra said, smiling at Tess and Bert. Everyone knew about his crush.

'Better rush out there, Vic. You don't want Petra stealing him off you. A man like that is best not left alone for a minute – you don't know who's going to come along and scoop him up.'

'Tess, I don't think Petra will be stealing him or anyone else off me,' Vicky replied, smiling and raising her eyebrows at Bert as she made her way towards the restaurant. 'And don't eat anything else!' she shouted imperiously over her shoulder as she exited. Tess looked at Bert and dipped her hand defiantly into the huge jar of olives she'd been eating from earlier.

'Better not. She counts those every day, you know.'

Tess smiled and put six large olives into her mouth arranging them so that they were stuck between her back teeth and the insides of her cheek. 'Why did Vicky say that Petra won't be stealing David or anyone else off her like that?'

'Very attractive. You look like a chipmunk.'

'Good. That's exactly the look I was going for. So go on, why did Vic say that like that?'

'Have you actually eaten the olives? Are those just the stones? They look huge. That's not a good look for you – you better make sure you never get mumps.'

'Shut up about the olives. I'm trying to break my record. Just answer the question.'

'You do have some interesting goals, don't you, Tess? A personal best for storing olive stones in cheeks. That's quite an achievement.'

'Buck off, Bert.' Tess found that the olives greatly impaired the clear pronunciation of Fs.

'Well, we think Petra's a lezzie,' Bert whispered, having finally decided to respond to Tess's question. Tess gave Bert a blank look. 'A lezzie, lesbian, you know, a woman who likes other women – like J-cloth.'

'I know what a "lezzie", as you so attractively put it, is, you idiot. You don't know for certain that J-cloth was a lesbian.'

'It's obvious – course she was. She was old, single and looked like a bloke. Everyone knew she was a lezzie.'

'God, you are pathetic, Bert. Being old and single does not make you a lesbian, and she couldn't help the way she looked. I expect she didn't *ask* to look like a bloke.'

'Why are you being so holier-than-thou all of a sudden? You were just as horrible to J-cloth as I was!'

'I was not! You made me join in. And, anyway, it had nothing to do with her supposed lesbianism.'

'Oooh, machwuuurre,' Bert drawled.

Tess was annoyed and spat the denuded stones, with great force, into the nearby sink.

'Better pick them out before Vic comes back in.'

'Look, I don't know why you're so obsessed with people's sexuality. Why does it matter whether Petra's a lesbian or not?'

'It doesn't, Your Majesty. You just asked why Vicky said what she said and I told you, OK? Anyway, why do you care so much if Petra or J-cloth are lesbians or not?'

'I don't. I just think always going on about what people are doing with their sex lives is a bit childish, that's all. Anyway, I bet she isn't a lesbian but because she doesn't spend her entire life talking about boys, like you and Vicky do, you both assume that she must be. She probably has more interesting things to talk about than whether some pathetic pseud is going to shag her or not.'

Bert realized that she'd touched a raw nerve and decided not to give Tess a direct answer. 'Yeah, OK. Look, I'm going out into the restuarant to see if everything's all right. Back in a minute.'

Tess got up and helped herself to a glass of wine from the fridge then sat back down grumpily. She'd allowed herself to get more irritated than she'd meant to. She didn't care one way or the other what her friends thought about Petra but she always preferred to underplay the role of sex in people's lives. She was perfectly well aware that sex loomed large in the world but she liked to think of herself as being in control of it as far as her life was concerned. Tess likened it to voting: if you were the sort of person who decided not to vote then you probably didn't think about politics much and it didn't matter that your everyday life was subtly affected by it. For Tess, if you opted out, then there was no reason why you should have to have your face rubbed in it all the time. She hated knowing that her friends spent so much time speculating about other people's sex lives – it highlighted her suspicion that she might be excluding herself from a huge chunk of ordinary life.

Evening Courses Are For Saddos

'Why don't you do a film course?' Tess's dad asked, sipping his coffee. He was over from France on one of his regular visits and had taken Tess to see the director's cut of *New York, New York* at their little cinema. It was the same quaint little run-down independent movie-theatre Malcolm had been taking his daughter to since she was a child. Tess was nostalgically fond of it, despite the creaking seats, rickety old projector and the sticky carpet. Having agreed that Robert de Niro had genuinely learnt to play the saxophone and that the film was all the better for the extra scenes, they'd come to the end of their customary debate. To Tess, Malcolm's proposition had come right out of the blue.

'Eh?'

'Why don't you do a film course? At a film school, you know. You could become an editor, or a director, or a critic.' Malcolm smiled at the last suggestion. Tess knew he wasn't serious about that one.

'I don't really want to go back to college, Dad.'

She was surprised: her father had never before raised the subject of what she was planning to do with her life. She wondered what his motives could be. In her view, she got by well enough, particularly as she had few outgoings. She'd been signing-on since leaving college, and the rest of her income was made up with dribs and drabs of cash Bert gave her for looking after Tabatha. This exchange had come about after some excruciatingly embarrassing – for both of them – discussions, which had verged frequently on rows. Tess had taken up the position that she should be paid but wasn't able to express this properly as she was reluctant to be seen asking for Bert's patronage. Bert had been of the opinion that Tess shouldn't want money at all because love of Tabatha ought to be remuneration enough in itself. Begrudgingly they had finally landed upon an agreement that was reasonably satisfactory to them both. It had the added bonus of being one that each of them had been able to fantasize was a big favour to the other.

'Well, you might like film school. Perhaps it'd be different from your other college.'

'Yeah, maybe,' Tess answered tersely. She wanted to end the discussion as quickly as possible. She was never comfortable talking about her future and the people she saw most frequently indulged her in this.

'It's just that I worry sometimes about what you'll do with your life. You can't live with Mum for ever. What if she were to remarry, for example? You wouldn't want to stay living there then, would you?'

Tess nearly spluttered her coffee out across the table. She wondered if the mum her dad was talking about was hers – for Tess, the suggestion of her remarrying was bizarre in the extreme.

'I don't think that's going to happen, Dad,' Tess responded, deliberately using the most unappealing tone of voice possible in an attempt to discourage her father from pursuing the topic further. The idea of talking about her mother's love life with her father, or indeed just talking about her, or anything personal, with him, at all, was making her squirm.

'Yes, well . . .' Tess could tell her father was becoming embarrassed too. 'What I mean is, I think you should be considering a career you're interested in and you're very knowledgeable on the subject of film and . . . Anyway, just think about it.'

That was probably what they call a fatherly pep-talk, Tess thought, as she rode home on the bus once they'd parted company. The picture of her father rehearsing his paternal speech made her smile. Neither of her parents had ever been given to parental talks, or parental anything, which Tess had decided long ago suited her just fine.

'Do you think I should do a film course, Mum?' Tess asked her mother, while they ate together later that same evening. She tried to make the question sound as if this was the sort of thing they talked about all the time. Bert was having one of her rare nights in with Tabatha, so Tess, for once, was at home for supper. Tess was feeling a little nervous. She rarely asked her mother leading questions, least of all about her future.

'A film course?' Rosemary replied dreamily, making Tess instantly regret that she'd brought the subject up.

'Oh, forget it. I was just thinking out loud, you know. It's no big deal, I just saw an ad on . . . on the tube that looked sort of interesting.' Tess wanted to drop the subject immediately.

'If you're interested enough in film then you should do a course on it, if that's the sort of thing you want to do. I'm not sure what one does afterwards, though,' Rosemary said vaguely. Tess guessed that her mother didn't really have any strong thoughts either way and quickly changed the subject.

Later that night, as Tess lay in bed watching a video of *42nd Street* – the film she'd seen with her father having given her a taste for forties musicals – she remembered with annoyance her mother's noncommittal response. Blimey, once in a blue moon you'd think she'd express an opinion, say something concrete. It's like living with an unexploded bomb! She must have feelings about *some* things one way or the other. It dawned on Tess that this characteristic of her mother's may have been a contributory factor in her parents' break-up. After all, it can't have been easy living in a supposedly intimate relationship with someone who reveals so little.

Tess didn't like dwelling on her mother's emotional weirdness and hastily turned her thoughts to her father's suggestion. She knew that because of her commitment to Tabatha she couldn't go back to college but she decided that it wouldn't do any harm, at least, to look into evening classes relating to film. It would have to fit in with everybody else, of course, she thought, as she scoured the synchronized tap-dancing drumming away on the screen in front of her for a foot out of place. One of Tess's favourite pursuits, when watching a film she'd seen a hundred times before, was to spot mistakes that had slipped by the director. As she drifted off to sleep she decided that she wouldn't tell the girls, or anyone else, about maybe doing a course just yet, in case it didn't work out and she ended up looking silly.

The next day Tess woke up feeling cheerful. She went to pick up Tabatha earlier than usual and wasn't surprised to find that Bert was still in bed. Tess and Tabatha had breakfast together and set off for school without seeing her. Tess greatly disapproved of Bert's inability to routinely rouse herself in time for her daughter's departure but she was glad to see that it never seemed to bother Tabatha. In fact, very little seemed to disturb Tabatha, who was contradicting Tess's fears about the possible effects of Bert's waywardness and growing up into a contented, bright child. While Tess didn't exactly want Tabatha to start speaking in tongues or attack her school chums with knives, she would have appreciated a smidgen of irrefutable evidence to back up her criticism of Bert's parenting skills.

After Tess had dropped off Tabatha she walked along to the local library to find out about evening classses. As she made her way she began to think that she was probably wasting her time and that nowhere was likely to offer the kind of course she'd be interested in. Having developed a rarefied knowledge of film on her own, in a vacuum, she was inclined to think of herself as better informed than practically anyone else and therefore unlikely to benefit from others' wisdom. This apparent haughtiness often irritated Bert, while Vicky excused it as merely a defence mechanism – a characteristically charitable view that also annoyed Bert.

Tess arrived at the library and, to her relief, quickly found a current copy of *Floodlight* without having to request it from the surprisingly trendy-looking librarian. She could just imagine the super-cool girl, who didn't have a single free evening for the rest of her life, snorting with derision while pointing out the magazine's location. Tess couldn't rid herself of the nagging suspicion that evening classes were populated largely by mad old women with huge teeth and booming voices, and forty-year-old male train-spotters who wore grubby anoraks and spent their entire day wanking over cheap porn. Her fear was based on a prejudice formed at school, when any girl contemplating voluntarily taking on more than the scantiest amount of work required to avoid expulsion was regarded as the most repulsive thing a person could be – a swot. Tess decided to put these thoughts out of her mind as she flicked through the publication's pages to see what was on offer.

To her surprise she found that a wide variety of film-related courses were available at numerous adult-education institutes, many of which were within easy reach of where she lived. She didn't really know what she was looking for specifically until she came across a course title that leapt off the page at her: Screenwriting for Film. Tess had never consciously thought of writing before but this looked as if it would suit her perfectly. Seeing as writing is a solitary pursuit I probably won't have to do hideous shared practicals with some bespectacled city accountant *and* I'll be able to write in my spare time without leaving the house! she thought excitedly, as she wrote down the details. She resolved to go and see about the course the next day after she'd taken Tabatha to school.

D.I.S.C.O.

'So what are we doing for your *twenty-sixth* birthday?' Tess asked Vicky the next evening, another of their regular nights at Bert's.

'Don't say twenty-six like that, like I might as well be seven hundred and thirty.'

'Well, me lady, you are still on the shelf and, gorgeous as you are, you're not getting any younger.'

'I am hardly on the shelf. More like sifting through offers at my leisure.'

Tess and Bert laughed, despite guessing that Vicky was half serious.

'So, assuming you can prise yourself away from the restaurant for one night, what are we doing?'

'Dunno. Thought we could go out for something to eat and then maybe go to a disco for a change. What do you think?'

'A disco? Is that a joke?'

'Yeah.'

Bert started singing and dancing round the kitchen. 'D-I-S-C-O, D-I-S-C-O, she is D-desirable, she is I-irresistible, she is S-super-sexy, she is C – such a cutie, she is O-ooooooh, D-I-S-C-O, D-I-S-C-O.'

'Shut up, Bert, you're driving me nuts with that stupid song. It's bad enough listening to you do it all day at work!'

'Bit of a cheat, though, isn't it – "she is C such a cutie"? You see, "she is D-desirable", fine, then, "she is I-irresistible", OK,

192

no problem there, "she is S-super-sexy" also fine, but then you get "she is C – such a cutie' and that's just not on. They've put in "such a" before "cutie", which is what the C stands for and officially it should just go "she is C", and then whatever they chose for C. So strictly speaking there shouldn't be anything else before the word, really. If you think about it, they've cheated, haven't they? They have flagrantly flown in the face of all accepted standards.'

'You've got a very good point, Tess. I'd write a stiff letter of complaint to the people in charge of overseeing sloppy pop-lyric writing, pointing out this hideous and offensive irregularity forthwith!' Bert advised, mimicking the Outraged of Orpington style of speech Tess had used to put forward her rant.

'Ah, yes, but to whom does one write?' Tess asked. '*Top of the Pops*? Kenny Everett? Who exactly is in charge of these things? It's so hard to know and there's so many to complain about. I mean, where do you start?'

'Well, personally I'd start with "I'm going to write a classic, I'm going to write it in an attic'! Now, whatever way you say it, "classic" does not rhyme with "attic". The "ics" rhyme, I'll grant you that, but the whole word has to rhyme, not just the last bit. I can see how, on the page, the bloke who wrote it thought it would, but sung out loud it simply does not rhyme and that is just not acceptable.'

'Am I going to have to spend the rest of the night listening to you two dissect crappy pop songs? I thought we were talking about my birthday.' Vicky was beginning to sulk.

'All right, keep your hair on, there's tough work to be done out there in the pop-lyric jungle and someone's got to do it. Wouldn't mind going out for a meal. So, are you paying, Vic?'

'How did I know you were going to say that, Miss Pile?'

'Because I'm broke and you're rich and it's your birthday.'

'In which case people should be paying for me. Anyway, I am

not rich, I work very hard and earn a decent but modest amount of money, which I'm sure you'd be able to as well if you put your mind to it.'

Tess decided that now wasn't the moment to tell them about the course she'd enrolled on that very day.

'Where did you get that speech? Is that something Darling David told you to say when the taxman knocks at your door?'

'David does not tell me to do anything,' Vicky said defensively. She was getting bored of the constant teasing about David, in whom she had absolutely no romantic interest.

'Oooh, touchy! Sorry I spoke. Anyway, here's an unusual idea. Shall we go and have a meal somewhere? Not at one of your competitors', Vicky – we're not going on a covert operation while trying to have an evening out, OK? And by the way we'll all pay, Tess, *va bien*?'

'Yeah, all right, let's do that, it'll be a laugh,' Tess replied. She spent so little money she could afford to splash out now and again. Vicky's birthday was a couple of weeks away and the first of the group's in the year. As such it always involved the longest discussions about how it should be celebrated, in spite of which they generally ended up doing the same thing every time.

Tess felt weird not telling her friends about the new course. She didn't like keeping secrets from them, but she had a suspicion that they'd make a bigger deal of it than it warranted. Then she'd feel pressured to build it up into something brilliant, when she reckoned it was probably going to turn out to be a bit of a wash-out.

Rosebud

The course was on Tuesday nights. In the interest of keeping quiet about it Tess hadn't sorted out anything officially with Bert, who often didn't work on Tuesday nights anyway. The restaurant was closed on Mondays and business was generally slow until later on in the week, leading up to the very busy weekends. Consequently, Bert was usually around on Monday and Tuesday nights. When, and if, I decide to stay on the course, then I'll tell the girls and set it up properly with Bert, but there's no point in jumping the gun, Tess thought, as she made her way to her first session of Screenwriting for Film.

When she got on the tube at her end she felt very nervous about the whole thing but by the time she'd got out at the other end and was walking towards the old school building that was hosting the class she had managed to supplant her uncomfortable nerves with her trusty superciliousness. It'll be full of nutty old film buffs and people who think remakes are worth doing, Tess thought, as she made her way along the hallway to the room in which the class was being held. There was no one in the room when she arrived – she'd made sure she was early so that she wouldn't have to run the gauntlet by walking in last. Tess chose a desk she thought was appropriately off centre: she didn't want to be too near the front and seem all keen but equally she didn't want to sit near the back and look like a right madam. Shortly after she had arrived more people began to drift in. Tess was relieved and slightly thrown to see that not one of them was wearing a grubby anorak or carrying their life in a plastic bag. In fact, Tess had to admit, none of them looked very different from her. One girl in particular, who arrived just before the tutor, caught Tess's eye. She looks like she could be one of my lot. That's a relief, Tess thought, not noticing that the tutor was now standing in front of the blackboard and had begun the class.

As Tess travelled home that night her mind reeled. She couldn't believe the last few hours she'd had. The class had been a real slap in the face with a wet fish. There had been nine other people in the class and virtually all of them had written something for either television or radio. Instead of the sense of superiority Tess had expected to travel home with, she had left the place feeling worried that she might be out of her league. However, she was able to comfort herself with the memory that she'd been the only one to know the significance of the last line from *Citizen Kane*. She arrived home feeling energized, excited, slightly insecure about what she'd taken on and, above all, really looking forward to the next class.

Footwear Factor

'So he's standing in the doorway of my house . . .'

'How come he's got as far as the doorway?'

'Because he'd dropped me off, you nit-wit. Now shut up and let me get to the good bit.'

'But why didn't you say goodbye in the car and get out, if you thought he was such a creep?'

'I tried to, but he obviously thought he was coming in, so he came up with me. Now can I finish my story, *pleeeeeease*?'

'Yes, get on with it, Bert. Honestly, you did say "in a nutshell, this is what happened", so come on, in a nutshell what happened?'

'Whenever Bert says "in a nutshell" at the beginning of a story you can guarantee it's going to take about seven years to get to the end of it.' Vicky, Bert and Tess started laughing. The three were celebrating Vicky's birthday in a Chinese restaurant near Vicky's house. The nationality of the place had been chosen by Tess and Bert confident that at least in the Far East cooks were allowed to stray from Vicky's rigid ideas of what one was allowed to do with a mange-tout. Bert was in the middle of telling them about her date with the good-looking bloke who supplied wine to La Cantina, known to them as Wine Man.

'Anyway, anyway, anyway, so I turn around immediately as soon as I've got the door open, you know, to make it obvious he's not coming in and . . .'

'Where was Tabatha?' Tess interrupted.

'This was last week when you were busy again, seeing your

secret lover or whatever it is you do. She was staying the night at her friend Josie's. Can I finish my bleeding story or do you also need to know what colour my pants were before I go on?'

Tess was duly silenced. She'd been attending her course for three weeks by now and she still hadn't got round to telling her mates about it. However, she found that she sort of liked the idea that Bert might think she'd got a secret lover. It made her feel like someone with an interesting and mysterious private life.

'Oh, wearing pants were you? That was an unusual move for you, wasn't it, Bert?' Vicky sneered good-humouredly.

'I only don't wear pants when I've got thrush, or – or –'

'Do you mind? I'm eating, thank you.'

'Tess, you are such a joke sometimes. You're like some pathetic bloke who can't bear hearing that women have periods and do poos!'

'No, I'm not. It's just that you always insist on talking about those things when people are eating. Vicky, aren't I right? Doesn't she only ever talk about her discharge and stuff when we're eating?'

'She's got a point, Bert.'

'No, she hasn't. Anyway, shall I finish this story or not?'

Vicky and Tess looked at each other and raised their eyes to the heavens.

Bert took this as a sign that she should continue. 'So he's standing in the doorway and I'm trying to say goodnight and stuff and he says, "Aren't you asking me in?" I say, "No, I'm tired and I've got an early start."'

'Did you?'

'Tess,' Vicky said, using the tone you'd use to control a persistently naughty dog.

'No, I just didn't want him to come in, I didn't fancy him, he'd been a right twat the whole evening.'

'Well, why didn't you just say that to him?'

'Good idea, Tess. "Excuse me you've been a right twat all evening and now I don't fancy you, so could you go, please?" I don't think that would have gone down too well.'

'I don't see that it matters how it goes down if you want to get rid of him. I think you never say that to all these twats you go out with because you want them to stay fancying you even though you're not remotely interested in them.'

Vicky saw Bert give Tess a murderous look and jumped in. 'Tess, it's perfectly normal to want to have people fancying you when you don't fancy them. Everyone does it a bit. Look, just tell us what happened, Bert.'

Tess didn't think that it was perfectly normal at all, but decided to let the matter drop. She often teased Bert about the huge quantity of men she dated and her indiscriminate selection process. But she also knew that Bert wouldn't put up with much dissection of her motives in doing so.

'So he goes, "I can't believe you're not asking me in!", super-cocky, and I'm thinking, Well, believe it, pal, but I say, "Oh, well, sorry but you know . . ." and just hope that he gets it. Then, and you're never going to believe this, he goes, "Well, you're making a big mistake because we would be fantastic together!"' Bert said, perfectly imitating Wine Man's confident, lad-about-town accent, and her friends burst out laughing.

'No, wait, listen, listen to this, that's not the end of it. He then says, "And I don't just mean me, I mean, we," and by this time, he's doing a sort of back and forth sweeping gesture with his index finger, you know, just so I understand that by "we" he means me and him! Anyway, so he's doing this . . .' Bert was doing the movement with her hand. To an onlooker it would have looked like she was conducting a tiny orchestra. ' ". . . we would be fantastic together. You are making one big mistake, lady . . ."'

Vicky screeched. 'Tell me he didn't say "lady", please tell me he didn't say "lady", I'll have to change my wine supplier if he did. *Pleeeeease* tell me that Wine Man did not say "lady"!'

'He did! If I'd gone out with him, he is definitely the sort of bloke that would have introduced me to his friends as his "lady"!'

All three girls shrieked in horror. Long ago they'd agreed that men who referred to their girlfriends as 'my lady' were as repulsive as men who wore clogs – or, indeed, any shoe deemed by them offensive, including, naturally, a sandal of any description. This particular method of ruling out a potential suitor had become known to them as the 'footwear factor'. It had all started at the airport the summer they'd gone to Italy together when Bert had spotted a gorgeous young American on their flight. She'd been about to find an excuse to strike up a conversation when Vicky and Tess had pointed out that, while he might be beautiful in every way, to the unsuspecting eye he was, in fact, wearing Jesus sandals and, as if that wasn't bad enough, his big toes were *hairy*. Bert had reeled back in appalled horror, saved by her friends from a fate worse than death – in their view – just in the nick of time. Now one of them only had to say, 'Footwear factor', when referring to a loss of interest in an otherwise promising new boyfriend and all was understood immediately.

'I felt like saying to him, "Do you keep saying, 'We'd be fantastic together,' like that because ordinarily you just mean *you*'d be fantastic but this time, lucky old me, you think we'd actually both be fantastic together?" but I decided against it in case he took it as an excuse to hang about.'

'Doesn't sound like he needed one,' Tess observed.

'Oh, he's very confident, this boy. The thing is, he is quite good-looking. He probably doesn't get turned down very often,' Vicky pointed out, aware that Tess had never actually laid eyes on the man.

'Well, he'd better get used to it, if he's going to carry on with that line of patter.' Bert laughed. She'd gone out with him knowing in advance that it wouldn't lead to anything, partly because he was so good-looking and partly because, Tess was right, she liked gathering scalps even if she had no use for them. La Cantina had proved invaluable in providing Bert with a wide selection of victims: she'd already worked her way through several including Parmesan Man, Napkin and Tableware Man and was looking forward to a date with Rat Man, whom she'd met after she and Vicky had mistaken a rotting potato nestling down the back of the fridge for a rodent.

Tess went home feeling as if she'd had a thoroughly satisfying evening. She loved listening to Bert's stories almost as much as she loved interrupting them. As she drifted off to sleep, she thought of how nice her life was at the moment. She was having a wonderful time doing her course and was feeling creative and positive for the first time since leaving college. She had meant to tell the girls about it that night but, somehow, a good moment had never arisen. She resolved to tell them next time they all met up.

How Long Has This Been Going On?

There were two main reasons that Tess was enjoying the course so much: one was that the tutor had a few credentials in the real film world, and especially that he'd written the first draft of a film that, although Tess had never heard of it, had actually got made. He also knew as much about films as Tess did, she was forced to admit, and to her that was almost as impressive. Deep down, Tess didn't really believe she was a genius but she had spent years building up her knowledge and understanding of movies and was aware that this was rare, at the very least, particularly for someone of her age. She was also glad to be surrounded by other lovers of film, none of whom, so far, had turned out to be the kind of person you'd cross the street to avoid if they looked you in the eye.

The other reason was that Tess had struck up a friendship with Helen, the girl she'd noticed on the first day. The tutor was a heavy smoker and, for this reason, he'd built a short mid-class break into his class; during one of the first of these breaks Helen had struck up a conversation with Tess. She'd turned out to be a radio producer who'd also written a couple of dramas that had been broadcast. Helen's real ambition was to write films and she told Tess that she saw her job only as an interim thing. Tess would no sooner have listened to a radio play than she'd have gone grocery shopping in the nude. However, she was very impressed: 'radio producer' sounded unbelievably grown-up, particularly as she guessed that Helen was only a few years older than her. Tess liked Helen, finding her friendly and open without being over-confident and, in a measured way, began to look forward to talking to her.

On the whole, Tess and her gang didn't tend to make new friends. They all knew people independently of each other, but they hadn't developed other friendships as intense or as satisfying as the ones they shared with each other – there'd been no need. As the weeks went by, and Tess got to know Helen better, she found herself liking the fact that anything she told Helen about her life and experiences wasn't coloured by additional, not necessarily welcome, information given by her closest pals. She hadn't taken to lying but she felt that having the power of editing meant that she could almost reinvent herself. The most obvious cut Tess had made was not to reveal that she was still a virgin and lived with her mother, fearing that Helen might think she sounded like a trainee nun. Tess discovered that Helen was originally from Edinburgh and had moved down to London when she'd found her job about five years previously. She had never been married which, despite the semi-feminist position Tess always took against Bert when discussing marriage, Tess found odd because she thought Helen was very pretty.

At the end of the fifth week as they were leaving the building after class Helen asked Tess if she'd like to work with her on a script idea she'd been developing. Tess hadn't had the confidence to start anything on her own as she still had no idea what on earth she'd ever write about, so she happily agreed to Helen's suggestion, relieved that she could finally embark on practical writing without having to take responsibility for the whole idea herself. They arranged to meet up an hour before next week's class to discuss the project.

'How long has this been going on? How long has this been going on?' Bert was singing, imitating the mock-pained crooning of the original singer.

'Only a few weeks. It's not like it's a huge big deal,' Tess replied. She had finally got round to telling her friends about the course. She was enjoying their surprised reaction: to her, it was proof that she wasn't as predictable as they might like to think.

'We thought you were having a torrid love affair with a door-to-door cleaning-appliances salesman or some other unde-sirable you dared not tell us about,' Vicky teased.

'Yeah, that or you were studying to become an accountant which, naturally, you would regard as a filthy secret.'

'Very likely, I'm sure,' Tess said sarcastically, preferring Vicky's version.

'So what's it like? Are you going to become a super-famous Hollywood scriptwriter?' Vicky said ingenuously. She always imagined that anyone attempting anything would have the same immediate success she'd had.

'I doubt it. No, look, it's just an interesting course which, you know, might lead to something, eventually, one day – but don't go on about it, it's nothing, really. I don't want you guys asking me if I've written *The Godfather* every week.' Tess was neither accustomed to nor comfortable with being centre-stage. She liked hearing about her friends' exploits. She didn't want them focusing too much on what she was doing.

'What are the other people like?' Vicky wanted to show interest without causing Tess annoyance. It was a fine balance to tread since she knew that Tess might get irritated if they didn't probe at all – and then think that they weren't interested in her life – but would get even more irritated if they asked too many questions.

'Yeah, they're fine, you know, just sort of ordinary. There's one person I've made friends with, who I might . . . I might try and write something with.'

'Ooooooooh, what's he like?' Bert cried out salaciously.

Tess instantly regretted having revealed any more than just

the absolute minimum. 'It's not a bloke, it's a girl, if you must know, called Helen. She's asked me to maybe write something with her. Not everything in the entire universe centres around sex, you know!'

Bert shot Vicky a shame-faced look; she really hadn't wanted to undermine Tess. 'Sorry, I was only mucking about,' she said sheepishly, then added encouragingly, after a short pause, 'but you're enjoying the course, yeah?'

'Yeah, it's all right.' Vicky and Bert knew when to give up and the conversation ended there.

Tess was satisfied that while she'd told them about her new activity she'd also managed to underplay it enough to be able now to carry on without too much interference from her pals.

Their initial meeting went well and Tess and Helen agreed to meet up the following Saturday morning to begin writing. Bert always spent Saturdays with Tabatha as she usually worked late at weekends. Helen had suggested that Tess come over to her flat, and despite it being on the other side of town, she'd readily agreed, having no desire to invite Helen to hers. While Tess resolutely refused to see anything unusual about her domestic set-up she wasn't keen to invite people over and expose herself to the assumptions they might make about it.

She made the journey in the grip of a barrage of nervous questions. How do we start? Who does the actual writing down? Who holds the pen? Maybe no one has a pen, maybe you just sit around and talk for hours . . . But someone must have a pen, someone must write something down at some point – you'd never get a script otherwise! By the time she finally arrived at Helen's flat – having decided not to buy croissants from the baker's she'd passed on the grounds that it would make her look too pally and unbusinesslike – she was almost shaking with nerves. To date, Tess had perfected the art of appearing aloof, fashionably unusual and very much in control of her unconventional life. But faced with discussing a proper work thing, like grown-ups did, and, what's more, with a virtual stranger, she felt like jelly wobbling on a paper plate.

Helen let Tess in and offered her some coffee before they started. Tess could tell that Helen had not whipped herself up into the same frenzy that she had. They chatted for a while and Tess calmed down, realizing that she'd let her sense of drama run away with her. After all, Helen isn't Orson Welles for Chrissakes! she thought, comforting herself by unfavourably comparing Helen to one of cinema's greatest ever talents. The exercise, on this occasion, helped Tess get things into perspective, but it was also something that she'd frequently done when questioning her own lack of perseverance. Citing examples to herself of great films or their makers helped her justify her inertia: 'What's the point in getting out of bed when somebody's already made *The Maltese Falcon*?' However, nobody, from the world of film or anywhere else within her sphere of knowledge, could have prepared Tess for the way her day at Helen's panned out.

Why Ask For the Moon? We Have the Stars

'Where the fuck have you been?' Bert shouted at Tess, the moment she burst through the back door of the kitchen at La Cantina, much later that same day.

'I know, I know I'm really sorry, I'm really and truly sorry. Is she all right? Is everything OK? Where is she?' Tess replied, looking around for Tabatha. She expected to find that, having had no choice, Bert had been forced to bring her daughter into work.

'I ended up taking her round to Josie's when I finally realized you weren't going to turn up. She's fine. What the fuck happened to you?'

'What did you say to Tabs about where I was?'

'I told her you'd got ill at the last minute and when I said she was going to spend the night at Josie's instead, she sighed, looked out of the window and said, "Why ask for the moon? We have the stars," whatever that's supposed to mean.'

'Clever girl. That's *Now Voyager*.'

'What?'

'*Now Voyager*, that's the last line from *Now Voyager*. Bette Davis says it when Claude Rains explains that, although they can't get married, she will be looking after his daughter and so he'll be free to visit all the time. Tabatha was letting you know that although she was disappointed not to be seeing me she was very happy to be spending the night at Josie's,' Tess explained as if nothing could have been more obvious.

'Really? Well, I wouldn't mind if she just said things like "wow" and "great", sometimes, you know, like other eight-year-olds. Anyway what happened to you? Where have you been? We thought you'd been abducted by aliens or run over by a truck or something.'

'I was at Helen's.'

'Whose?'

'Helen. The girl from my film course. Listen, you didn't ring Mum, did you?'

'Of course I rang your mum, I didn't know where you were. Why wouldn't I ring her? How was I to know you were in the middle of a secret love affair with this Helen?' Bert said, laughing at the idea until she turned to catch the expression on Tess's face. 'Oh, Tess, don't start having a go at me about everything not being about sex. It was a joke, OK?' Tess didn't respond and Bert didn't know what to make of her silence.

For a few minutes neither of them said anything and Bert busied herself preparing a plate of starters that one of her tables was waiting for, relieved that Tess hadn't turned on her. Finally Tess spoke. 'Erm, turns out that Helen's . . . erm . . . a lesbian.' She deliberately used a casual tone so that she'd sound like she was imparting information as banal as something like Helen having two middle names.

Bert was taken aback. She couldn't work out why Tess was telling her this. She was sure it was a trick and she was determined not to get caught out.

'Yes, well, that's fine, *chacun à son gout*. I'm sure it makes no difference to what she's like to work with or what kind of friend she is, OK?' said Bert, convinced that Tess was trying to trap her into saying something stupid about lesbians so that she could give her a lecture instead of having to explain where she'd been.

'So . . . she kissed me.'

'Eh?'

'Helen kissed me,' Tess said, plonking herself down in her usual place, the high stool that lived near the sink.

Bert crashed the plate she was holding on to the nearest counter. 'What?'

'She kissed me.'

'Yeah, I heard that the first time, but what I mean was . . . did you want her to? Did you kiss her back? Are you a lesbian?'

'Is who a lesbian?' Vicky said, entering the kitchen and catching the last bit of Bert's barrage of questions.

'Bert wants to know if *I'm* a lesbian,' Tess said, smiling at Vicky.

'Bert, stop this – Petra's going to come back in in a minute. Don't be going on about lesbians again.'

'Presumably she already knows she's a lesbian, yeah?' Tess asked.

'Yeah, but you know she –'

'Well, I don't,' Tess interrupted.

'You don't what?'

'I don't know if I'm a lesbian . . . now.'

Vicky was stunned and didn't know what to say. She looked at Bert who shrugged her shoulders. 'Oh, right,' she muttered eventually.

'Helen, my friend from the film course, kissed me, and I don't know if that makes me a lesbian or not.'

'Well, did you want her to? Did you kiss her back?'

'That's exactly what Bert asked.'

'Yeah, well, that's how you decide if you like someone. The first kiss usually sorts all that out, you know, sorts out the men from the boys, or in this case the – erm – the –' The three of them laughed as Vicky floundered over a suitable Sapphic equivalent.

'Thing is, I just don't know.'

At that moment the swing doors flew open and Petra entered. 'What's happened to those starters, Bert? Table six is going mad.'

'Sorry, here they are,' Bert said, nodding at the now dishevelled-looking plate. 'I was just coming through with them.' She looked at Tess and Vicky, not wanting to leave in the middle of the spectacular revelations. 'Look, Petra, will you take them in for me?'

'Why? Have you lost the use of your legs? It's your table, take them in yourself.' One of Petra's great qualities, as far as Vicky was concerned, was that she didn't let Bert push her around.

'Please, I'll do one of your tables' puddings or something, yeah? Come on, be a pal.'

'Yeah, all right. Blimey, are you three plotting a bank robbery or something? You should see your faces,' Petra said cheerily, as she picked up the plates and left.

'You could ask her,' Vicky hissed at Tess, nodding towards the space that Petra had just vacated.

'Ask her what?' Tess hissed back.

'You know, ask her if you're a lesbian.'

'Vicky, how on earth would she know if I don't?'

'No, she's right, Tess, she'll probably know. They can probably tell,' Bert joined in enthusiastically.

'Don't be so bloody stupid, you two. It's not a Masonic pact! There isn't a special handshake! Anyway, you don't know for definite that she's a lesbian, she just has short hair and doesn't talk about boys with the same relentless tedium that you two do. And neither of you'd better say anything to her either!'

'Yeah, all right, but you never know. If she is, which I'm sure she is, she may say that all first kisses for lezzies – sorry, lesbians, are like that. You know it may be a sort of lesbian thing.'

'Drop it, Bert. Just ignore her, Tess. Come on, tell us what happened.'

'Oi, it was your idea in the first place, madam!' Bert was

indignant that she was now being blamed for Vicky's suggestion.

'Well, I went round there and we spent ages discussing her idea and –'

'Did you think it was any good?' Bert asked.

'It's all right. It's a flashback, family-drama type of thing, set now and in Victorian times . . . not really my sort of thing but interesting, you know. Anyway, so we talked about it then tried to write a synopsis.'

'A what?' Bert butted in again.

Tess wore a longsuffering expression. 'A synopsis is a description of the film in a nutshell. Like how I'm trying to tell this story, if you don't mind.'

'This is exactly what you do to me when I'm trying to tell one of my stories.'

'Yeah, but not only do you have seven million new stories a week, and each one of them sounds exactly the same as the last one, but it takes you forty-nine years to get to the end of any of them!'

Bert was about to protest when Vicky jumped in. 'Great, so are you two going to row about who tells the most boring stories? Or are we going to hear about this momentous kiss?'

'It was not a momentous kiss, I don't want you two running away with some notion –'

Tess's protestation was interrupted once again. 'Am I working on my own for the rest of the night, then?' Petra asked, her head sticking between the swing doors.

'Erm, God, I'm really sorry, Petra. The thing is – erm – Tess's had a bit of a –'

Tess glared at Vicky causing her to stumble mid-excuse.

'– a – a – bad time – erm . . . thing . . . not really bad . . . just – you know – complicated . . . anyway, today, and we're just trying to help her sort it out.'

Bert, who had her back to Petra, stuck out her tongue and

rolled her eyes into the back of her head, indicating to Vicky that she thought her excuse was pathetic.

'So would you mind covering for us and I'll pay you a bit extra. Is that all right?' Petra agreed and left, giving Tess a sympathetic look.

'Thanks for making me sound like a loser. Couldn't you have said that I've just chucked my boyfriend or something like that?'

'Boyfriend?' Bert said, raising her eyebrows so high up that her eyes stretched wide open.

'Oh, you know what I mean. Vic made me sound like some awful old saddo –'

'Just get on with the bloody story, will you? Never mind what Petra thinks, unless you want to get off with her as well!' Vicky snapped.

'Very funny. So after we'd finished a rough synopsis, we had a break and then Helen asked me what I was doing tonight, which I did think was a bit weird, but, anyway, I said, "Babysitting," and then she said, "That's a pity because I was going to ask you to stay for supper."'

'Did you have any idea that she was after you at this stage? I mean, did you know she was a lesbian?' Bert interrupted.

'If you mean was her flat filled with dildos and books by Virginia Woolf then, no, it wasn't. I didn't have a clue. I'm not like you, I'm not constantly thinking the whole world wants to get off with me –' Tess broke off her flow to smirk at Bert then continued, 'So we talked a bit more and then she walked over to where I was sitting and just sort of leant over and kissed me. I completely froze – I didn't know what was going on. I mean, do blokes do that, just kiss you without any warning?'

Bert and Vicky looked at each other. They both thought about it for a moment then Vicky said, 'No, you can usually tell if someone's going to kiss you.'

'Well, I didn't know she was going to. Anyway, she did, and

then she said, "Is that all right?" and I didn't say anything. I mean, I didn't know what to say and then she asked if I'd ever been kissed by a woman before.'

'Did she say woman or girl?' Bert asked.

'Erm, I think she said woman . . .' Tess had to think about it for a moment '. . . yeah, she said woman. Why?'

'It's just that she sounds very grown-up, this Helen, you know, saying "woman" and then discussing the kiss and everything.'

'She is grown-up. She's a radio producer and I'm sure she's over thirty. She *is* very grown-up,' Tess confirmed.

They didn't really know any grown-ups, having worked out in their early youth that none of their parents qualified for the status. They occasionally teased Vicky that, of the three of them, she was the most like a proper grown-up person because she had willingly taken on professional responsibilities, but she always resisted the label.

'Didn't she mind it when you didn't say that you liked her kissing you?' Vicky enquired. Typically, she wanted to ensure that Tess hadn't hurt the woman's feelings.

'She didn't seem to. You see, that's what I mean about being grown-up.'

'So then what happened?' Bert was keen to hear the gory details, if there were going to be any.

'She kissed me again, and I sort of let go a bit more and we ended up lying around in her living room kissing for hours and I lost track of time and that's why I was so late. Sorry, Bert,' Tess said, suppressing a smile and blushing profusely.

Bert and Vicky exchanged knowing, indulgent smiles. They had often speculated that Tess might be gay but not know it.

'Well, sounds pretty much like you're a lesbian to me,' Bert said, nudging Tess in the ribs.

'Not necessarily, because, you see, I didn't fancy doing any-thing else. And, I mean, until you get your bits out and they become part of the action, kissing is just kissing, isn't it? I mean, you could be doing it with anyone – blokes have exactly the same tongues as girls, don't they?'

'This is typical of you, splitting hairs and not coming down one side or the other. You're not seriously going to resist committing to being a lesbian just because of a freak-of-nature detail? I assume your Helen friend has breasts, doesn't she? Well, men don't have breasts!'

'Darling David does,' Tess retorted, and the three girls all burst out sniggering. Vicky's admirer David's considerable excess weight was located in unfortunate areas and he sported luscious curves in place of where one, ordinarily, might expect to find his pecs.

'Obviously she's got breasts but *I* didn't touch them, so you know, she might as well not have had them. I'm just saying that I didn't mind the kissing but, you know, that I'm not definitely a lesbian or anything else for that matter. I don't know why you two are so determined to make me a lesbian anyway.'

'Tess, we're not trying to *make* you a lesbian –' Vicky was trying to be diplomatic but Bert wasn't having any of it.

'Typical of you, I suppose you're going to blame us. If you do become a lesbian, it'll be our fault!'

'Look, I'm just saying don't go rushing away with the idea that you can pigeonhole me straight away. I let a woman kiss me and that's all there is to it, OK?'

Vicky was prepared to leave it at that; Bert wasn't.

'No, you didn't *let* her kiss you. You, plural, kissed each other, unless you just lay there the whole time not moving like a block of cheese while she footered about with you.' Bert hung her tongue out of the side of her mouth and let her arms and shoulders droop giving her impression of a slice of Cheddar.

Vicky and Tess laughed. Then Tess stopped and continued to defend her position as the kissee rather than the kisser. 'What

I'm saying is, she took the initiative, she's got the main responsibility for what happened. Look, she's the one who knows she's a lesbian and I don't, OK?'

'Yeah, all right.' Bert decided to let the matter drop. She could tell Tess didn't want to be pushed any more and she'd lost the energy to keep trying.

Much later that night the girls finally went their separate ways having stayed late at the restaurant finishing off the dregs of various bottles of wine left by customers. It was a favourite pursuit of Bert and Tess's, and although Vicky insisted it was a disgusting habit, she could usually be persuaded to join in once they'd found an expensive enough wine to suit her more refined tastes.

Telephone Etiquette

After Tess finally got home she lay awake in bed staring at the ceiling, thinking about what had happened. She'd surprised herself by blurting out the whole thing the moment she'd walked into La Cantina's kitchen. Ordinarily, of the three of them, Bert was the one who inevitably reported to the group every single little thing that happened to her. Thing is, she thought, trying to give herself an excuse for behaving similarly to Bert, I had to talk about it out loud so that I could work out what I felt . . . not that I really know what I feel now, but still . . . I'm glad I've told the girls.

All the same, in the solitude and privacy the darkness provided Tess was prepared to admit to herself that she had been thrilled when Helen had kissed her. But, she reasoned, I've never kissed anyone before so I can't be sure that part of the thrill wasn't just from having a first kiss rather than who I had it with. She thought about Helen and knew that she liked her but she was hotly resisting what all of it might add up to ultimately. I just don't know that I want to be a lesbian, in fact I don't know that I want to be *anything*. Life is fine like it is. I don't want to turn into one of those people who worry about whether so-and-so fancies me and then start all that bollocks of who's going to ring who and then asking Vic and Bert if they think whoever it is has gone off me if they don't ring! Tess was whipping herself into a frenzy thinking about all the to-ing and fro-ing that starts once you've let sex sneak through the door. She couldn't help remembering the millions and millions of times she had listened to her pals analyse the calls they'd had with various boyfriends; going over and over whether calling him flagged up that you were keener than he was; under what circumstances phoning him was OK and what excuse you used for doing so; and what two consecutive days of hearing nothing from him meant. Sometimes she thought she was going to hurl herself out of the window if she had to listen to another conversation that started with the words 'So, do you think when he said . . .' Mind you, it must be great having someone else give you an orgasm – that must be fantastic, she thought dreamily, as she drifted off to sleep.

'Told you so,' Bert said smugly to Vicky, as they set up at the restaurant the next day.

'Look, she doesn't even know whether she is herself yet, so don't go patting yourself on the back.'

'Course she is. She's just being typically Tess-ish. Maybe Helen's just not a great kisser or something, and she'll only know for certain when she meets the right girl.'

'Oh, God, you don't think Helen did that disgusting thing of sucking Tess's tongue?'

'Yuk, no, I'm sure girls don't do that – only revolting macho men think that's attractive.'

'You're probably right. I can't imagine a girl doing that. Whoever taught anyone to suck someone's tongue when they were kissing?'

' "Mmm, darling, please suck my tongue so hard when we snog that it feels like it's being ripped out of its socket." Nope, just can't picture anybody actually *asking* someone to do that. I mean, where is the person who wants to do that or wants it done? Yuk, no one normal, that's for sure.' Along with 'footwear factor', what they classified as 'criminal kissing' had become another yardstick by which to eliminate suitors. Petra arrived, and further discussion as to a tongue-sucker's motives was brought to a sudden halt. Ordinarily the pair would have continued happily to mull over methods of exchanging saliva with Petra until the cows came home but Bert had something more pressing on her mind. She and Vicky had their backs to Petra and, as soon as she'd got her coat off, Bert started making wild faces at Vicky that she could not decipher, although she realized that they were connected in some way to Petra. In turn Vicky was making what-are-you-on-about? faces back at Bert.

Eventually frustrated by her friend's inability to read her mind, Bert decided to take the plunge unassisted. 'Petra, you know when . . . people . . . erm . . . well, actually, lesbians kiss for the first time? Do you think it's different from when girls and blokes kiss for the first time?'

Vicky raised her eyes to the heavens and let out a contemptuous sigh.

'Maybe, I dunno. I guess it depends on who's doing the kissing, I suppose, and on how much you want to kiss them in the first place, I dunno. Why? Are you planning on branching out and getting off with girls now as well?'

Bert laughed embarrassedly – she didn't want Petra to think she fancied her. 'No, no, God, no. I was just wondering if . . . you know . . . there was like a – a – lesbian thing – you know . . . that was different from straights.'

'I dunno, maybe. Anyway, why do you think I'd know?' Petra said, as she started to sort out tablecloths and cutlery.

Vicky and Bert shot panicked looks at each other: they were confused.

'Oh, no reason in particular. It's just that we were just discussing something and thought we'd get your opinion. It's no big deal,' Vicky chimed in chirpily, desperately not wanting Petra to be offended.

'Has this got something to do with Tess being gay?'

'God, how did you know?' Vicky and Bert cried out, in one amazed voice.

''Cos it's obvious, anyone could tell. Blimey, I can't believe you two *didn't* know.'

Bert gave Vicky a self-satisfied, told-you-so look. 'Well, we just thought you'd know for definite and that maybe you'd know whether lesbian first kisses were different from straight ones.'

'Still don't know why you think I'd know but anyway your mate Tess is definitely gay,' Petra shouted out, as she walked through to the restaurant with an armful of tablecloths. Vicky and Bert waited until Petra was out of earshot before they started arguing in frantic whispers.

'Oh, my God, she's not gay. You shouldn't have said anything!' Vicky hissed hotly.

'Of course she's gay.'

'She's not bloody gay! She just said, "I don't know why you'd think I'd know," talking about a lesbian kiss!'

'No, you idiot, it's obvious, she means she's never kissed a bloke so she can't compare lesbian to straight kisses, not that she's not a lesbian.'

'You're the bloody idiot! She means she's never kissed a girl, not the other way round. It's completely obvious!'

'Yeah, it's completely obvious that she *is* a lesbian and she's saying she doesn't know about kissing blokes. Look, she must be. Otherwise how would she know that Tess was definitely gay?'

Vicky paused, she had to concede that Bert might have a point, but she wasn't prepared to lose the argument hands down. She decided to pull rank instead. 'Either way, I don't want you going on about this any more. Tess specifically said she didn't want us to tell anyone, particularly not Petra, and what's the first thing you do the moment she walks in here?'

'Oh, shut up, I didn't say anything about Tess being gay. She asked if our conversation was about Tess – it's completely different!'

'Look, just shut up about this now. But if it all comes out I'm telling Tess it was all your fault!'

'Fucking typical!' The row ended at that point and the two girls went about preparing for the rest of the day, chopping vegetables and making sauce bases in as much ostentatious ignoring-each-other silence as they could muster.

Meanwhile, Tess was at home and unusually, for her, at a loose end. Tabatha was staying at her friend Josie's until tea-time, when Tess was scheduled to pick her up. In the meantime she was trying to divert herself by watching *Nosferatu*. It wasn't a particular favourite of hers, but she'd tried watching a number of other films from her video collection. However, she'd been forced to reject them all because, to her huge annoyance, every single one had featured lovers of some description: kissing, in love, separated or reunited. Whichever permutation came up, it had the undesired effect of making her think about Helen and what had happened.

She'd finally decided that a silent twenties horror film filled with spooky scenes of a man with a shaven head, fingernails down to his knees and fangs for teeth was not very likely to make her think about romance in any shape or form.

She was wrong. She couldn't stop thinking about Helen and the kiss and she couldn't concentrate on the film. It wasn't entirely her fault: she was interrupted by the telephone which, although she couldn't be bothered to answer it, kept ringing continuously. Eventually she decided to pick it up and discovered, to her surprise, that it was Helen. When she'd allowed herself to think about it Tess had been so consumed with her own feelings about what had gone on between them that it had never crossed her mind that Helen might have her own agenda. She had only thought about what had already happened, not about what might be going to happen thereafter. When she heard who it was, Tess couldn't help wondering if it had been Helen who'd rung all those times before she'd answered. If it was, then that's a bit keen. I'm not sure I like that, she thought, in spite of her determination not to indulge in telephone-etiquette analysis.

Helen suggested they meet up for coffee after Tess had told her that she was tied up from the afternoon onwards. Tess hummed and hahed for a bit and finally agreed, having decided that it didn't necessarily mean that she was going to run off into the sunset with her.

The Toss of a Coin

'Oooh, so she must be really keen then?'

'No. I don't know. Look, I don't care, we only had a cup of coffee together.'

'Yeah, but when they phone you up straight away, the day after, that means that they are officially keen and don't care who knows it to boot.'

'Don't start all that bollocks! I am not getting into all that what-how-many-days-between-calls means on the how-keen-they-are-scale shit! It's not the same thing at all, she's just a friend. The "they" that you're basing your brilliant theory on are half-witted morons looking to get their end away. No more and no less. I'm surprised most of them know how to use a telephone at all!'

'That's right, because you have to have a degree to know how to use a telephone, don't you?'

'Evidently not. You seem to have no trouble using one, night and day.'

'Do you two want to stop trying to score points off each other?' Vicky snapped in. 'Instead, maybe you, Tess, would like to tell us what actually happened, and perhaps you, Bert, might like to keep your trap shut for two minutes.'

'Oh, well, pardon me for breathing.'

'Darling, don't say "pardon". It's so *petit bourgeois*. Either say "what" or "I beg your pardon". If you must say anything at all!' As she'd intended, Tess diverted a row with one of her perfect imitations of Angela.

It was early Tuesday afternoon, a few hours before Tess was due to set off for her screenwriting course and she hadn't yet told her friends about the coffee she'd had with Helen since the kiss. This was usually the slowest part of the day for Vicky and Bert, who wasn't working that evening anyway, and the three of them were having a cup of tea together in a café near the restaurant. Vicky and Bert were very excited to learn that Helen had been in contact with Tess since the kiss. Their eagerness, which Tess still maintained was totally out of proportion to the event itself, was making her less and less sure she wanted to continue with either the story or, in fact, with seeing Helen at all. 'Listen, if you two are going to wet yourselves every time I tell you the smallest thing about anything that happens to be vaguely connected to – to – to –' Tess paused and looked around the café. It wasn't full but it wasn't empty either and she really didn't want to draw attention to herself.

'Shagging,' Bert said, in a voice that sounded unnaturally loud to Tess.

'Thank you, Bert, I don't think that old man at the end of the room quite got that. Anyway, to – to – sha – all that – then I'm never going to tell you anything. Honestly, stop making such a big deal out of it all.'

Bert looked at Vicky and crossed her eyes, aware that Tess could see. She wanted to show her that she was being a bit precious. Vicky frowned back at Bert to show her that she, as ever, was prepared to be as patient and supportive as Tess needed her to be.

'Sorry, Tess, we – and when I say "we" I mean Bert is just being over enthusiastic. Come on, we're all ears.'

Bert glared at Vicky but didn't say anything else. She wanted to hear the story too much.

'Well, I did think it was a bit . . . erm . . . a bit . . . keen to ring up straight away but, you know, I wasn't really doing anything until later so I thought it might be all right, just meeting for a coffee or whatever, and I didn't want to condemn her just for ringing up, you know.' Tess stopped speaking and looked at Vicky and Bert for some signs of agreement that she hadn't 'led Helen on' by arranging to meet her but, by now, her friends were so determined not to do anything that would give her an excuse to halt the story that they didn't dare speak. Tess was a bit puzzled as she was unaccustomed to an enraptured audience. 'Anyway,' she continued after a moment, 'we met up and every-thing was fine, you know, we chatted about this and that and that was all O K. Then, when we were saying goodbye, she kind of went to kiss me!' Tess came to an emphatic halt, giving her two friends an indignant and-well-what-do-you-think-of-that? expression. She was expecting an equivalent reaction in return and got nothing. She thought at least Bert would jump in with an expression of outrage to match her own.

'Is that it?' Bert finally said, after a few moments of bemused silence.

'What do you mean "is that it?"? She tried to kiss me, for God's sake, I mean just like that, she tried to kiss me! I mean what was she thinking about?'

'Tess, you *had* spent the whole of the day before snogging with her willy-nilly and then you *did* agree to see her again the next day. Of course she thought you'd want to kiss her again.'

'Oh, so I suppose I was "asking for it" then, was I?'

'No, don't be silly. What I'm saying is, what's so wrong with her trying to kiss you? She obviously likes you. That's O K, isn't it?'

'Well, she's got no business liking me before I know whether I like her back – at least in *that* way!'

'You feel like you're on a runway train to Lesbo Land and you didn't even buy a ticket. Is that it?'

'Yes, that's exactly it. I feel like I'm being railroaded.' Tess knew that she liked Helen. She even knew that she'd actually wanted her to kiss her when they'd met up again but she still could not get her head round the whole issue of being sexually active.

'What did you do when she tried to kiss you?' Vicky asked gently.

'Nothing. I said that I didn't want to in a public place and she said she understood.'

'God, she really is grown-up, isn't she? If you said that to most blokes they'd go into a sulk and accuse you of being frigid. Mind you, were there hundreds of people around?' Bert asked.

'She's not a dog on heat, you know, she can control herself. I'm sure she wouldn't have tried to kiss me if there'd been people around.'

'So what are you going to do now?' Vicky asked, ever mindful of Tess's spikiness.

'I'm supposed to see her at the course tonight . . .' Tess paused. Vicky and Bert didn't say anything, they could tell she was going to say something heavy. '. . . and she's asked me to go back to her house afterwards . . . to . . . erm . . . spend the night.'

'*Sacrebleu*!' Bert exclaimed.

'Yeah, that's what I thought,' Tess said.

'Are you going to go?'

'I don't know, I just don't know. It all seems so organized and planned you know, so . . .'

'Grown-up,' Vicky couldn't help herself finishing Tess's sentence with the adjective she found most fitting to the situation.

225

'Yeah, grown up and here I am, twenty-seven years old and I don't even know if I'm . . .'

'A lezzie,' Bert burst in.

'I was actually going to say "ready for this" but, yeah, all right, a lezzie. I mean, what if I am a lezzie? What if I spend the night with Helen and like it and then I'm trapped in Lesbo Land for ever and that's it? I mean, what'll my mum say?'

'Oh, well, if that's what's holding you back, then fuck your mum!' Bert said. 'Actually, on second thoughts, I'm not sure that's legal.'

'Thank you for conjuring up that lovely image, Bert. But, seriously, Tess, what are you going to do? Hadn't you better decide before you go to the course?'

'I suppose so. It's just that I don't know what to do. Look, let's talk about something else, I'll decide on the journey there. I'll toss a coin or something.'

'You can't decide whether you're a lesbian or not on the toss of a coin!' Bert cried.

'I'm not deciding *that* on a toss of a coin! I'll do that to decide whether to go back to her place or not, O K? Now, can we talk about something else, please? Bert, what's happened to that Spanish bloke who was after you? Do his accent again. Vic, have you heard this? It's hilarious, he says the funniest things.'

'Helen, my darling, I'm lying here with you now, you see, only because I chose tails first time and got heads so I ended up having to do best out of three and you won!' Bert was mimicking Tess when she spoke in her most matter-of-fact tone. 'Oh, I can see how pleased Helen is going to be to hear that!'

'Bert,' Tess said threateningly, 'do you want me to write to your mum and tell her that you've seen the error of your ways and you'd like her to come back immediately so that you two can make up for lost time and start being best friends?'

'Hah, hah. O K, my lips are sealed,' Bert said. She leant

forward, nearing her face to Tess's, and made a great display of pressing her lips so tightly together that they disappeared.

'Are you all right?' Helen asked, after a long silence.

'Yeah, I'm fine, fine,' Tess replied, not entirely honestly. What the fuck am I doing here? she thought, as she sat staring into the distance drinking tea in Helen's living room. She hadn't tossed a coin. She'd gone to the class having made no decisions at all about going home with Helen, it had sort of just happened. The class had finished, they'd got talking and somehow Tess had ended up back at Helen's place with not a tossed coin in sight. I wish I could just rip all my clothes off and dive straight in. Why can't I? I don't want to have to think about it. Why doesn't she just make a lunge for me so we can get the whole thing over and done with. God, then at least all this waiting about will be over. Tess fumed. She was too wound up to have any thoughts of romance. She was less concerned with the whole looming lesbian issue that had so preoccupied her earlier and more irked by not knowing what was going to happen next. Helen must have sensed what was needed because, when Tess eventually managed to tear her eyes away from the spot on the carpet she'd been glaring at, she turned her head upwards to see Helen walking towards her topless. Tess was taken aback. She was torn between being gobsmacked at the sight of Helen's splendid tits and wanting to run out of the room shrieking with embarrassment.

'Come here,' Helen said, stretching out her arms in welcome to Tess. As if in a trance, Tess stood up and obeyed. She fell into Helen's arms. Within seconds the pair were writhing about on the floor, kissing and caressing each other. A moment later, Helen tore off Tess's top and started sucking and licking her nipples. Tess was instantly catapulted into a frenzy of arousal, like nothing she'd ever experienced before in her life. The two women rolled around on the floor like a couple of mud-wrestlers, grabbing at each other's bits. In their passion they created a whirlwind of flashing breasts, nipples, hands, tongues, elbows, hair, belly-buttons. Tess was having the time of her life until suddenly a graphic image of a certain activity leapt into her mind and she froze stock still.

'What's the matter? Why have you stopped?' Helen said, disengaging her mouth from Tess's left nipple and panting breathlessly.

'I can't do this, I'm really sorry, I just can't do this . . .' Tess said, pulling her top back on and scrambling to stand up. 'It's not you, it's the whole thing, it's me, I'm sorry, I just can't.' She ran out of Helen's flat without saying another word.

Lunch In the Downstairs Restaurant

'Oh, my God, oh, my God, I don't believe this! You just ran out? Just left without a word? Just like that? You didn't say *anything*?'

'No. Yes. No. This picture suddenly popped into my head, right in the middle of it. Of . . . you know . . . of . . .'

'What? What?' Vicky and Bert asked in unison.

'Of that, um, you know, that thing people do,' Tess mumbled.

'What *thing* people do?' Bert asked impatiently.

'God, you know, the thing you call lunch in the downstairs restaurant.'

Vicky and Bert exchanged looks.

'Oh, *that*.'

'Yes, that. I just thought, I can't do this. I don't want to eat in the downstairs restaurant, I haven't booked a table, I don't even *want* a reservation! I can't do it!'

'Did you have to do it? I mean, is it compulsory?' Vicky asked innocently.

'No. I don't know. It just suddenly seemed inevitable and once I'd thought of it I couldn't get it out of my head. It was like in *Fawlty Towers* when Basil tells everyone not to mention the war and then he can't stop going on and on about it in front of the Germans!'

'You could have just gone down for a snack,' Bert suggested. 'Not even a snack! Couldn't you have just gone down there to see what . . . it . . . erm . . . Helen's "restaurant", as it were, was like, you know, no commitment to dine, just to have a look around? It happens all the time here and I don't mind. I see people looking at the menu in the window, then they pop round the door and then they go away, obviously having decided they don't like the look of it. I don't get offended. Couldn't you have done something like that?' Vicky chipped in.

'Vicky, it's a restaurant, not your fanny!'

'Vic, you know she couldn't have done that. "Hi, I'm just going down to see what it's like so if I come straight back up again you'll know I thought it looked revolting, is that OK with you?"'

'I suppose it is a bit different.'

'You see, I cannot get my head round lunch in the downstairs restaurant, I just can't.'

'Can't say I blame you. I don't understand people who say they love it so much.'

'Bert, you love it! You're always going on about how much you like it!' Vicky exclaimed.

'Yeah, having it done but not doing it. I couldn't do it. Sure, I like having it done, but I definitely could not do it. But, listen, you liked the kissing and stuff this time, yeah, Tess?' Bert asked, turning back to the most pressing topic on their agenda.

'Yeah, that was great, I mean, I really liked that. I could definitely do top halves only until the cows come home, no sweat, but bottom half, yuk, no, can't do that. S'pose that means I'm definitely not a lezzie, then,' Tess said, with some relief.

'Not necessarily. Maybe you're a kind of halfway-house lezzie. A sort of centaur lesbian, kind of thing,' Bert said, intending to tease Tess, who was looking increasingly forlorn.

'Oh, I don't know what I am,' Tess sighed.

'What are you going to do now? Are you going to see her again?'

'No, I can't. I'm not going back to the course. I don't want to see her again. She'll make me have an in-depth, mature discussion about downstairs eating and I don't want to do all that stuff.'

'Basically, you don't want to have it forced down your throat.'

'Hah, hah, very witty, Bert,' Tess said, half smiling despite her glum mood.

'Listen, don't worry. You know what? I bet loads of lesbians don't do it. Not every single one of them can like it! We should ask Petra – this might be a perfectly normal stage of finding your way along the road to lesbianism.'

'Bert, once and for all, you are not asking Petra anything of the sort! I just want to let the whole thing drop!' The three girls fell into a reflective silence.

After a moment Vicky spoke again. She'd obviously been thinking about how to help Tess out. 'You know, it might be a bit like avocados or something. Remember when you were young and they were the most revolting things on earth and now they're delicious?'

'What? You mean like an acquired taste kind of thing, yeah?' Bert chipped in.

'Yeah, it might be like that. What do you think, Tess?'

'I hate avocados, I've always hated avocados and it's more like saying you could get an acquired taste for slabs of uncooked meat.'

'Bleurgh,' Vicky and Bert cried out in disgust.

'Well, that's what it looks like,' Tess said defensively, slightly embarrassed by the lurid comparison she'd made.

'Not mine, and if yours does you'd better see a doctor soon – you've probably got some disgusting lurgy. Anyway, I'm sure it doesn't actually taste like uncooked meat otherwise no one would ever do it, would they?'

'Well, you know what I mean, I just can't deal with the whole . . . the whole . . . hip to thigh zone, bottom-half area, OK? I don't fancy it and that's that, so can we move on now, please, if you don't mind?' Vicky and Bert exchanged sheepish looks and remained silent by way of reluctant agreement.

Tess was not proud of the way she'd run out on Helen, but she didn't feel that she was completely to blame for the disastrous outcome of their heated snog. Tess spent all her time with people who knew her well. Although she realized it was unfair, she'd hoped that Helen could have been with her without pressing her own suit. Tess liked the idea of being loved without having to do anything. I just want to be. The right person could do what they liked as long as they didn't invade me, didn't annoy me, didn't make demands and were just sort of there, that'd be all right, she thought, later on that day, after the other two had gone off to work and she'd put Tabatha to bed. Oh, God, I'm asking for a kind of human equivalent of an amoeba . . . perhaps just not as boring. Tess groaned as she sat thinking about the kind of person likely to embody the requirements she wanted in her ideal person.

Her only love benchmark to date was the friendship with Vicky and Bert. She knew it didn't serve as a very useful comparison with which she could steam forward and hop on to the merry-go-round of sex, be it lesbian or otherwise. But, so far, she hadn't located the mechanism, the switch – which usually becomes obvious at some point in a person's life – that makes relationships, other than friendships, possible and desirable. As Tess sat munching her way through a packet of KP Discos and humming the advertisement's song in her head she realized that somehow she'd been well and truly fucked up along the way.

1986

Rats in the cellar

'Guatemala?!'

'Yup.'

'Are you winding me up?'

'Nope.'

'Your mum is emigrating to Guatemala?!'

'Yup.'

'I'm sorry I'm having a bit of a brain-ache but this is not computing. Can we recap? Your mother is upping sticks and emigrating to – to – Guatemala, just like that, without so much as a by-your-leave?'

'No. She's selling the house first. Well, actually she's nearly sold it already, apparently. And then she's emigrating,' Tess said nonchalantly.

'What about you? What are you supposed to do?' Bert asked indignantly.

'I dunno. Mum doesn't expect me to go with her. I don't think she'd want me to anyway. I am nearly twenty-eight after all, I guess . . . I don't know . . .'

'No, I mean, where are *you* supposed to live? Did she happen to notice that you've been residing in the same house as her since you were born, at all?'

'Well, she's kindly agreed to give me some money for the deposit on a flat and a few months' rent, and after that I guess I'm on my own.' Tess was delivering to Bert, in a very controlled manner, the information she'd been given by her mother that morning.

'Tessa, I'm going to live abroad for a while,' Rosemary had announced over breakfast.

'Oh. Where?'

'Guatemala.'

'Oh. Right.'

'I realized some time ago that I've reached an impasse in my creative development and I need a new non-Western inspiration.'

'Oh.' Tess was dumbstruck. Her mother hadn't noticed and continued in her characteristically detached way.

'I've decided that I need to immerse myself in another culture, another way of life completely. I want to live amongst the Guatemalan people and devote my time to exploring the ancient Mayan sculptures. I've given this plan a great deal of thought and have decided on balance that I may as well move there permanently to ensure unfettered artistic progress.'

'Yeah, but you failed to mention any of this to me while you were giving this plan such a "great deal of thought",' Tess muttered, but Rosemary didn't hear her. She carried on bringing Tess up to date with her grand scheme and the conversation had ended without Tess voicing any protest.

She had set off for Bert's feeling very peculiar. It was clear that once her mother had made the offer of the deposit money she'd seen herself as having fully despatched any outstanding maternal duties. Tess walked along in a mild state of shock. She couldn't work out exactly how she felt about the situation that had been thrust upon her or even if she had a right to feel anything at all. After all, she's a grown-up woman with her own life, why shouldn't she go and live anywhere she wants? It's not her fault I still live there, Tess reasoned to herself as she arrived at Bert's house.

234

'She should buy you a place. It's her bloody fault you're still living there!' Bert was shouting now.

'It isn't, really,' Tess said lamely.

'It bloody well is! She's held you back, ever so subtly, all these years while she needed you and didn't fancy living on her own, and then when it's time for her to move on, off she pops, thank you very much, be seeing you, *sayonara*, baby!'

'Yeah, well, it's done now.'

On the inside Tess felt numb, but in the meantime, until she could express herself, Bert was letting off steam on her behalf. As Tess watched Bert stomping around her kitchen in outrage she thought fondly, Bert's kind of like the valve to my pressure cooker. She decided to keep this to herself, guessing that Bert would tell her that she needed therapy if she had to rely on others to serve as her emotional equivalents of kitchen appliances.

'God, and I thought my mum was the worst mother ever. This takes the fucking biscuit!' Bert continued.

'Your mum's not that bad. You've just always had some stupid Fairy-Liquid-ad-Perfect-Mum fantasy of what mums are supposed to be like. Nobody's mum breaks off in the middle of washing up to show their child the sodding bubbles, as if the bubbles help anyway. And, anyway, she's *not* as bad as your mum – no piano-top shagging and maggots in our fridge that I can remember.'

Bert harrumphed loudly by way of response.

In truth, at that moment, Tess wasn't sure that her mother's desertion was any less appalling than some of Angela's antics over the years, but she didn't feel ready, just yet, to criticize her openly. She had a niggling suspicion that if she started she might never stop.

Later on that day, when Tabatha was home from school and having her tea, Bert made a suggestion. 'You know, you could always move in here, at least until my mum comes back from

India, if you liked.' The idea had already occurred to Tess but she couldn't put her finger on why it didn't appeal until Tabatha spoke up.

'Yeah, yeah, it'd be lovely, Tess. It'd be just like *Mildred Pierce*, except I promise never to be like Veda, the horrid daughter!'

'Who's Mildred Pierce?' Bert asked.

Tess and Tabatha exchanged condescending looks.

'She's a woman whose husband leaves her so she has to go and work in a restaurant and she lives with her two daughters, one who is horrid and one who is nice. You'd be her, Mummy!' Tabatha explained, in a clear, helpful voice. She knew her mum didn't know anything about forties cinema and thought she'd better spell it out.

'Thanks a lot, sweetheart.'

'Except you can't make pies and she makes lovely pies. But lots of men want to be her friend. So you are like her in that way,' Tabatha added. Bert laughed as Tess raised her eyebrows disapprovingly at her.

'Tabs, it isn't a good idea. I'll sort something out, it'll be fine,' Tess said.

'Why are you being like this? It's very unlike you to turn down a free offer,' Bert hissed. She wasn't desperate to have Tess move in to supervise her every move but, all the same, she was puzzled by her friend's unpredictable rejection of the idea.

Tess turned her back to Tabatha and replied. 'Because I think it'd be more like *Whatever Happened to Baby Jane?*.' She knew that it was one of the few films Bert was familiar with as they'd watched it together several times.

'Oh, yeah? And I s'pose you'd be the saintly one in the wheel-chair and I'd be the old slag bringing you your supper up on a tray, with a fag hanging out of my mouth, and cackling, "There are rats in the cellar, Blanche"?'

Tess sniggered mischievously and nodded.

236

Tess Books a Table

With Vicky's help and considerable flair for turning the cheesiest of things, be it a meal, a bedspread or a room into something lovely, within a few weeks Tess had set herself up in a small flat not far from Angela's house where Bert and Tabatha were still living.

Shortly afterwards, Rosemary set off to start her new life. Tess and she parted company with all the affection one might think normal when saying goodbye to the man who'd come to read the meter. Tess thought she detected a trace of moisture in her mother's eyes but couldn't work out whether it was emotion or the effect of the high, sharp wind that was blowing. Either way, I'd never know, she thought, as they awkwardly disentangled themselves from the cack-handed half-kiss, half-embrace they'd attempted, in lieu of a fond farewell, in front of the cab waiting to take Rosemary to the airport.

Tess still hadn't worked out whether she felt deserted or liberated. In the last few days, as her mother's departure approached, she'd made up her mind that she'd know for sure when her mother finally left. But as she stood there watching Rosemary disappear into the distance she couldn't feel a thing. Tess didn't want to carry on thinking about it and, as she opened her front door, she came to the conclusion that, as the whole operation had been orchestrated by her mother without her involvement at any stage, it would be pointless to feel anything anyway.

Tess walked around her new flat in a bit of a daze. It was early evening. Vicky and Bert were working, Tabatha was spending the night with Josie and Tess suddenly realized that she had nothing to do and no one to talk to. The room was bright and cosy but felt completely alien to her. Since moving, she'd contrived to spend the majority of her time, so far, away from it – either at Bert's, under the pretext of looking after Tabatha, or at the restaurant inventing new tricks to perform with assorted crudités. She sat down and turned on the TV. All her instincts were urging her to rush out of the flat and round to La Cantina, but a mixture of pride and confusion kept her welded firmly to the sofa. I've *got* to be able to manage on my own. This is ridiculous! It's not like Mum and me lived hand-in-glove! God, sometimes you'd never have known she was even there! Tess thought, hoping that she could berate herself into a more capable frame of mind.

Eventually she decided that a practical chore would divert her gloom and she set about sorting out the various boxes that had sat in the hall untouched since she'd moved in. Inadvertently, the first one she chose was the box of things her mother had asked her to keep for her. Tess sat on the living-room floor sifting through the contents. As far as she could tell it was mostly useless junk, and she thought how typically 'arty' it was of her mother to set such store by meaningless objects. Towards the bottom of the box she came across a bunch of old photographs held together by a moth-eaten rubber band, which snapped in half when Tess removed it. The pile flew apart and scattered all over the floor in front of her. It hadn't been touched for years. At first she didn't recognize the couple featured in the photographs, and then it dawned on her that it was her parents. Their young, smiling, hopeful faces beamed out of the dog-eared photos at her, looking relaxed, happy, in love and, moreover, completely unlike the same two people Tess had known. Over the years

Tess had seen the occasional photo of her parents together and had felt curiously neutral. This time she felt herself fill up slowly with sadness and anger. She picked up the last few photos and sifted through them. The back of one carried the inscription 'Happy Family! My two darling loves', in her mother's writing. She turned the photograph over and saw herself aged six or seven, sitting on a park bench. Her mother and father were sitting either side of her squishing her into their arms, which were wrapped around her and each other at the same time. All three were laughing and beaming at the camera. Tess looked at the loving scene, of which she had absolutely no recollection, and burst into tears.

I don't remember it ever being like that! I don't remember being cuddled, or tickled, or teased. I don't remember Mum and Dad larking around like that. Who the fuck are these people? Where did they go? What happened? How did they turn into those fucking zombies I was brought up by? All the anger and resentment that Tess had never allowed herself to feel, and never been allowed to feel, flooded into her mind as she stared at the unfamiliar family group. She couldn't remember ever being the smiling, happy-go-lucky little girl she was looking at now. Tess reckoned that that child had probably been crushed out of all existence. She certainly didn't live inside *her* any more. The Tess that Tess was now, the Tess who had never ruffled her parents' feathers, the Tess who had cheerfully accepted all domestic changes with calm, the Tess who had never pressed her parents for explanations – this Tess had been created by her parents' fucked-upness. The same Tess who had run out on Helen, the Tess who didn't want to be a lesbian, the Tess who balked at lunch in the downstairs restaurant, the Tess who thought Bert's fantasy of an ideal mother was ridiculous, the Tess who wanted the human equivalent of an amoeba for a lover, the Tess who had lived through her mates all these years, that Tess had been formed by her parents' inability to deal with adult responsibilities. Tess felt like someone had just lifted a heavy veil from her eyes. She saw that Bert and Vicky had been right all along: her mother *had* been holding her back. She had no business mooching around in the background all these years not saying anything but really meaning masses! Blimey, it's like I've been living with that spooky Mrs Danvers my whole life! Tess railed.

She chucked all her mother's stuff, including the photographs, back into the box and slung it out into the hall. She didn't know what she was going to do with it eventually but she didn't want her mother, as represented by the box, sitting in the room with her, judging her, when she made her first move as the new Tess. She knew what she had to do, what she wanted to do. In an extremely excited but nervous state Tess picked up the telephone. 'Please be in, please be in . . .' she chanted to herself as she listened to the phone ringing at the other end.

It rang for what seemed like an eternity. Just as she was giving up hope and was about to hang up she heard the person at the other end answer and her heart leapt into her mouth.

'Helen, it's Tess.'

'Oh . . . oh, right.'

Helen was very pissed off, Tess could tell, and she almost put the phone down but her determination to change spurred her on and she hurled all her inhibitions out of the window. 'Listen, I'm ringing to say that I'm sorry about – about – Oh, God, look, I really want to see you. Will you come over?' Tess blurted out. Guessing that Helen probably wouldn't be very keen to talk to her, Tess had planned on having a chat and then, when things had defrosted a bit, suggesting they meet up some time soon, but all her plans had crumbled into nothingness the moment she'd heard Helen's voice.

'Erm . . . I don't know. I don't think it's a very good idea,' Helen replied.

Ordinarily Tess would have been gutted, but she desperately wanted to sort things out and now that she'd got started nothing was going to stop her.

A couple of hours later Tess and Helen lay on the floor of Tess's new flat, naked and satiated after a frantic session of mutually satisfactory sex.

The Hills Are Alive

'*When will I see you again?*' Tess sang out, once Bert had finally picked up the phone at her end.

'*When will our hearts be together?*' Bert sang back.

'*Are we in lurve or just frie-e-e-e-ends? Is this beginni-i-i-i-ng or is this e-e-e-end?*'

'*When will I see you again?*'

'No, it goes *aga-a-a-a-in*,' Tess said, repeating the phrase but holding the second A so that it vibratoed heavily.

'Only at the end and we were doing the song from the beginning. I think you'll find I'm right, if you check your Three Degrees anthology. Anyway, you're in a good mood, what's up?'

'I'm a lesbian!'

'Eh?'

'I am a lesbian. I will happily eat lunch in the downstairs restaurant. In fact, I will make a permanent reservation and I don't care who knows it!'

'Tess, what's going on? Are you having a nervous breakdown?'

'Nope, listen, I've already talked to Vic. Petra is going to get a mate to help out so that you and Vicky don't have to work tonight. I'll see you back at your place after you two have finished setting things up at the restaurant, OK?'

Once Tess had organized the evening she threw herself into sorting out her flat. She put on some music and danced about arranging furniture and objects. She felt like Maria when she discovers that the hills are alive with the sound of music.

'So you had a full meal in the downstairs restaurant? I can't believe this! A full meal?' Bert asked again.

'Yup, starter, main and pudding.'

'Good for you, Tess, here's to you!' Vicky said, raising another glass of the champagne Tess had bought.

'This is amazing, I still can't believe it! What happened? I mean, what changed? Come on, we want to know everything!' Bert was flushed with excitement and the effects of the booze. Tess poured more drinks and told her friends about finding the photograph and the feelings it had uncovered. She didn't tell them they'd been right all along about her mother – she knew they'd be thinking that anyway, even if the end result had turned out to be totally unrelated to any of her parents' crimes.

'And she came over? Wasn't she super-sulky?'

'At first on the phone she was a bit, but, then . . . you know . . . I told you she was grown-up,' Tess said proudly.

'God, you really can tell she's not a bloke,' Bert said, with a certain degree of envy.

'I'll say! You should see her tits.'

'Tess!!!' Vicky and Bert shrieked.

'What?'

'Don't say things like that! Just because you've come out of the closet doesn't mean you now have to turn into some disgusting lesbo version of a man trapped in a woman's body!'

'Oh, Bert, don't be so prissy. You wouldn't mind if I'd slept with a bloke and said something about his prick.'

Bert shrugged her shoulders. She suspected Tess might be right.

'So, is that it? Are you Officially In Love now?' Vicky asked.

'Don't know about that, we only slept together last night, but we're definitely "in lust".'

'So, when are you seeing her again?'

'Tonight. She's coming back to my place later on when I get back.'

Vicky and Bert smiled at each other and cried out, 'Oooooooh, two nights in a row, it's official!'

Tess blushed. She was delighted that she had finally qualified as the object of teasing from her gang about her sex life.

After meeting up again that night Tess and Helen began to see each other regularly and passionately. Tess liked her a lot but, much to her friends' chagrin, she refused to confess to being Officially In Love – mainly because she wasn't. She enjoyed being with Helen but if she was in love at all it was with her new independence and the ability to spend time happily alone, skills she'd also discovered along with her sexuality. Helen was still attending the course, but Tess had decided to give it up. She had started to write on her own, which she found more satisfying, but also she didn't want to be tied down to doing a regular thing with Helen. During all her free time, when she wasn't tied up with Tabatha, Tess no longer lay around watching videos: she wrote. She wasn't sure yet if she was writing a novel or a film script but she scribbled down copious amounts every day and she loved it. The further into the past Tess's mother's departure became, the more the new, happier Tess emerged and Tess was very aware of this. She likened her 'pre-Guatemala life', as she termed it, to having been on a permanent, very slow bedside drip. She began to realize that, over the years, her mother had subconsciously been trying to turn her daughter into herself. Rosemary had never said anything overt but Tess now saw that each of the little comments her mother had made about her and her friends' endeavours to carve their own way along the path to being a grown-up had all contributed towards building up in her a strong reluctance, and ultimately a refusal, to get stuck in and see what it was like for herself.

At first when Tess thought about how her mother had behaved for so many years she felt livid, and often stomped around her flat letting off steam rehearsing out loud the bollocking she'd give her when and if they ever saw each other again. After she got tired of doing that (and worried that the neighbours might think she was off her head) she'd sit down and write her mother long recriminatory letters – but she never sent them. The lone ranting, interspersed with venting her rage on paper, seemed to be enough. As time went by, and she thought about it more, she learnt to accept that her mother probably hadn't chosen to behave like this: she'd just made it up as she'd gone along. On one occasion, when Tess was thinking about how much her parents had evidently changed between first meeting, feeling the way they'd obviously felt in the photographs, and parting company never to talk to each other again, she ended up feeling emboldened enough to confront her dad, and planned to do so next time they met up.

1987

Spanish Lober

'What? The olive-and-capers man, the one with the hilarious accent, the one who said all that you-wanna-catch-the-tiger-but-nod-pay-for-the-skin stuff?'

'The very same.'

'The one who said, "When I'm in lobe with a woman dere is noding I will nod do for hare"?'

'Yup.'

'Blimey!'

'Yes, and Bert was *so* sure she was a lezzer – sorry, Tess, *lesbian*,' Vicky said giving Bert a snide smile.

'You can say lezzer, I don't care. "Lesbian" sounds so right-on and sort of clenched-fistie-sisters-together-tweed-skirt-and-a-monocle, bleurgh! I'm definitely not that kind of a lezzer!'

'Just as well. We'd probably have been forced to throw you out of the gang if you'd started growing a beard and wearing Dr Martens.'

'Hah, hah, like you could do without me. Anyway, anyway, tell me more about Petra and the Spanish lober, this sounds fantastic!'

'Well, you know he was after me?' Bert said, her sleeves rolled up past her elbows in the middle of washing a huge quantity of salad stuff in the restaurant's largest sink.

'Naturally. He's a bloke, isn't he? He's got a pulse – how could he not have been?' Vicky said, smirking at Tess.

'Do they have to have a pulse? I thought they just had to be male.'

'Most amusing. Anyway, he kept coming in here and flirting with me, saying all that stuff that I dare say gets him laid round the clock in Spain, but he'd obviously translated all his chat-up lines directly into English and it just made me piss myself laughing, otherwise I might have got off with him. He's no slouch in the looks department, I can tell you.'

'Have you told Tess about the knickers?'

'Knickers?' Tess asked.

'Oh, God, wait till you hear this. I never told him I wasn't interested but maybe he guessed because one day he's obviously thinking he's got to really impress me so he goes to me, "I fink you should know that when I am really, really in lobe wid a woman dere is noding I will not do for hare. Por essample I will even wash her knickers if I am so in lobe wid hare"!'

'I suppose that's what passes for radical feminism in a Spanish bloke,' Vicky interjected.

'Can you believe that?' Bert continued.

'What did you say?'

'I said, "Oh, yeah? Well, big deal, because that's your basic foot-in-the-door stuff where I come from, matey." I don't think he understood, though – he's not that quick on the uptake.'

'Oh, in that case I'm really surprised you aren't interested in him. You usually like a half-wit, it makes you feel intelligent.'

Bert threw the heart of an iceberg lettuce at Tess, just missing her, but before she could retort Vicky spoke. 'Because before she'd decided that she definitely wasn't going to get off with him, you know, she was doing her usual dangling-him-on-the-end-of-a-string thing to see how keen and desperate she could make him before she made her final decision. He obviously got bored waiting around and decided to get off with Petra! Petra the "definite lesbian", and I quote, hah, hah! So much for being in lobe wid a woman!'

Bert turned to Tess and spoke using the tone one might use when talking about a mad person who was in the same room but not capable of being involved in the conversation. 'Poor Vicky, she's been dining out on this one since it happened. She thinks it's very funny. Thing is, I actually couldn't care less who he copps off with, but I refuse to accept that just because Petra is getting off with him it means that she's *not* a lesbian. Could be that she just fancied a bit of the other. You know, a post-match bath with the other team so to speak – it doesn't mean that she's not still a lesbian – sorry, lezzer – don't you think, Tess?'

Tess was preparing to tear Bert's theory to shreds when Petra walked in. She'd clearly caught the tail end of the speech. 'Oh, we're on lesbians again, are we? So, who's a lesbian this time?' she asked cheerfully, hanging up her coat.

The three friends exchanged hunted, guilty looks.

'Er – I am!' Tess piped up gallantly.

'Thought so. Well, I think your friends here think I am too, don't you, girls?'

'No,' Vicky and Bert replied hotly, and too quickly to be convincing.

'Yes, you do. Well, Bert definitely does, don't you, Bert?'

Bert's face turned a lurid puce. She stood stock still, speechless, utterly panic-stricken and feeling very caught-out. After a few moments she decided that she couldn't let Petra get one over her like that in front of her friends. All the bravado she'd acquired as a schoolgirl came to the fore. 'Yeah, all right, I did – actually do, as it happens. Aren't you?'

'Not as far as I'm aware but who knows? If I could have you, Bert, maybe I'd turn!' Petra said, wrapping an apron around her waist and swanning theatrically through to the restaurant via the swing doors.

Vicky and Tess burst out laughing.

'I told you, I told you,' Vicky cackled.

'That'll teach you, Bert!' Tess said, clutching her fanny.

Bert was deeply embarrassed and busied herself with the salad, deciding that ignoring her friends would be the most dignified response while giving her time to regain face. As she did so, a thought occurred to her, and once Vicky and Tess's laughter had subsided she turned to them and said, in an urgent whisper, 'Listen, you don't think she was serious, do you?'

When Tess got home later that night she knew exactly what she was going to write about from then on and what form it would take. She went to bed bursting with energy and inspiration. After a fruitless half-hour of thrashing around the mattress, twirling the duvet around her body and squeezing her eyes tight shut in an attempt to force herself to go to sleep she jumped out of bed. Tess spent the rest of the night feverishly hammering away on her new Amstrad computer, working on a film script.

Over the next few days she felt like someone who'd found an unclaimed suitcase filled with unmarked notes. She finally knew exactly what she wanted to say and how she was going to say it. Every available spare moment she had was taken up with writing. One day, after dropping off Tabatha at school, while racing home frantic to get the maximum use out of the couple of hours she had before picking her up again, she suddenly remembered something Vicky had said, years ago: 'It's not *doing* what you want to do that's hard, it's finding out what it is that you want to do in the first place that's impossible.'

Vicky was right. Once you know what you want to do, doing

it is easy! God, Vicky's wise sometimes, even though you'd never guess it most of the time, Tess thought admiringly, as she settled down to her writing.

Three's a Crowd

Tess, her dad and Marie-Anne sat in the Everyman coffee shop in total silence. Malcolm had made no mention of this Marie-Anne person when he and Tess had arranged to meet. In fact, Tess thought sulkily, he's made no mention of her *ever*. How long has she been around? Tess noticed that Marie-Anne was clearly at ease with Malcolm and assumed that they must have been seeing each other for quite a while. She was an elegant French-woman who was, Tess guessed, about forty-five. Tess had to admit that she seemed nice enough, but she wasn't feeling at all well disposed towards her because her being there had put the kibosh on Tess's big show-down. After much deliberation she had chosen today to challenge her dad and discovering him accompanied had completely stumped her. She'd arrived with a list in her head of complaints and questions, determined not to let him wriggle off the hook. Thinking about it all in advance Tess had been aware that it was slightly unfair of her to dump it all in her dad's lap, since her mum was as much to blame as he was. But Mum's scarpered to South America so I *can't* confront her and Dad's here. That's not my fault. Anyway, he did do a runner years ago, so it's sort of his turn . . . Tess had reasoned, in an attempt to shake off the burgeoning feelings of filial guilt she'd had on the way to the cinema.

'So, your father tells me you are quite an expert on film?' Marie-Anne ventured, obviously attempting to make polite conversation.

'Yes, well, sort of. And I am also a practising lesbian,' Tess replied. What the fuck? Her mind went into a spin. She couldn't believe the words that had just emerged from her mouth. During all her planning for today's seminal life-changing confrontation she had never once included the bit where she confessed to liking women. She'd entertained elaborate fantasies in her head wherein she would exact from *him* a humble and wholesale confession of what a crap dad he'd been, which would be followed (possibly) by a gracious absolution from her. They would then part company and Tess would walk off into the sunset feeling reborn, having shed herself of all resentment and bitterness.

Tess started playing with the sugar that was sitting on the table in front of her, not daring to catch her father's eyes. Bloody hell! Nice work! I come here all fired up to give *him* what-for and end up confessing to being gay! And, to make matters worse, I go and say 'practising lesbian', like it's something you need a licence for and I haven't passed my test yet!

She hadn't known how to backtrack and had decided, now that it was out, that she might as well just sit there and wait for the inevitable reaction. She was sure it would take the form either of a silence heavy with disapproval or of some woe-is-me-what-have-I-done-to-deserve-this? wail from her father.

Eventually Malcolm spoke up. 'And are you happy?'

Tess looked up to find that her dad's expression was sincere and loving. Well, as close to loving as he ever looks, she qualified, to herself. She was thrown and didn't know how to reply.

'Your mother and I made a lot of mistakes while bringing you up but finding out that you're happy now might go some way to helping me feel a little less terrible about how selfish we were,' Malcolm continued.

Tess saw Marie-Anne give him a look of sympathy and support. During all Tess's recent rants against the injustices enacted upon her by her parents it had never occurred to her that they might actually be aware of, and what's more feel bad about, what they'd done. It suddenly dawned on Tess that her father knew he'd been a crap dad and she felt a bit sorry for him.

Still, doesn't make up for it, she thought. Well, not completely, but I suppose it's better than nothing – or moving to Guatemala.

'Yeah, I am happy,' Tess said, 'and I did a film-writing course, Dad.' She hadn't planned on telling him about the course either, but she wanted him to know that she'd acted on his advice. His confession had made her feel generous towards him and as if she could afford to let him know that something he'd said had had an impact on her.

'Oh, that's marvellous, darling. Was it helpful . . . interesting?'

'Yeah, yeah, I learnt a lot, it was, ah, a real eye-opener.' Tess smiled and decided not to add, 'in more ways than one'. She also didn't add that she'd actually written a script and sent it off to a film producer friend of Helen's. Tess had felt unsure about showing it to anyone. She was proud of her achievement and hoped that it was good, but knew that that was a very long hop, skip and a jump away from getting a real film producer to read it.

Tess went home feeling quite pleased with herself. She hadn't confronted her dad, or reeled off her list of complaints, but she felt that, between them, they'd accomplished something of great significance. She decided that, given today's turn of events, she might even talk to him about emotional stuff in the future.

Take Three Girls

'Are you taking the piss?'

'No.'

'It's about three girls who are best friends?'

'Yeah.'

'One's a slag, one's perfect and one's a lezzer?'

'If you want to put it like that, yeah. But she's *not* a slag, the other one *isn't* perfect and the other *isn't* definitely gay, she's just not as active as her friends and you don't really know what she is.'

Vicky returned from the loo.

'Vicky, you know that Tess's script is all about us?' Bert shouted across the room, before Vicky reached the table.

'Sshh, you'll wake Tabs up,' Tess hissed.

'I s'pose I should be grateful the slaggy one hasn't got a child. That and not being called Albertine.'

'She did have one, but I cut it out. Didn't seem right, somehow.'

'Well, thanks a lot, I'm sure.'

'And I was going to call her Albertine, but it's too pretentious,' Tess said, smirking at Bert.

'Is it really about us, Tess?' Vicky asked, helping herself to some more wine.

They were mid-way through one of their evenings round at Bert's place and Tess had just told them about her script. She hadn't filled them in about sending it off to a producer. There didn't seem any point until something actually happened.

254

'Yes and no. Not really. It's a gang movie, sort of thing. It could be any bunch of girls who've been mates for years – it's not meant to be us three specifically,' Tess replied. She wasn't lying or telling the truth. The script was about three girls and it had been inspired by her friendship with Vicky and Bert, and the characters were similar-ish to them, but aside from that she'd invented a plot and made one of the girls American, so she felt justified in denying that it was based on their own relationship.

'Why would it matter anyway?' Vicky said to Bert.

'I dunno, just seems a bit of a cheat. I spend my life working as a cheesy waitress and Tess writes about it and becomes world famous!'

'Cheers, Bert.'

'Oh, you know what I mean, Vic. You own the restaurant while I am your mere slave. *Ce n'est pas la même chose.*'

'Yeah, well, I may not own it for too much longer,' Vicky said gloomily.

'What?' Tess and Bert cried out simultaneously.

'According to David, there's some cash-flow problem to do with the outstanding debts from before I took it over. It's all really complicated and I don't understand it. I'm going to have dinner with him to try and get it all sorted out.'

'Oh, I get it,' Bert drooled sarcastically. 'There's no *real* problem, Vicky. David has just finally lit upon some pathetic reason why you need to spend a whole evening with him. I'll bet there's nothing up.'

'Hope so. I'd rather sleep with him than lose the restaurant!'

'Well, fingers crossed it doesn't come down to either/or.' Tess laughed.

'I'd say it was a bit of a toss-up to know which was worse,' Bert added, squeezing her nostrils tightly together with her finger and thumb, as if she could smell something terrible.

*

Several weeks had elapsed since Tess had sent her script to Helen's friend, during which time, amongst other things, she'd alphabetized her video collection, cleared out her cutlery and pants drawers, taught Tabatha to knit and rotated the mattress on her bed three times. She'd thrown herself into every possible activity she could think of to avoid dwelling on the fact that she hadn't yet heard back from the producer. Tess avoided asking Helen about it, she didn't want to appear desperate (which she was), and she didn't want to look like she was asking Helen to phone her friend on her behalf (which she would have been).

Tess and Helen had been seeing each other for a few months now and, from Tess's point of view, things suited her just fine as they were. However, she was aware that Helen would have liked them to be more 'out', doing a greater number of activities together as a couple. Tess wasn't at all keen on getting into what she saw as a clichéd couple's lifestyle with anyone. Except for the addition of having nice sex on tap, she wanted her life to stay exactly the same as it'd been before she'd met Helen. She still hadn't introduced her to Vicky and Bert, and the truth was she couldn't really see any point in doing so. She had no intention of including her in their regular evenings together: she wouldn't be able to keep up, we don't talk about things she'd find interesting. God, Vicky and Bert would have to make conversation. I'd die! Apart from their girls' nights, most of her time was spent with Tabatha, writing, or hanging around the restaurant, and she couldn't see Helen enjoying that.

Tess was happy to go to the cinema with her now and again but otherwise regarded the whole two-people-who-have-sex-must-do-everything-together convention as a bit phoney and, quite frankly, surplus to requirements. I've spent a lifetime with my mum breathing down my neck and I'm not about to start all that bollocks again! Tess reasoned, whenever she felt bad about not wanting to be more we-two-are-one with Helen.

'You're really a man trapped in a woman's body, aren't you?' Vicky opined one day when the subject of why Helen had never been introduced had come up yet again.

'How do you work that one out?'

'Well, you know the way blokes really only want a woman at home, a wife kind of thing, because in reality they only *really* enjoy going out with their mates? Well, you're like that, aren't you?'

'No.'

'Yes, you are, Vic's right. Actually she's not completely, because you're like a married man with a mistress trapped in a woman's body,' Bert said, smiling.

'Eh?'

'You know, you've got a woman but there's no need for anyone else to meet her because she's only really there for one thing so you keep her hidden away – just like a man with a mistress!'

'That's pathetic, I'm nothing like that. I just don't see the point of bringing her round here to listen to you two argue about whether Petra's a lesbian, Wine Man is a wanker and whether you're going to get off with some new victim masquerading as a plonker who comes into the restaurant!'

'Ooooooh, machwuuurre!' Vicky and Bert cried out.

'And I suppose lesbians – sorry, lezzers – only talk about art and politics, yeah?' Bert sneered.

'Well, we don't talk about whether some cheesy turd is going to ring or not!'

'Erm . . . with all due respect, Tess, Helen is your *first* relationship and you said yourself she was quite "grown-up" so maybe you don't bring her round because you're ashamed of us . . . possibly?' Vicky ventured.

'Or her,' Bert added.

Tess ignored Bert's comment but was genuinely stung by the idea that Vicky could ever think she was ashamed of them. She didn't particularly like the suggestion that she might be ashamed of Helen either. She'd rather cut her tongue out than admit it but Tess suspected that what she might really be doing was trying to make it her friends' fault rather than hers that she didn't want to include her lover in her life.

'You wait, when you really fall madly, properly, hopelessly in love with someone you'll be waltzing down the street with whoever it is, hand in hand, singing at the top of your voice and smiling at strangers,' Vicky said.

'Well, don't hold your breath waiting for that to happen!' Tess laughed. She couldn't imagine ever being like that, even if she were to be more 'in love'.

'But that's only when you're OIL, Officially in Love, like Vicky was with Barney,' Bert said, raising her eyebrows at Vicky.

'And you were with Jonathon!' Vicky reminded Bert.

'Ah, yes wonderful Jonathon, mmmm. I wonder whatever happened to him . . .' Bert, followed by Vicky, fell into deep thought.

Tess looked at her two friends, taking in their pensive expressions. 'Well, neither of you has ever been OIL since that pair of –' She was stopped short of using her chosen term of abuse by Vicky and Bert's sharp looks.

'– so I don't know what makes you two think you're such experts,' she continued.

Vicky and Bert looked at each other. Tess was right. Of all their respective admirers and boyfriends since Barney and Jonathon, neither of them had met anyone who had got close to having the same effect on them as those two boys had managed to have.

Tess knew what they were thinking and it only went further towards shoring up her conviction that the whole falling-and-staying-in-love palaver just wasn't worth the trouble. I mean, here are my two best friends, centuries on from those relationships, and neither of them has been in love since! What kind of advertisement is that? she railed. She'd gone a long way towards building up her new post-Guatemala self but she had no immediate plans or even the slightest inclination to chart what she saw as the evidently perilous 'in love' waters just yet.

Uncontrollable Pubic Hair

Tess emerged from the meeting with Sarah Gunning, Helen's friend, the producer, and wandered around Soho in a daze. While doing so, she managed to walk straight into a postbox, and tried to cross the road while it was thick with moving traffic. She wanted to sit down but she couldn't find anywhere quiet enough. She needed a moment to let it all sink in. Never mind a moment! I'll need a bloody lifetime to let *this* sink in!

Tess wanted to pinch herself. She'd always thought people sounded stupid when they used that expression but for the first time in her life it made sense. She felt as if she was having an out-of-body experience, like she was sort of watching herself from above, as if in a dream. Just when she had been about to give up on ever hearing from Sarah and slink back with her tail between her legs into her pre-Guatemala destiny as a surrogate aunty, ruing the day she'd ever written the wretched script, she'd got a letter telling her that Sarah had liked it and asking her to call to arrange a meeting. A 'meeting'! A 'meeting'! Tess had read nervously. God, that sounds beyond me, too grown-up and professional. Fuck! What do people do in meetings? They probably all talk about fiscal shortfalls, projected targets and other stuff that means nothing to me. Help! Notwithstanding her hysterical reaction Tess had succeeded in fixing a date and it was from this meeting that she had just emerged.

Sarah Gunning had told her that they loved the script – Sarah was the only person in the room apart from her but Tess hadn't dared ask who 'they' were – and that 'they' would like to buy the rights and give Tess money to do some more work on it. After some discussion, during which Tess revealed that she was a complete novice in this world, she had left Sarah's office with the phone numbers of a couple of agents Sarah had suggested she talk to about representation and an agreement that they would talk again about how to develop the script further. Tess spent the rest of the day, until she had to pick up Tabatha, walking around the West End dreaming about her acceptance speech at the Oscars, who she'd take with her, what she'd wear and which movie stars would be right to play the characters in her film.

'Well, I want to be played by Olivia Newton-John.'

'She's shit.'

'She's all right. She was good in *Grease* and she's very pretty – I think she'd be brilliant as me.'

'Bert, for the last time, it isn't you – and, anyway, I'm telling you, she's shit.'

'Well, it's Julie Christie as me or no one.' Vicky joined in.

'Julie Christie? Julie Christie! Vicky, do you honestly think you're like Julie Christie?' Bert demanded.

'Well, I'm more like Julie Christie than you're like Olivia Newton-John. I'd like to see you get into those black satin Lycra trousers!'

'I think I want to be played by Debra Winger. I like her.'

'Who's she?'

'She's the one from *An Officer and a Gentleman* and that stupid film where she rides a pretend horse in a bar . . . erm, *Urban Cowboy*.'

'Isn't she the really short and hairy one?'

'Hairy? What do you mean by hairy?'

'Oh, you know that kind of hairy look some women have.'

'No.'

'When they look all hairy – like they've got masses of underarm hair and have to shave their legs six times a day!'

'Debra Winger doesn't look like that. You're talking about women like Golda Meir or the kind that hang around at Greenham Common!'

'No, I'm not. You know what I mean, the sort of woman who looks like she has masses of uncontrollable pubic hair, growing all over the place. Come on, Vic, you know the sort I'm talking about, don't you? There was a girl like that at school, she always wore her vest and pants in the showers . . . erm . . . Oh, what was she called?'

'That was Iona Sanderson, but Debra Winger doesn't look anything like that.'

'Anyway, never mind about who's hairy. Listen, is this film definitely going to happen, then? Are you going to move to Hollywood and become super-rich and famous? It's so exciting – we'll be able to say we knew you!'

Tess smiled at Vicky's barrage of questions. 'Well, my agent says – '

'Oooooh! "My agent"! I can't believe you're saying "my agent" like that – all casual and normal. It's so glamorous, Tess!' Vicky gushed.

'Not really. Honestly, you two, please don't get too hysterical about this. I've just got an agent, which isn't *that* big a deal, and he's organizing the contract and stuff with Sarah's company. I've just written a script that someone likes. It may never happen, for all I know. Apparently loads of scripts get bought all the time that never get made into films.' Tess was, in fact, thrilled to be able to say things like 'my agent' and 'the contract' but thanks to her friends' reactions she was able to keep a lid on the wild excitement she really felt bubbling inside her every single minute of the day.

262

'Are you getting paid tons of money for it?' Bert demanded.

'Typical of you to ask something like that. No, I'm not getting tons, if you must know, but enough to sign off the dole while I –'

'Enough to stop taking money off me any more for looking after Tabs, yeah?'

'Hah, hah, very amusing. No, I was going to say while I rewrite the script.'

'Blimey! Bet you're still taking money off me when you win your Oscar!' Bert whined.

'Bert, paying for a babysitter is part of taking your duties as a parent seriously. It's not about the money.' Amongst all the aspects of her previous self that Tess had shed so far, not included was her enjoyment of admonishing Bert for her continued inability, as she saw it, to fully absorb the responsibilities that being a parent entailed.

'Oh, God, you sound like Margaret Thatcher. I was only joking. Anyway, I expect you won't be interested in looking after Tabs any more now that you're going to be famous.'

'Of course I'm going to stay looking after Tabs. I wouldn't leave her to your devices! I'm only rewriting the script. I'm not going anywhere. Look, nothing's going to be any different from before!'

Tess was very excited about all the things that had happened to her but she didn't want her friends to think that everything was going to change as a result – it made her feel panicky and rootless.

Thirtysomething
1989

'It's not supposed to be like this. I'm not supposed to be starting out all over *again* at thirty. I thought your thirties were supposed to be the best time of your life!'

'No, I think that's supposed to be your twenties.'

'No, no, I'm sure they say it's supposed to be your teens. Didn't they always say, "Enjoy this, it's the best time of your life"?'

'Who? I don't remember anyone saying that when we were teenagers.'

'Excuse me, you two, do you think you could focus on my fucking problem? My restaurant is closing down! I need sympathy, not to listen to a sodding seminar about some stupid expression!' Vicky interrupted.

'Oh, God, yeah, sorry, Vicky.'

'Yeah, sorry, Vicky. It's just that I'm sure the expression is –'

Tess stopped Bert short with a fierce glare. 'So what are you going to do now, Vic?' she asked gently.

'I don't know, I just don't know.'

'Well, you'll always be able to get a chef's job, won't you? I mean, you are a brilliant cook,' Bert said, trying to throw a positive light on Vicky's bleak prospects.

'I don't want to work in someone else's restaurant! I couldn't after having my own, it'd be horrible. I don't know what I'm going to do. How do you start out again at thirty? It's *so* old!'

'What do your parents think about all this?' Tess asked,

knowing that she might have got some sensible advice from them. Jack, Vicky's father, still spent most of his time gallivanting around with female students he culled from the art school he now taught at, but her mother could usually be relied upon to behave in a modest and reasonably adult fashion.

'Mum thinks I should start a catering business. Can you imagine anything more ghastly than spending my life doing people's weddings and bar mitzvahs?'

'Well, that way at least I'd still have a job,' Bert said, smiling, and trying to give the impression that she was joking. Since the restaurant's recent collapse she'd been walking a fine line between trying to be supportive to Vicky and worrying about what she was going to do herself.

'Bert! Typical of you to be thinking about yourself. Honestly, you are so selfish sometimes!'

Bert was about to attempt to defend herself when Vicky spoke up. 'No, Bert's right, I do have to think about her as well.'

Bert was so humbled by how saintly Vicky could be even at a time like this that she was immediately prompted to encourage her in her reluctance to become a caterer. 'Yeah, actually, you're right. Private catering would be awful! Just think of the sort of people who'd employ you!'

'Well, I might end up having to do it. After all, if I don't want to work in somebody else's restaurant what does that leave me with? And it might not be so bad. At least I'd be my own boss.'

Bert was confused; she didn't know which way she should go now. 'Yeah, you know what? It might not be *that* awful. It could turn out to be a laugh, actually. Think of all the eligible young men we'd meet!'

'I think I've had my fill of eligible young men for the moment,' Vicky said forlornly. Tess looked at Bert and made a face; Bert wanted to kick herself for mentioning meeting men.

1987

Any chance of a grappa?

Vicky had thought that Tom was IT from the moment she'd clapped eyes on him. They had met at the restaurant when some of his friends who were regulars had brought him along. Vicky, who knew them well enough to say hello to, had had a quick chat with them that night and then gone back to her kitchen. The very next night Tom had returned alone.

'Remember that bloke who was here last night with those awful art-school types? He's here again. On his own,' Bert remarked, coming back in from the restaurant with an armful of dirty plates.

'What bloke?'

'That bloke, the good-looking one. You know, he was here last night with all those pretentious wankers you like so much. Even you can't have failed to notice him. Well, he's out there, sitting at the table in the window. On His Own,' Bert repeated, putting ostentatiously heavy emphasis on the last three words.

'And so what?'

'And so, so, he asked me if you were here, that's so what!'

'Oh, yeah?' Vicky replied, without looking round. Bert couldn't decide if Vicky was genuinely uninterested or was, as ever, playing it ultra-cool.

'Anyway, I said you were and that I'd send you out.'

'Did you? Well, you can go right back out there again and tell him I'm too busy to come out, and while you're at it tell him that I'm not in the habit of lounging around the restaurant during our most hectic period.'

'*Mon Dieu*, that's a bit strict! Vic, he is *really* good-looking. Don't you just want to go and have a look? You might change your mind.'

Vicky ignored Bert and got on with her work. She didn't need to go out and have a look, she knew exactly who Bert was talking about and she had absolutely no intention of going out to see him. Vicky had thought about nothing and no one else since the moment she'd laid eyes on him. She was completely smitten and simply couldn't face attempting to have a casual conversation with him. She was sure that what she felt would be plastered all over her face. Something about Tom had struck a chord in Vicky, and she was flushed with excitement to learn that he'd come back. She prayed that he'd returned because she'd had the same effect on him as he'd had on her – but she wasn't going out and that was that, she decided. Vicky hadn't discussed him with Bert and had no intention of revealing anything now. She knew that Bert wouldn't be able to resist letting Tom know, in some small way, that he hadn't come back in vain and she was far too keen to risk having Bert blow it all.

Vicky was usually regarded by most people, including her two best friends, as being cool as a cucumber. She was an expert at maintaining a smooth veneer of calm on the surface even when, underneath, she felt wildly passionate about something. Vicky had grown increasingly self-contained through her twenties, without becoming snotty, and this was partly as a result of the greater self-confidence she'd gained from her success. She often thought that it also helped having two best friends whose flamboyant personalities gave her the opportunity to be more reserved than she might otherwise have been.

She endured an excruciating evening. She couldn't concentrate on anything and, to make matters worse, Bert, behaving completely unlike her normal self, didn't mention Tom again. Vicky had been banking on her friend nagging her incessantly to go out and talk to him, so that when she finally did it could be under the pretext of shutting her up and not because she actually wanted to herself. As things began to calm down towards the end of the evening she realized that she didn't even know if he was still there. Oh, God, what if he's gone because I didn't go out? I'm such an idiot, I could have just gone and said hello. What if I never see him again? Vicky thought as she dropped a huge, dirty lasagne pan into the sink. Her panic was interrupted by a man's voice.

'Any chance of an after-hours grappa?' Tom said, peering round the swing doors. Vicky span round and turned bright red. She could feel her face burning up as she stood there, saying nothing but thinking, Oh, great, man of my dreams walks in and I look fantastic – purple face, hands covered in bits of old pasta and I can't even speak.

'Are you in the middle of something or could we have a drink?'

Vicky attempted a casual nod but it didn't seem to stop and she was sure she looked more like she was having a stroke. She still couldn't seem to get any words to come out of her mouth.

'I came back here to see you, you know.'

Vicky stayed rooted to the spot, practically shaking with nerves. I've turned into a mute, I've lost the powers of speech, he's going to think I'm brain dead! Say something, say something!

At that moment the swing doors flew open and Bert came in shouting, 'Oi, Vicky, are you –' She stopped in her tracks when she saw Tom, looked at Vicky and realized instantly that her friend had been feigning disinterest in 'that bloke' all evening. She snapped into action and decided to act like an idiot, knowing that this would break the ice between the awkward couple. 'Right. I'll . . . erm . . . get back to the restaurant and . . . er . . . do something absolutely vital that will ensure that I, er, don't come back in here for quite some time. If that's OK with everyone, right, OK . . . I'll be off, then.'

Once she'd left, Tom laughed and Vicky finally managed to force a smile.

'Subtle, your friend, isn't she?'

'Oh, yes, it's one of her strong suits,' Vicky said.

'So, this grappa?' Tom said.

Vicky found a bottle and some glasses and they sat down. After her wobbly start she felt completely at ease with him. They talked about anything and everything, and conversation between them flowed without any effort at all. After a few hours Vicky felt like she'd known Tom all her life. The pair stayed in the kitchen chatting until early next morning when they went back to his flat to make love.

'So is that it? Are you OIL now?'

'Well, don't know about OIL yet. It's only been three weeks but I'm definitely absolutely mad about him.'

'What does he do?'

'He's a journalist – freelance.'

'How old is he?'

'Blimey, Tess, all these questions. He's thirty-five,' Vicky said, with pride.

'Thirty-five? Thirty-five! God, he's ancient, that's . . .' Bert had to pause to work it out.

'Eight years, Bert. Take twenty-seven away from thirty-five and you get –'

'Thank you, Tess, I could have worked it out. Yes, so he's eight years older than us, Vic!'

'Seven years, actually, I'm nearly twenty-eight remember? Anyway, so what?'

'I don't know, it just seems really old. God, he probably wants to get married, have kids and wear cardigans.' Bert snorted.

269

'I don't think so just yet.'

'Oh, I see, but it's not out of the question?' asked Bert, half-seriously.

'Bert, I'm not thinking about marriage. We're just having a fantastic time, OK?'

Bert gave Tess a knowing look and said, 'And I don't suppose you're going to tell us about the sex, are you?'

'Nope.'

'No, of course not. Not if you're in the process of falling OIL. You wouldn't want to sully your perfect new love by telling your mates what he's like to shag, after all.'

'Bert, you know I won't talk about that kind of thing, so why do you ask?'

Bert made a face. 'Oh, God, help me! It's going to be like it was with Barney all over again. You'd better not turn into the creep you were when you were going out with him. Jesus!'

'I didn't turn into a creep. You were just jealous of us!'

'Jealous!?!' she spluttered. Of course, Vicky was right and they both knew it. Barney *had* come between them, and although Vicky had breezed through the whole episode herself, she knew it had been a terrible, anxious time for Bert and she didn't want to make her friend feel like that again. Vicky felt older and wiser now, and more able to manage a new relationship as well as keep up with her friends.

Vicky knew that Tess had found her feet. Her first film had never got made in the end but she was now having a reasonable amount of success as a scriptwriter. To Tess's amazement she'd found that, while working on her own stuff, she could earn a living either doing rewrites on scripts that other people had originally created or developing ideas that various production companies asked her to beef up for them. Helen and she had finally split up after Helen had given her a make-an-honest-woman-of-me-or-else ultimatum. Without a moment's hesitation Tess had opted for 'or else'. She'd cared greatly for Helen but the idea of setting up home with her or anyone else had made her shudder. She would often sing to herself, 'I'm fancy free and free for anything fancy' when spotting a girl who piqued her interest, an increasingly frequent occurrence, given her contentedly single state. On the other hand, Vicky felt that although Bert was happy enough gathering male scalps, bringing up Tabatha and casually hurling plates on to tables at La Cantina for a living, there was something missing in her life, a sense of purpose and direction.

As predicted, Vicky and Tom fell madly in love, and after a few months spent locked in each other's arms she gave up her flat and moved into his. She knew that her friends thought she was being hasty but she didn't care: it felt right. Vicky had always been happily unattached and fiercely independent. She had thrown herself into making the restaurant a success and during that time had never yearned for a relationship. But then Tom had appeared and that was that. Vicky often thought how lucky she'd been not to have had to kiss all the frogs that Bert was still kissing.

Tom's erratic schedule meant that he was often away or worked late into the night so his inclusion in Vicky's life never posed too much of a threat to the way the trio's relationship was set up or to their regular evenings together. After a while Bert and Tess grew to accept his presence in their friend's life as a feature of theirs. And they both liked him. He'd earned enormous respect by never trying to get into their gang by pretending he understood when one of them used a phrase only they understood, like 'footwear factor' or 'criminal kissing'. He didn't condescend to them or seem to think they were childish for having their own secret language. Tom just got on with his own life while clearly loving Vicky to bits. To Bert and Tess's relief, Vicky was completely herself with him, and wasn't putting *any* work into appearing Officially In Love, as she had with Barney.

As Vicky hit twenty-eight she decided that she was happy with her lot – her business was doing well, she'd met someone terrific and she still had time to have a laugh with her best mates.

1989
Ways To Leave Your Lover

Just before Vicky entered her thirties everything she had went arse about tit. She felt as if someone in life's Fate Department had taken a quick look at hers and decided that, all in all, she'd had too easy a ride of it and that pulling the plug on everything would be good for her.

'Tess, it's me. Listen, can you put Tabs to bed a bit earlier? I'm coming back with Vicky, she's in a bad way. Petra's going to hold the fort here,' Bert whispered urgently into the phone with her hand cupped over her mouth.

'What's up? You sound like you're twenty feet under water.'

'I can't talk properly, I'm at the restaurant, I don't want Vic to hear me. You'll find out when we get back.'

'Give me a clue. Has someone died? What's going on? I can't bear the suspense,' Tess whispered back.

'You don't need to fucking whisper. It's me that has to whisper, I'm the one trying not to be overheard, not you!'

'Oh, yeah, sorry. Whenever I hear someone whispering I always start whispering too. Sorry,' Tess replied, still whispering.

'You're doing it again. Stop it, it's driving me nuts. Anyway, no one's died, it's worse than that. We'll see you in about an hour, maybe less. 'Bye.'

Much to Vicky's relief, Bert had taken total control of the situation and virtually dragged her back to her house, despite her claims that she wanted to stay at work.

*

'He sent a *fax*?' Tess was incredulous.

'Yes.'

'A fax?'

'Yes.'

'He sent a *fax*?'

'Yes, a fucking fax. How many times are you going to say "fax" like that?' Vicky snarled.

'Sorry, Vic, I just can't take it in, it seems so – so – modern.'

'I don't think it's even included as an option in that "There must be forty ways to leave your lover" song,' Bert said.

'It's not forty, it's fifty. "Forty" – honestly, that'd sound really stupid,' Tess chipped in.

'Forty. Fifty. Who cares? Anyway, each suggestion for ways to leave rhymes with the name of a bloke. Doesn't it, Tess?'

'Yeah, it goes, erm . . . "you don't need to stay, Jay, get out of bed, Ned . . ."' Tess began to sing tentatively.

'It doesn't go like that. You're making it up. But what would rhyme with fax?' Bert interrupted. 'Ah, Max, it'd have to be Max.'

'Or Jax.'

'Jax? Nobody's called Jax! No, it would have to be Max, that's the only one that rhymes with fax.'

'Unless your parents didn't like the name Jack but wanted something near it so they called you Jax instead.'

'What kind of parents would call someone a made-up name like Jax? You're just doing that thing of trying to find a way that makes you right, instead of –'

'Hello! Jesus Christ, I don't believe this! Can't you two ever concentrate on anything that doesn't centre around either of you? My boyfriend has just chucked me after two years and you two are arguing over what fucking name rhymes with fax!!'

'God, God, I'm so sorry, Vic. Sorry, sorry. I think I was just thrown hearing that he'd sent a fax. I've never heard of anyone doing that before!'

274

'Well, the thing is, we don't know many people with fax machines. It'll probably become a perfectly ordinary way to chuck someone in a few years' time when everyone has one. Tom only has one because he's freelance. In the future it'll probably be as normal as having a telephone. I mean, we don't think it's amazing when people are chucked over the phone, do we?' Bert prattled on, oblivious to the inappropriate timing of her theory. Tess made a fierce face at her and Bert suddenly realized that she wasn't being very sensitive.

'I thought he was IT.'

'So did we,' Tess said sympathetically.

'So did he,' Bert added.

'Do you think so?' Vicky asked hopefully.

'Yeah, well, that's how he acted. I mean, not that I'm an expert on how a committed man behaves, but he certainly didn't act like someone who had a foot half out of the door the whole time.'

'I don't think he did. I think he just . . . wobbled out,' Vicky said limply. She was aware that her friends wouldn't really think that this sufficed as a reasonable excuse for deserting her after two years of near bliss.

'What did it say, Vic?' Tess asked. Vicky had left the fax back at their flat, where she'd discovered it flopped out on to the machine's feeder tray that morning before setting off for work. Tom had obviously sent it in the middle of the night. She'd read and reread it so many times she knew exactly what it said by heart. Vicky opened her mouth, intending to reel off its contents word for word, but instead her head slowly folded into her chest and she started to cry. Tess and Bert exchanged looks and with one synchronized movement picked up their chairs and shuffled round placing themselves next to Vicky so that she'd have a best friend on either side. Each put an arm around her shoulders. The three girls sat in silence, broken intermittently by Vicky's heavy sobs. Eventually Vicky composed herself.

275

'It said, "Darling Vicky, Can't go on, can't cope, can't face you, can't believe I'm doing this. I'm going to stay here for a while, take as long as you need to find somewhere else to live. I know it's not good enough but I'll always love you, in my own way. Tom."'

'Where's "here"? Where is he?' Tess asked indignantly.

'He's gone to San Francisco to do some article about that Aids disease.'

'God, that's an awful thing, isn't it? You want to thank your lucky stars you've become a lezzie, Tess. That disease is going to change everything for the rest of us,' Bert said, keeping her arm round Vicky's shoulder but leaning forward so that she could see Tess, her view blocked by Vicky's slumped form.

'Doesn't it only affect gay men?' Tess replied, also leaning forward.

'No, everyone thinks that. Straights can get it too.'

'Excuse me! What am I? The garden fence?'

'Ooops, sorry, Vicky, so go on.'

'That's it, Tess, there isn't any more. Just the fax. No warning, no nothing. I feel like one of those pathetic women we used to laugh at on that awful bit Our Tune on *The Simon Bates show*. Do you remember? Someone would ring up and tell a story about her husband who'd gone out for a packet of fags and she'd never seen him again.'

'Oh, God, yes, that naff tune was always playing in the background, wasn't it?' Bert started humming the tune, a slushy piece of pseudo-classical music. She made it sound like a track from the *Bobby Crush Greatest Hits* album.

'Oi, Bert, that happens to be the score from Franco Zeffirelli's *Romeo and Juliet* and it is not naff.'

'Well, *franchement*, it always sounded pretty naff to me.'

'That's because of how Simon Bates was using it. It's a classic piece of cinematic scoring which –'

'Excuse me? I am having a nervous breakdown if that's not too much trouble for either of you.'

'Sorry, Vic, sorry. So, listen, didn't you have any idea? I mean, has everything been OK between you two in . . . in . . . every department?' Tess interrupted, intending to be subtle.

'Yes, everything was fine, including the sex,' Vicky replied, giving Tess a weak smile to show that she appreciated her attempt to be delicate.

'So what the hell is the twat up to?'

'He's not a twat, Bert!' Vicky said angrily. 'He's just scared . . . I suppose.'

'Scared? Of what?'

'I don't know . . . maybe. Oh, we'd started talking about getting married before he left for America and – and – he seemed keen and it seemed like a good idea and . . . I don't know.'

'Oh, Vic, when did you start thinking marriage was such a brilliant idea?' Bert asked.

Vicky gathered from her tone that she felt like she'd been left out. 'I didn't, I don't. No, I do, well, did with Tom. It just seemed like the normal thing to do.'

'Not where we come from!' Bert cried.

'No, I know. That's why it seemed like a good idea with Tom, you know. It was going to be *different* for us.'

Neither Bert nor Tess knew what to say and the group just sat there hunched over in silence for a bit.

After a while Vicky sat up straight and shook her shoulders gently. 'Can you two stop hugging me now? I'm getting a bit hot.'

'So, no chance of a snog, then?' Tess said.

'I don't really fancy you, sorry.'

'I don't fancy you either, Vic, but I thought it might cheer you up. The word on the streets is that I'm a fantastic kisser.'

'Thanks, but no thanks.' All three laughed.

That night Vicky stayed on the sofa at Bert's. She couldn't face going back to the empty flat to the bed she and Tom had shared so happily until now. She couldn't sleep and spent most of the night staring at the ceiling, going over every recent conversation she'd had with him. She was sure it hadn't been she who had brought up the topic of marriage. She kept going over and over everything in her head. If anything he's always been the more romantic one. His parents are still married. He's the one who said he believed in everlasting love. It's not like I flashed my bare ring finger and talked about churches and flower arrangements the whole time! Why has he done this?

Vicky felt she had every right to assure herself that she'd never pushed for a commitment. However, she knew that way, way down inside her she had always hoped, ever since she was a little girl, that someone, the right someone, would simply insist that they be legally bound to each other. In her dreams, that 'right someone' was going to know exactly what he was doing and what he wanted and his certainties would allay all her fears. Rationally she believed, as did her friends, that marriages didn't last and were a waste of time. But as she lay in the dark, thinking about how things had been with Tom, she had to admit that with him she'd begun to hope that there might be a way to avoid the inevitable.

As dawn broke she wondered what the fuck she was supposed to do now. She didn't *do* anything at first and ended up staying at Bert's for the next couple of weeks. A few days after Tom's bombshell she went back to the flat to collect some things, taking Bert and Tess with her since she couldn't face going in alone. The fax was still where she'd left it, lying on Tom's desk; other than that nothing had changed. Vicky had hoped that there might be another, more recent fax filled with desperate regret and begging her to forgive him, but there wasn't, and she realized that it really was over.

A Casanova Complex

At first Vicky fervently hung on to her feeling of bewilderment, finding the state strangely comforting. It precluded any blame on her part and also any speculation about hidden problems she hadn't been facing up to. However, as time marched on, Bert began to ask questions about what Tom had been like in private. She was trying to help her friend find a rational explanation for his disappearance. Initially Vicky strongly resisted the notion that there must have been pointers. But eventually she was forced to admit that Tom had always had an elusive quality about him. Bert was right, it wasn't that she'd ever felt that he'd had a foot half-way out of the door but there'd been a freedom of spirit in his character which, until now, Vicky had never seen as a threat to their happiness.

'You know what? He's one of those types. He'll always be like that, going out with someone until crunch time and then he'll do a bunk,' Bert opined one night in the restaurant, when she could tell Vicky was thinking about Tom – again.

'Yeah, don't they call it a Peter Pan complex? Or maybe it's a Cinderella complex. Anyway, Bert's right, he'll always be like that,' Tess said, joining in. She had made a point of being at the restaurant as much as possible since the whole thing had happened, mainly to be supportive but also because she didn't trust Bert not to put her foot in it as per usual.

'No, I think it'd be a Casanova complex. Why would it be Cinderella? Or Peter Pan come to that?'

279

'Because Peter Pan doesn't want to grow up and Cinderella runs out of the party.'

'It's not a party it's a ball.'

'Oh, you know what I mean.'

'Anyway, she runs out because she's going to turn into a pumpkin not because she can't commit!'

'Well, maybe the pumpkin is a metaphor for commitment.'

'Tess, just admit you're wrong. It's a Casanova complex.'

'If this is your idea of being supportive I can tell you two that it's not helping.

'Oh, sorry, Vicky. Anyway, what I was trying to say is that I don't think you've got anything to blame yourself for, I just think Tom's like that. You could have been anybody.'

Tess winced as Bert came to the end of what she'd obviously imagined was a helpful analysis of Tom's character.

'Oh, well, that's good to know. Makes me feel much better. Anyway it doesn't really matter, does it? I'm never going to see him again and that's that.' Vicky wasn't being entirely honest. She suspected that she would see him again one day, one way or another, but she couldn't bear to keep going over how that might happen and in what circumstances. Instead she found it easier for the moment to blast him out of her thoughts every time he crept in – which was about every second.

Once Vicky had acknowledged Tom's elusiveness she decided that it was at fault for forcing him to do a bunk when the prospect of tying himself down had reared its head. She deeply regretted not having stayed true to her disdain of the institution of marriage. She blamed herself for not having been more guarded with Tom. She couldn't help feeling that if she had been, she wouldn't be in this unhappy position now. She felt that somehow she had asked for it by letting down all her defences with him. She'd had no choice. They'd fallen in love with each other so completely simultaneously that playing it cool with Tom had never once entered her head. There'd never been a single who's-going-to-call-who, he-hasn't-rung-for-two-days-oh-God-do-you-think-he's-gone-off-me? moment and, she knew, strategy would have been embarrassingly out of place. Vicky felt like she'd fallen down a massive hole only because she'd been looking in the wrong direction. Her previous view of Bert's life as lacking something changed, and she decided now that it would be much better to have a string of men in tow in whom she had no real investment, all pursuing *her*, rather than pining away for one person she couldn't have.

Life crept by like treacle for Vicky, Tom's departure having hammered the spring out her step. She found everything, even the most ordinary day-to-day activities, pointless, and went about her job like somebody on heavy-duty tranquillizers. Eventually this had an effect on the restaurant. Over the last few years, she'd always been able to surmount problems she'd encountered with La Cantina with a mixture of her own determination and flair, in combination with David's financial wizardry. The problems had mainly related to the outstanding debts attached to the restaurant's premises prior to Vicky's tenure. She and David had juggled things effectively for quite a while, but recently there'd been a major setback involving debts to suppliers and a dramatic rent increase. All this was topped off by Vicky's recent lacklustre approach to her cooking. The restaurant began to lose customers and with them went its trendiness and atmosphere. Given the whole sad picture, Vicky decided to give up. As she turned thirty she felt that her life was very much *not* going according to plan.

1990
Private Function

'David's nephew's bar mitzvah?'

'Yeah.'

'That's our first job?'

'If you don't count that dinner party Mum had – which I don't because she was only doing it out of charity – yes. What's the big deal?'

'Nothing. It's just that I can't help feeling that David has probably invented a nephew so that he can give you a job. I bet he's hired a boy actor and a fake family and a whole bunch of fake friends just so that he can help you out and sort of give you money without actually having to give you the money himself.'

'Which I'd never take in a million years!'

'*Exactement*. He knows that, so he's invented a family and found another way to support you without you knowing it. Can't you see his cunning plan?'

'Bert, you're being ridiculous. Even for you. David's not that soppy about me. Why shouldn't he have a nephew who's having a bar mitzvah and why shouldn't I cater it?'

'I don't know, just seems a bit odd. Has David mentioned this beloved nephew before?'

'Bert, why would he? Stop seeking out problems when there just aren't any. Look, anyway, I don't care if this job is a fake or not, I'm just glad it's not strict kosher – I can't get my head round all that pork and beef and shellfish and milk thing.'

'What? A nice Jewish girl like you?'

282

'Hah, hah. I was hardly brought up Jewish, was I? I don't think my mother would know what a rollmop was if it sat on her face.'

'Maybe not, but it's an attractive image all the same – your mother with a pickled herring lying across her mush.' Vicky laughed and Bert was pleased.

It was nearly six months now since Tom had left, and La Cantina had closed down. Vicky was still quite low. She had resisted the idea of becoming a private caterer as long as she could bear getting up in the morning with nothing to do, and the whole day yawning in front of her like an empty chasm. In the end, she'd faced up to the fact that it was her only option. The prospect had seemed so depressingly unglamorous, particularly when compared to running her own popular restaurant. 'Well, needs must when the devil drives,' Vicky's dad had said, when her future had come up the last time they'd seen each other.

'Yeah, I suppose so – whatever that's supposed to mean,' Vicky had muttered grudgingly. She knew that her dad was probably right but she hated his whole cut-and-thrust-pull-your-socks-up-stiff-upper-lip reaction to the – as she saw it – gargantuan disaster (disasters, plural, if I include Tom leaving . . . and I do, she thought) that had beset her. However, unlike her mother Julia, she didn't blame her dad for having got her involved with the restaurant in the first place. Although she accepted that it wasn't his fault the whole thing had gone pear-shaped, she did suspect that even if it had been he might not have acted any differently.

Jack had never been a great one for responsibility. He'd suited himself most of his life, having enjoyed a great time along the way. Now, in the first year of the nineties, he was a caricature of a swinging sixties hang-over. At sixty-four years old he was well past his best but blissfully – and mercifully, as far as Vicky was concerned – unaware of it. When they were young the way he'd dressed and acted had seemed unbelievably hip and appealingly unparentlike to Bert and Tess. At the time everything about him, from the clothes he wore to the people who bought his paintings to the places he ate, had been absolutely up-to-the-minute, he had *always* been a bit of an embarrassment to Vicky. But now, still wearing corduroy jackets, woven ties, bedding girls of less than half his age and driving around in a car that a provincial DJ might think was groovy, even Bert and Tess could see that he was a bit past it.

Dad's never committed to anyone since Mum and that was hardly a commitment, more of a lark and, anyway, she was pregnant with Jane so they had to get married in those days. Maybe Tom is like Dad, and I was choosing someone like my father without knowing it. They say that's what you do, don't they? You pick someone like your dad to try and change them to become unlike your dad, Vicky thought, as she sat making a list of suitable dishes for David's nephew's function. She'd got this theory from an article. She'd known that it was hardly a new concept but it made sense applied to Tom. She hadn't dared tell Bert and Tess that she'd taken to reading magazines like *Cosmopolitan* because they contained articles entitled 'Why Your Relationship Went Wrong' and 'How To Pick Better Men'. They hadn't bought those type of magazines since they were teenagers and, even back then, only when they'd offered free posters of David Cassidy or Les McKeown. They always con-sidered themselves much too sophisticated for that kind of thing. Vicky knew that they weren't going to provide any lasting answers. In spite of logic, she was able to take comfort in being reassured that men fell into a few specific categories, some of which should be avoided. It was all so easy: you needed only to follow the prescribed 'Ten Easy Steps' (the assorted magazines' plans varied sometimes but not widely) and you'd never get caught out again. She knew Bert and Tess would go wild taking the piss out of her if they caught her filling in the test question-naires also often included – 'Are You a Loser in Love?' and 'Do You *Make* Them Leave You?'. She knew it was all meaningless but couldn't help being pleased when she scored high, as someone who didn't encourage desertion. Vicky was, to Bert and Tess's relief, officially over Tom. Privately she still thought about him a lot but at least, by now, without the same acute, heart-breaking pain as before.

Tick-tick-tick

Vicky continued to live at Bert's while Angela showed no immediate signs of returning to England, having moved from her Poona ashram to another one her guru had recently set up in America. Vicky had finally got it together to move all her stuff out of Tom's flat a couple of months after the relationship had ended. She'd discovered no evidence of his return and, with some difficulty, had left her set of keys behind. She hadn't really wanted to: carrying them round in her bag had seemed somehow to represent that there might still be some life left in the affair, but Bert and Tess had forced her to do it, saying that it was cathartic – Tess's big new word – and a vital part of accepting that it was over for ever. Vicky had felt really terrible that day but was quietly glad that her friends had pushed her into doing it as she knew it was the right thing.

Bert and Vicky lived together in a state somewhere between harmony and hell, and both knew it would only do as a temporary measure. Bert thought Vicky was too finicky and Vicky couldn't get over what a slob Bert was. Since her mother had moved abroad Bert had become much more relaxed domestically. Her youthful neatness had, it turned out, been mainly a counter-reaction to her mother's slobbiness. Vicky refused point-blank to accept that she herself was fussy: she referred constantly to Tabatha's domestic dissimilarity to her mother as proof positive that she was normal and Bert was a pig. Tabatha was now nearly eleven and about to go to the same school where the three

286

girls had met. To Vicky's amusement, Tess's delight and Bert's amazement, she was different from Bert in every possible way. She had developed a quiet but confident character, she was studious without being an awful swot, and she showed no signs of having to be the centre of attention in every situation.

Although Tess was still very much in evidence as a second mother, Vicky was naturally spending more extended time with Bert and Tabatha than she'd done before, and it was having a very unfortunate side-effect on her. Vicky had greatly helped her recovery by readopting her formerly held disdain of marriage. She hadn't, however, anticipated or been at all prepared for the unwelcome arrival of an unfamiliar feeling. It turned out to be broodiness. She was slow to recognize it, never having thought about having children before, not even in the headiest days of being madly in love with Tom. She was stunned by its outburst and felt like she'd been hijacked by another, much more sorted-out and grown-up woman's loins. She found herself yearning for a relationship like the one between Bert and Tabatha which, although unconventional (Bert was more like a big sister to Tabatha than a mother) was, nonetheless, enviable in that it was loving and, more importantly, permanent.

Much to Vicky's annoyance the awful, hitherto laughable expression 'body-clock' constantly referred to as 'tick, tick, tick-ing away for the Woman Over Thirty' in the magazines she'd taken to reading, began to mean something to her. She, Bert and Tess were united in regarding thirty as really old. However, in Vicky's view, her friends' ancientness didn't pose the same physical threats for them as it now did for her. Tess worried about not having written a Hollywood blockbuster before she was dead or forty (much the same thing, as far as she was concerned), and Bert worried about having done nothing with her life other than serve people food and sleep with unsuitable men. But Vicky started to worry constantly about not meeting someone 'in time' with whom she could have a family. She deeply resented this assault because it meant having to think about men in a new and different light. Vicky hadn't turned into a bitter old bag by her unhappy experience with Tom. She hadn't turned into a man-hater, she just didn't want to be forced to think about them. She was recovered enough to contemplate having sex with a new person but she hadn't anticipated being compelled to weigh up the potential candidate's sperm count and genealogy first. I'm supposed to be sleeping around with wild abandon now! I'm supposed to be happy shagging any old bloke! Bloody hell – and just when I'd planned on turning into a slag! she thought indignantly, when she found herself unable to muster the vaguest interest in any bloke Bert suggested she get off with.

'Well, there's nothing for it, then. You'll have to marry the heavenly David after all! Bit of a waste but there you go,' Bert pronounced when, weeks later, Vicky finally confessed why she wasn't showing interest in any of Bert's suggestions for light relief – her description of the men she was proposing her friend divert herself with.

'A, why will I *have* to marry David? B, I might meet someone else, and C, David's not a gargoyle. He's been really loyal and nice to me over the last few months.'

'A, stop listing things using the alphabet. B, it's very naff, and C, it makes you sound like someone who's done a how-to-get-to-the-top-in-business training course. Now I see the worm is finally turning. So it was worth him going to all the bother and expense of hiring an entire cast of actors to pretend they were having this bar mitzvah.'

'He did not hire anybody! The worm, as you so nicely describe me, is not turning. I'm just defending someone who has been a good friend to me in my time of need.' Vicky and Bert were running behind schedule and, as they spoke, were hurling mounds of variously filled vol-au-vents on to silver salvers. They were in the kitchen of a large house in North London where David's nephew's coming-of-age was in full swing.

'I'm only teasing. Relax, I know you're not going to marry David. I mean, *zut alors*, pleeeeeeease, David!' Bert managed to make his name sound as if it stood for all that was depraved, twisted and repulsive about mankind. 'Mind you,' she continued, 'he looks quite presentable in black tie, doesn't he?'

Vicky squinted at Bert out of the side of her eye: she suspected her friend was trying to trap her into saying that she fancied David, which she didn't.

'Look, I'm not winding you up. Christ, I'm not saying he's Ilya Kuryiakin, I'm just saying that it's true what they say: men *do* look better wearing a dinner suit – and for an ugly porker, David doesn't look bad in his, O K?'

'Well, I'm sure he'd be very flattered to hear that, Bert.'

'Anyway if you must have a baby, *toute suite*, then why not have one with this Greg person? At least he's good-looking.'

'I don't think you have a baby by Greg if you can help it and I don't want to have a baby, like that, by just anyone. I want to meet someone nice that I like *and* fancy *and* want to have a baby with *and* think would be a good dad.'

'Oh, I see. Well, in that case, it'll have to be a gay man – the only problem being that he *may* not fancy you, gorgeous as you are.'

'Hah, hah. I'm sure that there are plenty of straight men who fit that description I just need to meet one . . . or two.'

'Well, don't hold your breath waiting for *that* list of particulars to materialize out of nowhere, especially if you're looking for it all in one man. A bunch of blokes cobbled together might measure up – but all in one bloke, I don't think so,' Bert sang out, picking up two huge trays in one swoop and gliding out of the kitchen.

Meaningless Sex

Vicky didn't really believe that there were plenty of available straight men who fitted her list of requirements wandering about on earth, but she wanted to. She minded terribly that she seemed to have become one of those women who thought about men in terms of types. She'd never pondered before about what kind of men were around. It bothered her that an unstoppable relationship radar seemed to have automatically switched itself on in her head and, what was worse, that it was trying to stand in her way of getting off with unsuitables. Vicky had selected Greg in a superhuman effort to deliberately defy the radar. She'd been doing her damnedest not to be relegated to the ranks of women-who-only-get-off-with-men-who-are-going-to-be-serious-about-them. Before now she had never had to worry about whether men would be serious about her. Even the Barney episode, years earlier, hadn't really thrown her. At the time, with Bert's help, she'd quickly come to the conclusion that, in fact, he was a wanker and therefore, no great loss. She'd always been one of those girls who take male interest in their stride. She'd never regarded it as something without which you had a sad, empty life or with which you had a wonderful, action-packed one. She was prepared to accept the broodiness but she was determined not to let it rule her life – for now, at any rate.

Greg was an actor who, like most actors, was in and out of work. Although he had movie-star good looks his finest hour, so far, had been punching the air as the mate of the bloke in a

Gillette ad, from which Bert had instantly recognized him. He had come into La Cantina during its final days looking for work and, not knowing the situation, had left his phone number in case anything came up. Going on his appearance alone, Bert had judged him to be the perfect little 'pick-me-up' Vicky needed to lift her spirits, but Vicky, not being Bert, had barely registered him. However, when it looked like an extra pair of hands were going to be needed for the bar mitzvah, Bert had produced Greg's number and Vicky had agreed to call him. She'd only intended to interview him but had found herself, totally out of character, asking him out instead. She put this down to having met up with him on a day that she was having a particularly aggressive power struggle with her radar. Their date had been arranged for just before the function so, acting on her natural sense of caution, Vicky had decided against hiring him, reckoning that she and Bert could probably cope on their own. Bert hadn't been at all pleased but when Vicky had put it to her that it had been a toss-up between an extra pair of hands or the potential for some meaningless sex, Bert had instantly seen reason.

A few weeks later, after they'd catered yet another bar mitzvah (this time for someone who'd heard of them via David's nephew's mum), Vicky and Bert made their way back to Bert's. Tess, who was babysitting, was waiting for them.

'So, dare I ask about the sex?' Bert ventured, once they were settled down with a bottle of wine.

'You had sex at a bar mitzvah?' Tess screeched in horror.

'Yes, it was great. He was only thirteen but very mature for his age and quite good at it, considering,' Vicky replied, maintaining a perfect dead-pan expression.

'Oh, Vic, that's disgusting. I mean, I'd expect that of Bert but what have you come to? A thirteen-year-old boy!'

'Excuse me, thank you very much! I am in the room, I do have the gift of hearing. She's winding you up. I was asking about the sex with Greg! She's been seeing that Greg and for the record I would not sleep with a thirteen-year-old boy, if you don't mind!'

'Well, I don't care either way, but the thirteen-year-old boy might have something to say about it!'

'Hah, hah, most amusing.'

'Anyway, who's Greg?'

'Greg, that actor off that "the best a man can get" ad. He came into La Cantina just before it closed down, looking for work. I told you about him. Don't you remember me saying that I thought he was just what Vicky needed?' Bert explained impatiently.

'Oh, yes, him, I remember – good-looking but stupid? Have you slept with him, then, Vic? I'd have thought, going by the description, he was much more Bert's kind of thing.'

'Thanks.'

Vicky and Tess ignored Bert's interjection.

'He is. But I've decided that something nice and fluffy might do me good, you know, don't want to go straight out of the frying-pan and into the fire, do I?' This was precisely the action that Vicky's radar was indicating she must take if her ovaries were to be heeded but, for now, she wasn't having any of it. 'As it happens,' she continued, 'the sex, if you're so interested, is pretty spectacular.'

'God, I can't believe it, you're actually going to tell us what the sex is like.' Bert was pleased: it looked like Vicky might be changing her ways.

'Well, not in the same graphic detail you retell everything, Bert, but up to a point I'm prepared to give you the high-lights,' Vicky said, in a gracious and deliberately condescending tone.

'OK, then, first off, did you give him a blow-job the first time?'

'Eurgh, no! Not on a first date, I hardly know him.' Bert laughed at Vicky's indignation.

'No, of course not. I mean, you'd fuck him on a first date, *naturellement*, but nothing so forward as giving him a blow-job.'

'Oh, I don't know, giving someone a blow-job always seems much more intimate than fucking them. I don't know why that is.'

'Actually, come to think of it, you're right. You can sort of contemplate fucking virtually anybody if you absolutely have to but giving them a blow-job is a whole different kettle *du poisson*,' Bert agreed, having thought about it for a moment.

'Don't know that I agree with you there, about virtually anybody but, still, you know what I mean. Oral sex seems a bit . . . oh, I don't know . . . exposing, I suppose, when you don't know someone that well.'

'Lucky you're not gay, Vic. There's not too much else on offer if you're not prepared to go below stairs,' Tess teased.

'As we well remember from your early am-I-aren't-I lesbian days. And look at you now – proper old carpet-muncher, aren't you?'

'Bert! That's a revolting expression.'

'It's all right, Vic, I'm used to her baseness, she can't help it.'

Bert gave Tess a huge false smile, baring her teeth and screwing up her eyes tightly.

'Anyway, do you like this Greg? Are you going to keep seeing him?' Tess asked. She wanted to show Vicky that she was pleased she'd finally got back in the water.

'Or are you taking him back to the shop as an unworn item?'

'Bert, he's not a pair of M and S tights! Yes, I am going to keep on seeing him. He's got a fantastic body and he's, ah, well, he's nice and quite –'

'And a good shag. Which, let's face it, is the only qualification required for the job in hand, so that's just as well, isn't it, Vic?

Even if he isn't as useful as a pair of tights,' Bert interrupted.

Tess gave Vicky a what-are-we-going-to-do-with-her expression and Vicky returned a noncommittal smile. Bert was both right and wrong as far as Greg was concerned. Vicky *did* fancy him and he *was* good in bed but he wasn't exactly a genius and she knew that, in the long term, she was wasting her time with him. For now, she was trying her best not to think about the future – it filled her with dread. Seeing Greg, she hoped, would help stave off the whole issue. She'd held her nose and jumped in feet first without looking down, sleeping with him the first time they'd gone out. She'd just had to: she'd known the radar would get the better of her if she waited.

Sell-by Date 1991

Slowly but surely, partly thanks to David recommending them far and wide but also through word-of-mouth, Vicky's catering business began to yield a decent living for herself and Bert. The trouble, for Vicky, was that it didn't provide her with any personal satisfaction. Her heart wasn't in it. She knew that people attending functions weren't very discerning about the kind of food they ate. They were there for the party or to be seen, not to marvel at her culinary skills. Vicky being Vicky naturally put her best effort into supplying delicious food but she couldn't help feeling it was all a bit pointless.

Bert, however, loved their new job. She was thrilled at always going to different places and meeting new people. For her, catering was a far more varied and interesting way of life than being stuck in the same place day after day, serving, by and large, the same boring people. But Vicky missed the every day sameness of the restaurant. To keep it successful had required a combination of sustained effort, application and imagination, and these constant demands on Vicky's time and energy had kept her active and creative. She missed the challenge and the drain on her resources. She found she had too much time to think now. Too much time to wonder how things were going to pan out for her and if they were ever going to go the way she wanted.

One day Vicky woke up and decided that she'd been living at Bert's for far too long. She resolved to find herself a flat. She was sure that if she didn't find something very soon she'd turn round and find that she and Bert were seventy and still arguing about what really constitutes a sell-by date. The argument had started when Vicky had discovered Bert head first in the kitchen bin retrieving a packet of biscuits that she'd thrown out, having used the sell-by date as her guide. Bert had protested that they were always a wild overestimation on the retailers' part. She was convinced that it was their ploy to ensure they never got sued for food poisoning and to make you buy more food than you needed. She hadn't even been deterred when Vicky had accused her of turning into her mother, reminding her of the rancid fare Angela had always kept festering in the fridge. Bert had refused to accept the comparison and simply accused Vicky of being ludicrously fussy. Her idiosyncratic interpretation of acceptable hygiene standards, along with her habit of forgetting to flush the loo, spurred Vicky's determination to find a place of her own.

Later that day Vicky bought every local paper she could find and set about scouring them for affordable flats. After several hours of phoning round, she had managed to make only three appointments. The first two places she saw were cheesy beyond belief. She couldn't imagine how they were ever going to be let. Consequently she entered the last place with a heavy heart. She'd been given the keys, so she was seeing it alone. Her spirits sank deeper as she opened the front door on to the flat's hall, which was only just big enough to accommodate the sweep of the door. It looked so grotty that Vicky momentarily contemplated not bothering to look around at all. Three doors led off the tiny hall and as Vicky turned to go she decided that she was being uncharacteristically defeatist and chose the door on her left. It led to a small bathroom: Yeah, just as I expected, bleurgh, she thought, as she turned to her right. This one opened on to a long, thin kitchen with a large window the width of the room at the end of it. Too small, yuk, Vicky thought, as she turned round and kicked open the last door. A huge, bright room was revealed with vast windows at either end. 'Wow!' Vicky said loud. 'This room's amazing! God, if I cleaned it up and filled it with my beautiful things it could be great.' She was delighted to see that there was a large fireplace with an open grate. It was filled with old cans and bits of rubbish and clearly hadn't been used for years but Vicky was already envisaging lying stretched out in front of a roaring fire. She left the flat feeling more cheerful than she had in ages.

Even considering the potential of the main room many people would have been put off by the grotty state of the place but it was exactly the sort of challenge that catapulted Vicky into action. She was the kind of person who, presented with an uneventful short cut or a scenic but tortuous route would invariably choose the latter. Bert and Tess called it her 'shirt-of-hair-bed-of-nails' trait. Her background hadn't honed this feature of her personality. For her, it was simply that the more blood, sweat and tears she produced in pursuit of something, however fruitless it might appear to others, the more worthwhile it made her feel as a human being.

Vicky signed a year-long contract for the studio flat, which ensured that she'd be forced to make a success of it, no matter how hard it proved. After a couple of weeks of relentless slog she'd succeeded in creating a showpiece. When Bert and Tess saw it first they were impressed and between them decided that their friend had turned the corner, she was going to be all right. To Vicky's satisfaction, they pronounced the finished product fit to be included in the pages of an interiors style magazine. As she settled down to her first full night alone in the flat she looked proudly round the big room that had previously looked so depressingly unpromising and thought, Imagine what I could do with a whole house! Vicky had put body and soul into producing a comfortable and elegant environment. However, once the work was over she was having to make every effort not to see the place as a stopgap. She was resolutely blinkering herself from the ever-present radar's interpretation of the flat as somewhere that would do 'for now' until she met *Cosmopolitan*'s Mr Right, moved into his palatial mansion and filled it with babies.

Shoulder Pads 1992

'*Sacre bleu!* What on earth are you wearing?' Bert howled, as Vicky walked into Tess's flat. Vicky ignored her and helped herself to a glass of wine.

'What's wrong with what she's wearing?' Tess asked, twisting her head round to get a look. She was glued to her usual prime position in front of the television, plonked right in the middle of the sofa. Their regular evenings were now dominated by *EastEnders*, to which they'd become addicted. Tess always tried to sit in the same place. It forced her friends to squeeze themselves in either side of her or sit on the floor.

'It's not starting for twenty minutes. Are you scared to get up in case someone nicks your seat? Better not laugh or you'll have to sit in your own pee for the rest of the evening!' Bert teased.

'I know very well that you *will* nick my place if I get up so that's why I'm not getting up. You always take the piss out of me for sitting here before it starts and then go and steal my spot when I get up. Anyway what's wrong with what Vic's wearing? She looks all right to me.'

'What's wrong with it? *What's wrong with it!* Look at those shoulder-pads – they're like house bricks!'

In spite of being irritated with Bert, Tess snorted with laughter, after which she immediately grimaced apologetically at Vicky.

'Bert, being the ignoramus she is, is probably unaware that shoulder-pads are back again and are *the* height of fashion. This

299

is a Joseph jacket and I am very pleased with it, thank you very much,' Vicky said.

'Bert is perfectly aware that shoulder-pads are back but not ones you could build a wall with!' Bert snapped.

'Yes, they are. Anyway, I don't care what you think. The jacket's great.' Vicky settled herself down as best she could next to Tess.

'Where did you get it?'

'Greg gave it to me as an anniversary present.'

'Anniversary present? *Mon Dieu*, have you been going out with him for a whole year?'

'Erm . . . yeah, a bit over, actually.'

'God, he hasn't done badly for a casual fling, has he?' Tess remarked.

'Well, you know, he *is* very nice and stuff . . .' Vicky said.

'Yes, but what about your breeding plans?'

'Nicely put, Bert. I'm not a prize cow. There's plenty of time left for me to have a baby. I'm just playing the field.'

'Vicky, sleeping with the same man for over a year is *not* playing the field, and you'd better watch out. You know what they say . . .'

'No. What do *they* say? Whoever *they* are.'

'Well, you don't hail a taxi with people in it, do you?'

'Eh?'

'What the fuck are you talking about?' Tess joined in.

'Look, you don't try and park your car in a space that's already taken, do you?'

'Park your car? What are you on about?'

'Oh, God, you two are so thick sometimes. It's obvious what I'm saying. I'm saying that if Vicky's already seeing someone she won't appear available to other people who might be more in the line of what she's ultimately looking for.'

'I thought you always reckoned that being unavailable makes

you even more attractive to the other person,' Vicky sneered.

'That's only when you're dealing with the sort of idiots I go out with! If you're after a proper grown-up type, like you need, then they'd probably just be put off if they thought you were with someone else.'

'Nah, bollocks,' Tess said, after giving it a moment's thought. 'Being unavailable always makes you more fanciable.'

'How would you know? You never go out with anyone any more. You just sleep with various girls here and there,' Bert said.

'Maybe, but I always fancy the girls who have girlfriends more than the ones who don't.'

'That's only because you want to see if you can get them to get off with you because you think that makes you more attractive than their girlfriends.'

'Either way, it proves that people who are officially unavailable are more attractive than those who'll go out with anyone . . . like you, Bert.'

'Hah, hah. Anyway, it's starting, shut up. But Vicky, u hiv bin varrned,' Bert said, in the kind of foreign accent only ever heard by actors in crappy horror films.

After that Vicky couldn't really concentrate on the soap, despite it being a particularly juicy episode filled with inter-family feuding and illicit sex. She was preoccupied. She herself couldn't believe she'd been seeing Greg for so long. She'd just drifted along with the relationship, knowing that he wasn't IT but not being able to see any point in giving him up. While she continued to see someone who, she secretly knew, didn't qualify as a potential father to her children, the relationship served its purpose in staving off the looming broodiness. However, it had alarmed her that Greg had given her an anniversary present, partly because she hadn't remembered that there was any particular day to be celebrated and partly because she didn't want to lead him on. By the time the soap opera's theme tune had started playing out another action-packed half-hour Vicky had decided that she was going to have to end it with Greg and confront head-on the wailings of her reproductive system.

To Vicky's surprise, Greg was shocked and upset to learn that she didn't reciprocate his feelings. He seemed to have thought they felt equally seriously about each other. Vicky couldn't help admiring the sheer gall of this assumption. The way he saw it, if he had feelings then it was signed, sealed and delivered that she reciprocated them. Maybe that's part of being an actor, she thought later, after she'd done the deed. Lucky old him, because although he was wrong this time, on the whole he's always going to assume that whatever he wants he gets. Greg had been absolutely sure that Vicky was having a momentary aberration and was mistaken in wanting to end the relationship. He was so confident of this that there'd been a moment when she'd even found herself hesitating and wondering if he was right. No, no, no. I can't spend the rest of my life with someone who wears hair-gel and spends forty minutes deciding which colour sweater to wear to an audition for a beer commercial! Vicky had reasoned to herself, when a little voice starting nagging away in her head, reminding her that, from now, she would have to heed the radar and all its transmissions.

Gratuitous Lesbian Sex Scenes

'You are never going to believe this. *I* can't believe it. Oh, my God, I'm so excited, you aren't going to believe it!'

'Tess, if you tell us what *it* is we can try. Just tell us what's going on.' Tess was panting: she'd raced round to Vicky's flat with the news the moment she'd heard – she hadn't wanted to tell them over the phone. She'd known they'd be in because she was aware that they were in the middle of preparing food for some do they were catering the next day.

'You are going to die when I tell you, just die!'

'Just bloody tell us, Tess. What is it?' Bert was beginning to get irritated with her. Vicky was smiling, waiting for her to calm down and reveal all.

'OK, get this. My latest script has been bought by a Hollywood studio, they're going to make it with a big star, it's going to be a proper movie!'

'Wow! That's brilliant, Tess, amazing, fantastic. God, good for you!' Vicky exclaimed.

'Is this the one with the woman who's married to the Mafia contract killer but she's realized she's gay and is having an affair with the woman lawyer they've got the contract out on and her husband is the one that's supposed to kill her?'

'Yeah, great, isn't it?'

'The one with all the gratuitous lesbian sex scenes?'

'They're not gratuitous.'

'But it is that script?'

303

'Yeah.'

'Brilliant! That is *brilliant*, Tess. Are you going to move to Hollywood now and get your tits done?' Bert remarked, making it sound as if the two events were inextricably linked.

'*My* tits don't need doing, thank you, madam. I don't think I'll be moving to Hollywood but I guess I'll have to go over there when shooting starts. God, it's so exciting I thought I was going to faint when I heard!'

'Well, sit down, tell us everything from the beginning – and don't eat anything,' Vicky commanded, gesticulating towards the one stool that fitted into her kitchen. Tess settled herself down and immediately started picking at the huge variety of ingredients strewn out over the counter.

'Well, my agent said I needed to write something more mainstream than the stuff I've been writing if I wanted it to sell for any real money, and after seeing him I was walking down that main road in town filled with porno shops, thinking, How am I ever going to write an action movie filled with blokes with guns and all that bollocks? because those are the sort of scripts people are looking for apparently. Anyway, I was sort of idly looking in the windows of all those cheesy shops and I suddenly noticed that most of the videos on display contain what they embarrassingly call "girl-on-girl action".'

'Yeah, all blokes love that stuff,' Bert interrupted.

'I didn't know that, did I? I mean, how could I? It seems pretty pointless to me, getting excited by something that completely excludes you but anyhow I started thinking – blokes would probably love a film with a traditional macho plot with guns and all that stupid stuff but with a twist. So that's what I wrote!'

'So basically you sold out your sisters for commercial gain?' Bert asked provocatively.

'No, I wrote about a topic I have no interest in, but from a perspective I *am* interested in.'

'And you put loads of saucy lesbian sex scenes in to make sure that blokes will want to watch it?' Bert was determined to get Tess to admit that she'd capitalized on her sexuality.

'No, I think the scenes are completely necessary. Anyway, what are you on about? Everything I've ever written has had some sex scenes in it and mainly between women!'

'Yeah, but a glamorous Mafia wife romping about on silken sheets with some gorgeous New York woman lawyer is *un petit peu* different from having to watch a couple of old trouts from the nineteen twenties frotting away in a ruined tennis pavilion!' Bert was referring to the one script of Tess's that had, so far, been made; it hadn't been very successful.

'It doesn't matter either way. Bert's just jealous. I think it's brilliant and you're brilliant, Tess,' Vicky said cheerfully. 'There's a bottle of champagne in the fridge. Get it out – we've got to keep going but let's have a drink.' Vicky was genuinely thrilled by Tess's news. But whether or not Bert was jealous, she couldn't be entirely sure she was wholly without envy herself. Tess's life was taking off in the most unexpected way possible, and here she was trying to invent new ways to make carrots look appetizing while attempting to ignore the deafening howls of her ovaries. However, it wasn't in her nature to spoil things and she wanted to celebrate properly.

Tess hopped off the stool and squeezed past her friends, pushing her way towards the fridge. 'What are all these flowers doing in here?' she asked as she pulled out the champagne.

'Ask Bert, it's her idea.'

'Yeah, I've had this fantastic brainwave. Instead of just doing the same old food, served in the same boring way, from now on we're going to branch out on new things. Everything will be wrapped in flowers and petals and leaves. It'll look really unusual and different!'

'Yeah and taste revolting. You couldn't persuade me to eat a daffodil even if it did have a hot sausage roll nestling in the middle of it!' Tess said, handing out the glasses.

'You don't *eat* the flowers, you idiot, they form part of the presentation, the look. It's a whole concept. Nobody's done this before. We're going to be the trendiest caterers in London.'

'Or gardeners, depending on which way it goes!' Bert stuck out her tongue at Tess.

'We'll see. Anyway, here's to your film, Tess,' Vicky said, raising her glass to toast her.

'And here's to your nibbles-cum-flora-and-fauna enterprise!' Tess replied, returning the compliment – sort of.

1993
A Purple Lycra Evening Dress

It hadn't taken much for Bert to persuade Vicky to let her try out her new idea. She'd agreed readily, not having strong feelings either way. The truth was that after plugging away at the business for nearly two years Vicky hadn't grown to like it any more than when they'd started. Bert, however, was becoming more and more innovative. Although she still couldn't cook and had no intention of learning, she was having increasingly ambitious ideas about how to expand the business and turn it into something different from a run-of-the-mill caterer's. Apart from one difficult moment when a guest was convinced the quiche slices had been wrapped in a blanket of poison ivy, their first experience with the new concept went well, and Vicky and Bert decided to persevere with it. Bert was very excited and managed to persuade Vicky that they should go the whole hog, having flowery business cards designed and placing advertisements in a couple of up-market magazines.

Until then they'd been catering on a local level for fairly modest functions. Bert reasoned that, along with being more adventurous with their presentation, they needed to set their sights higher in terms of the kind of people they catered for. Vicky was content to be swept along by her enthusiasm.

Little by little things took off and the requests for their service were coming from an ever more fashionable set of clients. Bert decided they'd definitely made it when they got a booking to do the wedding of an ex-model to a minor member of the aristocracy.

Two days before the wedding Bert and Vicky were slaving away at creating the medieval feast that the bride's mother had pretentiously, in Vicky's view, requested.

'I can't believe I'm doing yet another wedding!' Vicky moaned.

'At least we've never dressed a pig's head before so that makes a nice change!' Bert laughed.

'It's still a bloody wedding, though.'

'I think weddings are much better than cocktail parties. At least there's something to get stuck into. We get to put on a huge display, not fiddle about manufacturing all those little things people want when they're "not really providing food",' Bert said, imitating the instructions every client invariably gave when describing the kind of spread they wanted when they didn't want to spend money on proper food but didn't want their friends to think they were stingy.

'We seem to do nothing but weddings. It's like the whole world keeps getting married!' Vicky continued.

'Oh, I get it. Always the bridesmaid and never the bride, is that it?' Bert replied.

'Yeah, something like that.'

'Oh, Vic, you don't really want a big wedding with the whole dress-and-cake-and-flowers palaver, do you? It'd be a nightmare and, anyway, who'd do the catering?'

'I do. I want to have children and be married and be all safe and know what I'm doing.'

Bert looked at her friend and realized that she'd better tread carefully as Vicky looked like she might be serious. 'Vic, being married doesn't mean your life gets instantly sorted out. It just means that you're married. Nothing else changes, you know that.'

'Well, I'm going to marry David,' Vicky announced, and Bert laughed.

'Yeah, well, that's a good idea.'

'No, I am. I am going to marry David. I've decided.'

'Yeah, why not? It'll be a laugh!'

'Bert, I'm serious. I've made my mind up. I'm going to marry David.'

Bert glanced at Vicky for a moment. She didn't know what to say, she was waiting for her to crack a smile, which she didn't.

'Look, he loves me. He's kind, generous, loyal, faithful . . .'

'Fat, boring, unattractive, plodding, and more important than any of that – you don't love him,' Bert said.

'I do!'

'No, you don't!'

'I do!'

'Victoria Montague. Hello, have we met? You are not in love with David Winkleman. I would know if you were!'

'OK, all right, maybe not in love, *in love*, but I do love him in a deeper, more mature way . . .'

'Oh, yeah, right, in that deeper, more mature way when the idea of having to sleep with them makes you feel sick! That way, yeah? You are going to have to have sex with him if you marry him, Vicky. You do realize that, don't you?'

'Of course I know that! Anyway, the idea of sleeping with him does not make me feel sick. Unlike you I don't think looks are everything and anyway you can learn to have great sex with a person you didn't initially . . . erm . . .' Vicky struggled to find the right word to describe what she didn't feel about David. She didn't want it to sound too damning.

'Fancy?'

'Yes, all right, fancy. God, think how many blokes you've fancied in your life and then gone right off.'

'But I never said I was going to marry any of them!'

'Look, Bert, I don't happen to think fancying someone is the be-all or end-all. There are more important, lasting things than that. I want to have children. I'm nearly thirty-four years old,

I've hardly got any time left, David is devoted to me and I *am* really fond of him. Christ, plenty of marriages are based on a lot less solid ground than that.'

'Vicky, this is a panic buy!' Vicky gave Bert a blank look: she didn't know what she meant. 'You know,' Bert continued, 'like when you go to the sales all revved up to spend money and it's really annoying because there's nothing you want, so you end up buying a purple Lycra evening dress or something else you look shit in, just so that you've bought *something*. That's what you're doing. David is a purple Lycra evening dress!'

'No, he isn't! He's a considered choice based on – on – on – an adult friendship, mutual respect and admiration.'

'You don't love him like you loved Tom!' Bert hadn't wanted to bring Tom into this. She knew that being reminded of him would hurt Vicky but at this point she felt desperate measures were called for if she was to stop her friend from making the biggest mistake of her life.

'No, I don't, and thank God. That kind of love wouldn't have lasted – Tom couldn't have sustained a lifelong commitment.'

'That doesn't mean you'll never find the same sort of love again but with someone who could sustain a long-term thing!'

'Yes, it does. That kind of love has a built-in self-destruct – it's part of why it's so intense.' Vicky had become increasingly convinced of the truth of this theory over the last few years.

Bert didn't have an answer. She suspected that her friend might be right, but she didn't think that it justified settling for any old bloke instead. 'OK, well, what about David? Do you think it's fair? He's in love, *in love*, with you, remember? Will you be telling him that you're not actually in love with him or is that a minor detail?'

'He knows I'm really fond of him and he's too grown up to set much store by in-loveness and all the myths that go with it.'

'Yeah, well, he'll probably just be so overcome with gratitude that he won't dare quiz you about anything, like why you've suddenly come round after all these years.'

'Bert, don't make him sound like a lap-dog. He's a really decent bloke and I won't have you making fun of him!'

Bert gave Vicky a look of total incredulity. 'I can't believe that you, with all your beauty and talent and elegance and everything, are giving up like this.'

'I'm not *giving up*, I'm growing up. I'm facing the fact that you have to make compromises in life and that it's not all about doing exactly what you want, whenever you want and everything turning out fine regardless!'

'But don't you think you're taking the whole compromising thing a bit far? Doing something your heart isn't really in doesn't automatically make it *a good thing*. This is you taking your obsession with picking something really hard and trying to make it work to the most ridiculous extreme! David is a purple-Lycra-evening-dress-shirt-of-hair-bed-of-nails.'

'No, he isn't and I'm not going to discuss this any more. I know what I'm doing.'

'Well, it's your funeral,' Bert yelled at Vicky, who didn't respond.

After a few moments of deafening silence she and Bert continued with their work. Neither said a word to the other for the rest of the day.

The idea of marrying David had been lurking about in Vicky's head since she'd broken up with Greg. Every time she'd thought about it the arguments against had seemed less and less tenable. Her main objection had always been not fancying him even one tiny little bit. However, that had seemed like an increasingly spurious excuse, given that she'd fancied the pants off Greg but wouldn't have had him impregnate her even if he'd held a certificate guaranteeing that every single one of his sperm could produce a Nobel Prize winner.

There had been no dramatic change in their relationship but one day, when they'd met for lunch, David, seeing that Vicky wasn't her old self, had taken the opportunity to make it clear that he'd be there for her, come what may. He wasn't a fool and had wisely eschewed going down on bended knee or making a sudden display of wild passion. Instead David had engineered a conversation about the importance of building a family and the long-term commitment it required. Although he'd been careful to make his comments general, everything he'd said had been music to Vicky's ears. The lunch had ended with her telling him, to her own surprise, that she was going to give his proposal some serious thought.

Vicky couldn't help admiring David's tenacity and had come to appreciate that, in one way at least, he perfectly fitted the fantasy she'd always had about finding a man whose certainty would allay all her fears. As David seemed to know so definitively what he wanted, she was able to take comfort knowing that he wasn't going to be put off by her reservations. The more she'd thought about it, the more she'd become convinced that it was the right thing to do. Having decided that there was a distinct advantage in being with someone who didn't make her heart leap, she even managed to find a way round the not-fancying-him-one-tiny-little-bit problem. After the misery of the last few years Vicky felt that there would be a calm luxury in knowing that he'd be right there, rock solid as ever, irrespective of how she behaved. She made up her mind, and when Vicky did something, she did it right. She resolved that, far from playing fast and loose with David's feelings (particularly since he'd waited in the wings so patiently, for so long), she would reward him by turning herself into the Perfect Wife. Having made her decision she surrendered happily to David's offensive, feeling that he had earned her.

Vicky Tries to Make It Special

Vicky and Bert were back on speaking terms almost immediately. They had to be, given that they saw each other at least three times a week for work. Even when they weren't actually preparing for a do, there were always bookings and bills and other administrative issues to deal with. Apart from the cooking they'd shared all aspects of running the business and trying to do so separately now, they both knew, just wasn't possible. However, the atmosphere between them was tense. Vicky knew that Bert thought she was making the biggest gaffe of her life but she felt that, as one of her two oldest and best friends, Bert should support her in her decision, no matter how much *she* disagreed with it. Vicky had also made her mind up that Bert's objections were largely motivated by jealousy. Bert wasn't jealous. The possible negative repercussions of Vicky's marriage on *their* relationship hadn't yet crossed her mind. She simply didn't want her pal to settle for less than she deserved. As Vicky steamed away, going at full tilt with the grand plans for her wedding, Bert managed, with some difficulty, to hold her tongue as she watched her friend doing all she could to transform herself into the Bride of the Year.

Tess had been away in America for her first round of meetings with the studio that had bought her script and had missed the whole Vicky-turns-into-a-proper-girlie drama. The moment she'd returned Bert didn't waste a moment before filling her in with Vicky's plans. She was convinced that Tess would feel the same as her and might even be persuaded to help her hatch a plot to dissuade Vicky from slipping any further into her Mills and Boon fantasy. To her fury, Tess refused to agree with her view of what their friend's nuptials meant.

'This is that Barney-getting-a-blow-job-in-the-bog-at-that-party thing all over again and you're not going to say anything!'

'Bert, the thing is, I'm no sure that she *is* making such a big mistake. She's never really been happy since the restaurant closed down and Tom left and she does get on with David, you know. Maybe it'll work out.'

'Listen, if Vicky was a person who'd never been OIL properly then I might agree with you, but she has. In the back of her mind she knows what she's giving up!'

'There you go, you see? She knows what she's doing.'

'No, there *you* go. She knows exactly what it is that she imagines she can live without for the rest of her life – the Rest of Her Life, do you get it? Not just a couple of weeks, For Fucking Ever!'

'Look, I hear what you're saying –'

'Oh God, don't start speaking like an American. Of course you *hear* what I'm saying – you aren't deaf so it naturally follows that you hear what I'm saying.'

'Keep your hair on. Christ, it's only an expression. Anyway, you know what Vicky's like when she's made her mind up. Nothing we say will shift her now. The more we object the more annoyed she'll get and then we'll all fall out and then it'll be just you and me left and that'd be awful because you can't cook and you're always shagging about.'

Bert laughed in spite of feeling very irritated. 'Not any more! I haven't got time. The business is really taking off.'

'What? So people like eating flowers, do they?'

Bert smiled: she could quite happily let Tess take the piss now that things were going so well.

'So you've replaced meaningless sex with a career. That's good.'

'Eh?'

'That's what me and Vic reckon you've been doing all these years, shagging about instead of concentrating on a career. It's a great diversionary tactic is sex.'

'Well, hopefully they aren't mutually exclusive. I wouldn't mind having a shag at least once again before I die.'

'You might get one at Vic's wedding. David's probably got some nice cousins – perhaps even a brother, you never know!' Tess grinned stupidly at Bert.

'So that's it, is it? Instead of waiting for Mr Right, we're going to let our best mate marry Mr Oh-All-Right-Then, are we?'

'Looks like it. Are we going to be bridesmaids? I love the idea of getting all dressed up in chiffon and lace and carrying a posy.'

'Hah, hah. The way things are going between me and Vicky I'll be lucky if I get invited to the wedding at all.'

'Well, you're just going to have to make it up with her, Bert. I'm not spending the rest of my life playing go-between. Anyway, at the end of the day, who cares who she gets married to? We've never let a bloke come between us before – except for Barney and we were kids then, so it doesn't count. And honestly David, of all people, can't be the one who splits us up after more than twenty years of rock-solid friendship!'

'Yeah, I know you're right, it's just that it seems such a waste. Oh, and by the way, better not let Vic hear you say "David, of *all* people" like that. Remember, he's everything she ever wanted and not a purple Lycra evening dress,' Bert replied.

Tess laughed. She didn't know specifically what Bert meant but she got the general drift and the image of David as a last-minute mistake purchase struck her as very funny, if a little cruel.

The next time Vicky and Bert were alone together Bert decided to make amends. 'Listen, I'm really sorry. I haven't been very . . .

er . . . erm . . .' Bert couldn't think of an appropriately diplomatic word to describe her continued inability to see David as anything other than a total disaster '. . . er . . . enthusiastic about you marrying David. But, you know, if it's what you want and it's going to make you happy then that's good enough for me.' Vicky was deeply touched by Bert's climb-down. She suspected that her friend probably hadn't changed her mind but appreciated that she'd done the next best thing, which was to shut her trap. All the same, she couldn't help wondering how long Bert was going to be able to keep it up.

As the date approached for the wedding and the preparations became more and more elaborate even Tess was shocked by how much Vicky seemed to be metamorphosing. And never so much as the day she announced where the ceremony was to take place.

'You're getting married in a synagogue!'

'Yes – so? I *am* Jewish,' Vicky replied defensively. She'd known that Tess and Bert would go berserk when she told them about the wedding's recently decided-upon venue.

'A synagogue? You've never been in a synagogue in your life!'

'No, I know that, but David wants it to be a proper Jewish ceremony and . . . you know, that's fine with me. I've got no real objection to a synagogue. You wouldn't be surprised if I was marrying someone else in a church.'

'Yes, we would. We've never gone to church, in a churchy-religious way, apart from Founder's Day at school, and that doesn't count because they made us go. You've never been to a synagogue. Don't you think it's a bit hypocritical?'

'No, I don't, as it happens. David was bar-mitzvahed and everything, so it's important to him and that makes it important to me.'

Tess didn't say anything, but short Bert a look. This was the first time she'd voiced any form of objection to Vicky's plans. Bert hadn't got involved in the argument, having recently learnt her lesson already. Tess could tell from Bert's expression that she wasn't going to back her up. It was also telling her that, at this stage, opposition was fruitless anyway.

Vicky was enjoying herself immensely organizing the wedding. It was proving to be time-consuming, extremely hard work and all-encompassing – in short, everything that made her feel worthy. The more time she spent with David the more she convinced herself that she'd made a sound choice. Despite now being officially engaged they still hadn't slept together, which had been Vicky's idea. She'd put it to her fiancé that, as they'd succeeded in building up such a good relationship so far without having done so, they should save it until the wedding night, thereby making it extra special. Vicky chose not to tell Bert and Tess about this decision. She knew that Bert would interpret it as proof that she was admitting that fancying someone was, after all, an essential ingredient for a happy marriage. And Tess, she was pretty sure, would make her feel uncomfortable by waxing on about how romantic a gesture it was.

Vicky's decision to hold off was actually motivated by something else entirely. She was aware that the sight of David didn't send her into a frenzy of unbridled lust. She was also aware that the thought of sleeping with him didn't make her feel sick. Vicky's feelings were suspended somewhere between the two and she'd decided that delaying their sex life until after they were legally married would preclude any danger of going off him beforehand, causing her to wreck all her plans. Right from the start, Vicky had resolved not to worry about the impending physical side of their relationship. Occasionally, anxiety about what David looked like in the nude crept into her head but she quickly dismissed it and turned her attention to her wedding-cake and other matters of equal importance.

By her reckoning, she had made a sensible and pragmatic decision to enter into a union and there was no call for either slush or passion. Much to her relief, David seemed to be in agreement. His demeanour towards her had remained unchanged since she'd agreed to marry him. She'd feared that he might suddenly turn all lovey-dovey and sloppy but, as ever, he'd taken his lead from her. Vicky saw herself as a modern-day version of a Victorian bride, a sensible woman who was marrying for companionship and predictability, not for nightly bouts of rampant sex with a man who might send her a fax without a word of warning. And she was quite happy with this new self-image.

'Look I know you're in the middle of organizing the Wedding of the Year but we do still have a business to run and I can't do it on my own!'

'You're right, I'm sorry. You're going to have to hire someone to replace me.'

'What? You're giving up work as well?' Bert had been increasingly irritated by Vicky's failure to pull her weight when dealing with the business but it had never occurred to her that Vicky might give it up completely.

'For the time being, anyway. I really need to concentrate on the wedding full-time and then there's the honeymoon, so I'll be away anyway. But, listen, after I'm back and things have settled down I'll come back to work properly.'

'Mmm, well, you'd better,' Bert said grumpily. As far as she was concerned Vicky might as well go the whole hog, wear a veil and walk twenty paces behind David from now on if she was ready even to contemplate giving up her career on top of all the other alterations she'd made to herself in pursuit of becoming the Perfect Wife.

1993
No Sausages

'Oh, God, I hate this. I feel like a six-year-old in a party frock.'

'And you look like one too.'

'At least that's better than having my tits hanging out.'

'They are not hanging out. I am showing a pleasant amount of cleavage, which is well within the bounds of decency. You're just saying that because you're really a Mother Superior struggling to get out of some rampant-shagger's body.'

Tess laughed. 'Actually, do you think you can say shagger when talking about exclusive girl-on-girl action?'

'I don't see why not. Nothing in the word shag indicates a penis.'

'Bert, ssh, that woman in the awful hat just looked round. Don't talk about penises in here. Anyway, listen, seriously, do I look like a lampshade?'

'No, of course not.'

'Good, I'm not used to wearing this kind of thing. I feel very self-conscious,' Tess said, looking down at the cream and pale green patterned suit she was wearing.

'Not a *lampshade* – more of a loose-fitting sofa cover.'

'Fuck off.'

'Oh, so I can't mention penises but "fuck off" is obviously fine. Remember, you are in the house of God, there'll be no fucks here.'

'Or anywhere else today. Have you seen the rest of the guests?'

'You can't have been planning to cop off at Vic's wedding. I wouldn't hold my breath if I were you. Take a look around – we know hardly anyone here and they're not *exactly* your type.'

'There doesn't even look like there's anyone here that's *your* type and that's really saying something. I guess they're mainly David's friends and family. I haven't even seen any of Vic's awful mates from art college or anyone from La Cantina days.'

'Vic's dad's over there with his latest ten-year-old girlfriend and Petra's here.'

'Oh, I haven't seen her. Is she out yet, or did she marry the Spanish lober?'

'You'll be surprised to hear that I haven't got round to asking her that yet. She's on her own, at any rate, so if you get desperate you could always make a move on her.'

'Have you seen Vic's mum? I had a word with her on the way in, she doesn't look too happy, does she?'

'Well, would you? Your beautiful, accomplished daughter gives up everything to spend the rest of her life with a sausage roll. Not exactly how anyone thought Vic was going to end up, is it?'

'Bert! No penises. And definitely no sausages either – you're in a synagogue,' Tess hissed.

The pair had been sitting in their allotted seats for over forty minutes, awaiting the bride's arrival, and were having an increasingly hard time taking Vicky's wedding seriously. To their extreme relief, having guessed that they wouldn't do the job properly, she hadn't asked them to be bridesmaids, opting for flower-girls and pageboys instead. However, she had given her friends a stern directive as to what kind of outfit she deemed acceptable. Characteristically Tess had complied and was wearing a knee-length silk dress with a matching jacket. Her discomfort was mainly caused by how completely unused she was to wearing smart, well-fitting clothes. Notwithstanding, she looked very attractive and completely unlike her normal self. Tess had always gone out of her way to wear loose, nondescript clothes. Her wardrobe had greatly improved since she'd come out of the closet but its message had remained the same: judge-me-for-what's-inside-and-not-for-how-much-of-my-body-is-on-view-or-else. Bert, although never as effort-lessly elegant as Vicky, had always been interested in fashion and had chosen to ignore Vicky's attempt to dictate her manner of dress. Consequently she was wearing a voluminous lilac linen trouser suit. The jacket was close-fitting and buttoned up, revealing an inch less bosom than a saucy barmaid might think suitable for an evening pulling pints. Tess was confident their friend would disapprove.

Eventually Vicky arrived, looking serene and resplendent in a pale pink dull satin dress. Bert and Tess exchanged impressed looks and, affected as they were by the pomp of the whole procedure, managed to behave until almost the very end of the ceremony. As the couple came together for their post-vow kiss. Bert muttered to Tess out of the side of her mouth, 'Do you think David's squeezed himself into a girdle specially for the occasion? He looks a bit slimmer than normal.'

Tess let out a snort of loud laughter, causing most of the congregation to turn their heads sharply in her direction. Morti-fied, she produced a hanky and attempted to disguise her outburst as tears of joy while Bert succeeded in looking as if butter wouldn't melt in her mouth.

Afterwards, at the reception, Bert and Tess finally managed to get a moment with Vicky, who had been whizzing around controlling the caterers, the musicians and various guests' move-ments in her attempt to ensure that the whole thing went without a hitch.

'Relax, Vic, will you? It's all fine. You're supposed to be having a good time, not cracking the whip. That's somebody else's job today.'

'I just want to make sure everything goes to plan. But, anyway, I'm fine now, fine. So, are you having a good time?'

'Yeah, it's great, food's great, champagne's great. You look absolutely lovely by the way, really, really beautiful. David is very lucky,' Bert replied. She was being completely sincere – in fact she couldn't get over just how lucky she thought he was.

Vicky shot her a fierce look to check that she wasn't taking the piss. 'Yeah, well I'm lucky too,' she said, once she was confident that Bert wasn't winding her up.

Bert glanced sideways at Tess, who quickly changed the subject. 'I see Nil-by-mouth Nadine's here, and with a brood of kids.'

'Yeah, I thought I ought to invite some of my family.'

'Judging by the way she looks I'd say her Nil-by-mouth rule obviously doesn't apply to Danish pastries!' Bert piped up, blowing out the sides of her cheeks and folding her chin into her chest. Unable to stop themselves, the three friends hunched over and burst out cackling.

'Darling, are you all right? Hello, Bert, Tess.'

The trio looked up to find David standing in front of them looking disapproving.

Vicky snapped immediately into her recently adopted Perfect Wife mode. 'Yes, darling. Bert just made a silly joke, nothing worth repeating. How are you getting on?'

'I'm fine. You girls OK? Circulating all right? Meeting lots of handsome, eligible men I hope,' David said, giving his new wife's two friends a patronizing smile.

'Yeah, loads. My dance-card's already full,' Bert said, smirking at Tess.

Vicky narrowed her eyes and glared at her.

'Well, that's great, then. Victoria, my love, I wonder, if you have a moment, could you come over and meet an old colleague of mine? I'd like to be extra attentive to him, he doesn't know many people here and we've got a lot of mutual investments.'

Without a moment's hesitation Vicky said, 'I'd be delighted, of course, darling. I'll see you later, girls,' she said, not looking at them as she walked off.

'She'd only been here two minutes! Honestly.'

'Don't be silly, Bert. She's got to mingle, she can't stick beside us all day – we're not at school.'

'I know but, oh, God, it feels so weird. I mean look at all this – calligraphied place-cards, little net pouches filled with sugared almonds, a room full of freaks chomping away on smoked-salmon bridge rolls wearing pancakes on their heads. It's like something out of a corny fifties movie. And Vicky, look at her over there, pretending she's fascinated by some boring friend of David's. God give me strength. Tess, really, is this it?'

'Look, she's obviously trying to fit in with David's way of life. She might as well – she has married him, after all.'

'Yeah, I know, but I wish she hadn't. I never thought I was going to have to watch Vic, of all people, turn into Doris Day.'

'I suppose you both thought that was going to be me?'

'Nah, we were convinced you were going to turn into – who was it again?'

'Julie Andrews?'

'No, no, not her.'

'Deborah Kerr?'

'No, no, the other one.'

'Debbie Reynolds?'

'No, no, oh, I remember now, yeah – Norman Bates.'

'Hah, hah! And instead I turned into a gorgeous, fabulously successful lipstick lez – who'd have thought it?' Tess replied, as she swooped up another couple of glasses of champagne from the passing waiter's tray.

1994

Where the Fuck Is Totteridge?

'Where's Tabatha? I thought she was coming with us,' Tess said, climbing into the passenger seat of Bert's car which, apart from Bert, was empty.

'She decided not to come at the last minute. She wants to revise for her mocks.'

'Ah, that's my girl. I really did a marvellous job with her, didn't I?'

'Yeah, and all on your own as well. You are incredible.'

'Hah, hah. So fill me in, what's been going on while I've been away? Have you shagged that André yet?' Tess demanded, as they set off on their journey. They were on their way to visit Vicky and her recently born baby in the new house she'd moved to, miles away from their area. Neither Bert nor Tess had been there before.

'No, I told you when I took him on. He's a bloody good cook and I can't afford to lose him, especially now that it looks like Vic's never going to come back.'

'Wow, you really are a proper grown-up now, aren't you?'

'If choosing a good chef over a good shag is what constitutes "grown-up" then I suppose I am. God, how depressing. Do you know? I haven't had sex since . . . since . . .' Bert paused to think.

'Stop pretending you have to think about it. I know you know *exactly* how long it's been, down to days, hours and minutes!'

Bert laughed. She did know but she didn't want it to look like she'd been keeping count. 'Yes, all right, clever clogs, since just before Vicky's wedding, around the time I took over the business.'

'See? I was right. Sex *was* a substitute for success.'

'Well, why just for me and not you? You said you'd been having it off with that actress from your film and it doesn't seem to have affected your success.'

'That's different. Turns out that everybody in showbusiness sleeps around, which is great. But, more importantly, I didn't start sleeping with people until after I'd found out what I wanted to do with my life. You, my friend, started having sex *before* you had any idea what you were going to do with yours. Do you see how that one mistake changed the course of your entire life and destined you to be the sad washed-up old bag we see before us today?'

'You left out successful.'

'Sorry, the sad washed-up successful old bag we see before us today.'

'That's better. Anyway, I'm not sure I agree that things like that are mistakes as such. It's just the way it went, you know, sort of. Obviously *some* of my choices have been a little more dodgy than others but not all of them. At least I got the vast majority of my shagging out of the way before I started on a proper career.'

'Bert, it isn't homework! It's not something you have to get done before you can do something nice. It's not like there's a set quota of shagging you *have* to do. You know you could have always not shagged, did that ever occur to you?'

'Going on the available evidence, obviously not!'

Tess laughed. She liked it that Bert didn't feel the need to deny her former way of life. She found it particularly reassuring since it was very much what Vicky had been doing since she had decided to marry David. Their lavish wedding had taken place nearly a year ago, since when the three had not seen as much of each other as they used to. On the surface they put this down to their busy schedules: Tess was tied up with her film and a large amount of Bert's time was consumed by the growing catering business. However, both of them suspected secretly that Vicky's change in circumstances might be the real cause.

'Well, at least I didn't marry my lawyer and move to Totteridge,' Bert said, looking round contemptuously at the highly developed suburban countryside that was opening out before them.

'Where the fuck is Totteridge, anyway?'

'You've got the map. You tell me. I thought you had the directions. Vic told me she'd given them to you!'

'No, I can see where Totteridge is on the map, I know where we're going . . . I think. I meant *where* is it? What kind of place is it? What kind of people live there? How come we've all lived in London our entire lives and I've never even heard of Totteridge?'

'Oh, I see what you mean. People like David, I suppose – and footballers, the kind of person who wants to pretend to live in the country but really wants to be in London. I'm sure there was a girl at school who lived in Totteridge but she wasn't one of our lot.'

'She wouldn't have been if she lived up here!' Tess snorted, nodding at a couple of mock-Tudor mansions that stood back from the road. 'Blimey!' she continued. 'Look at the size of these houses. Even out here they must cost a fortune. I didn't realize David was that rich.'

'Well, that was partly how he got the job, wasn't it?'

'What job?'

'The job of being Vic's husband. He applied for a position he was massively under-qualified for, wasn't ever in the running, hung around being nice and it paid off – he got the job.'

'Bert! Vic didn't marry him for money, she married him because he was dependable and – and –' Tess floundered.

326

'Can't think of anything else, can you?' Bert interrupted.

' – and not like Tom.'

'Plenty of people could have qualified on that score. Anyway, part of being dependable is having money, isn't it?'

Tess supposed Bert was right. 'Oi, oi, slow down, stop, stop, this is it,' she said suddenly, waving frantically at a pair of brick pillars standing on either side of an entrance immediately to their left.

'Thanks for giving me so much warning,' Bert shouted, as she screeched to a halt and manoeuvred the car into the gravel driveway.

'Well, you shouldn't have been driving like a bloke!'

Bert was about to retort when Vicky's house loomed into view.

'Fucking hell!' they both exclaimed. Standing before them was a massive mock-Tudor mansion arranged on two floors, evenly spread out above a large porch and boasting a huge array of vast, leaded windows. It looked like a cross between a country pub and a golf club. They'd never known anyone who lived in a place like this. Neither Tess nor Bert could envisage their best friend residing happily in the hideous, ostentatious pile that stretched in front of them.

Vicky had obviously heard them coming up the drive for by the time they got out of the car she was standing inside the stone porch waiting for them.

'Fuck me, me old china, it's like Buckingham Palace!' Bert shouted across the expanse of the driveway in a loud fake-Cockney accent.

Tess laughed but Vicky's face turned sour and she hissed, 'Sshh, Bert, language! My neighbours aren't used to people like you.'

'People like me? What? You mean peasants?' Bert called, with exaggerated innocence.

'Oh, you know what I mean. Anyway, come in, come in,'

327

Vicky said, beckoning them over. She was genuinely trying to be friendly but Bert's theatrics had irritated her. Bert looked around and couldn't find another house in sight, let alone a neighbour. She and Tess walked towards the house exchanging desperate glances. Both knew exactly what the other was thinking: their friend was turning into an alien.

Vicky showed them into the living room, a large, sunny room spanning the entire width of the house. It was filled with the sort of plush furniture so brilliantly white that it looks like it's daring you to sit on it without making a mark. The windows stretched the length of the longest walls taking in the extensive panorama at the front and back. At the rear, a very well-tended garden spread out as far as the eye could see. It was so large it looked more like a small park. Once they were settled down, to Bert and Tess's utter amazement, a tea-trolley was wheeled in by a middle-aged Hispanic woman wearing an apron.

'Is that the staff then, m' lady?' Bert whispered using the same Cockney accent she had ill-advisedly used a few moments earlier.

'One of them,' Vicky replied, in an icy tone that instantly made it clear to Bert that she'd better not start taking the piss out of her for having a housekeeper. Vicky didn't want to make her friends uncomfortable but she also didn't want to have to start justifying her new lifestyle.

That afternoon was the most excruciatingly awkward the three had spent together since the day they'd met. The conversation was stilted and formal. They all felt as if the special knack they'd always had for instantly understanding each other had evaporated into thin air. At one point Tess momentarily contemplated talking about the actress she was sleeping with but everything about Vicky's demeanour forbade any kind of intimacy. It was clear to her visitors that any attempt at the familiar bawdy banter that had always been the mainstay of their relationship would be very unwelcome.

After tea, as if sticking to a timed regime, a uniformed nanny brought in Vicky's baby girl, Rebecca. Once the nanny had left the room, Bert, being Bert, couldn't help making a stab at teasing her friend into normality. She was desperately hoping that it might coax her into dropping her guard and letting even a tiny bit of her old self sneak through.

'Vic, she called you Mrs Winkleman!' Bert giggled.

'Yes. So what? That's my name,' Vicky said frostily, while bouncing her little girl on her knee.

'Mrs Winkleman? You've changed your name? I never realized you'd changed your name. You actually let people call you Vicky Winkleman?' Bert continued, ignoring Vicky's response, confident that she could crack her veneer.

'Why wouldn't I? It's my name now.'

'But, Vic, "Vicky Winkleman" sounds like an instrument you use for eating cockles!' Bert howled. Tess snorted with laughter, spraying soggy biscuit crumbs out of her mouth with tremendous force and scattering them all over the luxurious pale cream deep-pile carpet. Vicky looked down at the floor and then at Tess. Her expression was a mixture of disgust and dismay as she silently handed her a napkin.

Feeling very uncomfortable, Bert and Tess started to make all the appreciative noises about Vicky's baby that they guessed she expected them to make. Their task was made all the more difficult by the baby's uncanny resemblance to her not very attractive father. Her body looked like two white footballs stuck together, the smaller of which having a black loo brush stuck to the top of it. Luckily, Vicky was so enchanted by her child that she didn't seem to notice anything unnatural in the laboured compliments her friends were attempting to make.

The visit soon limped to a creaking end and they parted company with lame promises to see each other soon. Vicky closed the door on her departing guests, knowing exactly what they would be talking about all the way home: how much she'd changed. She knew she'd changed but, unlike her friends, she didn't mind. She resented the fact that, as she saw it, they only wanted her to be the way she'd always been. As far as Vicky was concerned it was their duty to accept her as she was now and that was all there was to it. Her current mindset did not allow for the possibility that their resistance in doing so might be attributable to her and not, for once, the fault of their customary opposition to outside developments in each other's lives.

Vicky guessed that they'd be busy dismissing her life as a sham but she didn't think she was kidding herself. She was prepared to concede to having made self-conscious efforts to be a certain way, the way that she'd decided a Perfect Wife should be. To her, they were the inevitable adjustments required for married life. But she wouldn't accept that this was proof she was living a lie. For her, reassurance that she hadn't made a mistake came in the form of how she now felt which, just as she'd predicted, was safe and cosy. No more and no less. The sex, her only real area of concern prior to the wedding, had proven perfectly bearable. As a lover, Vicky had found David competent and considerate without being slavish. Most importantly, to her enormous relief, he hadn't shown any grovelling gratitude for having finally been allowed to get his end away with her. All the same, Vicky had been relieved to discover that David was the kind of man who lost interest in sex when his wife becomes pregnant. Above all, once the baby had been born, every alteration Vicky had made to herself to rationalize being with him had instantly become a price worth paying.

After the housekeeper Maria had hoovered up the mess Tess had made, Vicky settled down in a luxurious armchair overlooking her opulent garden and set about planning that evening's menu. She turned a resolute deaf ear to the dissenting voices.

She had made her bed and she was going to lie in it, whatever her friends may think. This is the life I wanted and everything is going to be just fine, she resolved, as she pondered on what David might like for his supper.

Over the next few months, the threesome continued to drift apart. For Bert and Tess the considerable effort required in maintaining contact with Vicky had become increasingly difficult the more they saw her turning into an alien from the planet Married-People-Are-Just-Different. On the infrequent occasions they met up, nothing they found to talk about seemed relevant to her life and they usually ended up feeling embarrassed by how few mutual interests they all now shared. Once alone, neither Bert nor Tess was inclined to speak openly about the chasm that had formed. They didn't want to discuss it, finding it too unhappy and too frightening in case it proved permanent. Vicky was equally sad about the way things were turning out but she comforted herself with the belief that the blame lay squarely at her friends' door. Meanwhile, she threw herself into organizing a domestic and social routine so packed and tightly regimented that it wouldn't allow her a moment to miss her friends or the way of life they'd enjoyed together before her marriage. Vicky found that she could pack every day with a combination of coffee mornings and lunches with other local mothers, expeditions to a nearby massive shopping centre, overseeing the work of her housekeeper, gardener and nanny, and seeing to David's evening-meal and dry-cleaning requirements.

Traffic Calming

One day David came home and suggested they throw a half-social, half-work dinner party. To Vicky's surprise, as they sat together later that evening drawing up the guest list, he proposed that she include Tess and Bert. She knew that, while he didn't actively dislike them, he'd been pleased that they weren't around as much as before. She didn't blame him for feeling this way knowing that, as a bunch, they presented a clique that was virtually impenetrable to an outsider. Vicky also suspected that, at some point in the past, he must have guessed that her friends made fun of him. Now that they were married the memory made her uneasy and she hastily disassociated herself from ever having enjoyed or taken part in the piss-taking. Vicky was pleased that David wanted to invite them: it displayed exactly the kind of maturity and generosity of spirit she'd chosen him for. However, his real motives for wanting them present weren't quite as lofty as the ones his wife gave him credit for.

David was a deeply conventional person who'd always interpreted Vicky's tendency towards discretion as proof that she was much more chaste than the girls she hung around with. Far from causing confusion or irritation, her reluctance to sleep with him before their wedding had fallen in precisely with his view of conduct becoming to a nice girl.

As a couple they didn't really have single women friends and David certainly didn't know any who occupied the same moral vacuum as Tess and Bert. He wanted to have the dinner to woo a wealthy associate with whom he was keen to do business. The man had a reputation as a bit of a goer and, although married, his wife lived in the country. David was sure that his guest would become well disposed towards him once presented with a choice of not one but two available women as racy as Tess and Bert. The issue of whether or not they would be interested in him didn't cross his mind, assuming as he did, that women like them couldn't afford to be choosy – particularly as they were in their mid-thirties and getting on a bit. David was aware of Tess's sexuality but, to him, it simply added a saucy edge to her appeal rather than representing an insurmountable obstacle.

The night of the dinner Bert and Tess arrived early, for which Vicky was grateful. Despite having triple-checked every last detail from the menu down to the rose petals floating in the finger-bowls she was feeling very nervous. It was the first work-oriented dinner party they'd given and she knew that it was important for her husband that it went well. Although he hadn't apprised her of his plan to offer up her friends to his guest of honour, she didn't want to let him down.

David served drinks in the living room and the group stood around making awkward conversation. After a while, having heard in minute detail their host's plans for erecting a gazebo, Bert and Tess were very relieved to see the other guests arrive.

'So these are Vic's new best friends, yeah?' Bert muttered to Tess, as they made their way into the dining room once everyone was gathered.

'Looks like it.'

'A pair of fascists who run the Neighbourhood Watch campaign, a couple they play bridge with – *bridge*, God help me – David's partner and some awful middle-aged wanker who looks like he's modelled himself on Des Lynam.'

'Actually he's a real lech, don't leave me alone with him.'

'Fine as long as you shout, "FIRE," at the top of your voice when you hear that woman start to talk about security lights again, OK?'

Tess giggled and nodded as the assembled company took their seats.

'And I've also got a boat I keep moored at Marbella. Perhaps you'd like to see it, some time.'

'Ah, thanks, but I've, ah, seen a boat before.'

'Not my boat.'

'No, not your boat but still . . .' Tess had been placed – deliberately she guessed – too far away from Bert to elicit her help and she was getting desperate at trying to fend off the increasingly lurid advances David's associate was making.

'I'm a great lover of any beautiful thing that goes fast.'

'Really? The trouble is I'm not *that* interested in men's . . . er . . . boats, well . . . in men's . . . er . . . things in general. You see, I . . .' As she approached her revelation, Tess looked up and saw the silent entreaty in her hostess's expression. It stopped her mid-sentence.

Grateful that Tess had held back, Vicky was about to come to her aid when she was distracted by a conversation on her right that she feared was also about to take a dangerous turn.

'. . . the cars just come tearing along at incredibly high speeds, so I'm spearheading a crusade to have sleeping policemen installed.'

'Sleeping policemen, eh?' Bert responded, in a mischievous tone.

'Yes. Apparently they're very effective.'

Vicky shot her friend a look of warning. Bert ignored it: the main course was nearly at an end and she felt that she'd been well behaved for long enough. As far as she was concerned, the Neighbourhood Watch woman was lucky to still be alive: she had bored Bert to tears throughout the entire meal, droning on about open spaces, bus lanes and residents' parking permits.

'Well, never having slept with one I can't actually confirm that for you. But I've got my whole life ahead of me and there's always a first. So I'll let you know,' she said, smiling sweetly.

'Bert. Tess. Could you come into the kitchen and give me a hand with the pudding? Please,' Vicky barked, jumping to her feet.

'Both of us? Why? Is it very heavy?' Bert, staying seated, replied.

'No. I'd like your advice on whether it's . . . um . . . ready.'

'*My* advice,' Bert drawled, giving Tess a mock-incredulous look.

'Yes, *your* advice. So, if everyone would excuse us, we won't be a moment,' Vicky said, marching towards the door while widening her eyes fiercely at her friends.

'Look, for God's sake, you two, you've got to behave properly. You're ruining everything!' Vicky hissed, shutting the kitchen door firmly behind her.

'We're ruining everything? I've been a saint so far. I pretended to be fascinated by your Neighbourhood Watch pal's ranting for so long that I could stand in for her at tomorrow's night show-down with the sodding council if I wanted.'

'Um, Vic, I'm sorry if you think I'm not behaving very well. I'm doing my best but I've had to forcibly remove David's friend's hand from my knee twice already. I keep dropping subtle hints but I don't think he realizes I'm gay.'

'And for God's sake don't tell him! Or anyone else. And you, Bert, don't make another joke about shagging policemen. In fact, stay away from shagging completely. You've got to understand, these people aren't used to women like you. They'd never talk about sex and stuff the way you guys do.'

'Excuse me? "You guys do"? And you've never talked about that kind of thing, I suppose?' Bert asked indignantly.

'I'm just saying they wouldn't be comfortable listening to your exploits, Bert, and I'm absolutely sure they couldn't deal with lesbianism either.'

'Vicky, it's not our job to protect from modern society these freaks you've decided to make your mates. But I think we're both capable of making conversation that doesn't revolve around our sex lives, thank you very much.'

'Don't be so touchy. They're not freaks they're just . . . different.'

'Yeah, and buttock-crunchingly boring.'

Vicky decided not to respond directly. 'We've got to go back in now. I'll put you, Tess, where Bert was sitting, all right? And, Bert, you can sit where Tess was. I'm sure you can handle that bloke but, whatever you do, stay away from sex.'

'OK,' Bert and Tess replied, as they filed out of the kitchen behind their friend.

'So I'm not to ask him how much he'd pay me for a shag, then, Vic? Is that right?' Bert whispered, as they neared the dining room.

'Listen, I'm serious. This is important,' Vicky snarled between gritted teeth, before adopting a frantically cheery smile as she pushed the pudding trolley through the door.

Bert shook her head in despair, and looked at Tess, who responded by shrugging her shoulders in resignation. They were in complete agreement: Vicky had slid into Doris Day hell.

Stepford Wives

Less than a year later Vicky had had another child, a boy this time, Benjamin, and Tess and Bert duly paid a visit soon after his birth.

'So is this what you're going to do for the rest of your life – churn out babies year after year?' Bert said. She'd intended the remark to be jokey but she could tell from Vicky's face that she didn't find it remotely amusing. Bert's heart sank.

'Meaning?' Vicky snapped back.

'Er . . . nothing . . . Vic. I just meant, you know, you've had two in two years and, look, I really didn't mean anything.' Bert was stumbling for a diplomatic retreat. All the while half of her was urging her to fuck the consequences and tell Vicky exactly what she really thought while the other half was urging her to keep quiet and not rock the boat.

'Yes, you did, you meant is this *all* I'm going to do for the rest of my life, just have babies.'

'No, I didn't. Well,' Bert mumbled, neither half of the voices inside her having yet won.

'Yes, you did! I know you think I've sold out, I know you're convinced that I'm not in love, *in love*, with David. Well, I bloody well am! I wanted babies and that's what I've got, so just leave me bloody well alone, will you? Whenever you two come here, you always make me feel judged, you make me feel like my life isn't good enough, with your glamorous film-writing and the catering business you've made so trendy and successful. Well,

I'm doing exactly what I want to be doing and I wouldn't swap it for the world, so there!'

Tess was dumbfounded but Bert saw Vicky's outburst as her cue to let the home truths flow. 'Listen, Vicky, if you were that happy then you wouldn't be so defensive. If you were happy, I'd be happy for you but you're not. This isn't you. You're trying to live some sort of crappy fantasy life – you've turned into a fucking Stepford Wife.'

'I have not, I bloody well have not. I'm very happy!'

'What? You're happy when the most important thing you'll do in a day is choose new fabrics for curtains and organize a matching loo cover? You're happy planning supper menus for your husband? You're happy having nothing else to worry about other than whether your neighbours are going to nick Consuela, or whatever that poor cow's called, off you? If you're happy, you've had a lobotomy!'

'If you can't accept that I'm happy with my life then you'd better leave. I don't see how we can carry on being friends any more,' Vicky said, sounding steely, having regained her composure.

'Look, it's exactly because I *am* your friend, your best friend, that I'm saying all this. If it were anyone else I wouldn't bother. Do you think I want to fight with you? All I'm saying is think about what you're doing before it's really too late. You're going to turn around in ten years' time and look across the table at David and find yourself thinking, Who the fuck is this?'

'I think you'd better leave.'

'Oh, Vic, don't do this. Don't crawl into a shell and write off everything I've said. Think about it. If I'm completely wrong then fine, but if I've got a point admit it and have the courage to do something about it.'

'I've told you what I feel and you're not prepared to accept it. I'd prefer it if you both left now, thank you,' Vicky replied, in a terrifyingly detached, formal voice, standing up as she spoke. Bert and Tess had no choice but to comply.

'Well, I hope you're pleased with yourself. Top marks for tact and diplomacy,' Tess said, once they'd been driving for a few minutes.

'Don't start lecturing me. I know you think I'm right.' Bert seethed back at her, flaming.

'Maybe, but she only had that baby a couple of weeks ago. There's a time and a place for everything, you know.'

'I didn't mean for it all to come out, it just did. She started it. I didn't want to hurt her feelings but she *is* throwing her life away, I can't bear it. Did you see on her mantelpiece? There was an invitation to a Totteridge Young Mums Coffee Morning! An invitation! Somebody's life is so empty that they have time to write out invitations for a fucking coffee morning, Jesus Christ! That same person probably spends two days mulling over the momentous decision of whether to serve biscuits *and* cake or just biscuits. A few years ago Vic would have committed suicide if you'd told her the biggest thing she had to look forward to all week was a sodding coffee morning. I'm sorry, I just can't stand on the sidelines watching her turn into a robot and not say anything.'

'Sometimes that's what you have to do, Bert. Sometimes that's what being a mate really means.'

'Oh, bugger off! Where did you get that? Out of a fortune cookie?'

'No, I'm serious. All right, so you've said your piece and look where it's got you. You've made it virtually impossible to be friends with Vic any more. That isn't what you wanted, is it?'

Bert didn't reply. It suddenly dawned on her that Tess was right. She couldn't see how on earth she and Vicky were ever going to make it up again after everything she'd said.

*

Initially, following their flight, Vicky's indignation and fury at Bert's accusations served to keep all other feelings at bay. She regretted that Tess had been caught in the crossfire, but she didn't see how they could carry on meeting up without Bert. It didn't really matter, she reasoned, because she was sure Tess shared Bert's views anyway. With two small children, a large house to run and the rest of the busy life she'd set up she found that she didn't have time to feel sorry for herself anyway. Once the anger had subsided Vicky elected to be philosophical about the rift and simply accept that they'd all grown up and apart. She decided that they'd all been ridiculously childish, in the first place, to have ever imagined they could stay best friends for ever.

Occasionally reminders would pop up and give Vicky a jolt. It could be a programme on TV, a song on the radio or any other banal, everyday thing that to anyone else would seem ordinary but was absolutely hilarious to her and her friends once dissected by them as a gang. These moments would force her into acknowledging that she minded more about the split than she would admit. She had a particularly difficult moment when she came across a review of Tess's film, which was apparently doing very well. The reviewer described Tess as 'a pioneer in the traditionally macho thriller genre, breaking the mould of sexual stereotyping in film while maintaining a gripping plot and the leading characters' integrity and truth'. After she'd read it, Vicky's first instinct had been to get straight on the phone to Tess and screech with hysterical delight. She instinctively knew that Tess would be really pleased but would also think it was all a bit of a joke, especially given the pretentious language the reviewer had used. However, the days went by and Vicky found that she just couldn't make the call. She didn't know how to begin. It all felt too awkward. The knack had gone.

David Makes Demands

It was a totally unexpected development that finally triggered Vicky into admitting that her life wasn't as perfect as she liked to think. David turned into an arse.

During the first few years of their marriage David had behaved exactly as Vicky had predicted he would – which was precisely the same as he had before they were married. He'd been gentle, undemanding, indulgent and generally very easy to live with. Then, suddenly, out of the blue, David announced that he thought he ought to be getting more sex than the strictly controlled ration Vicky had him on. She had long since complimented herself on having succeeded in whittling it down to the bare minimum and his announcement horrified her. She'd known all along that apart from when she was pregnant he was keen to do it more often, and while she was not repelled by him, she was just as happy to avoid the whole palaver, if at all possible. After some heated wrangling it soon became clear to David that Vicky had absolutely no intention of turning into his nightly sex-slave and, as a result, he became grumpy, difficult and a pain in the neck to have around.

For her part, Vicky was no longer able to avoid facing the full implications of the life she'd chosen. She had to admit that she'd married someone on her terms only, to suit herself. She'd never considered that, in the fullness of time, there was a danger that her husband might make demands of his own. It suddenly dawned on her that all the effort she'd put into creating a dream home life had been her way of recompensing him for the fact that she'd never been in love, *in love*, with him. With shame, Vicky realized that having the Perfect Wife is no substitute for one who yearns to lick ice-cream out of her man's belly-button. She'd always hoped that whipping up heavenly soufflés and getting the carpets properly cleaned would divert his attention away from the fact that she'd never once given him a blow-job. The penny slowly dropped: she'd been hoping for rather a lot. Although she now accepted this, she wasn't prepared to take all the blame. She'd made it clear to David right from the beginning that she wasn't in love, *in love*, with him and she felt a bit irked that he was now expecting the kind of sexual attention normally reserved exclusively for the inhabitants of that territory. After a protracted stand-off, an irritated but slightly remorseful Vicky and a disgruntled but resigned David fell into a taciturn truce. Neither had any desire to divorce, nor did either of them, albeit for different reason, regard their sex life as a make or break issue.

A Greater Understanding of the Universe

There was nothing for it. When the news finally sank in Bert could only think of one person she could turn to for help. As she dialled the number, although she was mainly consumed by the disaster that had struck, she found that she was secretly pleased to have a real, proper excuse for making contact at last. The phone was picked up almost immediately.

'Hi, Vic? Is that you?'

'Who's this?'

'It's me – er, Bert.' It felt odd having to say her name. A lifetime spent chatting on the phone to each other had ensured they always knew the caller's identity the second they heard their voice. However, they hadn't spoken for over a year and that level of familiarity depended on the innate intimacy they had since lost.

'Oh . . . oh . . . erm . . . hi . . . er . . . how are you?'

'Well, *I'm* great, fine, thanks, but listen, something terrible has happened, well, actually, it's sort of funny but not. The thing is . . . er . . . the reason I'm ringing is that I badly need David's help. I don't know who else to ask.'

'Oh, right, OK.' Vicky was a bit put out to learn that Bert hadn't rung specifically to beg her forgiveness but, none the less, she was very pleased that she'd called. 'Well, he's not here at the moment. I'll get him to ring you when he gets back.' She momentarily considered keeping her cool and not asking what the problem was but instantly thought that would be too ridiculous. 'What's happened?'

Bert was very relieved that Vicky had asked. To her it was proof that, like her, Vicky was keen to use this opportunity to re-establish the friendship. 'Well, you're not going to believe it, but Mum's been arrested.'

'What?' Vicky shrieked.

'Yup, Mum's been arrested for fraud and tax evasion. Oh, yeah, I nearly forgot – and aiding undesirable aliens to enter the country.'

'Bert, it's a joke, it must be.'

'I wish it was. I thought it was a wind-up at first but it's true. She's in prison in Oregon pending someone posting bail. Luckily Tess is out in America at the moment. She's not in Oregon but she's arranging for some money to be transferred so at least Mum can get out of jail for the time being.'

'Does Tess live there now?' Vicky asked nervously. It felt peculiar not knowing what had been happening to either of her closest friends for so long.

'No, but she's always back and forth, you know, since her film.'

Vicky was relieved to hear that things hadn't changed that dramatically. 'Anyway, sorry, what's this all about? How did it happen? What's your mum done?'

'Well, guess what? Big surprise. It turns out that Swarmarjee Rarmarjee, or whatever her beloved guru is called, far from communing with nature and easing his disciples' paths to a greater understanding of the universe, has been easing his own path into their bank accounts, falsifying his books, not paying his taxes and getting loads of his mates into the country by pretending they were something to do with the ashram. Fucking twat!'

Vicky laughed, then said, 'Sorry, Bert, I didn't mean to.'

'No, you're right, it is funny. I'd be hysterical with laughter myself if it weren't for the fact that I'm having to sort the whole sodding mess out. God, I thought I might be having to go through all these kinds of dramas in a few years with Tabatha, not my bloody mother!'

'Why's your mum been arrested if it's the guru that's been up to no good?'

'Because, of course, Mum, who, as you know, can't ever leave well alone, has been helping him out for years on the administration side of running his bloody ashrams. I doubt that she knew he was siphoning off other people's money. I mean, she's a nightmare, but she's not dishonest. Anyway, apparently she's heavily implicated all the same.'

'Oh, God, this is awful.' Vicky paused. 'Listen, are you busy tonight?'

'No, not really.'

'Well, then, why don't you come up here and have supper? You can talk to David when he gets home.'

There was a moment's silence before Bert responded and Vicky feared that her friend was going to refuse.

Bert was actually taking the moment to decide whether she could answer characteristically or needed to tread carefully: she didn't want to inadvertently alienate Vicky again. 'Depends. Will you be conjuring up something simple yet delightful?'

Vicky chortled. She knew Bert was teasing her but it felt great. The knack was back.

As she put the phone down she smiled and thanked God for Angela's errant ways which, despite having been a thorn in Bert's side for all these years, had now served to bring the gang back together.

Once he was fully apprised of the facts, David sprang into action, dealing with Bert's mother's predicament with ingenuity and professionalism. He took complete control of the situation, and while it didn't turn him into sex-on-toast, Bert was able to see, for the first time, some of his appeal. She was deeply grateful to him and felt guilty that she'd always written him off as nothing more than Vicky's lap-dog. As things began to get sorted out, Bert thought it would be a good time to make a few complimentary noises to Vicky about David. By now, their friendship was more or less restored to its previous state. There'd been a few awkward moments when Bert had managed to stop herself from making disparaging remarks about various abiding features of Vicky's life – like the Totteridge Neighbourhood Watch group and Stepford Wives' coffee mornings. But, despite her continued scorn for her friend's way of life, their mutual love was the greater emotion and Bert thought it would do no harm if she ate a bit of humble pie on the topic of David.

Vicky's reaction puzzled her: although she accepted the compliments with her usual grace, Bert was sure she detected a new note of hidden contempt for him. However, she was disinclined to probe, particularly as she didn't fancy inciting Vicky into a lecture on how married life isn't all about holding hands and skipping through fields of buttercups.

And although Vicky had indeed come to resent David for breaking his side of the unwritten marriage contract, as she saw it, she was not yet ready to confess openly that all was not as it seemed.

With David's intervention, using the contacts he'd established during some lucrative property deals, Angela was released and returned to England. Before he had the charges against her dropped, David had advised her to transfer ownership of her assets in case she was convicted and ended up having to pay huge bills. From across the ocean and faced with a long-term jail sentence Angela had readily agreed to sign over the house, her only asset, to her daughter. As a result when she came home it was as a guest in what was now legally Bert's house and not hers. As far as Angela was concerned this was a mere detail but Bert saw it very differently. As far as *she* was concerned the potential advantage this change might afford her in the future was huge. She welcomed her mother home with a much lighter heart than she would have had the boot been on the other foot.

1997
You've Got to Have Friends

'Vic, Vic, you've got to help me out. André's come down with some dreadful disease and he can't do my next wedding. I know you're a committed, full-time housewife with a frantically busy freezer-filling agenda and all that but you've got to help me out!'

'Insulting my way of life is not very likely to get me to help you out, you know.'

'Yes, all right, sorry, sorry, I was trying to be funny, sorry. Look I'm in a real panic, we're doing this unbelievably grand wedding and I can't manage with someone I've never worked with before. What if they cock it up? Please, Vic, you've got to help me out, please. I'll be your best friend in the whole wide world for ever and ever, cross my heart and hope to die, if I don't.'

Vicky giggled at Bert's use of the phrase they'd uttered a hundred times a day at school. She hadn't heard it for a long time. While Bert continued to use the language of their youth she had adopted a manner of speech she saw as more appropriate to her position as a wife and mother of two – a proper grown-up. 'When is this wedding?'

'Next Saturday, that's why I'm in such a flap.'

'Next Saturday?'

'Yes,' Bert said, trying to contain her irritation. She didn't see why Vicky was repeating what she'd said.

'The thing is I've always got a lot on on Saturdays. I'm not sure that I can make myself free at such short notice.'

'What? The most organized woman in the world can't arrange

348

a whole day off? Well, actually it'd be two days because we'll have to do a lot of preparation on the Friday. Please, Vic. Look, do you need to check that it's all right with David?' Bert took a calculated risk in mentioning the need for David's permission. She was banking on the contempt she'd noted a few months earlier in Vicky's tone serving to spur her friend into instantly rejecting the suggestion that she needed her husband to sanction her decisions. The risk paid off.

'No, that won't be necessary, we don't have that kind of marriage, thank you. OK, I'll arrange things so that I can help you out. But just this once, mind.'

'Yes, yes, it'll never happen again, Miss, honest.'

'And there'd better be no pig's head on the menu.'

'*Mon Dieu*, Vic, no! That's so *passé* now. No one does a medieval banquet any more. It's all very simple and elegant nowadays – much more your sort of thing. You'll love it. Listen, I'll fax you over the menus so you can get an idea of what we're doing, OK?'

'You've got a fax?' Vicky exclaimed. Although she had a fax machine in her house it was only because David needed it.

'Of course I've got a fax, I couldn't manage without it. God, it's not even a big deal any more, they're practically obsolete. Most of Tabatha's friends have computers with e-mails and mobile phones and pagers and all sorts of other bits of modern technology to make sure you never have to see someone in person!' Bert laughed. 'So listen,' she continued, 'I'll send it in a minute and by the way, Vicky, thanks a lot, I'm really grateful.'

As Vicky put the phone down she couldn't help remembering a time in their lives when private ownership of a fax machine had been very uncommon, and thinking of the one, in particular, that had facilitated swift and unpersonal delivery of misery to her.

*

'So, anyway we're in bed –'

'Whoa, whoa, hold up there, you've omitted a crucial detail. Was this before or after sex?' Bert interrupted.

'You're absolutely right, very important detail. After, of course, because she goes to me, "So are you going to write me a part in your next movie?" and I go, cool as you like, "Not necessarily, we'll have to see how things go . . ."'

'God, you are so grand now! I can't believe you've got Hollywood movie stars begging you to write parts for them,' Vicky called from the other side of the room.

'She's hardly a movie star, more of a starlet,' Bert sneered.

'I'll have you know that she's regarded as one of the hottest new talents around.'

'Ah, well, then, in that case, could be she's only sleeping with you to get a part in your film. You never know.'

'Thanks, Bert, I've only written one successful film but I'll take that as meaning my work is so fantastic it's even worth sleeping with a disgusting old hag like me to get close to being cast in the next one.'

'Good, because that's kind of what I meant.' Bert laughed. Having written a commercially successful film (the only key apparently that opened producers' well-fastened doors) Tess was now living high on the hog. A number of the small independent studios and two of the big established ones had started sniffing round to sound out her interest in various projects they had on the boil. Lesbian chic, as Tess called it, was very much of the moment. She was widely regarded, Tess informed her friends, as partly responsible for paving the way into the current fashion, particularly since her lesbian credentials were bona fide.

'Tess, can you not keep eating those chanterelles or, in fact, anything else? It's great that you're here but stop picking at everything.'

'Blimey, it hasn't taken you long to get back in the swing of it, has it, Vic? Then again, I suppose you've been keeping up your bossing skills with Immaculada or Contrathepthiona or whatever she's called.'

'Her name is Maria actually.'

It was early in the evening before the grand wedding, and Vicky and Bert were literally knee-deep in preparations. Every surface, including most of the floor, of Bert's kitchen was covered by sumptuous food in various states of readiness.

'Mum, can I borrow a tenner?' Tabatha said, walking into the kitchen, swooping up a mini crostini and popping it into her mouth as she spoke.

'Yes, fine, just go away. I can't cope with everyone standing around chomping through . . .' Bert said, turning around to locate her purse. She was stopped short by the sight of her eighteen-year-old daughter's outfit. 'You are not going out in that!'

'In what?'

'Exactly. "In what"? You're naked, you are literally naked.'

'Oh, Mum, I am not naked. This is a skirt.'

'Not, it's not! It's not even a belt! If you so much as smile it'll end up being a necklace!' Vicky and Tess exchanged grins. Tabatha was wearing a very short suede skirt.

'Listen, I can wear what I fucking well like! I am eighteen years old! Stop trying to ruin my life and control me. Now, where's that tenner?' Bert was about to respond when Angela walked into the room behind Tabatha.

'Oh, darling, you look fabulous! It's wonderful that those things are back in fashion. What lovely legs you've got, just like Granny's. You *must* have got them from me. Poor old Mummy, she could never have worn a skirt like that – legs like milk bottles.'

Vicky and Tess burst out laughing and Bert shot them a withering look. 'Mum, stay out of this. Tabatha is my daughter and she's not going out like that. The skirt is just too short!'

'I'm sorry, Mum, but it's not "too short", it's trendy and I am wearing it.'

'Darling, I don't want to interfere but Tabatha *has* got the legs to carry off that sort of thing. Might it not be that you're just a teeny little bit jealous?'

Bert thought she was going to explode with rage. Ever since her mother had come back to live with them she and Tabatha had become the greatest of pals. If Bert objected to anything her daughter did she could be sure that Tabatha would find support from her grandmother.

'Listen, Mum, I'm warning you, stay out of this,' Bert yelled at Angela, who responded by making a mock-scared face, encouraging more laughter from Tess and Vicky.

Bert turned to her daughter and adopted the listen-we're-all-mates-here stance she'd always used with her. 'Tabs, darling, I know you're eighteen, and of course I don't want to ruin your life. I'm just saying that I think nowadays you have to be very careful and in my opinion that skirt is too short. Now, I'd be much happier if you didn't wear it, OK?'

'I know what you're saying, Mum, but, sorry, I am wearing it and that's that. Slater. By the way, I might not be back tonight. Oh, Tess, can I come round to yours tomorrow and pick up those videos?'

'What videos?' Bert chipped in helplessly.

'Oh, just some hard-core porn I asked Tess to get for me in America.'

Everybody was laughing now, except Bert, who felt like she was being outwitted by a super-hip, late nineties reincarnation of her own teenage self.

'Yeah, fine, whenever, just give us a ring first. Have a good time tonight and don't do anything I wouldn't do!'

'Well, that leaves pretty much everything open then, doesn't it? Cheers!' Tabatha said, skipping out of the room, waving goodbye with the ten-pound note she'd extracted from Bert's purse.

'Well, thanks for the support, girls. I would have thought that you, Tess, might at least back me up on the skirt thing. Jesus, she might as well have been going out in her knickers!'

'Relax, Bert, all young girls dress like that these days, it's no big deal.'

'Darling, you're frightfully uptight with her. You should try being more laid-back. It's the only way. You know, constantly battling with someone never gets them to see your point of view.' Bert twisted her head round towards Tess and Vicky, who were smiling, gritted her teeth, crossed her eyes and growled.

'She's a sensible girl, she knows what she's doing,' Angela said, as a parting shot, picking up the glass of wine she'd come in to get and leaving the room.

'That woman is dangerously close to being made homeless,' Bert seethed theatrically once her mother had exited.

'I heard that!' Angela called, from half-way up the stairs.

'You were supposed to!' Bert bellowed up after her.

She turned round to find Vicky and Tess laughing so hard that no noise was coming out. In spite of her double defeat Bert started laughing too.

Of All the Bars in All the World

'God you weren't joking when you said this wedding was grand. There must be six pageboys out there. They're all wearing tiny little velvet suits. They look so sweet.'

'You'd better not have been walking around gawping at everyone. I knew it was a mistake to let you come.' Bert sighed.

Vicky and she had worked so late into the night that by the time they'd finished there'd been no point in Vicky going home. She would only have to have turned round to come back almost as soon as she'd arrived. Tess was jet-lagged and had also ended up staying to lend them a hand. She'd decided to come along to the wedding to have a look.

'Bert, I think I know how to conduct myself in polite society. What do you think I was doing? Crawling about on the floor, fingering the gentry's silken cloth, drooling with envy and tugging my forelock? I just slipped out to see if your waiters were circulating the nibbles properly.'

'Canapés and crostini,' Bert corrected.

'Yeah, titbits, nibbles, deep-fried tulips, daffs in pastry, whatever.'

'Do you know, last night was the first night David and I have spent apart since we were married?' Vicky chimed in from the other side of the huge kitchen they were holed up in for the duration of the wedding.

Bert looked at Tess and raised her eyebrows. 'Getting a taste for it, eh, Vic?'

354

'No. I'm just saying I hadn't realized we'd never spent the night apart before, not even when I had the kids. I kind of missed him.'

Neither Tess nor Bert said anything at first. Eventually Bert couldn't resist. She was confident, now, that she and Vicky were on strong enough ground. She felt it was her duty to continue to poke fun at Vicky and David's marriage, particularly since now that she had a greater respect for David, after the help he'd given her, it could be done without malice. 'You know, I read somewhere that apparently you even miss a gangrenous leg once it's gone, if you've had it long enough.'

Tess let out a loud guffaw then shot Vicky a worried look, fearing that comparing David to a putrefying limb might be going too far.

Accustomed as she was to Bert's sense of humour, Vicky didn't react. She was thinking about something else. She had missed David and this had surprised her. She was in the process of deciding that it was a sign that the marriage was in a perfectly healthy state – if you didn't count the controlled-ration-sex thing.

'The food's marvellous. Everything is going terribly well. Thank you so much. I just popped in to leave you this – thought you might like a drink while you're stuck in here slaving away.'

'Thanks very much, that's lovely, thank you,' Bert said, to the departing brother of the bride who had just deposited a bottle of champagne on the table.

'Cor, they treat you just like one of them, don't they?' Tess said, attempting a Cockney accent but sounding more like Dick Van Dyke in *Mary Poppins*.

'Oh, bollocks, I can't find any glasses. I'll go out and get some,' Bert said, as she went to open the champagne.

'Do you want me to go and get them? I'll check on your waiters again, if you like.'

'No, thank you, Tess, I don't want to give you any more fuel for your cor-luvaduck-stone-the-crows-how-the-other-half-live act,' Bert said, smiling, as she left the room.

'Vic, you should go out and have a look. Seriously, they must have spent a fortune,' Tess hissed, the moment Bert had gone.

'I saw it earlier, when we were setting up. Very impressive, but I can live without seeing another bunch of drunk hoorays,' Vicky replied haughtily. 'Do you know, they say, "The showier the wedding the less likely the marriage is to last"?' she continued. Tess didn't comment, recalling the extreme lavishness of Vicky's own wedding, and wondering if her friend was aware of the subtext of what she'd said. She was glad Bert wasn't in the room to bring it to her attention in full technicolor detail.

A few minutes later Bert came back in with three champagne glasses.

'You took your time. I'm gasping for a drink,' Tess said, opening the bottle. She caught sight of Bert's face. 'What's the matter with you? You look like you've seen a ghost.'

Vicky stopped what she was doing and turned round to see what Tess was talking about.

'I have, kind of.'

'Don't tell me, one of your old shags is out there?' Tess said, laughing as she filled the glasses and handed them round. 'You see, the thing is, Bert, if you make a random selection of more than fifty people anywhere in the Western hemisphere, by the law of averages you're bound to have had sex with at least one of them.'

'It's not one of mine.' Bert paused. She didn't know how to break the news. Deciding she needed some Dutch courage, she drained her glass in one gulp. 'Vic, Tom's out there. Apparently he's a big mate of the groom. I didn't know, I couldn't have known, I never met the groom, only the bride and her mum. Even if I had, how would I ever have known? I'm really sorry.'

Bert finished rambling and poured herself another drink. She and Tess turned to look at Vicky whose face had turned deathly white.

She was speechless. She realized that her reaction was probably blowing her so-happily-married cover in one fell swoop. She knew she was giving the whole game away but there was nothing she could do. Seeing Tom ought to mean absolutely nothing to her, she knew that, but she felt too stunned to attempt a show of indifference in front of her friends. Anyway, she admitted to herself, caught out as she was, they'd known everything all along.

'Listen, he really wants to see you. He said to tell you that he was here and asked if you'd go out and talk to him. Ah, he, ah, he also said to tell you that if you don't, he'll come in here to find you.'

Tess couldn't believe how romantic and how much like the plot of *Casablanca* it all was, but looking at Vicky's face she refrained from voicing her opinion.

Vicky's heart was racing. Part of her wanted to rush out and throw herself into Tom's arms but the greater part of her wanted to steam out into the middle of the party and run him through with a carving knife. She was furious that he'd popped back into her life without so much as a by-your-leave. She was equally furious that his reappearance had thrown her into such an embarrassing flap. Vicky stood rooted to the spot for what seemed like an eternity to all three of them.

'I'm leaving. Tell him I've gone. No, don't tell him anything,' she cried eventually, tearing off her apron and flying out of the back door leaving Bert and Tess lost for words. Bert felt awful but she couldn't help also being relieved that the food had been ready before she'd made her announcement.

The next day as soon as Bert was sure that she'd find Vicky alone, she called her.

'Vic, it's me. Are you all right?'

'Yeah, I'm fine . . . fine. Why shouldn't I be?' Having escaped back to the safety of her mock-Tudor mansion and everything it stood for, Vicky had regained her equilibrium. She'd put down her uncharacteristically dramatic reaction to the possibility of seeing Tom to the effects of having stayed up half the night.

'Vic, I'm really sorry about what happened. I had no idea he'd be there.'

'Look, it's fine, Bert, really, it doesn't matter. Water under the bridge. It's not your fault. And, you know, it's not a big deal. I completely overreacted, it was just exhaustion, you know.'

Bert had guessed that Vicky might try to dismiss the episode as meaningless, and it strengthened her resolve to go through with her mission. She'd been unsure at first.

'Erm, the thing is, Vic, he gave me a letter for you. I didn't know what to do. He came in looking for you, I told him you'd left but he went off and then came back with this letter. I don't know what's in it but, well, anyway . . . I've got it here.'

Vicky didn't know what to say. She guessed that Bert would be well aware of exactly how much she desperately wanted to read the letter but she was feeling too out of control to make a sensible decision. Although she hadn't dared face him she was ecstatic to discover that Tom hadn't simply shrugged off her sudden disappearance.

'So, what do you want to do with it?' Bert said, after a prolonged silence.

'Oh, I don't know. It's probably full of rubbish. Look, why don't you just hang on to it and I'll read it the next time I'm at yours, OK?' Vicky said, as casually as she could manage. She was going to resist jumping into her car and racing over to Bert's to read the letter if it killed her. She was determined not to get caught out again by Tom. This time there was too much at stake.

Bert felt terrible about the situation to which she'd inadvertently exposed her friend. A bit of her was secretly pleased that something had finally come along to wake Vicky up but she didn't want it to cause her any real distress. As soon as Tom had asked her to, she'd decided to give Vicky the letter, not thinking it could do much harm. Other than that she wasn't going to say anything. If Vicky genuinely wanted to stay the way she was then Bert had resolved that it was her job, as her best pal, not to steam in trying to whoosh everything up – those days were over. All the same, Bert couldn't help feeling bad for agreeing so readily to deliver the letter in the first place. She knew that, once Vicky had read it, she would be *forced* to face the music. In an effort to assuage her guilt, and convinced that Vicky needed to get away from everything, Bert decided to organize a holiday for them all.

1997
Everything Will Be Great in Moscow

'Princess Diana is dead.'

'Fuck off.'

'No, she is, she really is!'

'She is not.'

'She fucking well is.'

'She fucking well *is* not.'

'Look, shut up, will you? I'm telling you – Princess Diana is fucking well dead, all right?'

'Really?'

'Wow.'

'How? What happened?' Vicky asked, sitting up.

'Apparently she died in a car crash, I couldn't make out the rest. There was a picture of a tunnel somewhere – Paris, I think – and the wreckage of a car. But it's terrible, don't you think? It's so sad, she was so lovely. It's a terrible tragedy.'

'God, it's such a loss, she was such a wonderful person,' Vicky agreed.

'How on earth could you possibly know what kind of person she was?' Bert shouted, not moving. She was lying on her front and yelling out of the side of her mouth, which was causing her words to sound distorted.

'Can't you sit up? You sound like you've just been to the dentist,' Tess said.

'No.'

'Because of all the wonderful things she did for everyone,' Vicky replied.

'Yeah, and don't you think it's interesting that we knew all about them every time she did them? We had every single little thing she did stuffed down our throats, especially when it involved some great act of charity. A day doesn't go by without her being on the front page of every newspaper. God, even when she goes to the sodding lavatory it's supposed to be a matter of national interest.'

'I knew you'd react like this. You're so cynical and horrible and twisted. She was a fantastic person who did lots of wonderful things for lots of unfortunate people and I think it's tragic that she's dead.'

'Look, Tess, she's – was a modern-day fairy princess. She looked nice in some great dresses and talked about her pain in public so that people were fooled into thinking that she was a real person just like them. If she'd looked like Hattie Jacques or that Tory MP – erm, what's her name? Oh, yeah, Ann Widdecombe, and done the same things no one would have touched her with a barge-pole.'

'Either way, it's terribly sad. Charles is going to feel awful now, isn't he?' Vicky opined, hoping to divert yet another pointless row between Tess and Bert.

'Well, he shouldn't have married her in the first place. A loveless marriage is *always* a mistake,' Bert replied pointedly, turning to look at Vicky who was on her right, lying down again. Vicky, who was aware that it was to her specifically that Bert was directing her pronouncement, ignored her.

'So that'll be why you've never got married, then, will it? No one has managed to measure up to your high standards despite the legion of offers from all those wonderful men?' Tess said, picking up the blockbuster she was reading and settling herself into a beaten-up old cane armchair that looked as if it had been left out on the terrace since they'd first stayed at the villa.

'Plenty of nice men have wanted to marry me, thank you very much. It's just that I didn't see the point of settling for something that wasn't quite right. Much better to be on your own than with the wrong person,' Bert replied, turning her head again to direct the thrust of her comments at Vicky.

'Quite. Much better to be knocking on forty and still living with your mother and daughter replicating some sort of modern weird version of *The Three Sisters*,' Tess muttered, not looking up from her book.

'*The Three* what?'

'Oh, Bert, even you must know *The Three Sisters*. It's a really famous play by –'

'Chekhov, yes, I know. I was winding you up,' Bert interrupted, delighted that Tess had caught the bait.

'Mmm, most amusing. Still, bet you don't know what it's about.'

'Well, I can't be sure but, off the top of my head, I'm guessing it's about three sisters. Am I warm at all, Professor Pile?'

'Not at all, actually. It's about three people who want to be something and somewhere they're not. They spend the whole play wanting to go to Moscow, which is really symbolic of their unfulfilled dreams. They're living half lives and imagine that they'd have full, happy ones if only they could be in Moscow.'

'Mmm, sounds great. Is it a musical?'

'You know what, Bert? You are pathetic. I don't know why I bother sometimes.'

'Don't be so bloody pompous, Tess, the stuff you write is hardly high-brow!'

'Will you two fucking well shut up?' Vicky burst out. 'When I agreed to come on this holiday I said, right from the beginning, that I wasn't going to spend a week listening to you two rowing about every single subject on earth. This is supposed to be a rest and I am trying to do just that – recharge my batteries and have a bloody holiday, OK?'

Tess shot Bert a sheepish look and they fell into a chastened silence. After a couple of moments she sneaked another look at Bert whom she caught suppressing a wide grin and they both cried out in unison: 'Ooooh, machwuuurre!'

They were in the middle of their first proper holiday together since the momentous school's-over-for-ever-life-starts-here one they'd had almost exactly twenty years earlier. Bert had arranged the whole thing fairly rapidly once she'd discovered that the same villa was free. Tess had been up for it from the moment Bert had made the suggestion, but considerable powers of persuasion had been required to get Vicky to abandon her husband and children – even for a week. She had gone into freezer-filling overdrive since Tom's re-emergence into her consciousness. It'd given her Perfect Life a bad knock.

'So are we going to go to *ristorante favorito* tonight for our last supper, then?'

'Yeah. Why try anywhere new on our last night and maybe end up regretting it? That'd be really annoying.'

'God, Bert, don't say "last supper" and "last night" like that.'
'Like what?'

'Like we're going back to face a firing squad, like this is our last chance of happiness ever.'

'Vicky, I didn't say it like that. You're going back to your Perfect Life, I can't think why you'd hear something as gloomy as that in what I said. Very interesting reaction, you might want to look into that, I reckon,' Bert replied.

Vicky raised her eyes to the heavens and smirked at her friend.

'Anyway, we have to go there because otherwise Vicky

won't ever get to see the lovely Salvatore again,' Tess drooled.

'We can go anywhere you like, I'm not bothered about seeing him,' Vicky lied.

'Oh *so* untrue, methinks, Vicky,' Bert drawled. 'Just think, if you weren't married you could have spent the last week having hours of hot, pounding sex with the heavenly Salvatore.'

'I think, even if I wasn't married, that wouldn't have been very likely.'

'Are you honestly telling me that if you weren't married you wouldn't have slept with him? Blimey, if he'd been after me I'd have slept with him, married or not!'

'We all know that, Bert, but I'm not like that,' Vicky said serenely, turning herself over to do her back. Bert bared her teeth at Tess who grimaced back at her.

Vicky was still flouncing around with a slightly above-it-all air. Ever since she'd got married Bert and Tess thought she'd surpassed herself in that department. Despite knowing that they'd witnessed her dramatic response to the Tom news, to Bert and Tess she was still trying to pretend that being a Perfect Wife had always been her destiny. By this time she bore little resemblance outwardly to the girl they'd known for nearly thirty years. But try as she might to convince *herself* that there was nothing more she genuinely yearned to do than spend her days making pastry cases, running up chintz curtains and bossing staff about, Bert and Tess knew that deep down Vicky was the same person. When they challenged her, Vicky always denied it but, secretly, she knew that this was why the friendship between the three had endured through all the ups and downs. Bert and Tess knew who the real Vicky was and it made her feel very safe, especially after everything that had happened recently.

As they walked along the narrow, dusty road under the warm evening sky on their way to the restaurant, Bert turned to Vicky.

'So, listen, I've had enough. All this hanging about, waiting for you to tell us in your own time, it's no good, it just won't work, it's far too grown-up for me. Anyway, it was Tess's idea not mine. Right, out with it! Are you going to tell us what was in Tom's letter or not?'

'Not.'

'Oh, bloody hell! I knew I should have read it before I gave it to you.'

'It *was* in a sealed envelope, as I recall, Bert,' Tess reminded her.

'Yes, but she'd never have known that. I could have just told her that Tom had given me the letter folded up and not in an envelope at all.'

Vicky and Tess laughed at Bert's unashamed nosiness.

'But what if it'd come up and he'd told me it had been in an envelope?'

'Ha, ha! Caught you out! You *are* going to see him! I knew it, I knew it!' Bert squealed, breaking into a skip.

Vicky remained unflustered. 'Not necessarily. I am merely speculating that if, in the event of deciding to see him, the topic of sealed letters were to have come up, I might, knowing you as well as I do, have asked him if his letter had been sealed when he gave it to you.'

'Mmm, well, I think he's still in love with you, says so in the letter and begs you to forgive him for being such a twat and run away with him now and live happily ever after.'

'Well, you're never going to know – unless, of course, I do run away with him, in which case I'll send you a postcard,' replied Vicky.

'You know, whatever offer he does make in that letter has to be put in the context of him knowing you're married with children. He asked me at the party and I told him.'

365

'Bert, give it up. Stop trying to trick Vic into telling you what was in the letter. She's not going to and that's that. She's always been like this, you know that.'

'Yeah, a boring old spoilsport. That'll teach me for being so trustworthy and discreet.'

Vicky and Tess both broke into raucous laughter at Bert's description of herself as they arrived at their destination.

'I luf jew very mush.'

'You love Jews?'

'Yes, I luf jew.'

'Erm, right.' Vicky wasn't sure how best to continue the peculiar turn the conversation had taken.

'Do you . . . only love Jews?'

'Yes, I honly luf jew.'

'O K, well that's, erm, interesting and . . . er . . . unusual.' Vicky paused until something occurred to her. 'How do you know I'm Jewish?'

'I'm sorry, but what is jewish? I honly no thet I luf jew.'

Vicky was sitting at a table in the now empty restaurant with Salvatore. She was trying to leave but only half-heartedly. Once the meal had ended Bert and Tess had mischievously slipped out ahead of her, guessing that she might like the opportunity to linger while saying goodbye to the owner, who had become so enamoured of her. Vicky had no idea what to make of his confession until what he was trying to say dawned on her.

'Oh, you mean me, you, "Jew", you! No, right, I get it, right, sorry, I misunderstood, you see it's pronounced "you" not "Jew" but, erm, never mind. Oh, I see, well, erm . . . thank you, thank you very much.'

'No, but why thenk jew? Jew don't thenk me, I'm serious, I luf jew.'

366

'Look, Salvatore, I'm really flattered but I'm married I have children, I can't. Look, I must go, really.'

Vicky stood up and prised herself away. She was finding Salvatore elegant, charming, handsome and tempting in the extreme. However, she couldn't accept that she might be the type to have a holiday romance, no matter how alluring the candidate. Despite this as she walked back to the villa she felt absolutely thrilled to have been so passionately pursued. Later that night Vicky realized that the flirtation with Salvatore, apart from making her feel electrified, had served a separate purpose and a much more momentous one. It had impelled her to make a decision about Tom.

1998
The Last Supper

'Last one before you hit forty – eeeeeek! Better enjoy it while you can!' Bert said, raising her glass to Vicky, whose thirty-ninth birthday the three friends were celebrating at Bert's house, a few months after returning from Italy.

'It's just a number. I don't know why people make such a song and dance about it.' Tess groaned.

'Everyone who says that is actually secretly terrified of turning forty. They all try to pretend it's not a big deal and say things like "It's just a number, I feel exactly the same as I did when I was twenty. I'm much happier now than I was ten years ago." They just can't face up to the undeniable truth, that in the eyes of most of the planet you might as well be dead!' Bert laughed.

'Do you remember when we used to think that people of forty were really ancient? That it was the end of the world? That you'd be a complete and total failure if you hadn't done everything, had a fantastic career, been married, had kids, got rich, everything, *before* you turned forty?' Vicky asked.

'I still think that!' Tess said, sighing theatrically.

'Well, if you think about it, between us we have done everything – it's just that no single one of us has managed to do it all on their own. If you roll us together into one person, though, we're Superwoman!'

'Not quite the same, is it, Bert? Having to borrow bits from your mates' lives to complete your own.'

368

'Vic, have you been reading *Cosmopolitan* again? No one has it all. It's a myth perpetrated by the people who make anti-cellulite cream!'

'Eh?'

'Look, everyone knows in their heart of hearts that you can't really ever get rid of cellulite, that you've either got it or you haven't, but we keep buying these supposedly magic creams that dupe us into thinking they work. Every time a new one comes out, we think, Maybe this is the one, maybe this cream will get rid of my disgusting orange-peel thighs and *then* I'll have a fantastic life! It's an evil conspiracy worked out by the whole anti-cellulite industry in cahoots with the rest of their cosmetics cronies to con us into spending seventy-five quid on a pot of fucking cream!'

Tess laughed as Bert came to the climax of her much-vaunted theory.

'Ah, but you see, I've never had cellulite,' Vicky said, smiling.

'It's a metaphor, you idiot! I know *you*, Perfect-Person-chronologized-photo-albums-never-stuffed-your-face-never-puked-at-a-posh-party Victoria Montague, sorry, Winkleman, don't have cellulite and can't imagine what it's like to live with that not-quite-made-it feeling the rest of us snivelling mortals are haunted by night and day but . . .'

Tess couldn't stop laughing as Bert paused to draw breath.

'Well, maybe not so perfect any more,' Vicky put in, before Bert could continue.

'I'm not taking the piss, Vic. You are sort of perfect. You're the exception that proves the rule.' Bert was only half teasing. 'I'm just describing the phenomenon that is your average modern woman,' she continued.

'And that'd be you then? Correct?' Tess said.

'Well, I'm not describing you, am I? Personally, I wouldn't

369

say that a successful-scriptwriter-virgin-lesbian fits your common or garden identikit for the average woman, would you?'

'You know, I honestly thought I was going to stay a virgin until my wedding night.'

'Well, you did – you have,' Bert pointed out. 'You are a virgin, technically speaking, and you might still get married, yeah? I mean, girls are only lezzers because they haven't met the right man, isn't that right?'

Tess's laughter was interrupted by Vicky. 'Isn't either of you going to ask why I said I wasn't perfect any more?'

'I assumed you were joking, Vic. I didn't really think you thought you were perfect.'

'I didn't think *I* was perfect but I did think you could organize a Perfect Life, you know, if you tried hard enough.'

'Well, you have in a way, two lovely kids, rich, devoted husband, a huge –'

'Lover,' Vicky announced, cutting Bert off before she could get to the end of her list. Bert whipped round to look at Tess whose jaw had dropped open. 'Not a *huge* lover,' Vicky sniggered, 'but I have got a lover.'

'Is this a joke, Vic? Are you trying to convince us that you're flawed or something?'

'No, I've been having an affair since just after we got back from Italy.'

'With Tom?' Bert asked, already knowing the answer.

'*Tom?*' Tess shrieked.

'Yes, with Tom.'

'Then you *have* been reading *Cosmopolitan*!' Bert cried.

Vicky laughed. 'No, but I did read Tom's letter and then I saw him and then one thing led to another and . . . well . . . you know.'

'No, no, no. Completely unacceptable. You are not dropping that bombshell and getting away with one of your coy oh-you-knows. We need facts, details, photographic proof . . .' Bert ordered, counting off each demand on the fingers of her right hand.

'Just tell us what you want to tell us. How did it all happen?' Tess said, pouring herself another glass of wine.

Vicky embarked on the story she'd obviously been dying to recount. 'Well, I arranged to see him not thinking that anything was going to happen *necessarily* but . . .'

'Very likely, I'm sure,' Bert said.

'Yeah, well, you know how my mind works. I couldn't arrange to see him thinking that we were going to fall into each other's arms. Anyway, we met up and it was all a bit awkward at first. And then suddenly he said he'd never stopped loving me but that he hadn't been able to cope at the time –'

'So when he ran off it *was* all about commitment and stuff?' Bert interrupted.

'It's all so *Gone with the Wind-y*, it's fantastic. Go on, go on.' Tess sighed.

'I guess so.' Vicky wasn't familiar with that plot. 'I tried to reason myself out of it at first but I couldn't. And the longer I was with him, the more I remembered how mad we'd been about each other and then there just didn't seem to be any point in resisting . . .' Vicky trailed off, beaming with happiness.

'Did you sleep with him, then and there, the first time you saw him?' Tess asked. Vicky didn't reply, but her expression revealed that the answer was yes.

'Oh, this is wonderful. I knew something would come along eventually to wake you up out of your coma. Make you see that there's a bit more life to life than sleeping policemen and filling your freezer. This is great. So, when are you going to leave David?' Bert blurted out, assuming that it was a matter of when and not if.

'I'm not,' Vicky replied tersely, as if the question was ludicrous.

'What? Aren't you in love with Tom?'

'Yes, Bert, I suppose I've always been in love with him.' Bert turned to Tess and gave her a huge I-told-you-so look. Vicky ignored it and continued. 'But what I've also realized is that, I was right, life *is* a compromise. I chose David for solid reasons. We've got a good marriage and, OK, although I'm not in love, *in love*, with him, it's a partnership, and I'm not throwing all that away.'

'Blimey, that is *so* mature I can't believe it!' Tess interjected.

'I'll admit to a few problem areas but every couple has them. I don't want to start all over again with someone else just to find a set of different problems.'

' "Problem areas", Vic? As we're letting everything hang out here tonight, might I ask if, making a wild guess, these "problem areas" are in the bedroom department at all?' Bert couldn't resist. She'd been waiting years to get her friend to admit that passion was a vital component to a healthy relationship.

Vicky gave Bert a frosty stare. She had no intention of saying any more. And then, totally unexpectedly, her face cracked into a smile. She couldn't keep up the freeze and there was no reason to either, she decided. Bert and Tess knew her too well.

'I knew it! I knew it! You've got him on portion control, haven't you?'

'Might have,' Vicky replied, smiling sheepishly.

'I knew it, you've got him on strict portion control. I'll bet he only gets a blow-job once a year on his birthday!'

'No, not even then. I've turned into a Nil-by-mouth . . . well, with my husband at any rate.'

'Jesus Christ! I can't believe you've managed to get away with this! You really are the most amazingly organized person in the universe.'

'Bert, it's no different from what either of you two have done or, in fact, most people of our age. You just go through life the way you can, doing what makes you happy. In completely different ways from me, that's what both of you have done too. You've made lives you want that you can also deal with.'

Once Vicky had finished, the three friends remained silent, exchanging thoughtful looks.

'Yup. I guess you're right,' Tess said.

'Wise words indeed, Glasshopper,' Bert said, in a *Kung Fu* accent. 'So, basically, you've got Tom neatly filed away in your lovely-affair-with-great-sex-but-not-a-long-term-investment box and David safely tucked away in the marriage-is-a-contract-based-on-mutual-understanding-and-vol-au-vents-matching-curtains-and-loo-seat-covers file. Would that be about it?'

'More or less. And, let's face it, in the end, everyone makes the compromises they need to make in order to get the life they want,' Vicky said.

'Well, here's to you, Vic. I think it's great if you're happy!' Tess said, pouring out the last of the wine.

'Yeah, *bonne chance, ma vieille douche*. Here's to no one ever cross-referencing your files.' Bert said drowning the contents of her glass.

'*Douche? Ma vieille douche?* What's that supposed to mean?' Vicky asked.

'*Bonne chance, ma –*'

'I know what *bonne chance* means,' Vicky said. 'It's *vieille douche* I'm having a little trouble with.'

'God, I may have been shit at school but I'm the only of us lot who knows *anything* about languages. *Bonne chance, ma vieille douche*, is a word for word translation of "Good luck, me old Dutch",' Bert explained, raising her eyes to the heavens.

'Um, Bert, it isn't. French for Dutch is *hollandaise*, as in Hollandaise sauce. A word-for-word translation of what you've just said is "Good luck, my old *douche*, as in shower or, more accurately, the jet spray you use for swooshing out the inside of your fanny!'

Tess burst into loud guffaws. 'No, don't. "Good luck, my old fanny-swoosher!" Stop. I'm going to wet myself,' she cried, spilling her drink as her body shook with laughter.

'Oh, Vic, please say that isn't true,' Bert moaned.

'Sorry, but it is. Don't worry, you've only made a twat of yourself in front of us, and we already know you're a twat.'

'I don't care about you two. It's the old French lady who supplies my cheeses, she's moving house and . . . I said it to her.'

Tess's howling stepped up a notch. 'Stop, Bert, stop. I am going to wee, stop!' she cried, clutching her crotch, and before she could stop herself she did.